Jack Lench was born in Suffolk and now lives in Warwickshire. His writing started in the form of postcards and letters to his father while he was working in far out, far away places around the world. Over the years, he kept notes on storylines and plots, the inspiration for which came from the people he people met and an interest in history, politics and places.

Illicit Deception is his debut novel and is a thriller about espionage, secrets, diamond theft and conspiracy with a love story running through it. Essentially, it is about people not being who they say they are. It takes three, tiny pieces of history and adds/changes one small intrinsic fact. In doing so, changes the course of history.

To Val

Jack Lench

The Robin Ashurst Trilogy

Please see website for details of publication:

www.jacklench.com

First Published in 2020 by Sunflower Publications

ISBN 978-1-8380341-1-5

Cover design by Pete's Productions

Dedicated to the people who never stopped believing in me:

Dad (the original Jack) - without his encouragement I would have never started to write this book!

Wendy — without her support, I would never have finished this book!

Chapter 1

Hello! My name is Robin Ashurst. I have been told that everyone has a story to tell. This is mine! Various twists of fate led me reluctantly, on a journey which my life in ways I could never have imagined. Ordinary people like me do not get involved in matters of state, political intrigue, or get immersed in the murky world of organised crime. I believed without question, all my history lessons at school, those documented accounts were true and accurate. I have now discovered that facts and individuals may not be as they appear. People can be deceived, details distorted by self -interest; it becomes harder to find the truth than to expose a lie. I am no author, so please bear with me. This is the true account of all events as they unfolded.

Generally, I felt that I had been a disappointment to my parents. I got a job in a local hotel in my teens and never really moved on. Then, in my twenties, I worked in pubs, clubs, and hotels all over the country, always at work when others were partying and missing out on, well something! Now at the age of thirty-three, I had nothing to show for all my efforts, and what bothered me more was that I didn't know anything else other than hotel and bar work, with its low pay and long unsociable hours. My relationships were as short-lived as my jobs, cool in my youth as I was fearful of commitment to people as well as places. I always got 'live in' positions, but what little I had earned over the years had been spent, never saving anything. Yet, on reflection, I was not unhappy with my lot. I've had some fun times along the way, with fellow revellers and hotel guests, who I met over the years.

You see, I really did and still do, love the world of hotels. My father had worked abroad through nearly all of my childhood. Visits to see him and holidays were spent in some of the best hotels in the world. They were decadent and luxurious places, where the elite indulged themselves. As a child, I treasured my hotel visits. No household chores, no homework, just excitement, and glamorous people. Fast approaching adolescence, hotels were where I had my notable and memorable experiences. My first kiss, my first alcoholic drink, the loss of my virginity, and so I grew up.

I had now ended up in a sixteen-room hotel on the south Devon coast. Having been built around the twenties, The Limes was constructed in a grand colonial style, symmetrical and enduring with wrought iron columns and a balanced array of glass windows. It was well-appointed with an eclectic variety of Edwardian furniture. Almost every room had a balcony with a sea view. Surrounded by landscaped gardens, the hotel was prominently situated on top of a cliff with the beach some fifty meters below. At night, the waves could be heard pounding the shingle. The ships sailed through the breakwater into the harbour at high tide, plying their trade, moving in and out of the china clay docks. It was always a hypnotic sight and took not only my attention but also guests who avidly watched the giant steel monsters manoeuvre into spaces that didn't appear large enough for their great structures and passing in between other pleasure vessels, tiny in comparison.

 The hotel had been named The Limes, after being built on the site of an old lime kiln. But now, age and a lack of investment over the years had, unfortunately, given the place a rather threadbare and dishevelled feel, which meant that the once Edwardian grandeur of The Limes had degenerated to shabby and 'tired.' It would have been a nineteen bedroomed hotel if three of the rooms had been in a fit state to let out to guests, but roof repairs were long overdue.

I was called manager! What a joke! I was 'Jack of all trades. My duties included managing everything and not just the hotel services but catering and accommodation, loosely referred to, in my contract of employment. It ranged from general maintenance to front of house, bar work to emptying the bins. I even had to do some cooking when our hotel chef Jermaine, an idiosyncratic Frenchman, was indisposed due to an overindulgence of one of his country's finest liquid exports. Jermaine was a small delicate man, with a full head of long black hair, who could only be described as 'highly strung.' He had been employed in some of the top hotels in London and Paris. Jermaine was a true craftsman of his art, indeed, the finest chef in Devon, when he was sober, that is! The proprietor just tolerated his moods and unreliability, as it was good for his ego.

The owner was an enigmatic, red-headed authoritative figure with an accent that I assumed was South African. His name, Hansen Mulhenny, described the fellow so well. I understood that he had come here at the end of apartheid and, with some cash on his hip, had purchased two hotels in the West Country. Hansen then flitted between both. He was an easy man to work for but not an easy man to know. My boss certainly had a mysterious side and often disappeared for long periods. Once, he arrived with a female partner, but she lasted a month and then vanished. We presumed she had gone back to South Africa, never to be seen or heard from again. Hansen was easy to work for because he didn't worry if the hotel made a profit or not, only that it didn't make too much of a loss. My job was comfortable and easy because I was never under any pressure to increase turnover or reduce expenses. I was content to a degree, as it allowed me to live in such a beautiful part of the country and by the sea.

The Limes was kept going by regulars; these were not locals. We didn't have many of them, even as paying guests in the restaurant. The generations of old Devonian natives regarded The Limes as the place where people went who had more money than sense. The newer stream of incoming inhabitants, the ones who were seeking quiet retirement in their dotage years or wanted to get away from the city hustle and bustle types, considered The Limes as a tourist hotel. They generally gave us a wide berth and ranked us in the same tacky 'grockle' fashion as the caravan parks and amusement arcades on the pier. Somewhere not to be seen. Rarely then, did they cross our threshold. Apart from our summer visitors, we had a very strange mishmash of individuals from every continent. These people kept coming back, and I think many were Hansen's friends or certainly acquaintances. Often, they stayed for weeks at a time during the season or out of it. So, this was my situation on a very pleasant day in early April. The daffodils were out and the fresh smell of spring was in the air, which was early this year after a mild but wet winter. The warmth of the sun streaming into the hotel was a pleasure and lifted my spirits.

The bell went in the lobby, a rather grand name for a small space, all it accommodated was a reception desk, which was not even big enough for two people to stand behind. I was bottling up in the bar. Unhurried, I sauntered over to see who was disturbing my morning duties. Today my mood was good, but I felt pressured as it was about ten o'clock. Breakfast had finished, all the checkouts had departed. I had been up since half past six to start work. Mr. Summers, who was posturing as an ardent beach walker, had been with us now for ten days, always greeted me on the dot at seven, the second that our breakfast service was supposed to start. Jermaine had been in the bar the previous evening, with some guests, so I hadn't closed before two. Now, I really wanted an hour or so in my room before my lunch shift. This had to be a pesky morning coffee order from ramblers. As if I didn't have enough to do!

A strange couple greeted me at reception. Nothing new in that at The Limes! Through the open front door, I could see George Tibbs, our local taxi driver. A rather portly man in his early sixty's. Tibbs was an acquaintance rather than a friend, but we generally got along. He was unloading numerous suitcases and trunks. George had taken off his jacket as the exertion was making him sweat somewhat. The elderly lady standing in front of me was well wrapped up in a heavy, fox fur coat, which had an extremely high collar. She wore a dark brown, wide-brimmed hat so not much of her face could be seen, except a pair of faded blue eyes and a small but pointed reddish nose. Poking out from under her bonnet was a crop of wispy, grey hair.

The lady was short in stature and somewhat resembled an ageing teddy bear, totally overdressed for this time of year. Her companion was a young girl of eighteen, maybe twenty. She stood with her feet pointing together, looking bored, and holding a small vanity case. With both hands in front of her, she had the manner of a petulant child. She wore no makeup, and her unruly hair was shoulder-length, mousey brown in colour, giving her an old-fashioned look, certainly not in a modern style befitting her age. Did grandma bear have a little girl as a companion? They didn't look at all like two people who would be travelling together. The old crone's coat had to be real fur and expensive, but it fell off her small shoulders and didn't dress her as a good cut should. My feeling was that the fur had some age to it, maybe like the owner. Old money, gone tattered! Expensive tastes, but without the means to support the former lifestyle. This was a little game I played trying to suss out guests. With Hansen's oddball visitors, I was well indulged at The Limes. But these two didn't fit the 'friends of Hansen' mould either.

My best friend, the gardener, Roy Collard, always said that my little games would get me into trouble one day. But amusements were not easy to come by here. This couple was undoubtedly going to be a challenge!

I was greeted with a bark.

"Are you in charge here?"

"Yes, madam," I replied. The teddy bear went on, in a very affected voice with a distinctive European accent.

"My granddaughter and I are here to check into this establishment. My name is Madame Aguirre and this is Miss Antonella Walford."

Weirdos, for sure, I thought. What a name! Sounded French but rhymed with squire. No more peculiar than some of Hansen's usual houseguests, I mused. Then as I glanced at the register, something strange caught my eye. There was a booking under the name of 'Aguirre' but what was odd was that I recognised the handwriting. It was Hansen's. He must have answered the phone to take the booking, which was certainly a first.

"I am sorry, Madam, but check-in is after two. Can you come back?" I was rebuffed at once.

"Now look here, young man! We are accustomed to staying at more superior hotels than this one. The concierge at the Ritz does not tell guests to 'come back later!'" There was an emphasis on the 'later.' George, who was hovering in the background, came forward.

"S'cuse me miss, is that everything? That's twenty-two pounds, please."

She fumbled in an inner pocket of the dead animal she was wearing and brought out a man's wallet then extracted two crisp notes and two coins. No tip, I noted.

"Thank you, mm.. missus."

George left off the title of 'miss' after the hostile look he got the first time. Still red in the face from his exertions, he shot a glance my way, which was an unmistakable, 'she's all yours mate!'

"Madame Aguirre, if you would like to have some refreshments in the lounge, I will see if the chambermaid has finished preparing your room." I addressed her in my poshest manager's voice, knowing full well that Mrs. Kemp didn't come in until mid-day. I looked at the booking again. A twin room! So, these two were going to share! Said so much in many ways and substantiated my first thoughts. No money. She can't afford a room for the girl. I got a dismissive wave of a worn leather-gloved hand, and the pair wandered into the lounge.

I followed them in,

"Will that be tea or coffee?"

"Brandy! A large one," she snapped.

I went upstairs. Room six had not been used for about two weeks. It was a twin room on the smallish side, overlooking the sea. Well, that's what it says in the brochure. But room six gave the best possible view of the china clay docks over on the other side of the estuary. The open sea view was on the other side of the hotel. She may prove to be a demanding customer, I thought to myself, so I put my 'difficult guest' protocol into action. This involved giving my guests an unsatisfactory room, and then I could change it for a better one. Guests don't usually complain twice. It also made them feel that I was a very attentive and hospitable manager worth tipping. I put fresh bedding on both beds and left clean towels in the en-suite, then returned to the lounge.

"Your room is ready, after all. May I ask you to check in now?"

"Another brandy first! I assume these are not going on my account?"

I noticed the girl didn't get a drink but sat upright in a Lloyd loom wicker chair, doing as she was told like a timid child, but I had an uneasy feeling with these two. I couldn't help noticing that she was attractive in a girlish, innocent sort of way.

"Here is your key, madam. You are on the first floor just to the right, at the top of the stairs. How long will you be staying with us, Ma'am?" I went for a middle of the road pronunciation of her title. I received a curt reply.

"Indefinitely!" She caught my eye; we held the position for more than a moment then she snapped again.

"Our luggage?"
"It will be brought up to your room directly."

I stared at the assorted bags and cases. Mentally, I sighed; my heart sank as I realised that I wasn't going to get any time to myself this morning. Two of the items were metal strapped wooden trunks, which appeared to have some age. They looked as if they had circumnavigated the globe on several occasions, and were extremely heavy, so I decided to get some help.

"What the fuck's in 'em?" said Roy. His West Country accent sounding thicker than ever.

"God knows! Certainly not buckets and spades for the beach!" I replied with a wry smile. Roy went on, "Feels like books!"

I wondered if they could be more of Hansen's strange acquaintances, but then, they didn't seem the type. However, if they were big readers, the couple wouldn't be bothering me too much. After the bags were deposited in room six, I returned to the lounge bar.

"I have a secure storeroom for your trunks. Would you like me to put them out of your way?" The old lady looked quite flushed, which I attributed to the two large brandies.

"That will be acceptable. We are going up to the room. Could you bring me a glass of water?"

Minutes later, I knocked on the door holding a small tray with a carafe of water and crystal glass. She opened the door and spoke.

"This room is rather small." I waited for more complaints about the room, but they never came. She took the tray and closed the door, so I left them to their unpacking. Through the window, on my way downstairs, I could see Roy outside mowing the front lawn somewhat haphazardly. I went to find the hotel's old wooden sack barrow so I could deposit the trunks in the garden store without any help.

Lunch at The Limes was in full swing with as much activity as one could expect for a Tuesday in April. We had two drinkers in the bar, one elderly couple and a family with unruly children eating in the restaurant. Mrs. Kemp, our 'housekeeper,' had stepped into the breach for kitchen duty as Jermaine was still recovering from last night's excessive sampling of a new Sauvignon, but Mrs. Kemp was now off upstairs with hoover in hand. Then the annoying Mr 'on the dot' Summers was back and wanting his regular sandwich order. It had to be cheese and pickle with a half pint of bitter. Nothing else would do, but at least he took it in his room, thank god! Then at precisely one forty-five, he went out. Always back at six, he would go to change and then appear in the restaurant by seven. After consuming his evening meal, he allowed himself a whole thirty minutes in the bar, boring me with the variants of rock pool life he had found that day. Throughout my fifteen years in the hotel trade, I had learned how to be civil to the most tedious of people. They were usually men. I now considered it to be an occupational hazard. Mr. Summers though had to be the worst for many years!

I looked up to see, Ms, Madame 'whatever' entering the bar, so I braced myself for a protest over the room.

"I would like some tea. Black with a slice of lemon?" she carried on without a pause.

"Where is your menu? You do have food here, do you not?" A peculiar thing to ask, since this is a hotel, I thought.

"And a wine list!"

No 'please' or 'thank you' was added with her curt demands. Why do some people have such an inability to be civil? In the hotel business, you become hardened to the rudeness. The young companion still hadn't uttered a word, but she had changed. Gone was the schoolgirl pleated skirt. Now she wore jeans and a sweatshirt with the words 'Hampstead College' emblazoned on the front. Her hair was pulled back into a ponytail. She didn't look so much like 'miss simple' anymore and I was reappraising my nickname for her. I settled on 'Matilda.'

Roy had taken over from Mrs. Kemp in the kitchen and was now plating up two children's meals. I offered him a bet. I knew he would be up for it. He had mentioned the young girl when they arrived, later during the effort getting the luggage upstairs, and I could see she fascinated him as much as she did me.

"Fancy a wager, Roy? First one to engage Matilda in a full conversation wins a tenner!" I said teasingly.

"You're on! Fifty quid to be the first into her knickers." The thought was appealing, but the young girl had trouble written all over her, so I felt it might be best to give the proposition a wide berth. I didn't want to complicate my life at the moment as I had been seeing a local schoolteacher called Amy. I had hoped that the relationship would develop further. But with all the entertaining lately, it had depleted my finances to the point where the lack of fifty quid could be a problem.

"No," I said. "Not fair. Oddball women are always attracted to you."

Roy Collard was as much as a mate as I had here at The Limes. He had been in the army, lower officer rank, I was led to believe, but he was always vague when asked about his past life. Apparently, he got invalided out, or so he said, but I never really found out why as he seemed perfectly able-bodied. I guess some sort of break down. Totally rubbish gardener, though! He had something of an inability to keep any form of plant life alive. Then the lawns! God knows how he could make such a mess of grass. It seemed to turn brown and wither every time he went near it. We had extensive grounds around The Limes, so Roy was a full-time member of staff with Jermaine and me. I got on well with him and for some reason, I could never fathom, he was closer than the rest of us to Hansen, which had its advantages. I assumed that his friendship with the hotel owner was the only way he kept his job.

Madame Aguirre was in the snug, a small room in between the bar and the restaurant. I was getting more and more intrigued by this lady and her companion. They had finished their meal, a salad each and a bottle of red wine. From the order, I certainly didn't have to worry about them being food critics. The old lady appeared to be lecturing the girl, but I couldn't understand what was said, as they were talking in a language, foreign to my ear. Not that I was any linguistics expert, but recently we had so many different nationalities staying, it was getting easier for me to distinguish between them.

My mind was now on tomorrow's plans for my day off. I had decided to get out of the hotel, away from work completely, have a day in town then see Amy. Staying in my room was not an option, as someone would bother me to perform some minor duty during the day. I had been dating Amy now for nearly a year, and she was my sort of girl, kind and honest. She knew her own mind, which I always liked. Attractive without being stunning, dark hair and a petite figure, she looked quite young for her age. Originally from Hertfordshire but had ended up in Devon because she got a job as a teacher at the local primary school. Her passion was cricket, which unfortunately was an interest I didn't share.

We had met through chef Jermaine. He told me he had found a beautiful English girl and was in love, but the affair only lasted for one date.

"Mon Dieu! All she talks about is cricket!" She came to The Limes a few nights later with two tickets for a one day international at the Rose Bowl, Southampton. I was attracted to her at once. Jermaine hid in one of the larders, so I did a deal with him. I would take her off his hands if he would cover me for the day. He quickly agreed. Even the cricket wasn't so bad thanks to rain and no play in the afternoon. However, things hadn't been going so well of late. I guess she was looking for more attention than I had been giving her. We had got into a routine of seeing each other once a week on my day off, then, end up in bed. In term time, she rarely got home before five-thirty, so our work commitments didn't allow for much more. The sex had got less exciting over the last few weeks. I was getting the feeling that the affair was coming to an end. Not that I wanted it to. I was really quite fond of her.

The next day, as I had a day off work, I considered trying to make the evening a bit more romantic. I resolved to pop over with a bottle of Hansen's best, a perk of the job. It would be billed out to an unsuspecting drunk who would receive a bottle of cheap house wine, which I paid for! I can't say too much and give away some 'tricks of the trade.' I mulled over my plans for a relaxing day, which had the potential to end up extremely intimately. A feeling that I was at a crossroads in life had been building up for some time. Something needed to change and I wanted Amy to be part of this transformation. An urgent distress call from the snug distracted my thoughts.

"Hello? Can someone help me, please?" It came from a quietly spoken voice, but with a note of anxiety in it. I looked up to see the girl Matilda, standing next to her grandmother who was slumped over the table, the fur coat bunched up in such a way that it looked like a dead animal just about to be butchered. I went over.

"What happened? Is she OK?"

"She just collapsed. Now she isn't moving."

I found her wrist and checked signs of life. The old lady felt extremely hot, but there was a faint pulse.

"I'll ring for an ambulance!"

I went to reception to call the emergency services. Mrs. Kemp was coming down the stairs, so I got her to go over and help. A woman's touch is much better in these circumstances, I always feel. My first consideration was that I wanted to get her off the premises as soon as possible. Strokes, seizures, fits and heart attacks. I have had to deal with them all, so I know from personal experience that they are not good for business or the smooth running of any establishment. When I returned, Mrs. Kemp had managed to prop her up in a chair, but she was still unconscious. Other guests were now milling around with interest and concern, which was not what I wanted.

"Where is that ambulance?" I muttered under my breath when Roy came out of the kitchen, grumbling.

"I am supposed to be the bloody gardener here, not the cook!" He stopped mid-sentence when he saw the scene.

"What's this, then?"

"Medical emergency," I said and went over to speak to Mrs. Kemp.

"Not sure what's occurring with this one," in her deep Devon tone.

"You're a star, Mrs. K!"

"Don't expect me to finish my work now." She grumbled on.

"I still be goin' home at 2! Got my little grandson to collect from school I 'ave."

The paramedics finally arrived and after what seemed like a prolonged period of time, Madame Teddy Bear left The Limes in an ambulance, lights flashing and sirens screaming, thoroughly breaking up the usual humdrum Tuesday routine.

My hotel guests settled back down. I looked at the evening diary and noticed a party booking in the name of 'Pilchard.' Shit! They were a group of London bankers, a totally arrogant bunch. Two or three times a year, they descended upon The Limes to spend a couple of days fishing and drinking heavily. In the evening, they would stagger back to the hotel for dinner. I have never met a more demanding and insufferable group of self-important guests throughout all my years in the trade. The trouble was they always spent so excessively, it was difficult to challenge their behaviour, even when they left their rooms in the kind of mess that Mrs. Kemp gave me a hard time over. What a day this was turning out to be!

Chapter 2

Halfway through evening dinner service, the rowdy Pilchard party were their normal obnoxious selves. I noticed Matilda walking up to the bar.

"Could I order some food here?"

"Yes, of course. What's your name, by the way?" I asked with a helpful smile as I handed her a bar menu.

"Antonella."

"How is your grandmother?"

"I don't know." The answer surprised me somewhat.

"Are they keeping her in then?"

"I'm not sure." As I continued to attend to this demanding bunch of morons, Matilda sat uncomfortably at one end of the bar awaiting my return.

"I would like this chicken' whatever' and a coke, please, but I have no money to pay for it."

"That's Ok. I'll put it on your room," but as I took her order, the proverbial penny started to drop.

"Did you go to the hospital with your grandmother?"

"No, I've been in my room." "Why?"
"They don't take passengers in the ambulance." I was astounded as I thought they did, but now it gave me something of a dilemma. It might mean a problem for me if the grandmother had an extended stay at Torbay General

hospital and Matilda had no cash. With their early arrival and the entire goings-on, I never took a card swipe. Bugger!

"Give me a minute and I'll call the hospital from my office." I tried not to sound overly concerned that I could have a non-paying guest on my hands.

"How kind of you." It's just that grandmother always arranged things and paid for them." Her tone was almost apologetic.

So, Matilda was either very cosseted or just a plain simpleton, although I felt that I was now ten quid up on my bet. As the pilchard party was getting rather raucous, I went into the kitchen to have a chat with Jermaine.

"That large group from London would like to compliment the chef," I said, grabbing his arm. My volatile and animated Frenchman might be throwing flames on the fire, but he was always up for an ego boost and this would give me some time to call the hospital.

Getting through to someone in casualty was easy enough.

"I am calling about a Madame Aguirre. She was admitted this afternoon."

"Are you a relative?"

"I am the manager of The Limes Hotel and I'm phoning on behalf of her granddaughter, who is with me. They are staying at the hotel."

"The lady has left casualty and is now in clinical assessment. Please hold and I will transfer you." The conversation was repeated several times before being finally transferred to a Scottish nurse called Sheila. She confirmed that the patient had arrived in her ward and was not very well at all, Sheila then asked to speak to the relative, so I handed the phone to Matilda.

The girl said little and then gave me back the phone.

"They want me to go to the hospital now, Ward 21."

Christ! The expression of total helplessness she exhibited pulled at my emotions. Matilda looked so lost, but this situation was getting out of hand somewhat.

"Shall I call you a taxi?" Our eyes met and she pulled a face. Her mouth twisted and she looked away from me.

"You haven't got any cash, have you? She shook her head. I tried to reassure her.

"Don't worry; I'll put it on the room." A flash of inspiration and not the first time I had done this. The Pilchard party would more than likely be so pissed that they wouldn't know how many cabs they ordered so I could give them one extra. I knew I shouldn't, but the moment of guilt abated quickly when I observed the arrogant and inebriated bankers. I called George to make arrangements and told him to collect the girl again when she phoned from the hospital. I returned to the loud group in the dining room. Surprisingly, Jermaine had calmed them down with his French humour and some fishing anecdotes.

The next morning was the start of my day off, but I was anxious about Matilda. After all, it was my balls on the line here. With no reply at her door, I phoned George Tibbs.

"What happened to that girl I sent to the hospital?"

"Dunno! Never got a call. Couldn't 'ave gone anyway. That party of bankers? One threw up in my cab, filthy bastard. That Frenchman is to blame if you ask me!" George was never one for the French, especially Jermaine.

"Left them trying to get onto the pier last night."

"The pier George? It's locked this time of year."

"I knows that and you knows that, but tell your froggy mate, will ye? Not surprised if the law weren't called. Heard alarms, I did and who's gonna pay to clean my cab then?"

I was getting exasperated with the conversation.

"Well, is it French puke or English puke? If it's French, then send the bill here, if it's English then you know where you dropped them off."

"How'll I know that then?"

"Easy! If there's garlic, snails, or frog's legs, then it's French!"

"Huh? Ye can study puke if you want, I got better 'n things to do."

A knock at my door interrupted this debate over the finer points of regurgitated haute cuisine.

"Have to go George. Someone's at the door." I put the phone down.

"I knows it's your day off, Robin, but I wants words with you."

"Come in, Mrs. Kemp. What is it?"

"I only does kitchen duty once a week so as you can 'ave a day aff. We all needs a day aff. I only does it for you. I have enough to do 'ere as it is for what I gets paid!" I needed to be wearing my diplomatic managers' hat now to deal with this. I took a deep breath.

"Mrs. Kemp. What is the problem?" I tried again.

"It's the kitchens you see. Nothin's been done from last night, nothin.' It's disgustin!'"

"I know very well. I saw the mess at breakfast. Where's the chef? He should have surfaced by now!"

"Not no sign of him." At that point, my phone rang. It was Jermaine. He garbled on without making much sense. Apparently, he had been arrested for breaking and entering. Mrs. Kemp, overhearing the conversation, let out a shocked utterance and then said, "I 'ope they throws away the key!" She scurried off as this would be a good source of gossip for her daughter Faye and friend Lucy who were also part-time employees and came in to help when we were shorthanded.

It was all I need, I thought, during my drive over to the local Police Station. This was not an unusual duty for a hotel manager of The Limes. Not just with Jermaine, but some of Hansen's friends had been known to get into trouble with the local constabulary after drinking too much. I even had a case of public indecency or flashing. Some guy of middle eastern descent had been arrested for exposing himself in front of a crocodile of school children. The embarrassed fellow claimed he was only relieving himself. Although his English was poor, his story didn't hang together, as my girlfriend Amy was the escorting teacher and witnessed it all. I had to get Hansen to sort that one out. He did so, surprisingly quickly, which was rather odd at the time as Sergeant Webster had been adamant when he spoke to me, that he was going to throw the book at him. I hoped it was George Webster who was on duty on this occasion as he was a decent copper. He came in for a drink and a meal at The Limes every so often, but today, there was a different custody sergeant.

"Hello. I've come about Jermaine, my chef at The Limes⌐?"

"Well, my boy, have you now?"

All I can tell you is that he is being held until he sobers up enough to make a proper statement. He will then be charged with breaking and entering and assaulting a police officer."

"He can be a little, well 'French!'" I offered an explanation for his behaviour.

"Can he now? Why don't you leave matters of policing to us!"

I didn't carry on with the encounter with the officer as my mood was waning by the minute. I wondered if I was going to get to do anything that I had planned for my day off. The situation gave me other matters to deal with. I had to get an agency chef in for tonight's service and the more I thought about Amy, the more I decided to sort it all out between us, one way or another. It meant wholesale changes in my life. I would tell her tonight with the wine and flowers. Yes, definitely flowers.

Back at The Limes, I first buttered up Mrs. K, which was easy, with an added titbit of gossip about Jermaine 'assaulting an officer of the law,' then I made a call to Hansen. I always deliberated on why he had purchased two hotels. He was not like any proprietor I had ever worked for or with. I put it down to him needing a business in the UK for residency purposes, that was conjecture on my part. I felt that he always pined to be somewhere else, presumably his country of origin, South Africa, but he never went back there. Maybe he couldn't. Or perhaps our Hansen was a wanted man. But wanted for what? Had he killed a man perhaps? Now my mind was racing into the world of make-believe. There was no mistaking his Cape Town accent, yet I had an inkling it might be fake. So, where did Mulhenny come from? Did I really care, so long as he paid my wages?

He took my call well, which was to my relief because it wasn't always the case. Often he sounded indifferent and regarded my issues as trivial. He told me to hold fire on the agency as he would get Jermaine out and back in the kitchen. To my astonishment, Hansen even said that if he couldn't, he would cook the meals himself as he was coming down that day to stay for a week or so. My boss then questioned me about the lady who been taken to the hospital. I wasn't sure how he knew about Madam Aguirre and made me feel there might be a spy in the camp. I dismissed that thought and focused on my next call to Amy's school. It would be break time.

Hi Amy! I've got to see you. I have things to say."

"Ok. Say them. You've got five minutes! I've got to get some art stuff ready for twenty-five eight-year-olds!" Her tone was impatient.

"No, I don't mean on the phone. Well, what I mean is, you're right. I've been thinking about what you said and I need to make a lifestyle change." Before she had time to reply, I jumped in again.

"I'll come over tonight. Is five-ish, OK?"

"No, that's too early, Rob. I've got parents evening, so pick me up from school at half seven." That gave me a jolt. Less time to fit everything in.

It wasn't till mid-day that I suddenly remembered the innocent Miss Matilda. There was still no reply from her room. Surely, she couldn't still be at the hospital? I called the main switchboard number. Eventually, the Scottish nurse came on the phone.

"Can you come and collect Miss Walford, please? We don't quite know what to do! Her grandmother died this morning and the girl seems to be in a state of shock. She sits there looking lost. We can't get any details from her. Do you know anything about them?"

"Oh, my God! No! I don't. I'm just the manager of the hotel they checked into yesterday. I only know her name, that's all. But my problem is that I still have their luggage at the hotel. This is nothing to do with me!" I pondered about what to do. I should really make another call to Hansen, but I couldn't face calling him again. He will be coming down, so I'll leave a note for him.

I have to get out of here. After all, this was supposed to be my day off. I wanted time to think about Amy. A romantic gesture was called for. I would get some flowers from that lovely little florist on the high street. I headed off to do some shopping. I could call into the hospital on my way into town and see what I could do for Matilda. I don't usually get to the shops much, as the hotel provides my food. As for toiletries, they are always left behind in rooms. It never ceases to amaze me what turns up in hotel bedrooms, and it wasn't just shaving cream and toothpaste. Hotel guests leave an assortment of goodies from laptops to sex toys, pills, and potions, some essential, some lifesaving and some illegal. Most of my wardrobe featured a discerning selection of items from lost property.

The thought sent a shiver down my back. What have I come to? Some men of my age are millionaires by now and I have nothing but an eight-year-old car, a collection of other people's clothes, lots of hair products, five packets of steradent and a lot of botheration to go with it! My resolve was strengthened to change my life. Tonight! This evening was going to be so important. I had to sort out a way forward and it had to include Amy, who was in many ways, not the easiest person to have fallen in love with. She was a touch old fashioned, knew her own mind for sure, but had an absolute horror of any of life's excesses, especially drink and drugs. Not that I was into that scene, but an odd joint or two did tend to relax me after a long shift.

As I arrived at the hospital, I spotted Matilda sitting on a bench near the entrance to A&E. She was looking down at her shoes.

"Hello!" I said. "I am so sorry about your grandmother." She looked up and I could see her eyes were red from tiredness. She was also quite pale.

"Were you close to your grandmother? The girl didn't answer, just kept gazing into space.

"I don't know what to do."

"Well, you can't sit here. Have you got any other relatives you could call? What about your mother or your father?"

"I am an orphan."

"Oh! I am sorry. Any other family or friends then?"

"Not around here. I have never been to Devon before."

"Listen! You need help from someone. First, there are the arrangements to be made for your grandmother's funeral, and then you will need to find somewhere to live. Park benches get cold at night!" She looked up and gave the slightest glimpse of a smile.

"Come on. I'll take you back to the hotel."

"Tell me about yourself. Where are you from?" The flood gates opened on the way back in the car but in stunted sentences as if she remembered each part of her seemingly bizarre life story in chapters, like a book, or a script.

"Not sure. I went to a boarding school near Brighton. My grandmother has looked after me after my parents died in a car crash. I had just finished junior school at the time. Grandmother moved around. Canada, Geneva, Lugarno, Paris, Milan, Switzerland. Nevermore than a few months, then she moved again." I noted that it was always 'Grandmother' not Nan or gran, and it had a touch of coldness about the way she said it as though she didn't like her that much. Geography wasn't her strong point either as the names of cities and countries rolled off her tongue, but she didn't appear to be sure which was which or even if there was a difference. I wonder where Lugarno is, I mused to myself.

"How old are you?" I asked a direct question.

"Twenty-six." The answer surprised me. Not a teenager, after all! Why hadn't her grandmother let her grow up?

"What are you both doing here in Devon? On holiday?"

"Grandmother had an appointment to see a lawyer around here. Someone called Davis, I think. He had promised to help with some legal stuff about an inheritance. And I think there was someone else we were supposed to be meeting."

  This was promising, so perhaps we could make some connection.

"Mr. Davis. Is he in Torquay?"

"Think so. Why?"

"I'll give him a call. He might be in a position to help." I struggled with my own motives for assisting her. Up until now, my interest in this was solely as the hotel manager. I needed the bill paying on the room and I wanted to get rid of their belongings, but I was warming to this shy girl who was, in her own way, quite intoxicating. She didn't appear to be at all streetwise, but Antonella had also sparked my curiosity. I loved to know about people which was one of the reasons I liked my job. I guess I am a nosey sod.

"Antonella is an unusual name. I have never met one before."

"It's Italian," was all I got as we pulled into The Limes car park.

 "Have you had lunch?"

 "No."

"Where did you sleep last night?"

"Didn't. I was at the hospital, so I just rested in a chair." Awkward, since technically neither of them stayed at The

Limes. I was now wondering how much I could charge. I disguised my thoughts in a display of concern for her.

"Antonella! You must eat and keep your strength up!" Goodness, what was it about this girl? Even my reprimand sounded a touch motherly.

"I will send up some sandwiches and then you can get some sleep. In the meantime, I'll try and find this, Mr. Davis."

"You are kind." She hesitated, then said,

"What's your name?"

"Robin, but my friends call me Rob."

"Rob, it is then!" She put out a hand and touched my arm as if she wanted me to cuddle her but quickly pulled away. The poor kid was dead beat.

I felt frustrated when I checked the time. My day off was diminishing rapidly. A quick search on my phone listed only one lawyer named Davis, but that drew a blank. I tried it again. There was another solicitor in Torrbridge, also called Davis. I called. He wasn't in. The office wouldn't give me any mobile number, but the receptionist said she would give him a message. A few minutes later, a man called me back.

"This is Mr. Davis. How may I help you?" I was startled to get such a quick call back. He must have been in his office all along.

"My name is Ashurst. I am sorry to bother you. It may seem a strange question, but do you know a Madame Aguirre?" The line went silent for a few seconds and then he replied,

"Client confidentiality, sir. I am not at liberty to say." Then he added,

"Where did you get my name from? And why do you ask?" His answer surprised me as I had expected a yes or no and his tone felt somewhere between defensive and confrontational.

"I have to tell you that she died this morning from a heart attack. I am the manager of the hotel where she was staying. Her belongings are here along with her granddaughter, who is in a state of shock. It was she who gave me your name but precious little else."

"Oh, I see!" The tone changed in that one syllable. He went on,

"Take my advice, Mr. Ashurst. Ask her to leave your establishment and have nothing to do with the matter. She is trouble with a capital 'T.' Good day to you. Please do not call me again." I was so taken aback, and I didn't know what to say. I sat holding the phone to my ear with my mouth wide open, dumbstruck. Was Davis a nutter? Did I imagine it, or did he sound a bit frightened? What the heck was this all about?

I looked at my watch again. I wanted to get ready for my evening with Amy. I was writing a note for Hansen when he walked in with a very sheepish looking Jermaine who had a very bruised and swollen lip.

"I thought you were going out for the day?" He sounded like he was just off the plane from the Transvaal.

"Had things to do, but I'm going out shortly on an important date with a lady!"

"Lady? I'll only delay you for five minutes then! What happened last night?"

"How do you mean?"

"Jermaine said you took a girl to the hospital and left him with some unruly customers."

"What?" I turned on Jermaine.

"You lying shit!" I faced up to Hansen squarely and made eye contact. I was fed up with covering for Jermaine and I was furious. I was certainly not going to take any blame for last night.

"I was here all night, Hansen! I got George Tibbs to take the girl to the hospital, so I left the restaurant to make the call from the office, that's all. The rest of the time, I was here! When I got back to the bar, half the fishing party had gone and Jermaine with them. I didn't know he had left the kitchen in a total mess until breakfast and Mrs. Kemp was not at all happy about having to clean up. The rest of the merry group weren't in till half two in the morning when I locked up! Gone to hospital with the girl! What crap!" I didn't think even Hansen could dispute such a defiantly argued testimony of the truth.

"Is this true, Jermaine?"

The petulant chef knew the game was up as he saw from my tone that I wasn't going to defend him, but he shrugged his shoulders to demonstrate that he was capitulating begrudgingly. Then Hansen took us both by surprise. He addressed Jermaine directly.

"You are sacked with immediate effect. No-one lies to me. Go and clear your room and leave by ten tonight! You are finished!" Jermaine looked pale. I wasn't sure if it was due to the excesses of the previous night or the news that he had just lost his job.

"Monsieur…. Please! Where do I go?" I had never seen Jermaine in begging mode before.

"That's your problem, Frenchman. Now get out of my sight!" He dismissed the chef and turned to me.

"Robin! What is the story about the lady who died?" Hansen had been well informed by someone.

"I was just writing a message for you about that." As Jermaine walked away, he looked over Hansen's shoulder at me and gave me a threatening glance. His lips snarled like he was cursing me under his breath. He thinks I've let him down, does he? Well, if he hadn't tried to blame me first! Hansen was right; he had brought it all on himself. My thoughts about Jermaine were diverted by Hansen's persistent line of questioning.

"I don't want a note. Tell me now, Robin."

"She booked in yesterday late morning, had a meal then collapsed in the snug. I guessed at the time, maybe a heart attack or something. I called the medics. They took her away. That was it. Her stuff… belongings whatever and her granddaughter are presently in room six."

"Granddaughter? What granddaughter? I didn't know she had a granddaughter!"

"Yes! The booking was a twin room!" Hansen paused, seemingly to digest the information.

"Has she said what they were doing here?"

"Apparently, to see a solicitor by the name of Davis." I reminded him that he had taken the booking, but he ignored that comment.

"Do you have any other information about them?"

"That's all I know. Just what the girl told me." It was a difficult interchange but strange in that I saw it as a problem with a customer not being in a position to pay a bill. It wasn't her fault or mine that she had died. Yet, I felt Hansen was grilling me over the circumstances and why they were here at all. I was more familiar with his usual '

just deal with it' approach. I then added,

"I will get her out tomorrow."

"No, no. Leave her here. For the moment anyway."

"Won't we need the room for the Easter break? Bookings are up because the Devon and Exeter races are on. What about the bill? It might take ages to settle and I don't think the girl has any access to cash!" As I ranted on, still angry from being dobbed in by Jermaine, Hansen's tone softened to the extent of being friendly.

"Don't worry about the bill Robin! It is my money to lose, not yours. Now, get yourself away on your date! Keep me informed of any developments. I'll be staying in my flat for the next few days and I will sort out a new chef!"

Hansen kept a suite at The Limes exclusively for himself when he had guests, but it was not often that he used it. The staff or me, in particular, weren't too keen on him staying over for various reasons. My own uneasy feeling was that I could lose control of my little side-lines. It was only my personal activities that kept me sane. I never actually stole from anyone, but a surprising number of guests seemed to misplace their personal belongings in the lounge or restaurant, which, rather strangely, always ended up in my lost property cupboard. I can't tell you how grateful and generous they were with their tips when I told them that their stuff had not been stolen but been safely recovered and was waiting to be reunited with the owner. They commended my honesty! However, at least I didn't have to worry about Antonella, for now anyway. That was peculiar too. Maybe Hansen had a heart after all.

I altered my focus to Amy. It was half-past five, so I needed to shower, change then get over to her school. The flowers! Oh, bugger! I forgot the flowers. No point buying any now! Women always know if they are purchased from a petrol station, which are grabbed as an afterthought as you are rushing to see them. They just never have the same effect as a florist wrapped bunch with a card. You can see the look of disappointment, yet flowers are flowers. Aren't they? Why do women read so much into actions? They are not louder than words and things don't always have a meaning. Often, they are just things.

At ten to eight, I was sitting in my car in the school car park. I had seen parents come and go. Several teachers had come out and got into their cars but not Amy. It was a warm night, the warmest so far this spring. I had the window open, just going over the events of the day in my mind, staring at the daffodil stalks parading in a long row beside the road. Daffodils were my favourite flowers. They heralded the start of spring yet they never seemed to last for long and then they had such messy stalks. The grass which grows through them never gets cut so I considered whether the untidiness was worth the few days of glorious yellow.

My mind switched back from yellow to grey. Jermaine was always on roster for breakfast, the morning after my day off. It gave me time to see Amy as she left for work if I stayed over and then I wasn't needed until the lunch shift. But with no Jermaine, it was looking like it would be down to me. It was unlikely that Hansen would prepare the breakfasts and be up for seven, as I know Mr Summers would be.

"Mr Summers and his wife, 'Anne'!!" That was Roy's smutty little joke as he would announce their arrival to the kitchen staff. It was mildly amusing the first day but was quite predictable after a week. How my mind is racing! God, I have got to switch off from it all. I was jolted from my thoughts when the passenger door opened and in jumped Amy.

"What a day! I swear the parents are more stupid and difficult than their kids!" Amy ranted on for some while about the trials and tribulations of teaching. I waited for this outburst to subside.

"So, how was your day?"

"Different." She raised an eyebrow. Then I added some heartfelt words.

 "I've missed you so much!" She looked at me intently. It took the wind out of her sails.

"Really! I didn't think you cared anymore."

"I have always cared. More than you think, Amy. It's just that I know what you want and it's a big change for me. A bit daunting, that's all, but I have come to a decision!"

"OK!" was all I got in response. It crossed my mind that a bit of honesty seemed to be working better than any floral arrangement. We sped along the Devon lanes to Amy's house, which was a lovely old former railway cottage. A little close, for my taste, to the main London line, especially when two trains passed. It felt like a 10.2 on the Richter scale in the front garden.

Nevertheless, it had all the attributes of a quaint English country cottage with lilac clusters of wisteria cascading down the front wall and soft pink roses climbing around the door. It was Amy's pride and joy, but the mortgage was a real burden for her on a primary scale three salary. She used to have a lodger; another teacher called Sarah, who worked with her. She paid good rent, which gave Amy a little spare cash for coming over to The Limes of an evening. Since the friend had moved in with her boyfriend, Amy was finding money tight.

"Have you eaten?"

" No, not since lunch." As I drove on past her house, Amy gave me the second sideways look of the night.

"Where are we going?"

"The Sparrows Nest?"

"But you don't like eating out!"

"My treat!" I said. She was dead right about that. I'd spent my life eating out, working in hotels and restaurants as I did. To have a lovely, home-cooked meal was always a treat for me, just like it was for everyone else to go and have dinner somewhere. But I had got lucky with a guest recently. A rather pompous gent, a former town councillor, Mr. Adderley, had booked a room for two at The Limes just for one night. There was no sign of Mrs. Adderley, a charming lady who I knew quite well. She was prominent in the local amateur dramatics and they all used to call in The Limes after rehearsals. Mr. Adderley lost his coat, or so he thought. Surprisingly, it ended up in lost property. He left it on a chair when he went into the restaurant, with his female 'companion.' I knew who it belonged to and thought I could work it to my advantage along with his keys and some personal stuff which included a neatly wrapped little purchase from 'Boots the chemist! When he checked out, I told him I had found his coat. He quickly rifled through the pockets. When he saw everything was present, he rewarded me with a £50 tip.

"Keep this between ourselves, Robin. There's a good chap. Eh, what!"

"I certainly will, sir. I hope everything was satisfactory. I hope to see you here again soon."

Yet another hotel guest successfully exploited! I still had Adderley's crisp new fifty in my wallet, which I was now putting to good use.

The open log fire season had finished, so we sat at a table for two, almost inside the inglenook at the Sparrows Nest, an old coaching inn which hadn't changed for years, locally famous for its carvery. Simple traditional food and all home produced. I did most of the talking and laid my cards on the table. So much so, that I even took myself by surprise, with the things I was saying. How much I wanted to share my life with her, that I needed a new job or career which didn't include unsocial hours. But perhaps she could help me find an alternative as I had only ever worked in hospitality. I laid myself open and at Amy's mercy to see if she would help me. It was quite a speech, which appeared to go down well. Amy's hand came over the table to hold mine. Then we got onto Hansen as the food arrived.

"I don't trust him," I said.

"Thought you liked him?" said Amy, tucking into a well-cooked hunter's chicken and chips.

"You can like someone and still not trust them." I paused to give this some thought, then continued. "Nothing about Hansen ever really adds up!" Snippets of the day's events came flooding back into my mind. Amy interrupted my thoughts as she recalled a particular incident.

"Remember when he got that flasher off? Our head, Mrs. Winstanley, made a formal complaint to the police. She definitely did because Joyce, the school secretary, told me."

"You were there when it happened, weren't you?"

"Yes! With all those kids coming back from swimming lessons but nothing ever came of it. Did Hansen ever mention it?"

"Just told me that he had contacts." Amy continued to press her point.

"Mrs. Winstanley was furious when she learned that no charges were brought!"

"What are you getting at?"

"Rob! Hansen had only been in the country for a matter of months. How could he have made contacts with the sort of people who can do favours like that in such a short space of time?"

"I can't argue with that. You're right!"

 "What else do you know about him?"

 "Who? Hansen or the perv?" This brought a laugh from Amy.

"He didn't have much to flash from what I saw!" We burst into laughter at this and many of the past few days' exasperations were released for both of us. After a delicious supper and a bottle of red wine, we felt full and wonderfully mellow. I reached out and held her hand.

"Let's go home?"

"I have a friend who could help you with some re-training. Do you fancy computers?"

"Not as much as I fancy your naked body!" She giggled and grinned lovingly at me.

"Charmer you!"

Chapter 3

It had been a good night. Not only was it the best sex
we had ever had, but I felt we had addressed the issues
between us in a positive way. Now I was on my way back
to The Limes with a smile on my face. It was a lovely day
and nothing cheered me up more than driving along the
coast road with the blue sea on one side, interspersed with
random lines of white breakers. I felt at peace with the
world. The sun was out and the air was clear on one of
those all so infrequent days in Devon when I could see Hay
Tor on the skyline, a distinctive granite effigy on
Dartmoor.

I pulled into the manager's space only to find it had been
taken, but even a selfish parker couldn't dampen my mood.
In front of the terrace, we had a clifftop grassed area with
benches looking out to sea. I spotted Antonella staring out
over the ocean, so I went over to her.

"Nice to see you up and about." She looked up from her
gaze and just said,

"Hello!" so I tried again to engage her in conversation.

"What's happening about your Grandmother? Have any
arrangements been made yet? I didn't get anywhere with
Davis." Antonella frowned and her eyes moved back to the
sea.

"Questions!" she said irritably. "Why does everybody keep asking me questions?"

"Who has been asking you questions?"

"The boss of the hotel. Him with the weird accent, tall man with red hair!" That was Hansen sure enough, but he was behaving completely out of character at the moment. Interrogating hotel guests in this way was even more peculiar. The girl clearly had no answers to give.

A seagull landed at the feet of a mother and little boy just in front of us. The lad had some crisps and was feeding the bird, but his mum was getting agitated as more gulls were arriving and she started shouting at her son to stop it. We both sat and watched the scene. I wasn't sure what to say next. After all, Antonella wasn't my problem, so why did I feel responsible? I was sorry for her, I guess.

"How can I get a train to Norfolk?" The question took me by surprise.

"There is a station over the river in Torrimouth with trains to London. You go via London then change stations for a train to Norwich." I was pretty well informed about public transport as many guests asked about the local train or bus services.

"Why do you want to go there?"

"I want to go back to Burnside Hall. It's in Norfolk."

"What's Burnside?"

"My friends are there. I lived there." The conversation appeared to be unwrapping her mysterious life, so I tentatively enquired further.

"You didn't live with your grandmother then?"

"No. I did when my mother died but only for a short time. Then she sent me to a school by the sea. When I was eighteen, she took me to Switzerland, but I had problems there, so I went to Burnside. My grandmother came to Norfolk last Thursday, we spent three days in London and then she told me I had to come to Devon with her and meet this solicitor called Davis." There was a pause then she went on,

"I was happy at Burnside. I didn't want to come here. Grandmother said it was to settle our future so I could have what was mine." She was talking in riddles and I really felt that this poor kid was unhinged. I left it there and she turned her head back out to sea again.

As I walked across the lawn to the front entrance of the hotel, I thought that she had to be the most immature twenty-six-year-old I'd ever known. I'm usually a good judge of character, but I just couldn't work her out. Possibly a bit backward but also confused and frightened. I made a mental note to check out Burnside Hall. The idea of a little sleuthing appealed to me. Anyway, I could work the situation to my advantage.

As I strolled up to the bar where Roy was serving, I noticed Hansen in the corner with a young couple. His back was to the door, so he missed my entrance. Roy spotted me and gestured that he wanted a word, so I lingered while he had finished pulling a pint for a customer. I was quite chilled, the night away from the madhouse, which was The Limes, had done me good.

"Jesus Rob! Am I glad to see you!"

"Why? What's occurring, mate?"

"We have a new chef for one and it's as plain as the nose on my head; he can't cook!" Roy paused, but before I could say anything, he rambled on.

"The boss is frazzled to hell! Did you know that Mr. Summers and his wife were kicked out this morning! Literally thrown out of the door with their things!" I was gobsmacked at this news.

"What?" I said in disbelief. This news hit me like a slap on the face. My most profitable side-line was gone. I was the only person who knew what Summers was up to and why. He was working undercover for some authority and the rock pool story was just a sham. In fact, he was watching the local fishermen, making sure they didn't exceed their 'time at sea' quotas, EU regulations, or something. His watch was at half seven or just before full tide. It was why breakfast had to be on the dot. He had confided in me and asked me to keep it under my hat. When he went to his car, he would either go to several of the clifftop locations, sit and watch the sea traffic. Then, I would make a quick call to the lads on the quay to let them know which way he had gone. Either up the coast or down, so they sailed in the opposite direction. I was rewarded with the freshest fish ever to be sold to The Limes, and in turn, the hotel was paying me wholesale fish prices. Everyone was a winner and we were getting a reputation for the seafood served in the restaurant. Even Summers admitted to me that he didn't like prosecuting the local fishermen, so I guessed it was why he had taken me into his confidence.

"There was no-one on breakfast duty, so he went to Hansen to complain and he just slung him out! Be warned, mate! The boss is ultra- jittery right now."

"Oh! Thanks for the warning, but it's face, by the way!"

"What?" said Roy blankly.

"Plain as the nose on my face. It's not head, you idiot!" I corrected him.

"Rob, mate! Aren't you listening? Something's going on here. I don't like it. It's odd, very odd. An old lady dies, new staff arrive, the boss is behaving oddly. And another thing. Suddenly, the hotel is full. We weren't full three days ago and the races aren't until the end of next week. That's odd if you ask me!"

"Look, Roy! The only thing that's odd around here is how you ever got a job as a gardener and you owe me ten quid! Did you see me talking to the girl on the bench? Her name's Antonella!" Roy looked at me, knowing I wasn't taking him seriously, but he got in with a parting shot.

"You may take my words in jest, but it's all very odd!" Roy left off as another customer came up to the bar. He caught my eye, a short man with an eastern European look, dressed in a business suit but not tailored. It was 'off the peg,' trying to look expensive but not quite getting there. He ordered something from Roy. I glanced at his group. There were three other gents with similar appearances sitting around a bar table drinking coffee. 'Coffee for four,' I thought. 'That's odd. Four men wouldn't order coffee. At least one would have had tea unless they were foreign, that is. When we get groups of blokes, it's usually fishermen, golfers, racegoers, ramblers, but not businessmen, not here at The Limes. They tended to stay in The Grand or The Regent. How odd! I smiled to myself. Oh, dear! Roy has got me at it now.

Hansen must have seen me going up the stairs so he ran after me.

"Robin! I am glad you are back. I've been trying to call you. Where have you been?"

"It was my day off, remember? I didn't want to drive back, so I stayed at my girlfriend's house last night. Can I have a shower and change?" I never took an overnight bag to Amy's, as I knew she would think it was presumptuous of me and send me packing.

"Don't take me or sex for granted!" she once told me,

"No! I want to speak to you for a minute, please!" Roy was right. Hansen was definitely stressed. I turned and came down the stairs almost petulantly but followed him into the office. Technically my shift didn't start till after lunch and I knew that Hansen's minutes could last for hours, but I wasn't in the mood to stand my ground on this. I guessed there might be more profitable battles to be won later with him.

"We have a new chef and his name is Ravi. He lacks experience with this sort of establishment, so can you show him the ropes? I am here to cover all your front of house duties."

"Hansen, I'm no chef! You know that."

"Robin, you know what to do better than anyone. This is a favour I am asking of you. It will only be for a few days." Being in the kitchen meant disruption to my routine, with no side-lines whatsoever. I thought about protesting, but 'what the hell.' I had other things on my mind, but the look in his eye made me think again. It was something I hadn't seen before.

"He needs help getting ready for lunch, so go into the kitchen straight away!" That was it. I was never one to be shat upon.

"Hansen! I need to change! I'm in the same clothes as yesterday." I gestured to the staff rota on the wall.

"I don't come on duty until 2 o'clock! Look!" I grabbed the list and handed it to him. Hansen picked up a pen and changed the time from 2 pm to 10 am. I was building up to go off on one at such a long shift ahead, but he looked like he was going to throw his pen across the table. Then he thought better of it and kept hold of it. He looked at me and tried to contain his agitation.

"Then, change the evening rota!" That meant locking up, which could be any time after midnight. I was getting quite exasperated.

"Change with whom exactly? Are you doing the last shift?"

"Of course!" he said, quite aggressively, then followed with,

"In these difficult times, Robin, we all have to make sacrifices. Be in the kitchen in ten minutes!" With that, he stormed out. What the hell? Difficult times! What difficult times?

I took a deliberate fifteen minutes before returning downstairs again. This was my defiant retaliation against his officious directive! As I entered the kitchen, Hansen was chatting to one of the coffee drinkers in a language that I didn't recognise. The man was short in stature and had an extremely poor posture. He was casually leaning against the work surface and dressed in a suit, so inappropriate for kitchen work. I also felt his clothes hadn't seen the inside of a washing machine for some time. Hansen gestured to me.
"Robin, please? A word?" He took me aside.

"Ravi's English is not too good and he is a little volatile." He tried to make a joke by comparing him to Jermaine, but I didn't see anything funny in this flippant comment and I saw red. I replied as forcefully as I dared to muster with Hansen.

"Nothing like Jermaine? Look at the guy! He's not a chef. Just what is he wearing? That's not kitchen attire. Where are his whites? Look, Hansen, is he illegal? Why does he not speak any English if he is working in this country? I am responsible for hiring all staff, which makes me think you are having problems with money. Is that why you are taking on these sorts of people behind my back?" So many questions, but Hansen did not answer any of them.

"None of your goddam business! I pay your wages, so do as I say!" His tone was threatening as he glared at me, but then he softened a little.

"Robin, my friend. Use him as you like for the time being. I'll see about hiring a proper chef."

 "I want him in whites, Hansen!" His retort matched my insolence with vexation and severity.

"Whatever!" He barked at me. "See to it then!" The tone changed again.

"The girl in room six?" His complete change of subject took me off guard.
"She seems to talk to you. I can't get anything out of her. Has she said anymore?"

"No. I told you. They came to see a local solicitor called Davis." The whole situation at the Limes was making me nervous. I could sense something heavy was coming down, which made me somewhat cagey myself. I decided to be a little more economical with the truth and with Hansen's intervention, I hadn't had time to do any research on Burnside Hall.

"Davis? Are you sure? Did she not mention anyone else?" I shook my head, but Hansen would just not let it go.

"Where is she now?"

"I really don't know. I wasn't here last night!" I was getting irritated and confused by this line of questioning and then sarcastically added,

"She certainly wasn't in the shower with me!" Hansen turned and was aggressive.

"Don't get smart! Your job is to run this hotel when I am not here. When I am, you follow orders. Do you understand me, my friend?"

"Clear enough," I replied. Unwittingly, Hansen was making my decision easy. I had decided to quit after everything that I had discussed the previous evening with Amy, so now it was just a matter of timing. Maybe I could move in with her. What had I got to lose? If I left and he let me go without a fight, then it confirmed that Hansen had cash problems. If he backtracked and really needed me, then my position was strengthened. I would be out of the kitchen. I played my trump card in a calm and relaxed voice.

"You have no right to speak to me like this. Can I leave straight away, or do you want me to work a week's notice?" You'd thought that Hansen had been hit by a ten-ton truck with the expression of disbelief on his face. His mouth opened. He went to speak then stopped. The silence between us was deafening. At last, he replied in a softer tone.

"Robin, Robin! Let's not quarrel like this! You are a good guy. I value you as my manager. I am sorry if I have offended you. I only want some teamwork going on here!" He clapped both my shoulders and then walked off.

"What the hell do you make of that?" Roy's voice came from behind where we had been standing.

"Did you hear all of that then, you nosey sod?"

"Every word. Would you walk out? Just like that. No word even to your best mate?"

"Yes, Roy. I would." I replied with conviction.

"Jump before you're pushed, mate. That's my philosophy. I've been caught out before in this trade when an establishment where I was employed went tits up, owing me wages and I'm not letting that happen again." Roy looked alarmed.

"That's it, isn't it? You do know something. The Limes is going bust and we'll all be out of a job!" He was starting to sound panicky.

"Roy! Get a grip, man! I don't know any more than you do."

I set about finding some whites for Ravi. I gave him a set of Jermaine's, which I found in the laundry. They were not a good fit, although the two men were the same height. Jermaine was pencil-thin, Ravi was stocky, but what the heck. I guessed after my encounter with Hansen, we would soon be having another chef anyway. I got Ravi preparing salads. It took me less than a minute to see that the man had no kitchen skills whatsoever. His use of our Damascus steel kitchen knives was nothing less than dangerous. I attempted to demonstrate how the celery and spring cabbage should be chopped then diced, but in the end, I gave up. If he cut himself, then that would be another problem for Hansen. I knew Jermaine had batched cooked some beurre blanc sauce for the fish, so I went to find them in the fridge.

Luckily, Thursday lunchtime was not busy. I tried to make conversation with Ravi, looking to discover if he knew anything, but his lack of English was a barrier. I was suspicious of the guy as he was a nervous fellow. On edge, all the time and kept looking around as if he were expecting something to happen to him. I wondered where Hansen got these bizarre people from. It certainly wasn't from a reputable catering agency. I phoned Mrs. Kemp and asked if her daughter was available for the afternoon to do some kitchen preparation, also to look after the afternoon teas and coffees. The lovely weather would encourage a steady flow of thirsty walkers. After all, I was still manager of this hotel and after my set-to with Hansen this morning, I thought he wouldn't challenge my authority on this point of staffing.

We also had two large group bookings in the restaurant this evening, so an extra pair of hands would be useful. Hansen was right about one thing; the kitchen was no problem for me. I just didn't like being in there. Food preparation, then the cooking, then service and cleaning down after were monotonous and uninteresting chores. I am a people person, I guess, not an artist. Over the years, being in the trade, I've had to fill in everywhere. In fact, most of my friends have been chefs, some of the best. Chopping up vegetables, however, did give me a little time to consider the recent events without any distractions and the more I thought about things, the more I couldn't get this young girl out of my head. There were so many things that didn't square up. I kept wondering why there were no funeral preparations. My natural curiosity drove me on to get to the bottom of what was going on.

Later that afternoon, I had some time to myself to make some calls. Ravi had vanished, which was no concern of mine. I phoned Amy first, to be sure of my ground as I couldn't walk away from The Limes if I had nowhere to go. Amy was a little reticent at first, then, in the end, said she was not sure. This came as a blow after everything we had talked about the previous day. Our conversation left me feeling somewhat subdued, so I started to re-evaluate my position. The phone rang again some minutes later. It was Amy.

"Rob, I'm so sorry, but it never occurred to me that you would move in here, but of course, it's fine. Are you serious about a career change?"

"It might take me a little time to find the right thing, but I want to give it a go."

I was really hoping that moving in would mean coming together much more, but Amy now started to talk about making a list of household chores that could be divvied up between us. Ever the practically minded Amy.

My next call was to my fisherman friend, Steve. I gave him the low down on the Summers situation and said I would try to find out where he had moved to, as I knew most of the hotel trade in the area. Then, some internet digging into what Antonella had said about, 'Burnside Hall,' Norfolk. It didn't take long to find out what I was looking for. It was a Christian retreat, near Fakenham.

'With beautiful surroundings, Burnside offers peace, tranquillity and time for inner body reflection and devotion. The perfect place to experience the beauty of God's creation. Residents can participate in the everyday duties of the establishment or enjoy many diverse recreational activities on offer.'

The home page showed a large hall in acres of woodland and photographs of residents engaged in creative tasks like basket weaving, painting, and cooking. They had such contented looks on their faces; it reminded me of the film, The Stepford Wives, which I once watched with Amy under protest. Far too sickly sweet for my liking, but maybe I shouldn't be so cynical.

It was clearly a place to go for people who couldn't cope with the modern world. Now Antonella was starting to make a little more sense. She'd had some sort of breakdown, maybe in Switzerland. Gran couldn't cope, so shipped her off to some backwater retreat out of harm's way. It also might explain why she was so naive. I looked out of my window, but the beach top bench where Antonella had been sitting was empty. I went outside and found Roy hacking at the edges of the lawn with blunt shears.

"Have you seen that girl from room six?" I asked.

"Not you as well! The boss has been asking me the same question every hour on the hour. What's Hansen's interest in her? Do you know?"

"I have no idea. It's just that I spoke to her this morning on the bench over there."

"Well, I think..." I quickly interjected,

"Roy! If you say the word 'odd' again! I'll cut your balls off with your blunt shears! Why don't you sharpen them, you will make a far better job." He laughed and walked away from me, holding his crotch.

I felt slightly concerned that Antonella might do something silly. I went back inside the hotel and promptly bumped into Hansen. He looked a little uncomfortable to see me but was pleasant enough.

"Is everything ok, Robin? Look, my friend, I need you here, '*you son of a bitch.*' You're the best manager I've ever had!" This was a clumsy compliment aimed to butter me up.

"I'm fine, Hansen." I kept it short as I wasn't going to answer any more of his questions about Antonella, but he then changed the subject completely. He carried on,

"I have been looking at the restaurant receipts. They are up double for this time last year. What have you been doing?" I felt he was rumbling me. How could I tell him about Summers?

"It's the fish." He raised an eyebrow.

"The fish?"

"Yes," I added,

"I get it from the boys on the quay. It's caught and eaten on the same day. The only way to eat fish is fresh, not frozen." It was clear from the first day of my employment that Hansen was not a hotel man. I liked to play him with my superior knowledge.

"No food is improved with freezing except maybe peas, but it is especially true of seafood. Hansen, all the specials are fish dishes and they are the days catch, whatever that might be. It appears that the diners love the quality of our food and keep coming back." An idea gelled in my head to overcome the minor problem of no receipts while not being sure Hansen wasn't doing some fishing of his own.

"I take some petty cash to pay the lads direct. That way, we get a really good price and what's caught doesn't go on their quota." True or not, I didn't care, as I knew Hansen would have no idea what I was doing. We went into the office where I could show him the figures on the office computer.

"Here, look! These costs are for fish purchased." Hansen looked intently and asked,

"How many meals does that make?"

"The fish comes in at 50p to £1 per portion. Any leftovers go into the Fisherman's pie which has been selling really well. Jermaine's been using up the smoked haddock and cod, which he's topped with fluffy potatoes and parsley. Customers love it!" To emphasise the point, I continued,

"The wholesaler charges nearly £2 per portion, so we get a much better product and cheaper. In fact, I was just off to the quay now to get tonight's catch." Hansen looked extremely impressed by this.

"Good work Robin! What can I say! You get along now. I will tell everybody tonight in the hotel that we have the best seafood in the southwest! By the way, who is on kitchen duty?"

"Faye, the student," I said. "She's doing afternoon teas with Ravi. With a pause, I added, "He's the pot washer!" Hansen moved close, he towered over me and stooped to whisper in my ear.

"It is a favour to a friend of mine, that's the only reason he is here. To be honest, Robin, I don't want the 'mother fucker' either!" Hansen's tone was almost apologetic. Then he said,

"We don't need anyone else new around until business is sorted with that 'little bitch!'" It took me a moment to figure out to whom he was referring. Such language from Hansen was new to me and directed at technically, a hotel guest. It all confirmed my doubts that all was not well at our Devon idyll and my future should lie elsewhere. I was also concerned about Antonella as in my opinion she didn't deserve Hansen's wrath,

It only occurred to me in mid-conversation that now, I had the chance to slip out for an hour so that I could find the girl. I drove into town and parked up outside the station. It didn't take me too long to find Antonella. She was sitting in the platform café watching the trains. The station café was a rather shabby establishment. A chalked-up list of refreshments was displayed over the counter. Two mature women were busy with a coffee machine and a line of three customers queued at the till. Other people sat at the tattered wooden tables and chairs on the platform.

"Figured you might be here," I said. Her face lit up when she saw me. "What are you doing?"

"Thought I might jump onto a train, but I forgot where you said I had to go. I'm not sure if I could get away travelling without any money!" After some thought, she said that she didn't want to go back to the hotel with 'those men' around.

"Men?"

"The ones at the hotel. They said they were policemen, but I don't believe them. They scared me."

"I have seen them hanging around the hotel and I can only guess that they are interested in the circumstances around your grandmother's death. There has to be an inquest." I said, reassuringly. I didn't want to alarm her, but I could not see why police would be involved at this stage, especially as it was just natural causes.

"I'll give you a lift back to the hotel if you want, but first, I have to buy some fish." We walked in silence through the shopping streets down to the fisherman's huts. So many squawking seagulls were about, pecking ferociously at whatever they thought might be food, we almost had to kick them out of the way.

"Will they still be at the hotel?"
"Who?"

"Those men?"

"Well, I didn't see any police when I left, but you will need to sort things out with them or the authorities at some point. You can stay with me for a while, though." She reached out and slipped her arm in mine.

"That would be nice. I like you, Robin, sorry, Rob!" I couldn't see how this could profit me in any way, but a sloppy form of compassion from inside me took over.

The sight of fresh catch on the harbour quayside seemed to fascinate Antonella. At first, she was put off by the wriggling and squirming mass, saying she couldn't look, but then the different shapes and textures started to interest her and she asked about their names. Dean was gutting a good box of mackerel, which he had caught, his long knife slitting them speedily down the belly, amazingly, he was not taking any more than five seconds over each one. The blood and entrails were being dropped into a bucket accompanied by the ever-present noise of the gulls, eager for any titbits. In the end, I got my bag of fish. We headed back to The Limes, the strong smell of the sea permeating through my vehicle. I opened the window.

"I quite like the smell!"

"You're a strange one!" I turned and smiled at her. "No-one else I know likes the smell of fish!"

"It reminds me of when I was a little girl and the stuff my dad did."

"Was your dad a fisherman then?"

"No. Not sure what he did, but he used to go away a lot." I was learning that these conversations with Antonella often led nowhere, so we sat in silence the rest of the way.

Hansen saw us arrive, and with him were three of the four coffee drinkers. Antonella noticed them too and rushed up to her room to be out of the way. After our earlier and rather heated exchanges, Hansen was choosing his words with care and showing more civility towards me.

"Robin, I thought you were going for fish?" He stopped mid-sentence as it was evident from the smell permeating the lobby that I was carrying a bag of the local catch.

"And where's the girl?" Trying not to give too much away, I mentioned briefly that I'd seen her in town and given her a lift back.

"Good man Robin, good man!" I scurried away to the kitchen. It was my sanctuary. I didn't want to get into any deeper conversations with Hansen or his mates. There was enough going on to consider. I was genuinely worried about Antonella because I couldn't understand why Hansen was so interested in her. He followed me in. Ravi made such a comical figure with his poorly fitting whites standing in front of the sink, washing pots. Hansen opened his mouth to speak, but I butted in.

"Ask him if he can fillet fish." A conversation then ensued. Hansen could evidently speak Ravi's language. It started to get a little heated. Ravi was gesturing to the sink, obviously complaining. Hansen put up his hand to signify that the exchange was now at an end. Then he turned to me.

"No. He can't. So, what did you talk about with the girl?" I sighed. Here we go again with this interrogation. I tried to divert his attention.

"Mostly about food and types of fish. General stuff." I replied.

"Stuff!" Hansen had a way of spitting the last word you said to him, back at you. He did it all the time. So much so, that I had more than a few bets with Roy what his first word would be in a conversation. After I won several times, Roy spotted the habit himself.

"Yes! Just stuff! We went to the harbour to find my friends who own the fishing boats. I don't think she has seen fish before unless it was in a breaded finger! But she asked me about recipes and that kind of thing. I think the girl has an interest in cooking." I thought that if I could discourage

Hansen's fascination with her, maybe I could make out that she was not worth pursuing.

"Look, Hansen! In my opinion, she's not all there!"

"Not all there?" He did it again.

"Yes! Slow, dense! Do you know she is twenty-six?"

"Twenty-six!" I got distracted, dreaming how much money I could make from this conversation.

"Anyway," I carried on. "She has no understanding about what to do about her grandmother, funeral arrangements, death certificates. All of it." Hansen thought for a moment before he spoke.

"I do not believe you are correct in your assessment of her, Robin, which could make things very difficult!" I didn't have a clue what he was talking about so

I took the bull by the horns and demanded to know what was going on.

"Hansen? Please tell me why you have this interest in her?" As I started to fillet the fish, Hansen's eyes went to my knife work and hand movements, seemingly fascinated by my actions.

"You do that well, my friend!" Then there was a pause.

"Look, Robin! I'm telling you this in confidence. I am sworn to secrecy and you must keep what I say to yourself. The old lady was being followed. I have the police here, not local bobbies but big guys from London. Apparently, the old woman stole a lot of papers, not sure what, but all extremely sensitive, high-value stuff. The transaction was going to take place here at The Limes. She had a buyer ready. The owners want it all back and they also want to catch the criminals involved. But, they didn't know about the girl, who she is, or what her connection is. Even why she travelled here with the old lady is a mystery." Hansen paused then added,

"The unfortunate death has thrown everyone into a tail-spin, so now, your Antonella is the only link. We are not sure what the buyer knows about the demise of his contact, maybe nothing. They might still show up here." His explanation confirmed to me that something out of the ordinary was going on, but I still didn't get why Hansen, as a hotel owner, would be so involved.

"Anything she had is still in room six," I informed him.

"Room six?" He shook his head.

"They had a quick look while you were entertaining the girl at the harbour. Now they want to have a more thorough search, so, Robin, my friend, tomorrow, you take her out for a few hours!" I was uneasy and started to object but bit my tongue when it suddenly occurred to me that no-one except Roy and me knew about the two travelling trunks! In any case, what sort of police just searched rooms without any kind of warrant?

"Err. Ok. I guess so." Never one to miss an opportunity, I was going to be the first one to look inside the trunks. There might be an earner in it for me, so I kept quiet.

"Good man Robin. I know I can trust you. I want this business sorted and then we can all get back to normal." Ravi started moaning again, obviously unhappy with something. I finished preparing the fish and then I went in search of Roy. He was nowhere to be seen, so I tried phoning him.

"Hi mate, where are you?"

"I'm in Exeter. It's my day off. Why?"

"Just needed a lift with something. No worries. It can wait until tomorrow."

"Been given some errands by the boss to do when I'm next in."

"Oh? He didn't tell me. I've got you down for a couple of bar shifts."

"Sorry, didn't have a chance to say. Its cash flow, isn't it? That's what's going on. Tell me straight, Rob! The hotel is going under. Right?"

"No, Roy. I don't think so." I left it at that for the time being. I put the phone down.

Faye came in with the rest of the evening staff, our usual two waitresses.

"Do you want me to stay on later?" Faye enquired. With Roy's absence and me in the kitchen, who was going to do the bar?

"I'll just check with the boss." I couldn't find Hansen anywhere, so I made the call to give her extra shifts.

"Please. If you don't mind, it's going to be a busy night, so can you do the bar until late?"

"Great! I need the money!" Faye was a university student, home for Easter.

"Tomorrow afternoon as well, then?" I changed the rota in the office. Sorted.

Something was still bothering me about all this, so I went to get a world map from the bookshelf in the snug, then found Ravi outside by the bins having a crafty fag. I pointed to a map of Europe and made some gestures.

"Me here. Home! You? Where you from?" He appeared to understand what I was asking as he thumbed through the pages and stopped at North Africa. His finger went across the page, but before he could indicate anything, a Transvaal voice boomed out from behind me.

"What are you doing, Robin?"

I was thankful for my ability to think on my feet.

"Just looking to see if he is Muslim. Can't give him the pork to prep, can I?"

"Pork?.... I see, no, he can't work with pig flesh." Hansen didn't even ask Ravi, which meant he must know the man personally. I thought of a new way to make myself appear indispensable and capable.

"Are you helping out in the bar tonight, Hansen?"

"Why?" he spat at me.

"Well, you let Roy go! I had him assigned for bar duties, so now we are short-staffed and it looks like it's going to be a busy night with all our restaurant bookings." This appeared to be new information for Hansen. It took some moments for it to sink in.

"I have other duties for Roy, which are far more urgent. Sorry, Robin. It slipped my mind. I should have told you."

I then pressed my point home.

"Don't worry. I'll see if Faye's friend is free to do some extra shifts and then re-do the rota."

"I know my hotel is in good hands, my boy!" Hansen always turned to flattery when he had been shown up. As he left, I thought to myself, 'he hasn't a clue about running this hotel.'

The atmosphere around the place that evening was tense, but things went well and we managed to get through service without too many issues. The guests never realised what chaos was going on behind the scenes. The following morning, I was in the kitchen at seven. Ravi was there too. Give him his due, he couldn't cook, but he was prompt on the job. I got him frying eggs, a task which required minimal talent and he even seemed to enjoy it. As he sweated over the heat of the pans, he wiped his brow and grinned at me. I popped to the lobby just in time to meet the paperboy. The headline of the local rag jumped out.

Body on beach……..

I read on….

The body found yesterday on Briscombe beach has now been identified as prominent Devon Solicitor, Gyres Davis, a 42-year-old divorcee from Torquay.

Chapter 4

My mouth went dry. I had to sit down. A shudder ran down my spine. Surely, this couldn't be connected, could it? I had spoken to this man only two days ago and his words still had so much resonance. What was the sentence he used? '*trouble with a capital T*.' He was frightened, that was for sure. Did Hansen say something about Davis? Yes! I remember now… 'Davis knows nothing.' Was Davis the buyer? Somehow, I didn't think so. Maybe a middleman who was being squeezed? This was getting heavy. Guyres! That's a strange name. Was he French? My head was spinning with all these notions, and then I saw Antonella coming down the stairs, which distracted me. I greeted her pleasantly.

"Would you like some breakfast?"

"Yes, please."

"I didn't see you last night."

"No. I stayed in my room. Are those men still here?" she was genuinely scared of these guys and I didn't know why. Somewhat hesitantly, I told her that they were in the next room to hers.

Just then, the three mysterious so-called policemen appeared in the lobby. It occurred to me that not one of them was mother-tongue English, which made it obvious they weren't coppers from Devon or London.

"Breakfast gentleman? Would you like to sit together?" I ushered them to a table in the bay window overlooking the sea. Antonella just stood by the juice counter looking rather agitated.

"Don't worry!" I said as gently as I could.

"I'll get a tray ready for you. Do you want to go out later for a drive?" There was no 'where to?' or a 'maybe' just a lightning reply.

"Yes."

"OK. I have to do breakfast, but I go off duty at ten. Then I've got some admin work in the office to attend to. Have something to eat in your room, and then I will come and get you about elevenish. I'm not on again until late afternoon."

By this time, other guests were coming downstairs, so I quickly got Ravi making pots of tea and coffee. I called on the hotel phone up to Hansen's flat.

"Morning! Would you give us a hand? We've got an early rush on for breakfast."

"Breakfast? Ok. I will be down." Hansen was already up. This was evident as he came into the kitchen minutes later, unshaven. It didn't look as if he had been to bed either, judging by his crumpled and dishevelled shirt and trousers.

"I've arranged to take the girl out at eleven."

"Eleven! Good man!" He paused then added,

"Right. I'm all yours. What do you want me to do?" And this guy owns two hotels! It was not right. Every hotel owner should have to pass the, *'I'm not an imbecile test'* before they were allowed to buy one!

"Just take orders. Ask them what they want, take the orders into the kitchen, then take out the breakfasts to the right tables." I tried not to sound too sarcastic. Hansen gave me a sideways glance and went into the restaurant. I watched him through the window in the service door as he went straight to the table with the four middle eastern men.

My senses were now in overdrive, taking in as much as I needed to. I was getting spooked myself by all the goings-on. I figured that any information I could glean might be vital. I saw the way Hansen chatted with them. I wasn't stupid. I knew they weren't police. I had known many coppers in my time, from the local plod, who came in the bar for a pint to district commissioners who attended prestigious dinners. These, most definitely were not 'the old bill.' Who exactly they were, I didn't know, but I was sure Hansen did. The only edge I had in all of this was that they didn't know about the trunks and I had Antonella's confidence.

I always like doing breakfast service. You never get complaints at breakfast. It's generally at checkout when it's time to pay. That's different. The thing with an early breakfast rush is that later on, it gets quiet. It gave me the opportunity to examine Hansen in action. He was undoubtedly a congenial host. Letting the guests know that he was the owner, and always on hand personally to attend to their every need. They responded warmly, but I saw it as sycophantic and insincere. It was an act. He was new to the hospitality industry, that was clear. You get a nose for the trade when you have been in it long enough. Instinctively, I know which guests want to be left alone and which ones like to chat, which owners have a business head and ones that don't.

Antonella had long since run up to her room with one boiled egg, a piece of toast and a glass of milk. She turned down my offer of a hearty, Devon cooked breakfast. No wonder she was as thin as a pencil. The effect of the Davis news had worn off somewhat, but I decided to make my move.

"Hansen? I need to pop into the village. Johnsons have messed up the bread order. Too much white and not enough granary. Do you still want me to take the girl out?"

"Out? Yes, I do." Hansen wouldn't know what the bread order was anyway, so it was a perfect guise.

"I'll take her for a drive on the moors for a couple of hours. It will give you plenty of time to search her room again, but I do need to sort out the bread first. Can you cover the front desk?" Hansen looked pleased.

"Excellent idea, Robin!"

With Hansen busy on reception, I got into my car and drove it round to the back of the hotel, where we had a big wooden shed. It was haphazardly stacked with surplus chairs, tables, sun loungers and garden furniture. Some were broken, some were good. I forced the door open with a lever. I had such an uneasy feeling about the Davis business. I reckoned it would be safer if I made it look like there had been a break-in if I were questioned later. Job accomplished. With a little time on my hands, I could make some calls in private. I thought I would phone the solicitors again. If he were there, I might be able to relax, as it was a bizarre coincidence if the town had two solicitors named Davis. I also thought I would call the hospital to see what the situation was, regards Madame Aguirre's funeral. I could say I was a friend and wanted to know where to send flowers. Now, what was that nurse's name?

Something in me made me act on an impulse. My heart was pumping ten to the dozen, never having done anything like this before. Checking that no-one was around. I quickly loaded the two trunks into my car. It wasn't easy and I had to put the back seats down. I walked round to the front and I could see through the open main door of the hotel that Hansen was still occupied. So far, so good. I went back to the car and sped off without looking back. My destination was Amy's garden shed. Running on adrenalin, I sped along the familiar back lanes of Devon. The trunks didn't feel half as heavy as when we had stored them in the first place. I started to wonder what I had got in my car. I rather hoped it would be some kind of treasure than musty old papers.

I drove quickly and pulled up behind Amy's cottage, delivered my load, then sat in the car to make my calls. Davis's number only had an answerphone, which told me nothing, good or bad. The hospital also drew a blank as the receptionist couldn't tell me anything, nor could she find the Scottish nurse called Sheila.

"It would be easier to locate the nurse if you have her surname, sir. We have nearly four hundred nurses here. Are you sure she worked here at The General?" This was hard work.

"Yes! Ward 21. An old lady died after she was brought in with a heart attack. I spoke to Sheila about it.

"Sorry, sir. There is no record of any recent death on that ward. Let me try the surname again. Did you say, Aguirre? One moment…. Is that the right spelling? … Sorry. I have no-one on the system with that name. Are you sure she was admitted to this hospital?"

"Never mind. Thank you for your trouble." I dropped the call then I had the idea of trying Sergeant Webster at our local police station.

"It's Robin here from The Limes."

"Hello, my boy, how are you?" He sounded cheerful enough.

"It is about the lady who died at The Limes?"

"Died? What lady? What are you are on about, son?"

"Well, she didn't die at the hotel exactly, but got taken ill and died in Torbay General. It is just that we have some of her possessions here. There has to be an inquest, I guess. Do you know how I can get in touch with some of her relatives?"

"This is news to me, Rob, but I never get to know about anything at the moment. Take that business with your chef!" I just realised that he meant Jermaine when he changed the subject back to the old lady.

"But if she died in Torbay then, it will be with Torquay station, not us. It might even have been transferred to her hometown. Where was that?"

I sighed.

"That's the thing, George. I didn't get an address or card swipe before she was rushed off. What did you mean about our chef or ex-chef, as he is now?" I briefly explained about the demise of Jermaine.

"He got the push then. Good riddance if you ask me. Had him banged to rights, even charged him! Caught red-handed breaking into the pier. Then he attacked Constable Harris! We're a man down now. Poor Harris. He's on sick leave. He lost three teeth, you know! That Frenchmen went mad!" I was getting a little confused with all this, as nothing made much sense.

"Couldn't you have held the guy any longer?" I asked. Webster rattled on.

"We had no choice. We had to release him. In the morning, we got a message from the Guvnor to let him go. Not to proceed with any charges. '*Not in the public interest*' we were told. What tosh that was. All I can say is that Frenchie had good connections!" He picked up a pile of papers to file away, then added,

"We got the other two, though!"

"What other two?"

"His friends from London. We did them for breaking and entering." I presumed that they must have been two of the Pilchard party.

"Thanks, George!" I looked at the time. It was nearly eleven, so I headed back to The Limes, mulling over the Jermaine business. As I recalled my conversation with Amy about Hansen's contacts and the flasher, it dawned on me that it wasn't Jermaine who was well connected but Hansen himself. But why on earth would Hansen get him off, then give him the sack? Every unanswered question led to another one. As I drove back along the narrow Devon roads, I thought I would try Davis again on the office number I had. This time a woman answered in a distressed voice.

"Have you not heard? Mr. Davis was found dead on Briscombe beach. It's been in all of the papers. All of his staff here are so shocked. The funeral is next Tuesday." The voice trailed off as the lady was clearly very emotional.

I pulled off the road, feeling sick down to my stomach. I was now certain his death was connected to the goings-on at The Limes.

"Where is the bread, Robin?" I had to think quickly.

"It's coming special delivery. Around lunchtime." The fact was that Johnsons delivery man always came about twelvish, but Hansen wouldn't have known that. He quickly moved on.

"Good work! Now, you take the girl up to the moors for a while. I have put Mrs. Kemp onto doing all the lunches with her daughter, so you don't have to rush back. See if you can get anything out of her."

"I bet Mrs. Kemp loved that, didn't she?" I said, jokingly.

"Talks too much, that woman." He got distracted by the phone, so I went up to room six. I knocked lightly on the door.

"It's Rob. Are you ready?" The door opened so fast she must have been standing behind it.

"Have they gone?" she whispered.

"The men?"

"Yes. Those creepy guys."

"They are downstairs, so stay close to me!" When we were on the way, I tried to get her talking.

"What is it that they keep asking you?"

"All sorts of stuff." I sighed. This was like pulling teeth and quite clear that Antonella was not going to give much away. Was it shyness, or was she on her guard? Conversation was not easy. I tried not to be pushy, which meant we sat in silence for most of the way.

The weather was now overcast and a little fresh for the time of year. I parked up at a local beauty spot known as Haytor. A cathedral-like structure of solid granite perched on top of a hillock. An optimistic ice-cream seller was trying to ply his trade in a vain attempt to make his day profitable. The guy had a homemade chalked up sign for '*Hot tea, coffee and soup.*' It certainly wasn't ice cream weather and our arrival doubled the number of cars. "Do you want to walk up to the rocks?"

"OK." This was all I got in reply. We set off at a keen pace, over the tufted moorland grass. The latest spell of dry weather made it easy going underfoot. A few abseilers were sliding fastidiously down The Tor on their ropes. A group of Dartmoor ponies grazed away to our left, knee-deep in the purple hue of the heather. I tried again.

"What do you want to do Antonella? You just can't stay at the hotel indefinitely." She paused for a moment and then said,

"I would like to go back to Burnside, but I know I can't. Grandmother was paying the fees for me. I don't have any money. Will you give me a job at the hotel?" Her request surprised me. I didn't know quite how to respond. It confirmed that she was not as slow as I had previously thought. Before I could reply she added,

"When those horrid men have gone."

"Well, I guess they'll have to sort out your grandmother's stuff first. Antonella, do you have any idea why she was here, the people she was meeting, apart from Davis?"

"No. Not at all." I believed her. I felt the girl had been caught up in something she had no idea about. Time to change the topic of conversation.

"What kind of work do you want to do in the hotel?"

"Cook. I used to do most of the cooking at Burnside." The home page for Burnside flashed into my head. Goodness, the management was onto a good thing. The guests pay to stay and do all the work. Somebody was making a financial killing. I didn't want to disappoint her, but I pointed out that cooking in a hotel for paying guests was slightly different from baking a few fairy cakes as recreational therapy.

"Don't be sarcastic! I'm experienced. College trained. Please?"

It was a strange admission after her reaction at the fish stall, but a thought came into my mind. If I got her working in the kitchen with me, she might open up more.

"Ok. I'll give you a try-out tonight." She had to be better than the kitchen help we had right now!

I figured I could get this past Hansen if I told him she was starting to trust me, the more time I spent with her. Then she took me by surprise.

"You put two of our trunks into your garden store. Are they still there?"

"No, they were moved. I decided to put them somewhere safe away from the hotel because I didn't want those men messing with them. I don't trust them either. Is there something you need that's in them?"

"No. Nothing special, just all personal stuff. That's all." She paused and added as an afterthought,

"Thank you. Just my parents' things." I did have the impression, though, that she was being less than honest, as the trunks were obviously more important to her than I first assumed.

When we got up to the base of the rock, it was quite bracing in the wind. The chilling bleakness of the moor dulled my emotions. With our backs against the colossal lump of solid granite, we stared at the vista in front of us. Standing together, both of us deep in our own deliberations, eyes fixed on the distant line of the horizon and the wild rolling countryside in between. I felt a strange connection to her then. We were two halves of the same puzzle. My mind was heavy with questions, while I felt Antonella must have some of the answers. As we strolled back down, she started to talk surprisingly freely. Most of it was what she had told me before, but with somewhat more detail and with some discrepancies which I put down to her present circumstances.

Antonella told me that she went to a catering college in Brighton then found work in a hotel in Switzerland, but she wasn't sure which city. There appeared to be a gap before she ended up in Norfolk, but I didn't press the point. Also,

Lugarno was mentioned again as a place where her grandmother lived, even though she was French. I made a mental note to find out where Lugarno was as I hadn't a clue. On our return to the car, we stopped at the ice cream van for a mug of deliciously creamy hot chocolate. Antonella still kept chattering away, holding the warm mug with both hands. It was quite a transformation. I asked her again what she thought the police were looking for.

"They said she had some papers, but I don't know what they were. There are no papers in my room except for 'The Times,' and that's four days old!" I recognised a wry attempt at humour. Not sure if it was intentional or not. She carried on.

"Grandmother didn't come with any stuff like that. Only clothes." I wondered if I should tell her that I knew something, but then I decided against it. What she didn't know couldn't hurt her. I felt that maybe the answer to her dilemma was in the trunks. I had to see what was in them. I resolved to sneak out tonight after dinner and take a look. Hansen had said not to hurry back, so I took her into Torquay for a mooch around the shops. It provided a welcome distraction from the onerous events of the last few days.

On our return, we ran the gauntlet of the mob as I had now named them, so Antonella scuttled up to her room. Hansen was there to greet me.

"Robin! Did she say anything?" I took Hansen into the office as I wanted him to feel that I was on his side and working as a 'mole' for him.

"The girl is definitely opening up." Hansen gave me a stare with expectation in his eyes. "But these things take time. She's timid and cautious. I have to get her to trust me." Hansen looked disappointed but said nothing. I could not figure out if he believed me. I continued,

"Remember, this is a strange place for her. She has just lost her grandmother, the only family that she seems to have." Still, he said nothing, maybe trying to determine if I was lying or hiding some of the truth. It felt to me as if we were playing mind games. I held my nerve.

"Antonella had no idea who they were meeting. I am sure of that. The old lady told her they had an appointment with a man. How did she put it? …oh yes. 'To secure her future.' That's what was said."

Hansen considered this new titbit of information as plausible, but before he could ask me anything else, I jumped in. "Do you know she is a chef?"

"Chef?" spit Hansen.

"Well, maybe not a chef exactly but certainly a trained cook. The girl went to a catering college some years ago, so she can work with me in the kitchen tonight. I can get her to trust me and open up." Hansen was clearly unsure about this idea. Maybe he didn't want my involvement after all, but I was more than just a pawn in this game of chess. I dropped my bombshell.

"Another thing, these guys that are here in the hotel?"

"They are police!" Hansen corrected me sharply. He certainly did not want me to think they were anything but cops.

"Ok. Antonella told me that they were asking about her luggage! When they both checked in, the old lady got me to put two large trunks into the garden store, so Antonella doesn't know where they are." I lied, quite deliberately, to protect her.

"Garden store! When? Why didn't you say so before?" He was almost shouting. I stepped back, trying to look as casual as possible.

"No-one asked me. I never thought about it until you said about the....." I nearly said foreign mob but chose my words, carefully, "err, the police, I mean."

Hansen seemed to take my explanation without much scrutiny, so maybe he thought that the prize was now in his grasp. A wry smile came across his face.

"Where is this place?"

"We have a shed at the back of the hotel where we store garden furniture and tools. Old broken stuff. That's all." They would find out at some point, if not from me, then from Roy. when he was back, as he saw the trunks arrive even if he didn't help me put them away. I was well aware that when the cases were found to be missing, a storm would erupt. Any suspicion would obviously fall onto me.

Hansen went over to the mob. They left immediately after he spoke to them. I sneaked off to my room and waited for the imminent explosion. It was like a countdown in my head. Ten, nine, eight, seven, six, five, four, three, two, one… minus one, minus two. They were slower than I thought. Minus three…..

"Robin!" Hansen's voice boomed from outside. As I opened the door slightly, he pushed it fully open with considerable force. I could see that he was quite red in the face. Was it rage or frustration? I wasn't sure.

"There are NO cases, boxes, or fucking trunks in that store!"

"Sure, there are. Two large steamer trunks like I said. Roy saw them arrive. He helped me take the smaller bags into room six, and then I put the trunks into the garden store the same day. I'll come and show you!" My stomach was churning. Could I keep up this act? They would soon suss out I was lying. He followed me into the storehouse. The mob was present. Even Ravi was stood around amongst the broken tables. Some stuff had been chucked out into the parking spaces.

"That's strange. I put them over there." I said, pointing to the far corner. Hansen was angry and it showed.

"I hope you are not dicking me about Robin?" I was now very much on the defensive.

"Phone Roy. He will tell you the same." I was shaking but tried not to show it. One of the four, the tallest member of the mob, spoke for the first time, with a strong accent.

"Do you always leave your store open like this? Not very secure for your guests, is it?"

 I turned to look at him.
"No, of course not. In fact, how did you get in? I have the only key!" The guy by the door picked up the broken latch with the padlock and chain connected to the other end and still attached to the door. He spoke to me.

"Looks like you have had visitors, doesn't it?" I feigned a look of troubled surprise.

Hansen then broke into the same language as Ravi. He was shouting fiercely. Four of them looked downbeat as if they were taking a rebuke, but the tall mobster was vehemently defending himself. Hansen turned tail and walked out. I was not sure if my ruse had worked. Perhaps for the time being, but the stakes were now much higher. Then he came back in and stared at me. His eye contact was undeviating and enduring as if he were trying to detect any untruths by telepathic means.

"I intend to check your story. I hope you are telling the truth, Robin. What's Roy's mobile number?"

"I have it on my phone, but it will also be in the office filing cabinet. Second drawer staff contact forms." He was still seething and I felt daggers from the four guys who were eyeing me with much suspicion. Evidently, I had got them into trouble. I followed Hansen back into the hotel, the men followed. I gave him the number, then I could hear Hansen talking to Roy from inside the office. Moments later, he had a word with the guys and then faced me.

"He confirms your story, my friend. Who else knew about the trunks?" My nerve was holding up well.

"There was Roy and me, then Tibbs the taxi man but he was long gone when I put them in the store. I don't think the girl knew anything about them except that they were full of her grandmother's stuff." I was lying, but I didn't feel she needed another grilling.

"The old lady and Antonella went to have coffee on arrival and left the luggage to me." Hansen interrupted.

"How long were the cases in reception for?"

"I guess, for some time, but I'm not sure exactly. I served them some drinks from the bar, then I went to check room six and get it ready. While they were in the lounge, Roy and I took the luggage up to the room, except for the trunks. Maybe I was ten or fifteen minutes. I told them the room was ready and suggested the store for the large cases. The old dear agreed and they both went upstairs. You know the rest."

The taller guy carried on the interrogation.

"What was in the cases? Did you see?"

"No," I replied.

"They were locked, but they were heavy, very heavy. In fact. I remember Roy commenting on how heavy they were." I wasn't too sure if Hansen and his men were believing my story, that much was clear from the expressions on their faces.

"Can I go and change? I'm on duty soon and I have a lot to do in the kitchen tonight."

I just had to get out of there and organize my thoughts. I was scared, that was for sure. I pushed my way out of the office, one of the men tried to follow me as I went to my room, so I shut the door on him. I had to shower and calm down. From my window, I spotted one of the mob leaving. So that was who had nicked my parking space.

There was a knock on the door. I was still wet. I grabbed a towel then opened it. It was Hansen. He came in with two of the gang and was surprised to see me dripping wet. No pleasantries now.

"What are you doing?" He said suspiciously.

"I'm going to prepare food. I always take a shower beforehand. Food hygiene!" I tried to take a managerial tone with him as if to say, don't you have a clue about the hotel business?

He ignored my comment.

"Did you notice anybody else in the lobby when the cases were there? We know the old lady stole more than papers, but I'm not at liberty to say what. Now the trunks have gone. Did this wretched woman speak to anyone else when she arrived?"

"There is nothing else I can tell you. I was busy. There were guests, walkers, people checking in and checking out, morning coffees." I threw in a few red herrings to keep them off the scent. Summers! He was there."

"Summers? Who is that?" Hansen asked.

"The little guy. The one you chucked out?"

"Oh, him!" Again, my inquisitors reverted into another language, but I did make out the name 'Summers.' I interjected.

"Then, the fishing party was here." It was the turn of the tall man again.

"What fishing party is this?" he enquired.
"You know. The ones who got Jermaine arrested. They had just arrived."

"You have any names?"

"They always book under the name of Pilchard. I guess we have credit card details for the one who pays."

"I can check that out." The grilling went on for some time swapping from English to whatever language they shared when they didn't want me to hear. All this time, I stood dripping in my towel. The discussion was now less and less being directed at me. I glanced out the window and noticed the same car returning. The guy came upstairs to give Hansen a message in English.

"Tibbs story checks." Hansen gestured to him not to say anything in front of me that I might understand.

"Look, fellas. Can I have my room back? I have work to do." I chucked my towel on the bed. It was a petulant gesture but had the effect that I wanted as they left me alone.

I went back into my bathroom to shave and finish my shower when there was another knock on my door, lighter this time. I grabbed my towel to protect my decency as I barked loudly to the closed door.

"Pissing hell! Now what?" I opened the door rather sharply to see Antonella standing in front of me. I couldn't decide whether she looked more shocked at the reprimand she got or the fact that I was naked apart from the towel.

"Sorry, I thought it was someone else."

No, I'm sorry. I thought you said I could start a shift with you this evening, shall I come back?"

"It's fine. Come in!" I grabbed my whites and slipped back into the bathroom to get dressed. It seemed quiet for a few minutes until I heard her voice.

"Someone has been in my room." I didn't dwell on the point as I knew she was right.

"I think it's those men who keep asking questions." She spoke quietly in case anyone was listening.

"They speak in a foreign language. Do you know what it is?" Antonella shook her head.

"It's not French. I speak French and Italian. My grandmother and my mother were from France, so we always spoke French when I was growing up. It's better than my Italian, which I haven't used for years. My father was English."

I was quite impressed and said without thinking, "You're not as simple as you look, are you?"

"What do you mean by that, Rob?"

"Nothing. Sorry. I apologise." I felt that perhaps my comment was a little harsh.

"Meet me in the kitchen in ten minutes, ok? I'll find you some whites." Antonella had been sitting on my bed, she jumped up and left the room.

Ravi was nowhere to be seen. Mrs. Kemp had gone home, but Faye had been holding the fort doing afternoon teas. When we went into the kitchen, she looked quite harassed, so I reassured her that help was on its way.

"Faye! can you find a uniform for Antonella here? She's here to help out."

"Thanks, Rob. It's been so busy this afternoon." Sizing up at Antonella, she commented. "Of course! I have a clean set in the laundry cupboard that will fit you." Antonella looked pleased to be included and they both scurried off to change.

As I started preparing food for the evening, the phone rang.

"Have you got a table for eight o'clock tonight?"

"I am sorry, sir, but we are fully booked." I had already checked the pre-restaurant bookings and knew we were not going to be that busy. I wanted to keep it like that. We would have the usual walk in's, but they were generally just couples. This group could eat elsewhere, and I didn't care anymore about the hotel's takings.

Hansen had loomed up behind me and was listening in.

"What was that?"

"Booking for a large party tonight," I said.

"Tonight? So why turn them away?"

"Too big a group. We can't cater for fourteen at such short notice." I doubled the size to cover myself and continued to explain.

"With the bookings and any stragglers that we get, we don't have the staff on duty or food for that matter."

"Oh!" Hansen gave my answer some thought and then said,

"So why say 'fully booked'?"

"It sounds far better. If you say you are fully booked, then the customer will think we are a popular restaurant and will book earlier next time." He didn't reply as he saw Antonella walk in with a tray of dirty crockery.

"What is she up to?" The disappearance of Ravi allowed me to justify my staff changes.

"Ravi is not here and Faye needed help with teas. Apparently, this afternoon has been really busy, but you can be sure I will keep an eye on her." I was learning with Hansen to change the subject quickly when things got awkward. I ventured to ask about our new, unqualified and inexperienced chef.

"Do you know where Ravi is?"

Hansen snapped back at me.

"Ravi is busy!" It took his mind off Antonella for the time being. I had guessed Ravi was associated with the other men as they all spoke the same language. Hansen said no more about her as a bell rang, signifying that the front door was opening. We both went through to the bar and watched two men enter the lobby. They sauntered up to the bar. 'They are definitely coppers,' I thought to myself.

"Can we speak to the manager of this establishment?"

"I am the owner. My name is Mulhenny. This is the manager, Robin Ashurst…. How can I help?" The policeman introduced themselves.

Hansen asked to see proof of identity which the two officers seemed unaccustomed to producing. It put them momentarily out of their stride, but they produced authentic Devon Constabulary warrant cards. Hansen nodded with acceptance.

"We are investigating the murder of a Mr. Davis, a solicitor in Torquay. We have identified from his phone records that he was called from a phone registered to this address. A total of four times this week, once on Wednesday, twice on Thursday and again yesterday. Did either of you have any business with Mr. Davis?" I had to act quickly to cover myself, so I offered a plausible explanation.

"It could have been a guest!" This had the desired effect of throwing them off balance as they looked at each other as if perhaps they had not considered that option. I explained a little further.

"We only have one line so guests can make a call from their room." I think Hansen was about to speak, but he didn't get the chance as the detective pursued his line of questioning.

"Do you have records for each room?" Again, I jumped in with an answer.

"No, not really. We tell guests that calls are charged to the room, but in reality, they aren't. Most people just use their own phones, so what we would take isn't worth the administration. The metered exchange packed up last year, but we never replaced it." I let them absorb the information then I made it even more vague.

"It could have been any guest, staff, or even casual visitor. The old payphone in the lobby is on the same line. As for me, I haven't had any dealings with Mr. Davis."

There was a pause as Hansen nodded in agreement but said nothing.

"Ok! Thank you, gentleman. That will be all for now." As they left, I regretted saying as much as I did, particularly as I felt Hansen's eyes were burning into me. He shook his head and said,

"You are in the wrong job my friend, if you can lie to detectives as well as that!" I barked back at him.

"I wasn't lying! I didn't know Davis and I didn't phone him!" I had to keep on the attack, to make the deception sound authentic.

"Maybe the calls were made by your friends, Hansen? Maybe they have something to do with the poor man's murder?" He was lost for words.

"Antonella gave me the name Davis which I told you about. All that stuff about the metered exchange is true and was actually mentioned in my monthly report about a year ago! Would you like me to get you a copy?"

"So, anyone can call from here for free?" Hansen casually cut in, dismissing the small point that I was claiming he was involved in a homicide. He could be such a cool customer at times.

"Yes! But very few if any do. Like I said to the cops, people use their mobiles these days. If anybody expects to pay and it's not on their bill, they are hardly going to own up to it, are they?" I returned to the kitchen after yet another difficult exchange.

I wondered if Hansen had noticed that of the four calls, I had made two and he or the goons two. Surely not! Hansen wouldn't have missed that for sure. But would he have suspected the old lady of making a call? Unlikely, as she was taken to hospital on the Tuesday. How long was it going to be before Hansen worked out that it was either Antonella or me made that Wednesday call? A cold shiver ran through me when I remembered that the second call was from my personal mobile and after Davis was dead. How would I explain that fact when the police checked further into the phone records? Shit!

It was only a matter of time before they came back. I was nervous and scared about the whole situation. Especially now, the local police were on the case, investigating a murder to add to the mix. Such a level of criminality was way outside my amateur league of scams, backhanders, and petty pilfering. I made the instant decision to get away from the hotel and take the girl with me. Events were moving on at such a pace. I didn't know who to trust if anyone and that made me uneasy. I tried Roy again on his mobile.

"Mate! Where are you? A whole load of crazy shit is going down here!"

"Yes. I heard. Who's been upsetting Hansen then?"

"What do you mean? Why have you been talking to Hansen about me?" I retorted. Roy stumbled around for a reply,

"Calm down! I am on your side, mate." He said these words with force, giving me some reassurance.

"Look, Rob! He just phoned to ask me to have a word with you about being a bit more co-operative." I was astounded.

"Co-operative? Me? What bollocks Roy! I haven't a clue what's going on. Nothing makes any sense. Some heavyweight guys wandering about pretending to be the law and two suspicious deaths which have to be connected somehow." I ranted on about Davis, about how the old bird had vanished from hospital records and that we had a gormless female who didn't know what planet she was on, now taking over in the kitchens as chef!

"Quite honestly, I'm totally mystified and bloody uneasy!" At that point, my legs went like jelly. I could not speak. Roy's loud and clear voice faded into hushed inaudible mutterings. I thought I was going to lose control of my bowels, as I observed one of the so-called police standing by the conservatory door. I saw the unmistakable outline of a gun poking into the ribs of another guy whose face I could not see.

"Rob? Rob? Mate? You still there? I am on my way back now!" With shaking hands, I switched off my mobile and made a discreet exit.

Chapter 5

The restaurant wasn't particularly busy with early diners, so I went in search of Hansen, thinking my best strategy was to keep him busy. I spotted him on the cliff top terrace with two of his fellow crooks. Giving the party a wide berth, as I had no intention of being questioned again. I walked round to the car park. My space was free, so I figured that the other two villains were not at the hotel. It was funny how I was now regarding my boss and his friends as a bunch of malefactors. I regretted cancelling the party of seven. If the hotel were busy, it would be better for me to execute my plan. Checking the office phone for the number of the last few calls received. One was a local landline.

"Hello. This is Robin Ashurst, from The Limes. You called earlier to book a table for eight tonight?"

"Yes. That's right."

"I want to let you know that we've just had a cancellation, so if you would still like a table, one would be available."

"Great, thanks! We'll take the booking," I heard the lady shout to someone else in the house.

"George! George? Are you upstairs? The Limes can fit us in after all. It's the manager on the phone!" I carried on. "Can I take a name, please?"

"Webster."

"I look forward to seeing you this evening then, Mrs. Webster!" As I put down the receiver, Hansen emerged from nowhere.

"Who was that?" My god, the man was jumpy.

"A booking for six!" I said.

"We have the restaurant staff, but can you do the bar again and any chance of Ravi on pot wash?"

"Ravi? He's gone thankfully and I don't want to be tied up. I'll lend a hand if needed, but Collard is on his way back!"

"Even if Roy is on the bar, we could still do with some extra help tonight." I shook my head. "It won't be easy getting a waitress at such short notice!"

"What about your 'little friend?'" Hansen replied. He almost spit out the word, 'friend.' His menacing tone made a chill run down my spine and left me with no doubt that he saw me now as an adversary.

"Antonella will be in the kitchen! I can't put her on the bar or give her waitress duties. I need her in the kitchen with me. She's never done it before. She isn't very bright, so she needs supervising."

"Bright? No, no, no, Robin. I think she is very clever! In fact, an outstanding actress! My assessment is that she is deceiving all of us!" He looked me in the eye and muttered,

"Or maybe it is you, my friend?"

I picked up the phone again and messaged Roy. I wanted to know when he was getting back. Hansen stood over my shoulder for a while and then went to serve a customer. Then I called Katie, a temporary waitress we had on our books. She agreed to come in with her fifteen-year-old brother who would be able to do some pot washing, but they had no transport. I told them I would pick them up in an hour. Hansen was back at my side.

"Well? What are you doing about your staffing problems?" He enquired.

"It's sorted," I replied with an air of smugness.

"Katie is going to work as an extra waitress and I've got her brother in the kitchen. I'll put Faye on the bar again until Roy gets back, then she can go where she is needed most. If there is a rush on, can you help Faye out?" Hansen nodded in agreement, as another couple came to the bar. I watched the man in action. If anyone could act, it was Hansen. He could scare you to death one minute then charm you the next.

In the kitchen, Antonella was busy preparing the vegetables. She certainly had the experience she had claimed as she displayed very efficient kitchen skills.

"They are outside!" she uttered in a low voice.

"Who?"

"You know. Those men!" She nodded to the kitchen door. I went out to see two of the crooks standing in the rear courtyard. Shit! That's not good, I thought. They are obviously keeping an eye on us. It was going to be much harder than I figured to get away. Not wanting to frighten Antonella, I chose my words carefully.

"I might go and see my girlfriend later. Would you like to come?"

"Yes, please! Don't leave me here with those creeps!" Her face changed from looking alarmed to looking reassured.

"You didn't say you had a girlfriend, Rob?"

"Sorry! Her name is Amy, a local primary schoolteacher!" Then came a strange question.

"Do you love her?"

"That's an odd thing to say! Of course, I do. Why did you ask me that?" Antonella paused for a minute as if she were deciding whether to tell me something or not, then commented,

"I had a boyfriend once. He said he loved me and we got engaged. Then one day, he just went away, disappeared. I was upset and cried for ages. Grandmother told me that all men do that."

"Do what? I asked, curiously.
"Tell girls they love them, but they don't really!" I wasn't sure where this conversation was going, so I was glad when Faye came over to ask if she could go on break.

"Of course. Take twenty minutes and sit down with a drink. You've been busy all afternoon and I think you'll be working hard tonight."

"Not half!" she said.

"I've walked ten miles already!" She proudly displayed the fitbit on her wrist.

"After your break, can you do the bar? I've got Katie coming in!" Faye went outside for a cigarette but soon returned.

"Rob? There are two men out back just hanging about. They look a bit suspicious!"

"I know. They are the boss's friends. I'm not sure what they are doing but ignore them! They are foreigners." She nodded as if that explained everything.

I set Antonella on batch making some prawn cocktail starters and yet again, her culinary skills really impressed me. She squeezed lime juice over the prawns then layered them in cocktail glasses with diced avocado and cucumber. Finally, she added her own version of 'Marie rose sauce' and garnished the glass with a slice of lemon. I went back to the bar where Hansen was busy serving some casual drinkers.

"Just sent Faye on her break, then she can relieve you!" I got a sharp reply.

"Tell her to be quick, then!"

"Faye's been rushed off her feet all afternoon, poor cow! She deserves her twenty-minute break. Anyway, it's the law!" He didn't respond and went back to pulling two pints of Guinness and pouring a gin and tonic. I helped with the backlog until everybody had been served. I went up to my room, threw a few clothes into a sports bag which I hid in the wardrobe, picked up my car keys and then went outside.

An arm grabbed me from out of the shadows. It was the tall friend of Hansen.

"What are you doing?"

"Sod off, mate!" I shook myself free, but then a strong pair of hands from behind gripped hold of me again. I was being held tightly and struggling to get free. I donkey kicked backwards and caught my assailants' shin. He swore but didn't let go. Hansen appeared with the other two.

"What the fuck is going on?" he boomed. Some customers observed the scene from the path and started to linger. Hansen pushed us to behind the garage. I was still being held.

"I was going to pick up Katie. The extra waitress? She doesn't have any transport. Let me go!" I was vociferous in my condemnation of the way I was being treated. He motioned to the heavies to free me.

"You are not going anywhere, Robin. I'll send someone else!"

"Why? What is this?" I demanded to know what was going on in the most indignant voice I could muster. Then I thought of a good reason.

"It has to be me. She won't get into anybody else's car!"

There followed a heated conversation in another language, and the guy behind me wanted to give me a good kicking in payment for his shin. The tall man had a lot to say, which he accompanied with hand gestures. It looked like Hansen was struggling to maintain his authority. In the end, he turned to me and said,

"He will go with you, Robin," nodding to the tall mobster.

"And in future, you do nothing without telling us. Is that clear?"

"I am the manager here and I want….." Hansen interrupted my tirade.

"And I am the owner. There are things you don't understand, my friend and for your own safety, it is far better that you don't. Just do as I say." My heart was running so fast I could feel the beats throbbing in my chest. The bruised shin grabbed me from behind and threw me against my car. I spun around quickly and landed a kick, aiming between his legs. His hand dropped instinctively to protect his crotch and diverted my kick to his knee. It hurt my foot, but the guy plunged to the ground like a sack of potatoes. Hansen was on me as quick as a flash. I was restrained in some form of arm lock before I could react. Jesus! This man has had combat training, I thought to myself. A heated exchange between them went on as they helped the fallen brute to his feet. Serves the bastard right. Hansen loosened his grip on my arm.

"Go and get the girl, then come back. No funny business. OK?" I firmly believed now that their act of masquerading as police officers was a sham. They were a bunch of menacing hard-line thugs. As the tall man walked over in the fading evening light, I saw something metallic in his hand. My stomach churned over, not for the first time in the last twenty-four hours. My mouth went dry. He had a gun.

I was shaking while getting into my car. Any doubts I had previously held about their involvement with the Davis murder, had now gone, and it showed me what horrors these characters could perpetrate. The guy climbed in beside me. The round trip took just over ten minutes. On our return, Katie and her brother jumped out. The chap watched my every move then gestured for me to hand over my keys.

I objected strongly. "What! No way, pal!"

"If you know what is good for you, just co-operate!" His tone was threatening. I just gave him a two-finger gesture and walked away surprised by my own bravado, but holding my body taut, all the time, expecting a blow from behind, which never came. I returned to the kitchen and saw Hansen on my way in, but he was busy with some irate customers in reception. I couldn't hear the specifics, but the man was complaining loudly and demanding to know where he was going to stay that night. I needed to remain alert and vigilant as unpleasant events were now unfolding. This pretence of running a professional hotel was clearly a sham. Hansen and his heavies had another agenda and it was increasingly apparent that what was important to them was the contents of the trunks. Did they really think that someone was going to turn up, to keep the so-called appointment with Madame Aguirre? The lady had been dead for several days now, so she could not have made contact with her accomplice. It was more likely that the mob would stay until the chests were found. Where did Antonella fit into any of this? It reinforced my plans about doing a runner. I waited, watchful for an opportunity to get us both out.

The kitchen was getting hectic. The warm weather for the time of year had encouraged people to socialise with friends and dine out. One of the gang had positioned himself inside the kitchen now, looking every inch out of place, his well-tailored suit hanging uneasily on him. A fellow perhaps more used to being in jeans and a sweatshirt or even combats. Yes, I could see him in combats.

"Robin! One of the customers wants a word with you!" Hansen barked from the bar door. I thought about saying I was busy but decided against it. I just obliged. The tall guy was in the bar, so where were the other two?

"OK! Who is it?"

"Over there. At the end table. Do you know them?" I glanced over the corner and made an evaluation, for the sole purpose of annoying him.

"A table of middle-aged folks, professional people, obviously friends. A birthday/anniversary celebration. Extremely well dressed for The Limes, so possibly going on somewhere else." Hansen looked impatient.

"Don't be clever! I didn't ask for a surveillance report. Do you know them, Robin?"

"No, I don't. They're not regulars." I heard myself saying. My goodness, the lies came easily now.

The use of the term 'surveillance report' was rather peculiar, even for Hansen and the words echoed around my brain as I walked over to the group in the far corner. George Webster or Sergeant Webster was unmistakable even from the back. I left Hansen smouldering and went over to the table, well out of earshot.

"Good evening George, how can I help?"

"Hello, Robin, lovely meal. Wondered if I might have a quick word with you?"

"Let me get you a tipple from the bar. Follow me!" I suggested.

We moved into the snug, well out of hearing range from the rest of his party.

We sat down together in a corner. George sipped his whisky.

"Rob lad! I'm just a local bobby peddling down to retirement. I don't know what's occurring, but something big is going down. I've had all kinds of noises coming from above, 'high above,' if you get my meaning. There is a rumour about the National Security Services being involved. The death of the old lady has spooked the senior ranks in the big city. Funny that you were the only person who asked me about her." He raised his eyebrows, knowingly. "Then I also heard your name mentioned by CID, in relation to the stiff on the beach, which I'm guessing, you also know something about." He took another sip. "This is a warning, Rob. Don't mess with these people. They are ultra-heavy duty. I will have to push this information up the ladder tomorrow, so you, my lad, are going to be in their sights, if you are not already! Is there anything you want to tell me, son? Off the record!"

"Thanks for the heads-up, George. Really appreciate it, but I am in the dark myself. All I know was that the lady who died had an appointment to see a Mr. Davis." I smiled at him nonchalantly. "It's all happening here, isn't it? Quite exciting!"

I was stunned, amazed at what I was hearing, but not surprised, following on from what had happened in the car park. I made some excuse to leave and went back into the kitchen.

Oh, fuck! Why had I moved the trunks? How was I going to get out of this situation? Local plod and now CID! But who could I trust? I wasn't even sure about George Webster. His little speech had undoubtedly been designed to get some information out of me. I felt like a pawn on a chessboard.

I was really surprised and pleased to see Roy standing by the sink.

"I am so glad to see you mate!" I said to him and clapped him on the shoulder.

"Hansen phoned and told me that you needed help. In the kitchen," he added quickly. "I've been tidying up and helping your girlfriend get the last few desserts out. She's just gone to get some more ice cream from the big freezer in the store." Then he started, somewhat hesitantly, to ask about the trunks. I was just about to confide in him, but then I held back. Was he in this too? Was I being paranoid? Maybe it was just the way he called Antonella, my 'girlfriend?' I looked him straight in the eye and lied.

"Mate! They've been taken! Someone broke into the store and took them. Christ knows who did it!" Just at that moment, Antonella came in struggling with five big tubs of assorted ice cream. She smiled at me. The girl looked so helpless, naïve and vulnerable, which was not unattractive to me. Despite Hansen's negative comments about her, I was convinced that she was completely oblivious about what was going on. Her words kept ringing clearly in my head.

"Grandmother was bringing me here to secure my future," but then other recent exchanges also resounded in my subconscious, playing devil's advocate. What had George said, *ultra-heavy duty*' and '*a matter for national security.*' I was mixed up in something big; we both were. I had seen what these brutes could do and they were dangerous. Was I at peril too? I considered very carefully, my options. Walk away from the poor girl or help her. At that moment, I made a life-changing decision. Not that I knew it at the time.

Chapter 6

I slipped up to my room and found all the cash I could lay my hands on plus my passport, not that I had any plan to leave the country. It was clean and crisp through lack of use. Ironic that I might need it now as a fugitive. I stuffed as much as I could in my pockets. Everything else, which I thought I might need, was shoved hurriedly into my sports bag retrieved from behind my shoes in the wardrobe. Then I threw it out of the window and heard it land in the rose bushes underneath with a thud. I put on jeans and a T-shirt under my whites. Adrenalin was pumping as I sprinted down the back stairs. I was determined to leave The Limes with Antonella.

Hansen's buddies had returned. They kept looking me over and whispering. My imagination was working overtime. I could envisage that when the hotel was locked down for the night, their evening entertainment included interrogating me and inflicting pain. I was feeling a lot more than anxious. The best chance I had to escape would be when I took Katie and her brother home. The sooner, the better. I told them to finish off and I would drop them back home.

"Robin, what are you doing?" as I grabbed my jacket. I wanted to avoid another aggressive contretemps with Hansen like the earlier incident, so I decided to be casual about it.

"Taking our staff home!" He stared at me and, as usual, repeated my last word.

"Home? No Robin. Call that cab man. What's his name? Tabb?"

"Tibbs!"

"They can't afford Tibbs' night rate! "It was a statement of fact, but then I added brazenly,

"Not on the wages you pay, anyway!" Hansen shot me a glare. No longer was I the obedient employee, the man in his pocket who did as he was told. Strangely though, he didn't challenge me.

"I'll pay for the taxi fare. Take it out of petty cash."

I felt infuriated and also worried that my best chance of escape had been thwarted. I had to come up with another plan quickly. It wasn't hard to picture who might be the next body on the beach. Hansen would have to find a new hotel manager, but I guess that was the least of his worries, right now.

I rushed back to where Antonella was talking to the other girls helping to clear up in the kitchen after a busy night. I was just reacting on impulse, offering personal protection. With no firm plan in mind and certainly not thinking about any consequences, I took Antonella aside,

"We are going to have to make a quick getaway!"

"Ok, Rob! What a pity! I enjoyed working here tonight!" I couldn't believe she showed such little resistance to being simply picked up and put down. Perhaps it was that she had no idea of how much danger we were in, but then Antonella was used to being told what to do. I had just replaced her grandmother.

"Do you need to get anything from your room?" She shook her head. "Do as I do and follow me!" I whispered to her.

"We're just taking the rubbish out!" I announced as we picked up a black sack, each from out of the bins near the sink. I led her out from the kitchen.

The security light was on in the yard behind the kitchens. The tall crook looked at me with animosity in his eyes. I gestured to the rubbish dumpster. He didn't move. We threw our waste bags into the skip and then nipped around the back through a hole in the fence. It was dark but not pitch black. There was a little moonshine which showed us the way, but I knew the footpaths well, so we hurried along. I was holding Antonella by the hand as we escaped through the gardens, between the beds of roses and spring pansies then we ran across Roy's lawn to the far corner where I knew there was a metal ladder, which dropped down about ten meters over the sea wall to the shore. I didn't dare look back to see if we were being followed. I went first, then Antonella came down behind me.

The beach was a combination of shingle with sandy parts. As we crept further around the foreshore, it changed, with less clear open areas. Then, closer to the cliffs which formed the headland at the mouth of the river, the going was strewn with large boulders, some as large as a car. Carrying further around it connected to the beach in the next cove.

The easy areas were gone as it was now just large rocks arranged randomly as they had fallen from the cliffs during winter storms. I had, in the past, traversed the way many times, but it was a challenge in darkness. We had to walk now as we had no chance of running. The big red 'dangerous cliff keep to shoreline' signs came into view in the murky half-light, so I had some idea where we were.

Progress was slow as we weaved our way around a multitude of obstacles in an attempt to find a route around the point and into the next bay. Seal cove was inaccessible from the town, but it had an old smugglers path that led up to the main road. My plan was to phone Amy and get her to pick us up there.

I could hear no noise from The Limes, which was strange. I thought our absence would have been noticed by now. It only takes thirty seconds to put the rubbish out. It made me start to doubt my feelings. I wondered if my imagination had been running away with me. Had I got everything so out of proportion? Were we on the run from dangerous criminals or behaving like some pathetic absconders?

We started to make our way over the boulders. Cloaked by the dark shadow of the cliff, we were well concealed, but our course wasn't easy. Antonella tugged at my jacket. She had caught some raised shouts from The Limes and the outline of blue flashing lights on the beach road going up to the hotel. The voices were carried down by the wind, but we were too far away to hear what was being said. No turning back now. I strained my ears to hear but didn't have time to dwell on them as I could perceive groaning noises far nearer than the ones from The Limes. I edged around a large boulder to get a glimpse of an amorous couple making love on a rock. We could see a woman on her back laying splayed across a table-sized rock, her distinctive high heel boots pointing to the stars and a man standing with his trousers around his ankles, rhythmically pumping his thighs. I backed off and took a detour to the water's edge, trying not to make a crunching noise on the shingle. We were skirting our way as best we could over the difficult terrain, all the time getting further away from The Limes.

As we stopped to catch our breath, it suddenly came to me. I recognised the boots, even in the dim light. They belonged to Julia, the landlady of The Mariners Wife. I chuckled to myself as she certainly had not been making 'rumpy-pumpy' with her husband. That wasn't Steve from the back, no way, with such a fat arse as that.

"What's funny?"

"I just figured out who the lady is on the rock!"

"We should have helped her." The reply seemed unexpected, but under the circumstances, I didn't give it much thought.

The going was becoming less challenging. Not only were there less big boulders as we rounded the headland but now we had more of the moonlight to see our way. I moved from the openness of the beach to the base of the cliff in an attempt to stay less visible. I tried to phone Amy but without success. Our exertions in climbing over the rocks had made me hot and a touch sweaty, but then I was wearing two sets of clothes. Antonella stopped a couple of times and held her stomach for a few moments.

It occurred to me that my bag was still outside in the shrubbery under my room window. Shit! I certainly couldn't go back for it. Seal cove was quite long and it was a good fifteen-minute walk until we got to the end. Walking was easier now, over the gritty sand. I tried to call Amy again. This time, she answered.

"Rob? Do you know what time it is? I was asleep. Are you finished for the night? What's up?" I didn't have the time to answer all these questions, so I interrupted harshly.

"Amy? Shut up and listen! I had a row with Hansen and I've walked out. I'll explain later. Can you pick me up at the top of Smugglers Lane? The pull-in, where the ice cream van usually parks?"

"At this time of night?"

"Please. It's important. I can't go back to The Limes."

"Rob! You're making no sense at all. Are you pissed?"

"No! I need you to do this for me. It's been such a shit night. Please, Amy!"

 "OK, calm down! Why there? Where's your car?"

"I've ended up here. I'll tell you everything when I see you!" There would be time enough for explanations later when we were safe.

"I'm in my pj's so I need to get dressed. 'Bout twenty minutes?"

"Make it thirty. I'm on the beach."

"The beach? In the dark, why? What on earth are you doing there?" The only way to fend off her questions was the usual bullshit about not being able to hear properly.

"I can't hear you… crap signal here. See you later!"

A text came in as I was talking to Amy. It was Roy, '*where the f** r u? It's all kicked off here!*' I switched off my phone and tried not to think about what was happening at The Limes.

We headed up the old smuggler's footpath, an uphill incline, tricky at the best of times, even in a good light. The track meandered its way up through brambles, bushes and at some points, it was very narrow, which made the going terribly slow. There was no solid base underfoot, only the dirt compacted with years of use, leaving it very muddy. Antonella was finding the going harder than around the beach. I couldn't hold her hand, as we had to climb in single file and it wasn't long before we had both taken a tumble or two in the mud. She again stopped a few times and appeared quite troubled.

Amy's British racing green Mini was parked up as we scrambled the last few meters into the lay-by. She was sitting inside with the window down. There was no one else about.

"Rob, you idiot! What the hell are you up to? For Christ's sake! Tell me what's happened?"

She was, understandably, annoyed and concerned, all at the same time. Still, it could have been worse.

Her rant trailed off as she saw that I had a companion.

"Who's this?"

"Err, Amy, this is Antonella. Antonella, meet Amy!" The two girls glanced at each other.

"She's part of the problem, which I'll explain when we get back to yours." Antonella said nothing and just slid into the back of the Mini.

"I'm sure she is Rob! Why are you both so filthy? I don't want mud and sand in my car!"

"The path up the cliff was really slippery!" The interrogation started immediately, unlike her car.

"So, what the hell were you doing on the beach at night in the dark?" She kept turning the key in the ignition, but the car would not start.

"It's complicated. Can we just get to your place, have a cup of coffee then I will tell you everything, I promise!" The tone of my voice was agitated but firm. The engine finally fired up. She released the handbrake so forcefully, I could see she was not happy. Amy was always one to have the final word in a disagreement.

"This better be fucking good, Rob!"

We drove quickly through the narrow back roads to the town bypass. Everything was shut up and quiet. The streets were empty. Jesus, it must be late. My watch confirmed my observations. It was half-past one in the morning.

The milk train was passing the cottage as we drove up. It's what the early train or late train was called in these parts. Not that I think it had carried milk for decades, but many slurred and jovial evening conversations in the bar had ended with 'Got to go before the milk train.' I was engrossed in thoughts about how I was going to explain everything to Amy. I was not looking forward to the cross-examination, which I knew was coming.

It was a fifteen-minute drive. Antonella had fallen asleep in the back or appeared to be. The lateness of the hour, together with the exertions of our beach adventure, had taken its toll on her. When we arrived at Amy's house, it all started quite amicably. Amy took Antonella to the spare room and all but tucked her in while I made coffee.

"Who is she? Your new kitchen scullery maid?" I ignored the sarcasm.

"A guest at the hotel and yes, a new member of staff. Can I explain this from the beginning!" Amy cut me dead.

"In the morning if you don't mind. I am back off to bed. The sofa is yours. I'm not being kept awake by your snoring as well!" It was her way of being in control, her body language was easy to read, 'I am very pissed off with you for getting me out of bed and bringing another woman into my house, but if this means that you are now no longer the manager of a hotel and we can be a proper couple, then I might not be so cross with you!'

I tried to sleep, but I was restless. The couch wasn't big enough for me to stretch out fully and my mind was spinning with everything which had happened, but I guessed I must have dozed off for a while. It was first light when Amy woke me up and her face looked pale and worried. She was as close to being hysterical as I had ever seen her.

"Tell me why the fuck are the police looking for you?"

"What!" I was stunned.

"Tim, a friend, has just phoned. He heard it on the radio that the police want to question you concerning the death of the man, found on the beach and the disappearance of a woman with learning difficulties, who, let me fucking guess, is the floozy in my spare room! What shit have you got me into Rob?" Amy was screeching. I put my hands over my ears. She grabbed at them and spoke in a more measured tone.

"You have ten minutes until I call the police, so make it good!" I was quick to outline the story of how I had got dragged into a situation that was not of my making. Then, how I now thought Hansen was a criminal and had used The Limes as some sort of legitimate cover. I went on to say that the answers might be connected to something in the trunks left by Madame Aguirre, which were now in Amy's shed. I didn't know why it was out of the hands of the local police. I also went to great lengths to say that I was so sorry that I had got her involved, but I didn't know who to trust. I told Amy about Antonella's role and what Sargent Webster had said. I pleaded with her to help me, also adding that I didn't have many answers either. The whole dialogue transcended two cups of coffee, at the end of which, Amy just looked at me.

"Fucking unbelievable!" then again,

"Unbelievable! I am a schoolteacher in a rural county school, Rob. This stuff with security forces, international gangsters does not happen here or to me!"

"I could say the same!"

"You've got to leave!"

"Amy, it's gone beyond that. We've all got to go. If they've put out a radio appeal for me, then it won't be long before the police or the bad guys come knocking on your door, as 'wanted man's girlfriend.' Remember! Hansen knows all about you!"

A look of absolute horror swept across Amy's face and she gazed out of the front window. I thought she would either hit me in a rage or burst into tears, but she did neither.

"Your plan is what then? Come on, brains! What now?" There was an edge to her voice, but before I could reply, she added,

"Don't you dare say that you don't know!" It was telepathy as Amy took the words right out of my mouth.

"OK. OK. Let's list our options." I tried to be calm and focused.

"Number one - You call the police and they pick us up here. The problem is. I'm not sure who would pick us up. Look what happened to Davis? Maybe he didn't know anything either.

Number two - The three of us make a run for it to some safe place. This gives us time to go through the trunks, find some answers and look for someone to trust.

Number three - Go back to The Limes and give up the trunks to Hansen. I don't trust him. I think he's a criminal.

And number four is…" I hesitated.

"I don't have a number four." Amy thought for a minute, then carried on.

"I could hand in Antonella to the police and you make a run for it on your own with the trunks. I'll tell them what happened last night. Then this morning when, supposedly, I found you gone, I act all surprised and ignorant. I don't mention the trunks as I don't know anything about them." She was trying to help but was missing an important factor.

"Yes, but Amy, the difficulty with that is that the trunks are as heavy as hell. I'm on foot."

"I see what you mean. Why don't you steal my car then?"

"Well, I suppose that gets you out of the firing line, but then Antonella gets interrogated. Poor cow!"

"Is she more important or something?" Amy asked.

"Yes, no! Well, the more I get to know her, I don't think so. The girl speaks three languages, but she is frightened, not worldly, that's all. She's been looked after and closeted all her life and is rather naive to the point of being pathetic. Hansen thought it was all an act, but I don't know what to think. She's had some sort of breakdown." I told her the Burnside story. I also told Amy about Julia, with her legs in the air and knickers down. It made her smile for the first time that morning.

"Perhaps your friend has been attacked, something bad happened to her in her past. Who knows?" It was all conjecture and not a pressing issue. Choosing an option, however, was a priority now.

"What then? One, two, three, or four? Which?" Amy shook her head.

"Rob! I came here to Devon for horlicks and hobnobs, not champagne and caviar. I didn't want James Bond, I wanted Jimmy Bloody Average, which is what I thought I had with you!" She looked at me in a pitiable way as though I had let her down. It was a strange speech to hear from Amy, but the events of the last few hours were changing our perception of each other. At that moment, I didn't know if she was going to be my redeemer. A few moments of silence. This was her call now.

"Somehow, I don't think I will be at school today. What excuse shall I give to the Head?"

"Err, up all night with diarrhoea and sickness? It always works because no-one wants a bug spread around the school!" I felt reassured in the solidarity of our relationship.

She went off to call in sick. I retrieved my phone and switched it on. As I thought, there were several missed calls, texts, and voice mail messages.

Then I had a worrying notion. 'Could mobiles be tracked?' I switched it off quickly without listening to any of them and left it there on the table. My gut reaction was to make a dash for it alone, leaving the girls here. It felt like it was the macho thing to do, but then what could I achieve and more importantly, where could I go. Amy came back into the lounge, looking very purposeful.

"It's sorted. My parents have got a holiday cottage in Wales and I know exactly where they keep the key!'" Option 2, it is then,' I thought!"

"I'll go and wake…. What was her name again?"

"Antonella!"

"Strange name! Sounds Spanish! She does speak English, doesn't she?"

"Yes, of course! Apparently, it's Italian. I'll go and get dressed. Don't suppose I have any clean clothes here, do I?" Amy went into the bedroom and came back with a carrier bag which she peered into.

"One pair of black pants….!" Amy had put herself in charge of making the decisions, which was such a relief to me after the last few days. I had every confidence in her ability to lead the troops to safety.
"I'm sure I've got something *Arabella* can wear and I'll try and clean off the mud from your jeans." She got her name wrong quite deliberately to make a point. As I emptied the carrier bag, out dropped a spare set of whites. Amy laughed.

"Heavens! I'm not going on the run with two chefs! That's a bit too conspicuous!"

We got to work with our escape preparations. I loaded the trunks in the car. One in the boot and one in the back. Antonella was up and now dressed in some of Amy's clothes, jeans, and a navy hoodie. The girls were the same size and, in some ways, not too dissimilar in looks. In fact, at a distance, they could pass as sisters. With our worldly possessions now packed into a couple of holdalls, Amy and I outlined the plan to Antonella. She nodded in agreement, still dopey from last night's hike. We set off. The atmosphere in the car was very positive as if we were off on some touring holiday. Little did I know then, what a dangerous and lifechanging adventure, it would turn out to be.

Chapter 7

Twenty miles down the road, I pulled off into a lay by, which had a tea van parked up in one corner. Two large union jacks flying above were showing the strength of the wind. There was a chill in the air and the sun was striving to make an appearance. Amy went to get us some hot drinks and bacon rolls. I hadn't eaten since yesterday afternoon and I assumed the same for Antonella.

I cautiously switched my mobile on again to listen to the messages and put it onto speakerphone. There were some random sales calls, one from a very agitated Hansen, which I deleted and one from Roy. I listened avidly.

"Man! Where the fuck are you? Shit has happened. They're saying you've run off with the night's takings and they're looking everywhere for you. After you fucked off, four cars pulled up. One was a police car from Exeter and one was from the Met. Couldn't believe it! Place swarming with cops and well-tailored men in suits everywhere giving orders. Hansen's guys tried to scarper, but they got two of them and Hansen was whipped away. They want to know where you are, mate, so I had no choice but to give them your number. Fucking be careful, Rob! Don't shit with these people! BTW- what happened to that frosty, dim bitch from room six? For God's sake… call me ASAP."

Antonella was listening in, rather unfortunately, as it happened.

"I am not frosty, dim, or a bitch!" She declared. This was the last thing she said as Amy got back in the car with our breakfast and felt her standoffishness as Antonella just snatched her food and didn't say thank you. Amy gave me one of her looks, as we drove off, I relayed Roy's call to Amy and then started to munch my way through a hot bacon roll.

We headed north up the M5. Our phones were now switched off as neither of us was sure if we were being tracked. The discussion went back to Roy's disturbing call. Amy tried asking Antonella questions about her role in all of this after she had assured her that Roy was a male chauvinistic ass hole, with all his brains in his bollocks and to take no notice. I wanted to stick up for my friend, but she did have a point. My general assessment of Antonella was changing. She was far more erudite than I first thought. It was just after ten and we were halfway to Bristol. Amy put forward her own theory.

"OK. This is how I see it. I think you're right about Hansen. He's a crook. The cops came to the rescue last night and maybe to arrest him and his associates. Whatever is in those boxes, we take a look. Then we hand them over. We've done nothing wrong!"

"Might not be as easy as that, sweetheart," I replied.

"Why do you say that? Rob? Is there something you're not letting on about?"

"No, of course not. I've told you everything, just that I've been thinking about what Roy said. Answer me this? Who got the feds out last night? It certainly wasn't Antonella or me, so who?"

"Christ knows. But didn't you say that Sargent Webster was there?" she asked, somewhat puzzled.

"Could have been George, I suppose. It just seems unlikely. You know, we always thought Hansen had some inside influence, didn't we? I mean, how he got the flasher off and the others, like Jermaine?" Both the girls let me chatter on and didn't respond.

"But then, Webster said there were heavy-duty guys involved. How will they view us? Is it just a simple case of telling the truth, or will we need some sort of proof that we're not involved? We've got to be sure who we're dealing with. Will they believe that we had absolutely sod all to do with any of this in the first place. There's so much crap going on now, which doesn't make any sense!" My discourse was over and it didn't warrant any debate from my passengers. At that point, we crossed the Severn Bridge into Wales.

As we did so, I was a touch uneasy, thinking that police could track number plates. I wondered if we should dump the car. Amy was also starting to think about the consequences, rather than this being a merry adventure to lighten up her life. To cheer up the atmosphere in the car, I switched on the radio. An eighty's classic, Sultans of Swing by Dire Straits blared out. Antonella had only spoken when asked a direct question. She gave nothing away and seemed rather subdued. Amy decided we needed some supplies if we were going to be fugitives on the run. So, a trip to a supermarket was ordered. I pulled up at a megastore and the two girls went in together. I waited in the car, looking in my mirrors to see if anyone were tailing us.

Amy returned to the vehicle with two well-filled bags of drinks and snacks.

"Stocking up for a siege?"

"Girl Guide motto - be prepared!"

"How did you pay for them? They can track your debit card, you know. Where's Antonella?"

"Gone to the loo, and yes, I guess they can, so they know we are in Wales, but it is a big country. Thinking ahead, I got some cash out at the same time". Then she lowered her voice to a whisper. "She asked me to get some sanitary towels for her!"

"Amy! Do I need to know that? Some girlie bonding moment, was it?"

"Kind of yes! Rob, she's a bit weird, isn't she? I think she started her period when you were on the beach and it had got a bit messy. She didn't even say anything about it even when we were at mine, so I've had to buy her some new knickers, as well. She's got nothing with her and no money. She's a bit weird!"

"Yes, I guessed as much. Shhh! She's coming!"

Antonella appeared and jumped into the backseat again,

"Better?" asked Amy.

"Much, thank you."

"Tell us about your Nan, Antonella?"

"My grandmother, you mean?" I assume that now she felt more comfortable, she was able to open up a bit and told us that she was related on her mother's side, but they didn't get on at all.

"Grandmother was strict and could be very scary, not like my mother. I only really saw her when my parents died in a car accident. She was the one who sent me to a college in Italy after I finished school. Three sisters ran it, but I only had basic Italian, so I found it difficult at first. Then one day, two men came to the school and weren't nice, asking me all sorts of questions. They hit me and made my mouth bleed. One of the teachers saw what was going on and called the police. They ran off, but I kept seeing them hanging about outside the college. I was frightened. They were just like the men at the hotel, you know foreign looking. Then one day, I was walking around the grounds and they were hiding, waiting for me. They put a sack over my head, bundled me into some car and did stuff!"

Amy and I could only imagine some ghastly sexual attack, and we felt the situation too delicate to probe any further. Antonella continued without any prompting from us.

"They left me in a park. Someone found me, I guess, and took me to a hospital. I don't remember much about that bit. Then, my grandmother came to help me. She took me to Burnside and left. I hadn't seen her for many years, which was fine with me. Now she is dead. I know I should feel something, but I don't." It was the longest speech from Antonella that I had ever heard and we both felt she was opening up to us. She continued, not in a very ordered way.

"Grandmother turned up out of the blue six days ago, saying that she wanted to take me on holiday."

Again, bits of the same story but altered. I vaguely remembered Antonella had said something about going to a catering college in Brighton. I wondered what had happened to that part. Or maybe I heard it wrong.

We pulled off the M4 following the GPS. Amy had put the address in, but I had no idea where we were going. I had never been to Wales in my life before. The roads got smaller and smaller as we turned this way and that, until we were informed by the sat nav that we were at our destination.

The cottage was at the end of a terrace. Stone-built with a sea view of sorts over two fields and through a string of tall electricity pylons. There was a big room downstairs, which used to be a shop and had a large kitchen behind. The narrow wooden stairs went up to two bedrooms and a bathroom. The walls were exposed red brick and the country style furniture was either pine or covered with

Laura Ashley, pretty floral prints. It had a country cottage feel but smelt quite musty and damp.

Antonella took our things upstairs while Amy and I unpacked the provisions and prepared a snack. We sat in the lounge, munching on pork pies and tuna sandwiches.

"Do your folks come here much?"

"Not really. Dad is getting more and more difficult about going anywhere. He lived for his cricket and now hardly ever goes. He hasn't been to see me in ages. Dad was always far too strict when I was little, so it alienated my brother and me. Everything had to be on his terms and the only time I could get close to him, was when we went to the cricket. My mother is different but controlled by dad. But for instance, dad won't let her use the car, or if she thinks for herself, then he gives her such a hard time. This is mum's house left to her by her parents. Dad never really got on with them, so I guess he never felt that comfortable coming here."

"Is that why I've never met your folks? I thought it was because you were ashamed of me!"

"Not at all, Rob. Nothing to do with you, but he would have made it unpleasant somehow. He always did if I took boyfriends home. Now, dad is developing dementia and it's getting worse. He's not the same man as he used to be, but I wanted you to meet them for my mum's sake. She's lived such a lonely life in her marriage that I thought it would be nice if she could have some good times with us.

It's the same with Karl and Bridget, my brother and sister in law. They only live three miles away but have little contact. Dad even refused to go to their wedding as he said Bridget had 'a reputation.'"

"That is cruel! Did she?"

"Did she what?"

"Have a reputation? Was she a bit of a bike, then?"

"Rob! What a horrible expression! No more than most normal girls growing up in the eighties. Anyway, what about your parents? You never mention them!" I noted the quick change of subject.

"Not much to say. They split up. Dad lives in Tunisia now. He was an oil rig worker and saw a large part of the world, mainly the Middle East, not offshore. He had an accident when he was about fifty and fell from a platform. Broke his spine in several places, then retired on health grounds. He suffers now with spinal arthritis, which was brought on by the accident, so the warm and dry climate helps him. My mother never liked the life and the long periods of separation. Hence, I had several 'uncles' while growing up. I was shipped off to boarding school to keep me out of the way from a young age. I guess dad knew what was going on and didn't care. They weren't well suited and had nothing in common. I was never close to my mother. She re-married a total bum who doesn't like me. I can't stand him either, so I don't see anything of them. Dad is very frail now as he lives with constant pain, but his mind is ok. The last time I saw him was a couple of years ago. I went out there to visit him."

"Did he ever remarry?"

"No! But he has some local woman who lives with him as a carer or nurse. Don't think he would be capable of doing much with her, even if he had the urge."

It was quite interesting that we were both talking about our respective families and our relationships with our parents. It was a conversation we had never had before.

"What made your dad stay abroad after his accident?"

"Not sure. Maybe he wanted to stay as far away as possible from my mother!" I grinned. "It's a cheap country to live in. As I said, the dry climate is good for his illness and he speaks Arabic fluently, which he picked up on his travels. He would never return to the UK now."

Amy nodded and then drifted away into her own thoughts. I grabbed the remote and switched on the telly. I flicked through the channels until I stopped at the news. My stomach tightened and I held my breath until it started to hurt. There was a police bigwig at a news conference. Amy looked up at the screen at the same time as Antonella wandered in with some mugs of coffee.

'*We are looking for a hotel worker by the name of Robin Ashurst. This is in connection with the murder of a Torquay solicitor, some days ago. We also believe he can assist us with our inquiries into the recent death of a woman in a Torquay hospital. But most urgently, we would like to apprehend Mr. Ashurst as we believe he has abducted two women. A primary school teacher by the name of Amy Gooch.'* Amy's picture flashed up on the screen. It continued...' *We understand that he was in a relationship with her. The other young woman is a Miss Aguirre. She was related to the deceased woman in Torbay hospital. Bloodstained clothing has been found at the home of Amy Gooch. We are now extremely concerned about the welfare of the two women and believe they are no longer in the Devon area."*

There was no picture of Antonella and I was about to ask Amy where they got the photo of her but the camera then turned to a mature woman, holding a handkerchief to her eye. Amy let out a yell of terror, which made me jump. The look of shock on her face was alarming.

"It's mum!" she started to cry, so Antonella went over to sit with her.

"I want to appeal to this man who is holding my daughter. Please tell the police where you are. Amy is such a wonderful girl and daughter!"

Her plea stuttered with emotion. A man who looked blank sat next to her, holding her arm. The report went back to the presenter. Amy just lost it in screams and sobs. This was just awful. I moved over to Amy, so I could hold her as well for comfort, as I tried to let it all sink in. How did they get the idea that I had abducted the girls and why was I now being linked to the death of Antonella's grandmother?

Antonella was the first to speak.

"Did you have anything to do with my grandmother's death?" I was astonished and angered by her accusation.

"What!! How could I? I only called the ambulance. You were there! Have I abducted you? As I recall, you were more than happy to come with me to get away from those men! It is all fucking bollocks. Bloodstained clothes? Where's that come from! It's all crap!" I was incensed and only swore when I was really stressed out. Which I was, right at that moment. I tried to calm down for Amy's sake.

"Sweetheart! Phone your parents now! Tell them that we are here and that you're safe." There was a long pause as Amy tried to stop sobbing and dry her eyes.

"Wouldn't they have asked my folks about this house or picked up the car registration plate with road cameras or something?"

I had made up my mind to call the police and hand myself in when Antonella suddenly shouted.

"My trousers!"

"What?" We both asked together.

"There was blood on my trousers. I changed them at Amy's house!" I knew why she had done this, but I didn't say anything. It was all sinking in. Amy was less hysterical now.

"Rob! You're right. It's all a load of bull. I can't have my mother frightened out of her wits like this, but before I call her, I think we should open the trunks. Let's do it, and then we call the police!" I nodded as it felt like the best thing to do, and with no other plan in mind, I went out to the car, looking down the road. It all looked clear. Nervously, I carried the first one in. I returned for the second, but something stopped me, a feeling that I was being watched. I looked all around, but again, no-one in sight. I locked up the car and went inside the cottage. One at a time, I thought.

There was a small metal clasp on the trunk, clearly of some age. It took me a while to find something to prise it apart. An old screwdriver did the trick. The top opened with a creak of protest from the little-used hinges. Inside was a strong steel box with three heavy-duty locks on the lid.

"We'll never get these apart with this!" I felt beaten by just a few deadlocks, and as I knelt beside the box, I started to weep. It was such an emotive outburst. Even the girls looked alarmed. I felt bad for Amy, with her sore red eyes and in a profoundly empathetic state had told me to go on with this madness. We all sat motionlessly. Nothing was said in what felt like several minutes, then Amy got up and surprisingly pulled me up onto my feet.

"I do love you!" That was all she said. We hugged. Even Antonella came to join us for a group cuddle.

"Sorry, I doubted you!" Antonella said in her soft voice.

"Forget it!"

We sat down and debated what could be the best way forward. We all agreed that we had to give ourselves up. Surely, justice would prevail. We hadn't done anything wrong except run away with two boxes, which were Antonella's property. Technically, then, they had not been stolen. It was evident that the key to all this was in the trunks, so I expressed the feeling that as long as we had them, we would be safe and wouldn't end up like Davis. This was up until the point where we could work out who we were dealing with, and who we could trust. I offered to hide the trunks, then Amy would call her parents and tell them where we are. Settled.

The only idea I had as a good place for safekeeping, was a lockup storage facility. Although it could be traceable, it might give us some time before we were rounded up. I had to act quickly. I found such an establishment outside Tenby and rented a small unit under the name Tim Squire. I paid upfront, in cash, for six months. The girl on the desk was more intent reading the text messages, which kept coming in on her phone, which suited me. Still numb with the shock of the news story and anxious with what was to come, I stashed the trunks into a small unit and purchased a shiny new lock.

Chapter 8

I had been gone for about three hours at a guess, maybe more, but the scene on my arrival back at the cottage was completely unexpected. There were police cars everywhere and two large dark blue vans. Two handcuffed men in army combats were being pushed into one of the vehicles with some force. My arrival triggered an alarm. Within seconds, I had several automatic weapons pointed in my direction.

From somewhere behind me, an amplified voice from a megaphone boomed out.

"Get out of the car, Mr. Ashurst. Lie face down on the road with your hands behind your back." This kind of scene was something straight out of an American TV cop series, not rural Pembrokeshire.

I did as instructed, but in doing so, I stumbled deliberately and threw my arms out to protect myself as I fell heavily onto the ground. I had the keys to the newly acquired lock-up in my hand. In one smooth movement, I quickly lobbed them over a hedge. I landed in a large puddle with a splash and I wasn't sure if anyone had seen what I had done. At once, I was handcuffed with my hands behind my back, and I could feel the cold water soaking into my clothes. It felt like I was on the floor for ages before I was roughly brought to my feet, my handler frog marched me into the second van. I sat on a hard-wooden slatted bench seat. I was so relieved that it was all over, at the same time still frightened by the unknown, which lay ahead. I started to regain my senses and felt uncomfortable from the cold dampness of my trousers seeping into my skin. My line of sight was limited, but I could clearly see the hedge. No-one appeared to be looking to see what I had thrown, so I started to feel I might have got away with one thing at least. I heard Amy's car being moved, as some guy in semi-military gear climbed into the van with me. I wanted to see the girls and talk to them, make sure they were OK.

It was ages before a second handler got in with us and we set off. We sat in silence for what must have been about an hour's drive. It was a nightmare experience. Worried about the girls and only keeping things together by the knowledge that I hadn't done any wrong. Then the van's progress slowed as it went around some roundabouts until it started to reverse into what I imagined was a secure area. Then the door opened. 'Mr. Happy,' my travelling companion, put a pole onto my cuffs and led me down some well-lit corridors passed several offices. After the darkness of the van, my eyes were struggling to adjust to the intense fluorescent light. With my arms being pulled about, I staggered like a drunk. We eventually entered a room that had a uniformed officer just inside the door. I sat on a chair, feeling very despondent. I was starting to panic about what was going to happen next.

"I am very wet. Is there any chance of a change of clothes?" This chap had a much kinder face than my travelling companions. He came over to check, and he put his hands on my legs.

"Oh, yes, I see! I'll call through and find out." He used the intercom on the wall to request some dry clothes. Within a few minutes, a uniformed policewoman entered, carrying trousers, a towel and what looked like paper boxers. She put them on the desk in front of me.

"Would you like a cup of tea, Robin? We have some on the way."

"Please," I mumbled. I rolled my shoulders and groaned to demonstrate the seemingly injustice of such restraint.

"Are these handcuffs really necessary?"

"Sorry! We can't remove them. Orders, I'm afraid. Only you while you clean yourself up and change!" As she removed my manacles, I could feel instant relief in my shoulders. Just as I was towelling myself down, another officer came in with tea and biscuits. I removed my shirt, changed my trousers and then had my restraints re-locked, thankfully with my hands now in front of me. My lady valet took my wet clothes and exited, leaving me much more comfortable. Drinking tea with handcuffs was tricky. After what appeared to be an excessive length of time, the kindly lady officer was back to ask if I wanted anything and my guard was changed. Boredom and frustration were starting to set in when, to my utter surprise and astonishment, in walked Hansen Mulhenny.

"Hello, Robin!"

My jaw dropped. I cannot express how dumbfounded I was to see him. I would have taken a bet that I was more likely to see Jesus Christ popping his head round the door than Hansen 'fucking' Mulhenny. I lifted my shackled hands but couldn't find the words to speak. He gestured to the uniformed guard who removed my cuffs and then left the room.

"I owe you an apology, my friend. I have used you and for that, I am sorry." I was utterly confused. My brain was desperately trying to make some sense of why he was here. Perceiving my bewilderment, Hansen delved into a jacket pocket and thrust an ID fob onto the table in front of me. I could see his photo and underneath was written,

'MI6 International Crime Division.'

"Does that explain everything?"

Anger and disbelief were both pounding through my head.

"You are a government agent?? You total SHIT!!" I spat the words out, but Hansen remained calm and composed.

"Sometimes, in the intelligence community, we have to do things we feel uneasy about. I can only repeat that I am sorry, but we were trying on two levels, to flush out both a big-league crime gang and a French anarchist group called *Action Française*. I'm not able to give you any more information than that, but needless to say, I saw an opportunity and I had to go for it. Then, when you unexpectedly got involved, I couldn't stop events unfolding.

"What about Amy and Antonella?"

"Your girlfriend is being reunited with her parents as we speak, and the other young lady is being questioned as we don't know the full extent of her involvement."

"What about my connection with the murders and......" He cut me off.

"Look, we knew all along you were at the cottage with the girl. We followed you from Devon. Amy's house was under surveillance, but the news story was simply put out to flush out the bandits. If we hadn't, they would be after you now. There will be a report out tonight on TV with pictures of your arrest. We have to make it look real to protect you!"

"Am I free to go then?"

"Free? Yes, of course, but after you have answered one or two questions. Then, you will be taken to wherever you want to go."

"Are they in the interests of state security?" There was an edge to my tone, which made Hansen stop and pause.

"Robin. You have been lied too so understandably, you feel hurt. I will try and explain, my friend. I am not the owner of The Limes. It's a government-owned establishment. We use it for many reasons. Let's say it's a kind of safe house, but not quite in the way portrayed on TV. You were not told for your own safety. The less you knew, the better. Now, the cover of the hotel is blown, it will be sold, so I'm afraid to tell you that you are out of a job. But I must say you are the best damn manager we have ever had. I would also like to offer you a job working for me. You are extremely suitable. Your ability to lie to the police so convincingly was top drawer!" I felt there was a touch of sarcasm in his voice.

"I don't know what you mean!"

"What you said at The Limes about the telephone landline?" I changed the subject because I wanted more answers from him.

"So, who did kill Davis then?"

"Davis? It was that jester Ravi. He got overzealous with interrogation. In truth, the whole thing went bad the moment the old bird toppled over. The four guys you met were the foot soldiers. Advanced guard, so to speak. We were waiting for the big cheese, so I played the role of a middleman called Davis. The four criminals are now in custody, looking at long stretches. Really, I should not be telling you any of this, as it is classified. However, under the circumstances, you have been through a lot and I owe you an explanation. Madame Aguirre was something of an obsessive. She claimed to have jewellery purported to have belonged to the French royal family, in particular, a diamond necklace which has never been seen since Marie-Antoinette had her head cut off. The only evidence, apparently, is in paintings, so it was most likely broken up, but the legend of its existence persists." I listened incredulously to this story.

"I don't think she had the necklace, but she did have other items from the pre-French revolution era."

"Like what?" I asked, feeling as if I had walked onto the set of a TV historical drama.

"Well, we also believe that she had some valuable documents. One is reported to be the last will and testament of Louis Philippe, the last King of France, who claimed on his death bed that he had a legitimate child with an Italian cook and that they married in secret. As their marriage was not acceptable to the royal court, the lady and the baby were dispatched to Milan. Louis then married an acceptable spouse and fathered ten children, but there are also claims that Madame Aguirre had evidence to suggest that Louis was impotent after a riding accident so that he couldn't have fathered any children." This story was getting more bizarre by the minute, I thought to myself. Hansen continued.

"Madame Aguirre has been a thorn in the side of French intelligence for decades, but in my opinion, she was just an obsessive eccentric. It all comes from the strange circumstances of the demise of her parents, her husband, and her only daughter. All the deaths were suspicious, but we found no evidence of foul play. If her French royal story could be proved beyond reasonable doubt, it would change the French inheritance claim, something the Bourbon and Orleans families have fought over for decades. There was even a court case as late as the 1990's."

"However, as far as we are concerned, this is a matter for historians and really would have little significance in today's world. What interests us in the department, is the pro-royalist group in France, called the '*Action Française.*' They keep popping up with various causes, such as wanting to re-instate the French monarchy. They don't commit terrorist acts for publicity like the IRA, so they are not well known, but they more subversive and have been associated with a string of assassinations and attacks all designed to undermine the French Republic. They had a try at the end of the Second World War to bring back their own nominated French-born leader as monarch. Now they have emerged again, this time more radical in their actions and approach. They want to rid France of all immigrants and undesirables. They are ultra-right wing. It is getting to be quite a problem for French security with their terrorist activities." I stared at him, my eyes wide open, concentrating on his every word. "This is quite a lot for you to take in Robin?" I nodded, like some juvenile standing up in court before a judge.

"Anyway, the AF were interested in the old lady's stories and claims because they were predominantly a pro-royalist group. So much so, the AF has been infiltrated by French intelligence officers for decades, and of course, the AF wanted to flush the French agents out. They had worked out that they had a problem with spies. They thought Madame Aguirre could help them with her contacts. It was me, in fact, who had set up the meeting with her. I was acting on behalf of French intelligence. There never was a solicitor called Davis, I was going to be the 'fake' Mr. Davis but events took their course. Unfortunately, someone in the department didn't do their homework very well and there was a real solicitor called Davis. He was a very unlucky man and didn't deserve his fate."

I sat and listened intently. It all seemed to explain everything, but I couldn't relate to any of it.

"So, where does Antonella fit into all of this?"

"Her presence is the strangest thing of all. We were unaware of her existence until she showed up at The Limes. If she is the granddaughter, then as the only living relative of Madame Aguirre, she stands to inherit whatever the old lady was hiding, maybe even a title. That would in itself piss off plenty of people in France. The current members of the Bourbon and Orleans families are not without influence. Then the AF might take an interest as she could be the next figurehead who knows how these cranks think." I was getting more confused.

"Sorry, I still don't get this. How did the old dear get hold of all these supposed documents and jewellery?"

"From the line of the illegitimate or otherwise the son fathered by Louis. The claim is that she is a descendant of his, but we have no proof. As I said, we believe that Madame Aguirre's daughter was mysteriously killed in a car accident, but we were unaware of any children. Adversity has affected this family throughout history because the AF do not want any claims to the French throne other than their own, so when they are more active like now. I think Antonella will become a target. I fear for the young lady's life."

There was silence.

"What can I do to help her?" I asked feebly.

"Robin, if you really want to save her life, you must answer my questions and I want you to be honest with me." I looked down and nodded.

"Number One. Why did you sneak out of The Limes with the girl that night?

Second. Where did you go to this afternoon?

Thirdly. Where have you hidden the two cases you put into the garden store at The Limes?"

There was a long pause while I composed my answers. I was trying to decide if I should keep to the story, which the three of us had made up or tell the truth.

Hansen waited patiently for a few moments then added,

"You, my friend, are an excellent liar, but let me tell you that I know when someone is telling me the truth." I had to give him an answer.

"Question one. I was scared for myself and Antonella because I didn't know who to trust. You appeared to be in cahoots with a bunch of guys who you said were police. They obviously weren't. I worked that one out!"

"Question two. This afternoon? After we saw the news about me being 'Britain's most wanted' I went to see if I could steal a boat or car or something. I figured the cops would have the registration number of Amy's mini, but I am no thief. I panicked, I guess. I had decided to give myself in, and then I ran into your lot.

Thirdly, I have no idea what happened to those steamer trunks after I put them in the store, which is what I told you then and I'm telling you again. I suppose somebody saw me stashing them and broke in."

He shook his head. "Sadly, my friend, only two out of three! Not good enough, Robin!" His voice became firmer.

"We need the contents of those boxes to assess what the old lady had. Then and only then, we can put an end to all this nonsense once and for all." He stared right at me. "Whoever has them now is in danger! These people, the AF, are not to be messed with!" He didn't believe me but was going to let it pass. For now, anyway. Hansen continued,

"The news reports will say you have been captured and are being held for questioning and for your own protection. We will put it out to the press, that the name of the abductor was incorrect. We will release a false name to the newspapers of a fictitious man whom we have in custody. You MUST not talk to anybody and keep a low profile for a few weeks. The hotel will pay your salary for the next year. If it were up to me, I would like to pay you more, but we are talking about public money. It should tide you over while you look for a job, but The Limes is now closed and will be sold in due course. If you want some accommodation, our other hotel, The Green Tree in Somerset, will accommodate you and your friends, completely free of charge. Lastly, I must reiterate that you must not communicate any of this for your safety, not even your girlfriend."

"Fine by me."

"One other thing. I need your phone as your old number will be in the wrong hands, I am sure. We have Amy's too just in case. Here is a new mobile for you and Amy with some of your contacts transferred over. Antonella didn't have a phone, did she?"

"No. I never saw her with one!"

"Surprising in this day and age. We need you also to sign a document." He slipped a file across to me. I opened the cover to see a heading of '*Official Secrets Act 1989!*'

"Yes, it is real! You must sign it as we do not want our identities leaked or anything disclosed, which I have discussed with you. Both girls have to do the same." I flicked through the file, which had the government crest prominent on every page. I made no objections but compliantly completed all the questions and signed, although not understanding the severity of the implications.

With that, he got up and shook my hand.

"Contact me if you want a job in the intelligentsia!" I was still not sure if he was being serious.

It was a strange feeling. The whole escapade started so quickly, drew me in so deeply and now it was over. I felt relieved but traumatised with it all. At least, I had some answers, though. I called Amy.

"Hi! It's me! Are you ok?

"I think so. What about you?"

"I have just been de-briefed by Hansen. Can we meet? I've been so frightened about you and Antonella." Overcome with emotion, I blurted out a torrent of words.

"Will you marry me? My hotel life is over. The Limes is closed. I've been given a year's salary as a redundancy payment. That means I will have to re-train for some office job now."

"Rob, Rob! Slow down. We have to talk first, get over what's happened. I can't talk about jobs and our future right now. I'm with mum and dad. We are all going to The Green Tree hotel for a few days to calm down and try and get over this, this horrible.....frightening..." she struggled for the right word. I interjected,

"Experience?"

"I was about to say nightmare!" My heart sank, as it occurred to me that I might not be welcome around her parents when she added,

"What time will you get to the hotel?"

"Don't know. I need to find some transport. What happened to Antonella?"

"She is with us." I didn't know why, after what Hansen had said, but I was surprised by that.

A mature lady very smartly and expensively dressed, with greying hair, came into the office. She gave me back my still damp trousers, plus my bag, the one I had thrown out of the window of The Limes on that eventful night. Now, I had some fresh clothes and my passport.

"We are currently making a big show of sending a police officer to London disguised as you. Then when the coast is clear, you can leave from a back door.

The whole thing seemed utterly over the top, but hey, it might be my only opportunity to play counter-espionage spy. She continued,

"You will be taken out of here in a parcel courier van. Where do you want to go?"

"My girlfriend is going to The Green Tree Hotel in……." I guessed she knew all about it. "Why do I need to go in a van, Mrs… Miss?" I ventured.

"You have been hi-profile front-page news for the last twenty-four hours, so the last thing we want is an innocent member of the public reporting a sighting, certainly not after all the trouble we have been to."

"My name is Penny Carter and I work for Mr. Mulhenny," she said, in a very Miss Moneypenny sort of a way.

"I am your contact. If anyone unusual tries to get in touch with you, or if you have any problems, please call me on this number. She handed me her card and gave me a reassuring smile.

"I used to work for Mr. Mulhenny too!" It was somewhat of a pointless remark which Ms. Carter ignored and continued.

"I will see if the coast is clear!" Echoes of 'Elvis has left the building' entered my head, all very cloak and dagger, which was novel although I did think that it would be rather cool to have a contact in British Intelligence.

I was going to be hidden in the back of the van until we were clear of Pembroke Police HQ. Well! That was Penny Carter's plan. As it happened, I got to travel upfront with the driver after about a minute on the road. The van door opened and for the second time in a day, I was completely astounded. The driver was none other than my old friend, Roy Collard.

"I don't fucking believe it, you bastard!!"

"Hello, mate!" He beamed at me.

"Don't tell me. You work for British intelligence too? Dog's bollocks! You don't have enough intelligence to work in 'Intelligence!' Do you trim their borders as badly as you cut ours?" Roy laughed. How many more secret agents were suddenly going to appear out of the woodwork?

"Sorry to disappoint you, Rob but, yes! The government employs me, too! Good to see you, buddy! You had me worried for a bit."

Suddenly, it explained everything.

"Let me guess! you were Hansen's eyes and ears at The Limes?"

"Maybe! But I never grassed you up about your scams, mate!" His comment almost raised a smile from me.

"Who else was in the know? I suppose everyone but me?" I went pale at the thought of Mrs. Kemp, the cleaning lady being some kind of '*Mata Hari*' double agent.

"No, no! Just me!" We made some small talk about the hotel, then he asked me directly, "So what did you do with the old lady's boxes you stashed in the garden store?"

"Oh, Roy! Not you as well? That's all Hansen wanted to know. Truth is, I have no idea. I never gave them a thought for a day or so when the old lady was in hospital. When I did, they were gone!"

'Slippy bastards!' I thought. So, this was why Roy was my driver. Mulhenny thought I might let slip where they were.

"Does explain a lot though Roy. You being a secret agent! You were such a rubbish gardener. I always wondered how you got that job and kept it!"

Roy filled me in about what happened after I had bolted with Antonella. He tried to bring up the subject of the boxes again, but once more, I pleaded complete ignorance.

"I thought you took them, Roy. You were the only other person who knew they were there!" Maybe I did have the makings of a secret agent, after all!

Chapter 9

The thought of being reunited with Amy lifted my spirits, but as I drove down with Roy, I pondered on what sort of reception I might receive. I needn't have worried as whatever was said to her during our detention in Wales, it must have been made clear that I was not to blame.

"Look! I'm so sorry for dragging you into all this." It was the start of a speech I had rehearsed on the way back, but she cut my line short with a passionate kiss, the kind that I had rarely experienced. Amy's action spoke volumes.

"Is this a good time to ask your dad for your hand in marriage? I want to meet your folks!"

"They've gone, thank God! Dad was getting worried that he had left the house unlocked as they left in such a hurry. He couldn't think that any purpose would be served staying in a hotel. He's getting worse. Poor Mum has her hands full and needs to do something before she's imprisoned in her own home. By the way, Antonella has gone back to Devon. They wanted her to sort things out with regards to her grandmother's funeral and all that. The old birds' big shot lawyer turned up from Switzerland. So! It is just you and me, babe! I've never made love to a 'wanted criminal' before!" Her grin was encapsulating and I went weak at the knees. Our passion reached new heights that night. The fears and anxieties of the last few days melted away in our desire for each other.

The following morning brought rain and plenty of it, but I didn't care. I was so full of ideas. A year's salary and no work! For the first time in my life, I could pick and choose what I was going to do. Amy kept getting the giggles over breakfast, but eventually, we decided to go back to the railway cottage in Devon by train. There were lots of reasons for this.

We knew from news reports that the police had raided her house, so we didn't know what state it was in. I also wanted to get my things from The Limes. I was assuming that my hotel keys still worked and my car was there. We were both concerned about Antonella, thinking that she would need some help, so we wanted to make sure she was alright. Amy was worried about her job. In particular, what her headteachers' attitude might be towards having an abducted hostage as a member of staff. Mrs. Winstanley could be unpredictable at the best of times. Amy would either be heralded as a heroine, showing the world the best of St Martins, or a villain bringing dishonour to the school.

Unfortunately, during the fracas of my arrest at the holiday cottage in Wales, and then the subsequent roundup of the gang of crooks that had tailed us, Amy's green mini had received a shunt from another car which rendered it unroadworthy. It was a line that Penny Carter had given us both. In a way, I didn't believe it and wondered if it was a ruse to have the car forensically checked. Or maybe, I had watched too many detective tv shows, but I held the view that if they were looking for forensic evidence, they would find some proof that the old trunks had been in her car.

Amy, on the other hand, had taken to the affable Penny Carter and didn't think she could be capable of anything so devious. We were poles apart on this. It made me wonder if there had been any hidden cameras or bug devices in the hotel. I didn't like to talk too much about my suspicions. It felt much safer to talk openly, only when we boarded the train to Exeter. Amy thought I was paranoid, but I wasn't so sure.

We exchanged our stories. Our interrogations were similar, although Hansen had given me more of an explanation of what had been going on. The three questions were more or less the same. Why had we gone to Pembroke? Where had I gone that morning and had she seen two large trunks? Her answers were so similar to mine, we were turning out to be very plausible partners in crime.

"I don't think he believed me, though!" said Amy.

"Why do you say that?"

"It was when he said, '*two out of three, Miss Gooch!*' How patronising! Like he was some kind of human lie detector?"

"Yes, but Amy, we WERE lying!"

She giggled. "I know. He is a strange guy, isn't he? I am surprised you got on with him at all, Rob!"

"Hansen was a very different man at The Limes!" It hadn't occurred to me at the time, but now it had some resonance and I wondered which question he didn't accept as true from both of us. Amy got her iPad out and started to check some facts on Wikipedia.

"'Action Française' is definitely listed. Can't say I've ever heard of it. Have you? Listen to what it says here." She started to read aloud.

"*A shadowy anarchist group which has been around for decades and in recent years has gone through a change of direction. Initially, they were all about reinstating the monarchy, but now their efforts are directed at destabilizing the state and ridding France of all immigrants.*' Jesus, a bit extreme, aren't they?" She continued.

"*Methods used are computer hacking, political agitation, and direct action against migrant businesses. They have been associated with political assassinations. In the nineteenth century and early twentieth, the faction was funded by Britain, but now it is thought to be from the proceeds of organised crime.*'"

"Pretty much tallies with what Hansen said about them," I remarked. Amy was surfing again.

"What was Antonella's last name?" The question took me by surprise as I couldn't remember.

"It was…." I hesitated. "Milford? No. Began with W….. Wexford?" I couldn't remember the exact name.

"The old lady's name was Aguirre. That was the name of the booking at The Limes." Amy had moved on to more interesting research.

"Oh, my God! Listen to this, Rob! I just googled French crown jewels. There are pages and pages about them. The jewels and all the coronation regalia were kept in eleven sealed cabinets but loads of stuff was stolen in seventeen something or other. Jesus!! There were over 9500 diamonds in the collection at the time, and five hundred of them were in a necklace, given by the Hapsburgs to the then queen of France when the infamous Marie-Antoinette got married."

"That will be worth a few quid!" Amy was utterly engrossed in what she had found and continued.

"According to legend, the necklace disappeared during the revolution and surfaced again at the time of Napoleon Bonaparte, but only in paintings, and the general consensus is from historians, that the artists could have copied it from other images."

The train finally pulled into Exeter station. We had to catch a taxi to Amy's cottage. On our arrival, we found the police had secured the house as a crime scene so that we couldn't get in. After half an hour's fruitless endeavours, I called Penny Carter and explained the situation. She said she would phone me back. We stood in Amy's garden in the spring afternoon sun. I hadn't figured the cottage would be out of bounds and I didn't know what to do next, but Penny called back as promised.

"Hello, Robin. I've made some calls so someone will be round in ten minutes. Anything else?" I was quite surprised at the speed of which she had organised this.

"No. That's kind of you." I was even more impressed when after only five minutes, a van turned up and two guys got out. They unscrewed the temporary front door and let us in. They said they would be back the next day to make amends for any damage they had caused.

"Our Penny certainly has the power! She says jump and everyone jumps."

Amy's mood changed when she saw the state of her beloved home, ransacked and disorderly. It was quite a mess and understandably, she was terribly upset.

"I feel like I've been violated!" I decided it was a good idea to give her some space.

"I'll go to the Limes, collect my car and some clean clothes. I'll get some provisions as well!"

"I can't think about food at the moment. The kitchen is a right mess. Ok. I'll make a start clearing up!"

Using my new mobile, I called for a taxi. George Tibbs was round like a shot. He opened the car door to let me in, then shook my hand.

"Gotta give a lift to a wanted man! What reward is there if I dob you in?"

"A slap in the gob, that's what you will get!" was my response. He laughed heartily.

"How are you, mate? I knew from the start it was a load of bollocks! It had to be Mulhenny. Never liked the guy. Always knew he was a wrong-un!"

I let George ramble on about events that night and what all the local gossip had been.

"Some people thought you needed to be banged to rights, but I put them straight!" I was nodding now and then. He had nothing to tell me that I didn't already know. The local consensus was that Hansen was a crook and had some smuggling racket going on, which had got discovered. I smiled to myself. If I had tried to tell George that Hansen was in the employ of her majesty's government, he would have never believed me, so I didn't even try.

As we pulled up in the hotel car park, my good humour waned. It was *my* hotel in everything but name. A '*closed*' sign on the door and a '*For Sale*' board already in place, presumably as a testament to the efficient Miss Carter. The whole scene saddened me, and for the first time, the enormity of what had happened became apparent. My secure little world where I was in charge had now gone, I was unsure of the road which lay ahead.

"How much do I owe you, George?"

"It's on me, mate! God, I must owe you? The number of fares you've put my way! I will miss you, you sod! Any plans, Rob? Why don't you buy the Limes?" He was rambling on, but I got the impression that he seemed genuinely upset. I could almost see tears forming in his eye.

"No plans, George, except spending some time with Amy." I felt a bit choked up myself. "Got a bit saved up, so I've some time on my side before I need to start looking for another job." He shook my hand like it was going to be the last time he would ever see me.

"I am just up the coast, George! Not going to Timbuktu!" I tried to make light of it, but I think we both felt it was the end of an era. At that, he drove off. I took my keys out of my pocket and unlocked the front door.

The Limes was creepy, all so familiar yet so strange. No guests chatting. No staff milling about. No noise. No movement. I went into my office and it was just as I left it, with the last evening's takings still in the safe, not an inconsiderable sum. The old Rob would have pocketed the cash, but now I just left it there. The events of the last few days had changed me. The kitchen was in a right state. Dirty pots and pans everywhere, boxes of vegetables had been left on the floor, food scraps scattered around. It was sickening to see. I walked away and headed up to my old room to collect some of my belongings. My idea was to get the rest when there was more time. I did pop into room six and looked for a set of keys that might fit our mystery boxes but to no avail. The room was in complete disarray with clothes and belongings strewn all over the place, evidence that her room had been searched. I was concerned about leaving Amy for any longer than necessary and I needed to get to the supermarket in town for groceries. Time to leave.

I was just starting to come down the stairs when I heard a noise from outside. I shot up back to the landing and looked out of the window only to see my old friend, Jermaine, the chef. He looked very dishevelled, unkempt and with some effort was dragging a heavy box or something behind the hotel towards the clifftop. Very strange, I thought. Surely he is not living rough. We had parted with some ill feeling and I didn't know what state he would be in. He was argumentative at the best of times, even when sober. I didn't let him see me as I slipped out, loaded my car and drove off quickly. It was nice to have my car back, my old Toyota estate.

Amy had been busy and it showed. Her little cottage was looking more like a home than it had done, a few hours earlier. I arrived with two bags of shopping and a Chinese takeaway.

"Why have the bastards taken up the floor in the spare room and the bathroom?"

"I've no idea." It was all I could say.

"What about the front bedroom?" I didn't want to say 'our' bedroom. Despite our beautiful night of passion in The Green Tree, I needed to play this softly.

"Have you had the floor up recently in the back bedroom, the room where Antonella slept?"

"No! Why would I? What makes you say that?"

"Well, these people are thorough, and if the floorboards have any sign of being recently moved, they can tell and will look for anything hidden." Then I told her about spotting Jermaine moving something heavy through the garden.

"Maybe you should phone Hansen and tell him?" He kept rattling on about your boxes. It might throw him off the scent?" I pondered for a few moments to think about what she had said.

"Not a bad idea, love! Not bad at all!"

I had liberated a fine bottle of French red from The Limes. Not the usual accompaniment to a Chinese takeaway, but it slipped down well. We talked about what the contents of the trunks might be and our way forward if there was one. We chatted about so many ideas. We were going round in circles. In the end, we decided to sleep on it. However, the one thing we both agreed on was to find Antonella. I still had an uneasy feeling about being watched but didn't share it with Amy.

Tracking down Antonella was left to me and finding her turned out to be difficult. I dropped Amy off at school for her meeting with Mrs. Winstanley, an appointment that she had been dreading. My first port of call was the hospital where her grandmother had died. An immensely helpful woman on the enquiry desk put me through to the morgue, who informed me that the coroner had not yet released the body to the family. This was such a contrast to a few days before, when they had denied all knowledge of her existence. I could only put it down to the work of the security services. They had no other information which they could give me.

So, another call to Penny Carter. After thanking her for sorting out the locks, I relayed the Jermaine story, which she seemed very interested in. I asked her about Antonella, giving a tale about needing to return some clothes and belongings. I was put on hold, which I assumed was so she could check with Hansen. Not surprisingly, when she came back, she said that they did not know where Antonella was.

Penny changed the subject quickly. We had some chitchat about Amy's house and I told her about the damage that had occurred. She apologised and assured me that workmen would be round immediately to do what was necessary. She didn't have an answer as to why the floors had been taken up and suggested it must have been the local police. The whole conversation increased my anxiety because I felt she was lying to me.

I returned home to find a team of carpenters working at the cottage. Sometime later, Amy called me for a lift home from the school.

"Well? What happened with the Head then?"

"Not too bad! She gave me a lecture on the reputation of the school, which is paramount, obviously, but told me to have the rest of the week off! What a relief! Anyway, I did some more research on this '*Action Française*' while I was waiting for you. It's really fascinating! I've learned so much. What about you? How did you get on? Did you find Antonella?"

I recounted my day's events but didn't have very much to report that was positive. Amazingly, just as we were talking about Antonella, a cab drew up. The door opened and she got out.

"Hello! We were starting to worry about you!" She smiled at us, reassuringly. It was good to see her again. With the cottage full of workmen, we decided to de-camp to the local pub, The Sparrows Nest, where I had taken Amy just a couple of days before. Luckily, they had a couple of rooms available. My feeling was that we would be safer talking there. I still couldn't shake off the idea that Amy's house might be bugged. I told myself that electronic surveillance was a ridiculously farfetched notion, but the uneasy feeling didn't diminish.

Over a comforting fish and chip supper and several drinks, Antonella told us of a conversation with her grandmother's lawyer. Il Signore Colidato, from Lugarno in Switzerland.

"Lugarno! Why does that place keep cropping up? Where is it exactly?"

"The Italian part of Switzerland. It's on a large lake called Lake Lugarno!" I picked up on an unusual tone of sarcasm in Antonella's voice. As she continued, both Amy and I noticed how much more confident she appeared and how she took the lead in our conversations. Quite different from the timid, shy girl we took to Wales.

"He wants me to go to his office in Lugarno for the reading of the will. I would like you both to come with me." My life for the past few days had been a series of surprises, but non-more so than this, a trip to Switzerland.

"When?"

"Next week, please! I am feeling so anxious and I hate to ask you to help me again, but you are the only people I can trust and call friends. I am not sure I can face the journey on my own. I'd give anything to go back to Burnside and hide away from the world, but I don't think I can. Look!" She made this emotional appeal while fumbling in her bag for a flimsy, folded piece of paper, which with some ceremony, was spread out on the table. Amy and I curiously leaned forward to see what it was. A gloriously elaborate, handwritten calligraphy style, family tree in blue ink was set out before us, with so many branches and names attached to each. Almost at the bottom was Madame Aguirre, then her own line of succession, which included her daughter, Antonella's mother. Going up through the generations, which were concisely marked until at the top, the name '*Louis Philippe*' was written. Neither of us was quite sure what to say.

"This is what it's all about. Grandmother gave it to me just before she died. I don't quite understand its significance yet, but this man here, Louis Philippe, was the last king of France." She pointed to the collection of names and lines at the top.

"He married this woman, here, called Marianne and they had a son called Leopold, who, apparently, is my direct descendant." To my complete surprise, Amy responded immediately.

"Wait a minute, though! After he became king of France, Louis had ten children from his Italian wife, daughter of the King of Naples!"

"Amy! How are you so well informed?" I was stunned.

"That was the research I was doing. It's amazing what you can find out online!" Antonella carried on unravelling the family history.

"That was my grandmother's big secret. Marianne was an Italian cook in a boarding school where Louis Philippe worked while he was in exile in Switzerland. They had an affair and she got pregnant. The school cook was not considered suitable marriage material for a king, so the poor lady was dispatched off to Milan. But it seems they were secretly married, which makes Leopold his legitimate son and heir." Amy and I were still trying to work out the significance of all this. Then, Antonella provided the last crucial piece of the jigsaw.

"The rumour was that the ten children he was supposed to have had, later on, were not fathered by him. All of this was supposedly documented in his will."

We were both open-mouthed at this revelation. Amy was trying to take in all this information, and I was amazed because it all fitted with what Hansen had outlined to me when I was in custody. I even remembered Hansen saying that in later life, Louis Philippe was a 'Jaffa.'

Amy was the first to speak,

"So, if this is correct and if…. and it's a big 'if,' that it can be substantiated, YOU are the only legitimate heir?"

"It looks like it, but what that means exactly, I've no idea." I really believed that Antonella was oblivious to the consequences of her position. Amy jumped in excitedly.

"Some people are obviously prepared to kill for it, but maybe the implications will all be explained in your grandmother's will? Maybe all the answers are inside the trunks?"

"I am sure they hold many secrets, but at the moment I feel they are best out of the way. If British Intelligence gets an inkling that we are heading back to Wales, then we would be in shit creek." I put my case for leaving the trunks where they were, quite forcefully.

"I am with you, Rob," said Antonella. I diverted my mind to the excitement of the upcoming trip, but Amy interrupted my thoughts.

"I have to be back at school on Monday. Sorry. I've had so much time off. I really can't push it anymore with Mrs. Winstanley." Then she added,

"But you two must go!" Another shock as I didn't want to leave Amy on her own, so I tried to think of an excuse.

"Antonella, I would love to help, of course, but this sounds expensive. I've got no job now.

"That's not a problem! Mr. Colidato has organised a credit card to cover all necessary expenses, flights, hotels. I'll pay for everything, even tonight's rooms and the supper is on me for what you have both done!" The notion of Antonella knowing how to pay for anything struck me as rather surprising yet, her plea for help was so heartfelt, it was difficult to ignore.

"Please, Rob? I can't do this alone!" She took the wind out of my sails. I agreed to go. Amy went into travel agent mode and whisked her iPad out of her handbag.

"Great. It's sorted then! I'll check the flights and book some hotels. What's the date and time of the meeting? "Amy's organisational skills were in full use as she began checking airline websites.

"To get to Lugarno, I reckon the best route is to fly to Milan, then take the train. I won't ask you, Rob, as you have just demonstrated to us that your geography is lousy!"

"I have travelled extensively, the Middle East, Africa and more!"

"When you were a boy, maybe, holding your mother's hand!" The girls giggled. I was so out touch with international travel, I left arrangements in Amy's capable hands.

"Two nights or three, Rob?"

"Two! It's not a holiday, Amy! We'll go and get back as soon as possible. Do you want to get rid of me or something?" I picked up the family tree again and studied it carefully. It would be good to speak to this lawyer guy. If nothing else, it might throw more light on the situation. Then I had another thought.

"Antonella, did your grandmother have any effects or belongings at the hospital?"

"I don't know, but I have some items to collect from the chapel of rest, so I've been told."

"A bunch of keys, maybe?" Amy looked up from her iPad.

"Clever old thing! Are you thinking what I am thinking?

"It's possible, isn't it? Why don't we all go tomorrow and find out? What about the funeral, though, Anton'? Did your grandmother want a cremation or a burial?"

"The undertaker says he can't make arrangements until it is all cleared by the coroner. I don't know why. I will just have to wait and see. Maybe there is something in her will. We weren't close, so I am unsure about her last wishes."

The conversation subsided. It was getting late and raining heavily outside. The drinkers in the pub were leaving, one by one.

"Let's get off to bed," said Amy.

"Anton. We booked a double room for us and another room for you. Is that OK? See you in the morning."

We retired to our rooms. As my head hit the pillow next to Amy, it was filled with thoughts of a trip to Switzerland, a country that I had never visited or knew anything about.

Chapter 10

The next day we visited the undertakers, Marsh and Co. A youngish man with bad acne and a weasel looking face greeted us, then led us to a back room where he went through a box of personal items. The old ladies' mothball coat and hat. As he took them out, something jingled from inside the lining of the pocket. He pulled out a smallish gold ring holding an assortment of keys. Some grubby antique-looking ones of various sizes and thicknesses and a modern silver chubb key. I felt excited. Surely, these keys had to be the ones for the trunks. Antonella had been quite chatty in the car on our return to the railway cottage, but when I told her what we had learned about the *Action Française* from the internet, she went strangely quiet.

Amy had booked flights and rail tickets for the following Monday, on the basis that we would be away for two nights. The plan was to fly in, attend the meeting on the second day and fly back on the third. I left the girls together at Amy's and went back to The Limes.

I was not alone when I arrived, but the only change from my last visit was a large skip placed outside the front entrance. The place was a hive of activity. A company was busy cleaning and tidying up the public areas. It was nice to see the kitchen had been scrubbed and anything that might decompose had been thrown out. After explaining who I was, they let me in.

My room had not been touched. I packed up the rest of my personal items, mainly clothes. Depressingly, very little to show for over six years of work at The Limes. My meagre haul of possessions fitted into just two holdalls and one cardboard box, but it still took me an hour or so to round up everything. I looked into Antonella's room again and tried to work out which of the scattered chattels were hers, but the place still resembled a rummage sale. I filled some bags, leaving stuff that was clearly the old lady's. While I was busy doing this, I wondered if anything important had been found during the searches.

"Where's our house guest?" I asked, on my return to the cottage, newly restored to its former self.

"Gone for a walk. I think she wants to clear her head. You know Rob, Antonella has really opened up." Amy disclosed details of the conversation she had just had with Antonella.

"Well, she was abducted and held by four men for three days when she was in France, about five years ago. They kept asking her questions about her family and her life. She couldn't tell them anything and when they didn't get the answers they wanted, each bloke raped her in turn".

I was horrified at hearing this.

"She told you all this, Amy? Do you believe her? It is just that we heard a similar story from her, which happened when she was at school. Remember? Surely it can't be true! But how horrific if it is though!"

"I don't know. I think so! I've read about horror stories like that. It also might explain why she is a bit strange! She mentioned that it was '*dirty rape*'"

I shuddered.

"What the hell is 'dirty rape?'"

"Use your imagination, Rob! Anyway, it's irrelevant. They finally let her go. But the worst of it was the way they left her."

"Left her? What do you mean?" I was beginning to wince even before I heard the answer.

"She was tied to a bench in a small town completely naked, in the middle of the night. She had been defecated on and covered with a flag. That's what these people do! They always cover their victims in shit. I read about it online. When she was found, she was completely traumatised. That's why she was taken to this retreat in Norfolk."

"Jesus!" Was all I could say. The full horror was so out of any sphere of life, I had ever heard of or experienced.

"Anyway, Rob, Antonella said it's the first time she's told anyone. She feels at ease in our company and thinks it all might be connected with what's happening now. She remembers seeing *Action Française* literature in the flat in London that she went to with her grandmother some days ago. When you mentioned it earlier, then she understood the significance. Rob, please don't say anything. I guess she will tell you in her own good time!"

"God, no! I thought there was some mental breakdown in her past. Who can wonder why the poor kid was so frightened"?

"She also said that she was a virgin too, at the time of the rape and wouldn't be able to cope with a sexual relationship now. It's put her off any interest in guys, but she does feel extremely comfortable with you as a friend!"

"Christ!" Then something occurred to me.

"Amy, that doesn't exactly ring true! She told me that she was engaged once!"

"Well, I believe her! Maybe it was her catholic upbringing then! 'No sex before marriage'?"

"What? In this day and age? Anyway, that's beside the point. We have to be careful, you know! Hansen said these people were brutal! No wonder they have come to the attention of the intelligence services." Amy agreed. Then she thought of something else.

"Another thing which I don't understand. How did grandmother stay at liberty and die of old age? Surely if they knew she had…. whatever, wouldn't the old lady have been targeted?" I thought about what Hansen had said.

 "Hansen told me that she was a thorn in the side of French intelligence!"

"Yes, he said that to me as well. We have to tread carefully, don't we? We don't know the full facts".

"Mulhenny lied to me for years about who he was, so I'm sure we are only being given information on a need to know basis." Amy nodded in agreement. I continued, "He also said that the old lady had evidence to prove that the AF had been infiltrated. So, she could expose the French intelligence agents working undercover for them. It could explain why they went for Antonella, but of course, that doesn't tell us why the old lady wasn't a target. Maybe she had been attacked, like Antonella, when she was younger. Who knows if she did have concrete proof and it wasn't just a theory? Or was it so well hidden they didn't dare knock her off? If she were killed off, they would never know which of their members were spies!" We were going around and around in circles of conjecture, hypothesis and just plain guessing games.

"It's all extremely complicated! But we definitely know that it was an objective of the AF to restore the French crown, don't we?"

"Yes! That was always their great cause, but with their own heir, not someone else's?"

"Think about it, Rob, perhaps it is what the AF wanted all along. To have 'it' lost forever?"

"What do you mean, Amy? What's the 'it'?"

"I'm not sure. The stuff in the trunks, I suppose!"

"How can we know? It might just be old clothes and books."

"That's true!"

We puzzled over all the questions and wondered if we had worked out any answers. I had bought ingredients for a meal, so started to peel and chop onions, while Amy was doing more research and had even in her efficient way, started a folder. Anything she felt relevant, was being printed off. I poured us both a glass of wine and went over to her.

"You know what, Amy? We could sort this out once and for all!" She knew what I was going to say. "If we open the two trunks, now that we have some keys?"

"You *think* you have the right keys! But I don't know where the trunks are. Do I, Mr. Detective?" Amy laughed and sipped her wine.

"On a more serious note Rob. If we assume that the contents are important, then while they are still hidden, there is a status quo. Nothing changes. Don't you see? If there is some proof contained in the documents or 'whatever' and it all comes out." She was quite serious now. "Then it will cause huge eruptions. One side stands to gain, but the other side will lose. Who do you think will be in the firing line when Pandora's Box is opened? To my reckoning, it could well be us!" She finished off her wine with a final gulp and held out her glass for a top-up.

In a way, what she said made perfect sense, but I couldn't figure out why it did. We both went quiet as we tried to fathom the significance of not opening the trunks. Then, something occurred to me.

"Amy! You asked why the old lady didn't get knocked off. Don't you think it was because she was the link to what they all wanted? She was the 'key holder' so to speak. The legend, the truth, the myth, and the lies. No-one dared to bump her off, so they all tried to get at her through her family but not her directly!"

"My God! Rob, you could be spot-on! That's got to be it! Now, we have the goods under our control. All the more reason we should keep the boxes under wraps!" I continued with my theory as I sweated the onions in some of the red wine.

"I reckon the only reason it worked for Madame Aguirre was that everybody who mattered knew. The boxes won't protect us because no-one knows for sure that we have them. Plenty of people have their suspicions, which is why they keep asking us. Hansen, I guess, is fairly sure." Amy watched me cooking and said nothing for a while. Then, she had a eureka moment.

"Rob! I've got an idea!"

"Reveal all, my darling! Will I like it?" Amy spluttered, almost spilling her wine as she wanted to share her flash of inspiration with me.

"Tell the world that you have the boxes!" I stared at her.

"What? You mean like a double-page spread in the Times?"

"No! You arse! You write a book."

"Get real! What do I know about writing a book? I've hardly ever read one, let alone write one."

"We have an amazing story! British intelligence, jewels, spies, murders. It's got to be as good as a John Le Carrie novel. Flower it up a bit and get it published!"

"Sweetheart, you're crazy! Do you have any idea what it takes to get a book published?"

"I do, yes, as it happens. You need publicity and we've just had shitloads of *that*, haven't we?" At such a tense moment in our conversation, Antonella came in, so we let it drop.

"Smells good!"

"Anton, I think Rob should write a book about our recent adventures!" She disguised any surprise she might have had with a big smile.

"That's a great idea! I'll help."

"What! You are both crazy! It is a massive undertaking to get a book into print!" I got on with my lamb stew and gave no more thought to such nonsense. When Amy brought up the subject again over supper, I refused to talk about anything to do with books.

Antonella did not want to keep any of her belongings, which I had brought back from The Limes. She binned most of it and was most emphatic about why.

"I want a fresh start to my new life."

The next few days were really enjoyable. The two girls went shopping for clothes, luggage, and 'girlie' things for Antonella. Some new cosmetics, jewellery, and perfume. In between daily chores and activities, talk was never far away from our shared adventure. It bound the three of us together. Amy continued with her online investigations, almost to an obsessive level and kept finding articles that generally supported what we had learned. I knew what she was up to. Compiling a research archive for this book idea she had come up with.

After the police returned Amy's mini, I gave it a good look over. Going back to the time when I was in the police van, I never heard anything like a car being bumped, so I always felt that it was a ruse. Now, it was as immaculate inside as out. This was not to say Amy had a messy car, but this was super clean. I am no panel beater, but I couldn't find any signs of repair. There was no overspray, no new panels. No sign of anything you would expect after a shunt. It confirmed to me that they had kept the car for some forensic investigation. I sighed. More unanswered questions which exacerbated my uneasy feeling that we were still under surveillance. It crossed my mind to call Penny Carter, but somehow, I didn't feel I would get to the truth. Instead, I shared my concerns with the girls. They, like me, drew a blank as to why.

Monday came and with it, our trip to Lugarno. It was also Amy's first day back at school and she was quite apprehensive. I, on the other hand, was looking forward to my sojourn. Antonella was in a talkative mood and chatted freely on route to Gatwick. I assumed she was aware that I knew about the rape story, which cropped up, albeit briefly. She was also very keen on the book idea. She reasoned that it would be a cathartic and emotional release for her. I wasn't so sure.

Getting to grips with the Gatwick complex was a little daunting, as I was not a seasoned traveller but Antonella was happy for me to take the lead. Once we had successfully grappled with the complexities of parking the car and getting a bus ride to the terminal building, it seemed easier. With time on our hands, I was starting to feel relaxed for the first time that day. We were laughing and joking as we checked in our bags and headed off through the security and hand luggage check.

The queues moved quickly until I was at the front. A bright-faced, young Asian lad in a turban, took my passport, but he seemed to spend ages examining it. He said something into the microphone on his lapel, but we couldn't hear the words. He turned back to speak directly to us.

"I have to talk to my supervisor, sir. I won't keep you a moment. Are you traveling alone?"

"No! I am with a friend." Antonella stepped forward, so she was now beside me. He gestured for her passport, only to go through the same routine. A uniformed and somewhat overweight 'Border Control' officer appeared and visibly scanned our documents. I felt restless and incredibly guilty about holding up the people behind us.

"Mr. Ashurst?" He asked and looked again at the passports.

"Miss Walford?" We nodded.

"Can you both come with me please?"

"What the hell for? We have a flight in half an hour!" My hackles were up. What's the problem?"

"We won't detain you long, sir!" The 'Sir' had an annoying tone but not one I dared to challenge. Two other officers arrived, evidently to form our escort and the tubby bloke, who appeared to be in charge, tapped the young lad on his back as he left his area. We followed the three men down a corridor and were ushered into another brightly lit office. There was a table with two chairs on each side. It resembled my detention room in Wales, even to the point that there was a red plastic strip around the room halfway up the wall. This was an emergency alarm. Our minders didn't come in with us, but I heard the key in the lock. We sat in silence for some time.

Antonella was clearly upset and frightened. My feelings were now more of anger. Our plans were clearly out of the window and I was concerned by the notion that we had been prevented from going. It added to the increasingly long list of unanswered questions. The hefty fellow from Border Control came back into the room.

"I have a few questions that…."

"And I have more than a few for you!" I interrupted him sharply.

"Will we be able to leave today?" The man looked uncomfortable.

"Please don't make this difficult, sir. I am not in a position to tell you very much, simply because I do not know myself. Your passports have been revoked, and in such circumstances as this, it is our job to detain you and report to the relevant authorities that we have you in custody. There are many reasons for cancelling passports without the knowledge of the holder." I shook my head in disbelief but did not say anything. He continued.

"Can you confirm that you are travelling together?"

"Yes."

The interrogation carried on like this for a while. He wanted names, addresses, where we had come from and where we were going to, the last time we left the country, the reason we were going to Switzerland. He listened and recorded our answers twice. One for me and one for Antonella.

"And, can you confirm the nature of your relationship?" This was getting me really irritated and wound up.

"Friends!" I barked at him. Antonella just nodded in agreement.

"We have to ask you this, sir, but do you have an intimate relationship?"

"Why! For fuck's sake! It's none of your bloody business! She's a friend but not my girlfriend!" My tone was so severe, he didn't pursue his question. I took the opportunity to ask some questions of my own.

"What about our luggage? It was checked in!"

"Your bags have been taken off the plane and so we must examine them together. If you would both accompany me?" Antonella was now visibly distressed and her answers were softly spoken. We followed our interrogator through a maze of offices into a small hall. There, on two stainless steel tables, were our three bags.

"Are these items your property?" I felt like saying 'what do you think, prick?' as two very new, fuchsia pink Samsonite suitcases lay next to my shabby old rucksack.

"The old blue rucksack is mine and the other two are Antonella's."

"Is that correct, Miss Walford?"

"Yes."

"Did you pack all the items yourself?"

"Yes."

"Please can you open them and remove the contents."

This was a strange and nerve-racking experience. I felt like a criminal. Even though I had nothing to hide, the whole situation made me feel very apprehensive. What if they found a stash of drugs or something which someone had planted? Two more Border Agency Personnel stood opposite with blue plastic gloves and white disposable aprons. I wanted to shout at them 'You dumb shits, you *won't catch any germs from me and Antonella's stuff is all new!'* but kept my cool. We did as we were asked and produced a neat spread of belongings. After it was all sifted through by the blue gloved hands, it became a dishevelled pile of crumpled clothes and torn boxes of toiletries. They also had some probe that resembled a magician's wand. Our empty cases got a thorough inspection too.

Just as things could not get any worse, they did. We suffered a further indignity by being escorted into two small separate cubicles. These consisted of plastic curtains which were drawn on three sides, like the ones you get around hospital beds. We had to remove all our clothes and give them to one of our blue gloved friends. In exchange, we were handed a white towelling bathrobe, not the fresh smelling, fluffy type you get in a hotel spa, but rough textured thin cotton. I emerged into the room a full five minutes before Antonella. When she finally appeared, the spark which she had in the last few days had gone. She was sobbing openly. As I went over to her and hugged her, she clung on to me so hard that I could feel the contours of her body through our temporary garb. A lady official asked if we wanted tea or coffee as she carried our clothes out. After noticing Antonella's anguish, the lady official assured us that it was all strictly routine.

We were both dressed for the sauna when to my surprise and almost relief, Hansen Mulhenny appeared. I turned away and stared at the wall to compose myself, or I would have lost it with him. I took a deep breath and turned around. I had worked it out. The security services had put a stop on us leaving the country.

"I might have known you were behind this!" I said, with sarcastic brazenness.

"It is purely procedure Robin. Under section 7 of the Terrorism Act, 2000, the police can stop, search, fingerprint, question and detain anyone for up to nine hours. Lucky for you that I arrived when I did!"

"What the hell are we supposed to have done?" I shouted. My anger was now evident.

"I must apologise to you again, but we had to do it for your own safety."

"You take our clothes and subject us to this humiliation!" I spluttered. "For our own safety?" He didn't answer my question, but Hansen's tone softened slightly.

"Robin, can you please explain to me what you were doing?" I was in no doubt that he knew precisely which flight we were booked on, but I humoured him anyway.

"We were going to Lugarno. We had an appointment to see Madame Aguirre's lawyer, for a reading of her will. Antonella didn't want to go alone, hence my presence in this almost naked state!"

Hansen looked at me with a familiar stare. No-one spoke. He left the room but returned very quickly with the fat controller, holding our clothes in a neat pile. He allowed us to get dressed before the interview resumed.

"Your grandmother's lawyer communicated with you recently. Did he not, Miss Walford?" He knew that Antonella had been in communication via the phone, so really, he didn't need to wait for her answer.

"I regret to tell you that the lawyer Colidato has been reported missing. Yesterday, we learned that a savagely beaten body had been found by Lake Lugarno. The teeth have been smashed and the fingers burnt, so identification is proving difficult for the Swiss police. We do, however, have reason to suspect it is the body of your lawyer. So now, do you understand why we couldn't let you go?"

As the news sunk in, I felt utterly wounded, not for the loss of another unfortunate man whom I had never met. But, because this horrendous situation was still evolving, rather than at an end. We were right back in the middle of our nightmare. Hansen's voice brought me back from the dark thoughts inside my head.

"Robin! You and Antonella need to do two things. Firstly, I think you know where Madame Aguirre's trunks are. I suggest you hand them over before our little subterfuge of you being arrested is discovered and the AF come after you again. Then and only then, can we protect you."

"And the second?"

"You have to change location. You can't stay in your girlfriend's cottage. It is not safe!" I was trying to think clearly about what to do. My instincts told me that holding onto the boxes was our best protection, yet another voice in my head considered it as sheer stupidity. It was now or never to make the call. I just blurted out.

"How many times do I need to say this? I don't have them. They were taken from the garden store at The Limes. I've no idea where they are now." Hansen's voice was stern.

"Robin. I must warn you that the longer this goes on, the more people will get hurt!"

"Hansen. Tell me, truthfully, please. Are we under surveillance?"

I got the look again, but she didn't answer.

"Please keep me abreast of any plans in the future. It will prevent any unfortunate incidents like this!" With that, he got up and left. We collected our bags and went back into the main hall of the airport. The journey back to Devon was uneventful, the mood subdued. Little was said as both of us were lost in our own private and troubling thoughts.

Chapter 11

Amy was surprised to see us back, but she had her own unnerving experience to report. We swapped stories.

A man who claimed to be a reporter had approached her, looking for a story about the abduction. He was willing to pay handsomely. Amy felt uneasy about him, as it happened for a good reason. When she checked up on the guy, the newspaper he purported to work for, had never heard of him. Yet another mystery to add to the already large stack. She did, however, manage to get a photo of the bogus man on her phone. We messaged it to Penny Carter.

Antonella went up for a bath.

"Is she ok?" Even Amy noticed how quiet she was.

"I'm not sure. She's gone back into herself. The worst time was at customs when we had to get undressed with an officer present. It freaked her out!"

"Why! Was it in front of you?" asked Amy.

"No, of course not! Separate cubicles!"

"Who watched her get undressed then? Was it a bloke?".

"No! Female, but she didn't want to do it. It really upset her."

"Did you get an internal inspection?"

"No, I didn't suffer that degradation, thank God. I guess she didn't get one either. Do you know that other than a cup of tea before we left the house, she hasn't eaten or drunk anything today? I'm worried about the girl."

"I'll have a chat with her tomorrow." I felt reassured that Amy's natural compassion and empathy would help. Then I made a statement that was something of a surprise to her.

"I've decided. I'm going to write this book that you keep going on about. Well! I'll qualify that, I am going to write the first three pages and then we'll see!"

"Great! How come you changed your mind?" It was a hard question for me and to be honest, the only reason I came up with it was that I had no clue what to do next. This book plan, however crazy, was the only idea we had on the table. To show my intent, I picked up Amy's folder and started to read the first few printed pages. It was a gesture of my resolve. The article was about *Action Française* and it quite seized my attention.

My transition from hotel manager, to wanted criminal and then to author was proving not surprisingly, rather unsettling. Not only that, the mood in the camp was low. We felt we were all walking around on eggshells. The once easy relationship between the three of us had been irrevocably damaged by the airport experience and another brutal murder, which, although still unconfirmed, was likely to be Colidato. Antonella now only made fleeting appearances, choosing to stay mainly in her room. Even Amy was unable to break through the barriers. Antonella told her that she was the last person that she could talk to.

Understandably, Amy felt hurt. We offered to take her somewhere else, but she pleaded with us to let her stay.

The atmosphere was awkward. Not conducive to any writing. Still, I persevered and over the next few days, I became engrossed in more research. Amy would add to my reading list most evenings when she got home. I was also making copious notes from which to work from. Trying to put any words onto a page, was not easy for someone untrained and inexperienced. Then after about ten false starts, I had written the first page, then page two and three. Not exactly a masterpiece, but I was happy with it. I showed the girls. Instantly, Amy was my number one fan as she said it showed promise. Antonella was aghast at the way I had described her. Feeling somewhat disheartened, I rewrote some of the paragraphs. However, Antonella did say that my description of her grandmother was perfectly accurate.

To my surprise, the promised years' salary had been paid into my bank as one lump sum and it was more money than I had expected. My account had never been so healthy. I felt quite rich for the first time in my life, but Amy dampened my high spirit. She was unsure about the payoff and the reasons for being given it. It might prove difficult to explain how I came into so much money. She was probably right. I had no idea who might be looking into my bank account or, for that matter, who to ask for any advice. I wasn't sure of anything anymore.

The next morning, I had the house to myself. With Amy's reservations firmly set in mind, I decided to sound out Penny Carter.

"I appear to have a large amount of money in my bank account!"

"Yes, that is correct, Robin. We paid you a full year's salary and a bonus. I was sorry about what happened at the airport. You should have outlined your plans to us. We only have your best interests at heart. How is the young lady? I heard she was terribly upset?" I ignored the last question.

"It doesn't feel that way, Penny! I've been lied to again and again. If there is something you don't want us to know, you should say so and not give me a load of crap!"

"Point taken Robin, but it works both ways. We believe you have lied to us!" I wondered if I was pushing this too far. This lady had the power to crush me.

"May I suggest we are a little more honest with each other? Tell me then, did you take the trunks?" I took in a breath.

"You know I did!" There! I had finally admitted it.

"Can I ask where they are?" Penny would not let go.

"I don't wish to disclose that information." I could play the tough negotiator too.

"And the reason is?" I outlined our thoughts about being safer. How Madame Aguirre had lived out her full life by keeping them hidden, while all around her fell to some misfortune." Penny's reaction surprised me.

"I fully understand your position, Robin. If I were in your shoes, I might even do the same." This was not what I expected her to say.

"May I ask if you have examined the contents?"

"No. We couldn't get them open. There are several locks on each one and we don't have the keys!" The last part was a blatant lie, but she didn't respond. I could almost hear her thinking down the phone, probably about the keys, so I continued quickly,

"The man we were going to see in Switzerland. Was it his body?"

"Yes! We've had it confirmed now. Aren't you glad we didn't let you go there?" Without waiting for a reply, she tried again.

"You said you don't have the keys?" I gave a short reply.

"No!" Then, in a quick change of direction, I asked,

"Was he covered with excrement?"

"What a question, Robin! I honestly don't know. It is a matter for the Swiss police and unfortunately, our influence doesn't reach that far. Why on earth do you ask?"

"It is a calling card used by the AF. I read about it somewhere, that's all."

"I see! Yes, it could be interesting! I will certainly make a note to find out." Changing direction again.

"Penny? How would you or your establishment react if I were to write a book?"

"I must say you are full of surprises. Where did that idea come from?"

"Just a notion we've had. How would that sit with you?"

"You have all signed the Official Secrets Act, which makes it illegal for you to disclose certain facts, you know that?"

"I know. I want to have a record of events. I'm told it is a cathartic process of dealing with what happened. I don't have a job anymore, so I need to keep myself busy."

"Can I ask if this is for your own consumption or a wider audience?"

"I want to tell the world."

"I see! Well, good luck! It's not going to be easy for you. You will need a professional, with good contacts to get anything into print. Maybe I can help. I can recommend Rowena Kerry. She's an investigative journalist and I believe she has written a couple of books. The lady has a web site. If you want, I will put it to her!" I was feeling more positive now about the book idea. I had assumed the security services would be against it, but here was Penny Carter trying to help. Strange!

"Robin? I'm so glad you called me. I think we've cleared the air somewhat?"

"Yes. Me too! I want to add that the cases are now somewhere where I can't go and get them. If you understand my drift? It would be very difficult." I would try and let her think that I had disposed of them, dumped them in some random skip or something.

"That's interesting!" I had started, so I finished,

"We just wanted to be rid of them. They were bringing us such bad luck, so that's what I did."

I recounted all this to Amy when she got back from school. Antonella was out on one of her long walks. She was upset I had let on about the boxes as she still didn't trust anyone, but I disagreed. We had to start somewhere to end this. I also asked if she had made any progress with Antonella.

"Some, not much. Rob? Something happened at the airport, but I don't know what. Maybe they gave her an internal examination at Gatwick. You know, to look for stuff?"

"I don't think that they did! Why would they? They didn't give me the rubber glove humiliation and anyway, don't doctors have to do that?"

"I don't know. Maybe it was because she was a female. Who knows? I'm not sure. But I think it brought back the memories of the rape. She hasn't shown her body to anyone since that day. She's told me that when the gang rape happened, the bastards stood over her when she was naked, tied her to a table and talked between themselves, *'your turn next'* and *'no, you go first, she's got such a disgusting body, I'll struggle to get it up.'* And so, it went on." I was stunned, hearing what this poor girl had been submitted to.

"Every woman wants to feel attractive. These scumbags were helping themselves to her but saying crap like that! Can you imagine? The mental scars run far deeper and have lasted far longer than the physical assault. It's left her with a self-image that even rapists find her ugly and repulsive!" I shook my head and closed my eyes, listening to the horror of what she had gone through.

"Antonella suffered all that embarrassment and torture? For what? They didn't get what they wanted, did they?"

"That was all she told me. I get the feeling that although she knows she's safe here, living here with both of us is becoming uncomfortable for her. Do you know what I mean? Two's company, three's a crowd syndrome and Rob…." Amy took a moment and then said,

"I think she is falling in love with you!" I was stunned.

"What! For god's sake! I haven't done anything to encourage it. You believe me, Amy! Don't you?"

"I do, but come on, think about it! Two women and one bloke in a house? You must admit, you walk around half-naked some of the time! I can see the way she looks at you! You and she get on so well together!"

"Well, yes. Of course, I like the girl, but I don't see her in that way!"

"Rob! We both do, but it's our house, well mine actually. Antonella is a guest and can't live with us forever. When all this shit is over, what's she going to do? Where will she go? I think that's why she goes walking. To try and figure out her future."

"My god, Amy! You should be a psychiatrist!" With that, she gave me a long, lingering kiss on the lips. Then she pulled away.

"I am a bit uneasy with her, though. I keep getting niggling doubts about what she says sometimes. You don't think it's all an act, do you? I was so sure I saw her using a mobile the other day. I was driving home and saw her walking across a field holding a phone to her ear. It was only for a split second, but when I asked her about it, she told me that she didn't have one."

"I don't know what I think! We can hardly search her room looking for a phone! Yes, some of her stories change, but the girl has been through hell, even if you only believe half of it."

I emailed Rowena Kerry that night. Amy admitted she hadn't thought of anything along those lines, but enlisting professional help was an excellent idea. We were both impressed with Rowena's website and credentials. The next morning, I had a reply from her, expressing interest in our project and asking me to call her. We had quite a positive discussion. Firstly, I spent some time summarising the ideas we had formed for a book and outlined the story so far.

"I saw the news about the manhunt! Let me get this straight, are you saying that you feel like you have been shafted? By whom exactly?" Rowena asked.

"I wish I knew! Let me go over the main points! We have French and British Government interest. We have the Secret Intelligence Services, certainly a department of MI6 involved. Then there's this anarchist or terrorist group, Action Française and a bunch of crooks or international crime gang. We have two confirmed murders and an old lady who died of a heart attack. Then to add to the mix, missing historical documents and maybe some stolen royal jewellery!" Rowena was clearly impressed but came up with reservations.

"Your story is unbelievable and almost impossible to prove. I think a book on this subject has got to be one of fiction, even if it is based on historical fact. An area which is not at all my speciality!" I didn't agree.

"No! It's fact and very real! It happened just like I said, but I do admit that it's complicated. There's some stuff that we can't disclose as they got us to sign the Official Secrets Act. The bottom line is that now, right now, we feel that we are in a position which is potentially dangerous and our only option is to tell the world." I paused, thinking about what to say next to convince her to help.

"When the story is published, anyone who is interested will know that I have the documents, they are safely hidden away and that's where they'll stay. Then and only then can I stay safe and live out my natural years." I felt she was tempted.

"Robin! It certainly sounds fascinating! I've done some work on the AF before. Not had any dealings with the MI6, though. Look, all I can say at this stage is that we should meet up and discuss things in further detail. No promises. By the way, you said it was somebody in MI6 that recommended me?"

"Yes, I did."

"Really, how interesting! Can I have a name?"

"Sorry, no! I promised I wouldn't let on!"

 We finalised details of a meeting for the following morning and left it at that. Antonella was not keen to go. Amy and I both felt it was because she wanted to give us some time alone, but we managed to persuade her that she was part of this project and, as such, needed to be there. It was Saturday. We left early and drove to London. On route, Amy started to express doubts about Rowena. She thought she might be a plant, having been recommended by the International Crimes Department. I couldn't disagree with her theory. However, it was a little late to cancel.

 Rowena was everything I expected. Smart, efficient, outgoing and focused. Her auburn hair was cut neatly into a bob with a side fringe. She was wearing a classic navy suit, giving an air of sophistication and her manner business-like. She had rented some expensive hotel office space for half a day, functional and very corporate, an image that I guess the workplace didn't have. The boardroom table was huge. Rowena sat at one side and greeted us with a firm handshake, plus a broad display of some expensive whitening dentistry. There were files set out neatly on the table next to her iPad, voice recorder and a large notepad.

"Welcome! I thought it best we meet here. OK? Tea, coffee anyone, or shall we crack on?" Rowena had a strong Essex or east London drawl. I started with the story outline, much as I had done on the phone. Rowena sat and recorded it all, making notes at the same time. When I had finished, I handed her the first two chapters that I had written and Amy got out our folder of research from her bag. She flicked through the documents.

"Can I keep hold of this?"

"Not really. Rob's using it for his writing. You can make copies if you like?"

"Yes, of course. There is a photocopier in the entrance to this suite." Surprisingly, Antonella spoke for the first time and offered her services.

"I'll do that." She picked up the folder and left. Rowena scanned my first few pages.

"What a story! I would like to help, but I am more of a freelance journalist than a writer. I honestly believe, looking at your work Robin, that you need the help of a professional writer!"

"You mean it's rubbish?" I was quick to say.

"Not exactly, but it's not particularly good for book purposes. Did you do English at school?"

I was a little insulted, to say the least by her remark.

"Yes, of course I did. What's wrong with it?" Somehow, I felt that she was not going to hold anything back and I was right.

"It's written like a school essay. It lacks detail and jumps about. You don't paint a picture of the scenes for your reader, so it's vague. Far more like a report on what is needed to repair a boiler. Not enough adjectives. You don't express yourself very well. You take for granted that the reader knows what you want them to see. The grammar is dreadful, in particular, your punctuation and you swap tenses so much I feel dizzy! Need I go on?" Turning to Amy, I said,

"Told you, I couldn't write, as you see! This is hopeless!" However, after such a damning critique, Rowena proceeded to build me up again.

"Robin! Your writing can be improved. What you have is a story that people will want to read. It's a good starting point, but you need a professional person to put it into a form which is more reader friendly. You need somebody who will ghost for you."

"A ghost? What do you mean?"

"It is a collaboration of sorts. You sit down together. You tell your story to the ghost, who then writes it down in a suitable and correct form with structure. Get my drift?" She carried on, despite my attempt to interrupt her flow.

"Time is of the essence here. You want to tell the world or certain people anyway, what you have, without saying so directly. You must make use of the recent publicity with your arrest. I would suggest getting to press as soon as possible. The whole story interests me. Like I said on the phone, I have been doing my own work on the AF. The signs are that they are now linking up with anarchist groups within the UK. I haven't got any concrete proof of that yet."

Amy, listening intently, jumped in at this point.

"Are you sure? From my research on the AF, they want France for the French and they would build a wall around the country, keeping every other nationality out if they could. They are so French centred they wouldn't look outside of France or to any foreign associations."

"That's an interesting view. Have you got anything to support that theory?"

"Yes. It's all in my research notes."

"OK. Good. I'll go through it all later. Right! Practical stuff now." Rowena fired off an agenda at top speed.

"First, I'll get you a ghost writer. I have a couple in mind, but it depends on how they are fixed up, with short notice and all.

Second, I can write some articles for the press to build up some interest. I can see the headlines, something like, '*MI6 agent bungles clandestine operation, resulting in the death of an innocent man*'. Then, '*Hotel manager wrongly accused of being an abductor*.'" It was certainly impressive. It would have taken me weeks to have thought of such headings. The lady was in full flow.

"Or '*UK intelligence services in covert meetings with French terrorist groups.*' "That sort of stuff will get into the broadsheets, I am sure. I could get a serialisation, but the book would have to be really good. Any pre-publicity will at least cause some ripples in the establishment." She carried on without pausing for breath.

"Now, as the author, Robin, you will have to give a presentation to potential publishers. It is how things are done. If they go with it, there will be plenty of media stuff, interviews, talks, etc. What are you like at public speaking?" I didn't want to admit that I had no experience whatsoever and look like a complete amateur in every aspect.

"Not done too much!"

"Well, even if the book is first class, I'm afraid that if you don't present well, they won't take you on. I'll get some media help to give you the once over and coaching in due course. Our first priority is to get the book written".

At that moment, Antonella entered the room with a tray of drinks accompanied by a plate of biscuits. Rowena seemed irritated with the interruption.

"Yes?"

"They are just getting me some more paper. For the copier?" She explained. "They gave me this tray."

Rowena, oblivious to the refreshments, had already moved on to other items.

"What's your accommodation like?"

"Amy has a two-bedroom cottage on the Devon coast."

"Sounds enchanting?"

"Well. We have the main west country railway line in between us and the beach, or estuary, to be exact!" Amy glared at me.

"You've never complained about the trains before!"

"I'm not complaining, just painting a picture." I couldn't resist adding a petulant comment directed at Rowena, "I've been told I don't do it enough!"

"Let's not debate this. The cottage is not big enough. I have a house near here in Slough, which you can use." Amy was looking slightly worried.

"Slough! No, it has to be in Devon. I am a schoolteacher and I can't take time off."

"OK! We will look for a house with four bedrooms, maybe five. There's me, the ghost, you two, Antonella and we might need housekeeping!" Amy and I looked at each other.

"What do you mean by housekeeping?"

"Isn't it obvious! Someone to cook, make tea, go shopping, that kind of thing?" Antonella looked enthusiastic for the first time in ages.

"That can be me! I have nothing to add that Rob doesn't know already and I would like to keep busy."

"Good. I assume you can cook?"

"I've been to catering college and not poisoned anybody yet!" There was that sarcastic tone again from Antonella, which I had seen once before. I got the feeling Antonella didn't like Rowena much, but I don't believe it bothered Rowena whether people liked her or not. I also noticed something else rather strange. The catering college was mentioned again, which just didn't fit in with her other stories. I was distracted from these thoughts by Amy's protest.

"Why do we need this house, Rowena? Can't we work from home and meet up somewhere?" Amy asked a valid question. She was thinking more clearly than me. I was being swept along by the excitement of this adventure.

"Time is the answer to that! We need a place where we can all eat, sleep and work on the book. No travelling, no distractions, nothing. If we keep to a tight schedule, it should be finished in a month. Rob, Antonella and the ghost need to work on it twenty-four seven. I will pop down for two or three days a week to monitor progress, come back to London to work on publicity articles and to find a publisher. I have friends in the trade, so it might not be such a problem. So long as the book is good and the exposure is building up. Now, let's address the gritty question of costs."

I was feeling really motivated and certainly felt we had the right woman behind us. Rowena had not yet finished and reeled off some figures effortlessly.

"Right, rent for one month to six weeks, £3k with expenses, food etc.

A ghost will be £4k a month plus a percentage of book revenues, so maybe 5%. You may get one for £2k if you give them 10% upfront, but that's only if they feel the book will sell well. Then I usually ask for 5% of the book revenue, but I will only require expenses on this project. I'll keep full payment from the articles and if it goes big, the serialisation. Antonella is doing housekeeping, so £1500 for that. In total, then, about £12K, which includes a contingency."

"Will we get any advance?" Amy asked, very sensibly. Rowena shook her head.

"Unknown author with no previous publication. Just a synopsis! It's not very likely!" I stepped in with a bold gesture.

"Cash is not a problem. I am happy to fund this!" Amy turned on me.

"Just a minute, Rob! What are you saying? This is your savings, in fact, our savings!"

"We have to take a chance sometime and why not with this. It is all about our future life now. Who knows, we might even make a buck or two!" I was being carried along with the euphoria of this project and Rowena was the most positive and motivated person I had ever met. It was hard to see how it could possibly fail.

"Do we have a deal?" asked Rowena impatiently, sensing Amy's reticence. We all nodded in acceptance while Antonella left us to finish the photocopying.

"I am going to like working with you guys. I can feel it!" she said. As I picked up my first two chapters from the desk, I asked with a wry smile.

"Do I keep writing this crap then?"

"For sure and it's not crap! Like I said, it's more of a factual statement. A good ghost will turn it into a great story." She stood up, which was the signal that our meeting was at an end.

"I'll get contracts drawn up for everything we've discussed and send them over for you to approve. In the meantime, there is one thing you could help with. I'm not familiar with the area so can you start looking around for some accommodation on a short-term rent, say two months? Do try to get one fully furnished. Give me a call if you need anything!" She walked us to the door.

"Robin? You said on the phone that somebody inside MI6 recommended me. Are you sure you can't give me a name?" This was the second time it had been mentioned.

"Sorry, Rowena. I can't. Maybe I can ask them to call you, without falling foul of any treason laws or giving away state secrets!"

"If you could, that would be great!"

"When are you looking to start this project?"

"Right now, with publicity. I will get the wheels in motion asap. The faster we can get the book out, the better chance we have." Amy was now thinking of her own timescale.

"I teach in the week, but my weekends are free. I'll have a week off soon with half term coming up, although I was planning a visit to my parents."

"That's fine. Help with the research whenever you can. Its Rob, who has to do the hard work now." As she opened the door, Antonella was waiting with a large pile of photocopies.

Chapter 12

The girls spent a great deal of time discussing Rowena on the way home. Although they agreed her ideas were sound, she was not a lady with whom they naturally bonded. '*Bossy cow*' and '*overbearing bitch*' were a couple of terms, banded about. I kept out of the discussion. If I joined in, I would be seen as defending her. Amy kept asking the question, "Why is she so willing to help us?"

I didn't have an answer but thought she was able to recognise a good story when one was put in front of her. As regards the girls' attitude, I put it down to a clash of personalities. That night was the first in some time that I felt relaxed enough to watch the TV. My housemates disappeared upstairs together for a while. It left me alone for the evening. A good thing for a couple of reasons. I hoped Antonella was finally coming out of her shell after the awful Gatwick experience and I was expecting hard times over my somewhat reckless decision to fund everything.

Monday brought a change to the weather, as a cold front had passed over during the night, bringing heavy rain. It also brought a progress report from Rowena.

"I've placed two articles in broadsheets going out tomorrow. The Telegraph and The Guardian, mainly questioning why the AF might be currently active in the UK. I've also got The Express interested in the botched

MI6 operation, but my legal advisor thinks it is too circumstantial and not enough fact. Is there anyone who can give more strength to the story?"

I was impressed. This woman was certainly dynamic. I tried to think of someone.

"George Webster, the local policeman. He was at The Limes the night when it all kicked off. He might have some ideas about the police investigation into the Davis killing?"

"The police are not always interested in the media. If they are, it's usually because the press is in a position to return the favour. Anyone else?"

"Some things I was told in confidence, so it is difficult. I can't think of anyone offhand. Let me give it some thought. I am working on the accommodation problem, though."

"That's good! I might have found your ghost writer. A lady called Sandra. I'll confirm later today. If she can move one or two things around, she will be able to start next week." Another 'female' in the camp! I wondered how my housemates would react to that after what had been said in the car.

As the week progressed, my house search with local agents was proving fruitless. One suggested trying a web site where people moved out of their homes for short periods. Possibly an expensive option, but one property popped out as fulfilling Rowen's criteria. It was available at a whopping £4k per month. Spending large sums of money was such a detached notion to me, I almost ruled it out. However, when I spoke to Rowena, which I did on a daily basis, she advised me to grab it. The ghost writer, Sandra Pegg, was available and booked. Rowena suggested staying in a local hotel until we could all move into the house.

I shared my concerns over costs with her, but she dismissed them as irrelevant and insignificant in the grand scheme of things.

"Focus on the bigger picture, Rob!" She was more interested in reporting the reaction to her articles. Questions were now being raised by some politicians, which was precisely what she wanted. She planned to increase the pressure. Much as I was impressed with results so far, I had niggling concerns over my diminishing bank balance. I mentioned my worries over the finances to Amy and she agreed that we should rein in spending. She would call Rowena after work.

Antonella and I went to view the property. Her bounce was back and in a chatty mood. I thought it was the time to brace a difficult subject with her in the car.

"Antonella. Can I ask you something?"

"Sure, what?"

"When you read my opening pages, you weren't happy with what I'd written about you. My description, I mean.

You are the main player in this. I am writing about me and you, so how I perceived your character when we first met, is relevant to the story." She frowned, so I wondered if she was offended at my comment.

"Well! You weren't exactly flattering, were you! You saw me as some halfwit! A little girl holding a teddy by his ear in one hand and her grandmother's fur coat in another, wearing sensible shoes with the toes pointing together and sucking a gobstopper, which had just been given to me so I would be quiet!" It was quite an amusing account. I could understand why she found it a little insulting.

"Ha! I didn't say that, but I wish I had done!" She gave me a playful punch on the arm.

"Rob! I've got over it, OK? If that's how you saw me, so be it. Yes, I was hurt, but I feel differently now." I felt relieved.

"You know. I felt safe at Burnside. They take fragile people like me and wrap them up in cotton wool. I guess my mother did the same, trying to banish the past from getting anywhere near me. But what's happening now is my destiny. I am twenty-six and not a child anymore. I have to address all these things that my family has gone through, no matter how unpleasant, before I can find peace. I am fine with what you said. It's helping me come to terms with my past."

"What about your assault and rape? Are you sure you are Ok with this stuff going in the book?"

"I will try to be. How much more detail do you need?"

"I can make some stuff up, which won't affect the story if you like?"

"Rob. Do you know why I was so upset at the airport?"

"Kind of, yes. Amy filled me in." I slowed down as I approached a red traffic light.

"On Saturday night, Amy took me into your bedroom and took off all her clothes. Everything. She made me look at her body. All over. Then she made me take off mine. We stood hand in hand, looking at each other in a full-length mirror." The lights turned green. I took a deep breath as I released the handbrake and raised my eyebrows. I wasn't quite sure what was coming next. She reassured me.

"No, we don't fancy each other! Neither of us is gay! Do you know what she told me?"

"No!" I was intrigued.

"That she has a sexy body that men find attractive, whereas I have a body that men find repulsive."

"Right." I was listening intently.

"Then she asked me if there were any differences between her body and mine."

"And there weren't, were there?" I could finally see what Amy was trying to do in this body issue therapy session.

"No. That's what Amy kept telling me, too! But that's the first time I've ever seen it for myself."

"Wondered what you were both up too! Why didn't you ask me to offer an opinion?" Antonella laughed and gave me a flirtatious smile.

"I am not ready for that! I still feel I have a repulsive body, but I now think it may be a problem in my head. You know, something I can work on. It's all down to Amy. It's the same with the book. It's making me face up to everything. It's a road I need to and want to take." With some thought, she added,

"I owe everything to you and Amy. I couldn't have found any more wonderful people to do this with! Friends, true friends!" This emotive little speech nearly brought a tear to my eye.

On arrival at the house, we were greeted by the owners. Mr. and Mrs. Saul, a retired couple. Mr. Saul, a rather stout man with very distinctive facial hair on his top lip. The grey hairs made his moustache look like a used paintbrush, stuck onto his face. He was pleasant, chatty and gave us the grand tour. The property was suitable. A little old fashioned in its décor, not that the condition wasn't good. The hall and downstairs rooms had recently been re-decorated. We ended up in the lounge and Mrs. Saul came in with a silver-plated tea tray. It was clear that our business would be concluded over loose-leaf English tea and lemon zest shortbread biscuits, adhering to strict etiquette rules.

"Can we ask what you need the house for?" It seemed a fair question.

"We are writing a book. We need a place to work with no distractions. There are five of us." Mrs. Saul poured the tea using an antique silver tea strainer.

"How interesting!" She handed me a bone china cup and saucer and a dainty teaspoon. "How many sugars?" She picked up the matching rose-patterned sugar bowl and took off the elegant lid.

"We haven't had any authors before, have we dear?" They were turning out to be a sweet couple but rather 'Darby and Joan.'

"No, dear," she replied. "Milk?"

"Can we ask why you let out your house like this?"

"It helps with our finances, you understand. Our pension doesn't stretch very far these days. We really should downsize, but somehow, we can't bear to move. Such an upheaval. The house was a wedding present, you see. We've been here now for fifty-three years." Mrs. Saul echoed her husband again. "Fifty-three years!"

"Where will you go?" Antonella asked.

"We have a holiday cottage in Cornwall. She changed the subject back to writing.

"Have you written anything we might be familiar with?"

"I don't think so. More technical stuff. No appeal to your everyday reader. A more specialist market." I fended off any more questions and addressed timescales.

"We're looking at six weeks but could be longer depending on how things go. Would that suit you?"

"That is not a problem. We have a minimum let of one month."

"Fine! We want to move in next Monday. Would that be possible?"

"That's rather sooner than I anticipated, young man. I need to get everything ready, but maybe we could call on Mrs. Richardson. What do you think, dear?" He looked over at his wife, who was pouring another cup of tea from the Royal Doulton bone china teapot.

"Is Mrs. Richardson your home help?"

"Yes, bless her!" answered Mrs. Saul. "I do not know where I would be without her in this big barn of a house!"

"Perhaps we could hire her services for cleaning and laundry duties?

"I will ask, but I am sure she will say yes. Mrs. Richardson needs the money, poor thing. With that delinquent of a son, she has to support. Do you know, only last week, he ...." I jumped in to stop her rambling. I was familiar with the Mrs. Saul's of this world from being in the hotel trade.

"As I said, there are five of us staying, but two of them are a couple so that we will be using four bedrooms." Mrs. Saul was clearly put out of step by my business-like approach.

"Right, you are dear. We would charge an extra £500 for such a short notice arrangement." I smiled to myself. Doddery she may be, but sharp as a tack when it came to money. I looked at Antonella. She nodded in agreement.

"We accept. I'll do a bank transfer this week for the full amount. Can I have your bank details, please?" She got up, rummaged around in a drawer in the sideboard for a scrappy piece of paper which she handed to me.

"This is a list of the things we do not allow, my dear." I scanned through it quickly, wondering if it included anything about abduction, jewel theft, or fleeing from the police!

"That's fine." Not wanting to get embroiled in all our yesterdays, I glanced at Antonella and got up to go.

"Monday, then. About nine?"

"We can go through everything when you arrive. In the meantime, I will have a word with Mrs. Richardson."

Business completed. We were shown out. I fancied having a pub lunch and knew just the place. It was a charming oaked beamed Devon pub, which had an excellent reputation for my weakness, which was 'real ale.' Antonella said she didn't do pubs, but I convinced her that a 'pie and a pint' was a necessary part of any rehabilitation process. She laughed. As we pulled into the car park, my mobile rang. It was Penny Carter.

"Robin! Penny here! We have a situation, so please listen carefully." The lady had my attention immediately.

"Two suspected activists of the AF have entered the country this morning. We got the news from the French authorities, but it was too late for us to detain them at Dover. A car trace has tracked them heading along the M4, we assume to the West Country. We have dispatched some personal protection officers to you and will be at Amy's cottage within the hour. Where are you now?"

"I'm at The Sparrow's Nest pub in Silverton with Antonella. Amy is at work."

"We know about Amy. Another officer is on his way to her now. The school has been informed about the situation."

"Oh, my God! Amy isn't going to like that!"

"It can't be helped. We can't think of any other reason why they would be heading to Devon. They must have gained intelligence that our ruse about your being in custody was false. Your journalist friend has been stirring things up in the press so much recently!"

"Rowena? But I thought she was more your friend than mine?"

"You are mistaken, Robin. I've never met her. I only know her by reputation!"

"Penny! I have only met her once myself. She wanted to talk to you, but I told her I couldn't give out your name."

"I'll get Hansen to call her, but he won't disclose his true identity. Tell her to expect a call from an Andrew Johnson.

Anyway, to more pressing matters. This pub? Where is it again?"

"Market Lane, Silverton."

"Stay there! It gives our men more time to secure the house. Our people will come to you when it's ready. Your girlfriend will be escorted to the pub. These people know who you are so, please don't advertise yourselves!"

"OK!" Antonella looked genuinely concerned and was tugging at my arm to know what was going on.

"I'll phone again if there are any developments." With that, she hung up. I outlined the call to Antonella then phoned Amy. Her voice was stuttering and panicky.

"I am in the Heads office now, Rob. She got a call from County Hall saying that one of her staff was a potential terrorist target. Mrs. Winstanley flipped! For fuck's sake! Can you believe it?"

"Shit! Amy! Listen to me! I need you to ...." I don't even think she heard me.

"It's crazy here, Rob! The police have arrived in abundance. It's bloody mayhem. All the poor children have been put in the school hall for their safety and Mrs. Winstanley is blaming me! What the hell has happened?" I tried not to scare her unnecessarily, so I just outlined the conversation I'd had with Penny Carter. Amy's only response was quite bizarre.

"You're both in the pub? Jesus. That's handy for you!"

"Look, Amy! If they are heading our way, they will go to the cottage first. According to Penny, it gives the security people more time. The bad guys won't know we are here, nobody does. Please just sit tight. An officer is coming to get you from school. Then he will bring you to the pub where a large glass of red wine is waiting!"

"Rob! I have to go. A policeman is coming over." The phone went dead. We both sat eating some lunch and not really speaking. It was a surreal situation. Being told by British Intelligence that we were targets of what only could be described as fanatical extremists.

"It might be nothing at all," I said, really trying to reassure both of us.

"Could just be two innocent Frenchmen going on a fishing trip." Antonella nodded, but in our heart of hearts, we both feared that trouble was brewing. I rang Rowena and told her to expect a call from an Andrew Johnson, giving her the good news that our house move was fixed for Monday. I didn't mention anything else as I guessed Penny would fill her in if she needed to know. Then Amy called again in another panic.

"This gets worse! The police have detained a man trying to get to the school. The kids are all up at the windows watching. Now they have a bloke on the ground!"

"What? Amy, are you sure there's only one guy? Where's the other one? How many police are there?"

"Twenty or thirty. Some with guns. Jesus, Rob, I'm so scared!"

"You poor thing! Don't do anything! I'll call Hansen." I got Penny again. I relayed the scene at the school, as Amy had described.

"Do you know who phoned the police?"

"It may have been the Head, Mrs. Winstanley."

"You say just one man and not two?"

"Yes! Just one!"

"OK. Sounds like it could be our chap who the police are trying to arrest. Will look into it." The call ended abruptly. Within seconds, the phone rang again. It was Amy.

"Rob! This is inexplicable! The arrested man is now on his feet and giving hell to the police. We can hear him shouting, telling them to put down their guns!"

"Amy! I think that's because he is the MI6 officer coming to get you!"

"Are you sure he's not one of the terrorists? I bloody hope he isn't. He's on his way into the school." At that, she hung up. I put the phone on the table as I waited for it to ring, but it was unusually silent.

"Can I have a Campari and soda, please!"

"A what?" I stared at Antonella.

"Campari and soda," she repeated. "Never had one, but I've always wanted to say that in a bar." Antonella's strange request brought me down to earth with a smile.

"Right! Do you want any dessert?"

"God, yes! Something big, sweet and sickly. I always get so ravenous when I am being hunted down by terrorists!" Does this girl comfort eat to deal with stressful situations, or does she have a weird sense of humour?

It was over an hour, before Amy finally arrived, still reeling from the events at school. With hands shaking, she picked up her glass of wine and drank it like it was water.

"Mrs. Winstanley is a broken woman. She got another call from County Hall, giving her a dressing down for involving the police. Then someone phoned the press and told them about an actual incident that was taking place at my school, so they showed up as well with cameras. OMG! Just when it couldn't get any worse, my hero Ricky here, who is not a terrorist, extracted me from the chaos!" She nodded at the broad-chested man dressed in a black tracksuit, wearing dark shades, standing by the door, busy on his phone. He looked like a fitness instructor rather than an anti-terrorist officer.

"You've both had plenty of time to eat everything on the menu, I see!" Amy joked, looking at the disarray of empty plates and glasses on the table.

"I always have an insatiable appetite when radical activists hunt me down!" I repeated what Antonella had said. She started giggling and it even raised a smile from Amy.

"Desperados! I don't think so! The only people who pursue you are some of your ex-girlfriends, Rob! What's that you are drinking, Antonella?"

"Campari and soda."

"Very civilised. Get me one too, will you, Rob?" Antonella held out her glass.

"Another for me, please,"

"That's four, you've had!" Don't' expect me to put you to bed!" The girls laughed again, but the mood changed when our guard Ricky came over.

"We might be here for a while. Was this venue a random choice, or are you regulars? I feel that this is the safest place for you all at the moment, as it is very public."

"No, not regulars. Every once in a while. They do a dammed fine pint here!" Ricky was evidently a professional and not remotely interested in the quality of the ale.

"At the moment, sir, my colleagues have not made the cottage secure. Can I have the keys?"

"Here have mine! Do you want a drink, mate?"

"No, thanks. On duty!" He went to the door again and made another phone call.

The next two hours were spent slowly getting more pissed, but what else could we do? Several beers, a bottle of wine and four campari's later, two other guys came to join Ricky. We left The Sparrow's Nest and headed home in convoy. Well, not that I remembered much about the rest of the evening.

Chapter 13

I awoke in the morning to the delightful smell of fried bacon wafting through the cottage. Opening the curtains, I noticed a man in the front garden and we also had a guard out the back. I went downstairs to the kitchen to make tea and to get something for my head, which was throbbing. There, I found the source of the wonderful aroma. Antonella was making bacon sandwiches.

"Coffee? Looks like you need it!"

"And you don't after what you put away last night?"

"I'm fine. I had a good time. I just thought I would get things going this morning. Dave has been to get some supplies, so I am doing breakfast sarnies for the guys."

"Dave? Who's Dave?" I enquired in my soporific state.

"Don't you remember being introduced to them in the pub? Ricky brought Amy to the pub yesterday. Dave, the one who drove us home in your car? He's the bloke out front. Pete is in the back garden and somewhere about is Kev. They are such nice guys!" She was buttering the baguettes.

"No, not really. I do remember that you had as much to drink as me, so you were no way sober!" As I snatched a hot piece of bacon from the pan, she playfully tried to smack my arse with her butter knife and grinned.

From a girl who previously struggled to engage anyone in conversation, suddenly, she was comfortable in their company of men she hardly knew. This therapy of Amy's was certainly working, but I had an uneasy feeling. I had a sudden flashback to what Hansen had said on that fateful night, '*she is a very fine actress indeed.*' I put the thought aside and grabbed two mugs of coffee for Amy and me. As I went upstairs again, Antonella shouted behind me.

"Your phone's been bleeping like mad!"

"What time is it?"

"Half ten."

"What!!!!"

Amy was still fast asleep when I returned, so I left her coffee by the bed and went for a shower. I needed to freshen up, then I got dressed and returned downstairs.

Shit! Seventeen missed calls! I sat in the lounge and called the first. It was Penny.

"Sorry, Penny! Just got up. Touch of indigestion last night." I preferred not to mention the heavy drinking session. I was sure she would disapprove of such insobriety.

"The car has gone to ground in the Plymouth area, so we are still on red alert! What about you and your two companions?"

I outlined our plans to move into the rented house and gave her the details. She did say that the position of the railway line could cause problems for the security team, but if I could give Kevin the address, he would look it over and do an assessment. Penny also wanted him to check the inside of the house as a matter of urgency.

"I'll call Mr & Mrs. Saul and tell them to expect someone."
More expense, I thought. No doubt, they would charge
extra.

"Good. I will wait to hear back from Kevin. If it's a better
option than we have now, I suggest you move in tomorrow.
In the circumstances Rob, we will fund the
accommodation." Her last line lifted my spirits no end.
The next call was to Rowena. I summarised the current
situation which we were in, but she was far from
impressed.

"Are you telling me that we've got fucking security guards
following us around? How am I supposed to do my job?"
This was the first time I had ever heard her swear.

"Rowena! We're effectively under house arrest here.
We've got four of them stuck to us like limpets!
Apparently, it's your articles that are getting the AF tetchy,
so all I am saying is watch your back!"

"Ok. Ok! On that point, I do have some news for you. The
Express is going big on my *'Terrorists in the UK'* piece. It
will be front-page tomorrow unless the queen dies or
something. Publishers will be queuing up, boy! So, get
writing!"

I summarised Penny's remarks about the house and told
her that if the security people gave us the go ahead, we
would be in the following day. Rowena listened intently.

"Give me word, as soon as the decision comes through and
I'll bring Sandra over."

"You don't need to. She's been in touch by email. I've sent her what we've done so far and the outline I gave you. Sandra says that there is enough material to make a start and she's happy to work from home. Apparently, she has a problem with her dog." Rowena's reply was a severe rejection of my proposal.

"No, Robin! That is not acceptable. I want her there with you. The quicker we get this done, the better. I will re-negotiate her contract if necessary, with or without the dog. Has she never heard of kennels! For god's sake!" I offered a word of caution.

"Just be careful, Rowena! These are heavy-duty guys who will stop at nothing. It's you who is poking the hornets' nest."

"I can look after myself. Now tell me what you know about Andrew Johnson?" I knew she was talking about Hansen, but I didn't let on.

"Andrew Johnson?" I tried to look mystified.

"He told me he'd known you for several years," said Rowena.

"Oh, yes. That Andrew! I am not sure that I can tell you much about him. I only found out who he was and who he worked for a short while ago." She was pressing me hard for information and I wasn't having any of it.

"Surely you can tell me more than that." I tried to deflect her questioning.

"Did Johnson tell you anything useful?"

"Yes, but I want more info on him. Whose side is he on?"

"Let's keep it the way it is, for now. We are under threat of god knows what. I can't get a full grasp of this situation. We don't want to piss him off with stuff in the papers!"

"OK. I take your point but tell me this. Where are these trunks that Johnson says are in your possession?" Her direct question took me by surprise.

"Not sure I know what you mean!"

"Rob! Don't bollocks me. I want to know."

"I've no idea. I had no answer for British Intelligence when they asked me that question, so why do you think I can give you one?"

"I hope for your sake Rob, the answer will be in the book!" Her tone was intimidating and I didn't much care for it. It must have been discussed with Hansen and Penny. There was nowhere else it could have come from. My only option was to throw a curved ball and buy some time.

"Look! I'll tell you what I know but not over the phone. It might be bugged. If we get in the house tomorrow, I'll reveal all, but I warn you, I don't know as much as you think I do." It took the wind out of her sails and we moved on to discuss less controversial issues. By the end of the call, she had regained her professional modus. Amy was a good judge of character. She was spot on with Rowena.

After such an exchange, I went in search of Antonella's bacon sandwiches and more coffee. She was pleased to oblige.

"I think Amy's up. I heard somebody in the bathroom." I went upstairs to check.

"You alright, love?" As I popped my head around the bathroom door, she was sitting on the toilet completely starkers except for a pair of black lace panties around her ankles. Dishevelled strands of hair covering her mascara stained-face and her hands holding her head.

"God! you look sexy!"

"What! Oh! it's you." She groaned. "I don't feel it. I haven't been hung-over like this since college days."

"It was a good night, though, wasn't it?"

"Yea, right! A great celebration for losing my job!"

"What? You haven't?"

"I have! Mrs. Winstanley said I wouldn't be welcome in her school again."

"Rubbish! She made a fool of herself, not you. Anyway, she doesn't employ you, the governors do!"

"Maybe, but that doesn't stop my head from spinning." I changed tack.

"What's this about you stripping off in front of a mirror with other women?" She stared at me.

"Other women? Don't be stupid. Only Antonella. She told you then?"

"You've made a real difference to her life, so you must take heart from that." Her reaction was an emotional outburst.

"Of course, I do, but I'm talking about my job! I love teaching! I love Devon and I love the school, the kids, everything. You don't understand how important this is to me. I don't want all of your shit with bodyguards and murders and stuff jeopardising it. It's got to stop!"

"Have something to eat and you'll feel better." I didn't want negative vibes from her now, so I tried to be positive. "We could be moving in tomorrow!"

"What! No, no, no. I am not moving into a house with 'that' woman! I am staying here."

"You can't, Amy! The security situation is still well, a situation." I spoke calmly to her, but she was getting worked up.

"These big fish are just playing with us. Don't' you see? Do what we say, sit where we want you to sit, go where we want you to go! Behave like good little children and then we can protect you! Don't you get it? We are just the fucking bait to catch what they want!"

She was right. I had worked that out for myself. Before I had a chance to give a reassuring reply, she was raising her voice.

"You know I am bloody right. So why are you going along with it then?" Amy's tone was getting more agitated.

"I don't think we've any other option. These AF people are not going to go away just because we say we don't want to play anymore."

"Go away, Rob and shut the bastard door!" I got the message, so I left her alone.

Dave, the security man in charge, made an announcement just after lunch.

"We will be moving this afternoon, so please get everything you need. We will not be returning here and we do not wish to give any opportunities to be followed. We will be taking all the cars." He outlined the procedure to us. It came as no surprise that the move took place with exact military precision. I would have expected nothing less, even down to the synchronisation of watches, which was a little tricky for me as I don't wear one.

Amy was not in a good place when we arrived at the 'safe house,' but I tried to be as patient as I could. The episode at the school had upset her far more than we could have imagined and now she was in what she called' imprisonment.' She was also belligerent in her attitude towards the protection officers.

"Which is the master bedroom?"

"Top of the stairs on the left," replied Dave.

"That's mine then!" Amy retorted.

"Miss! We are just about to allocate the rooms."

"I don't give a shit! I'm having that room, or I will return to my cottage and you can look after me there!" Dave didn't press the issue, but you could see he was not happy. I followed her in with my bag.

"This is my room, Rob!" I, too, was in the firing line.

"Amy, love, we have to share. There aren't enough rooms to have one each." I pointed out calmly.

"But the protection gang aren't sleeping here. They're working in shifts, aren't they?"

"Yes! but the ghost writer needs a room and so does Rowena."

"You have this room and share it with Rowena then!" It was no good arguing with Amy when she was like this.

A man's voice shouted upstairs.

"I have a Mrs. Richardson here asking for Mr. Ashurst?" It was a chance for me to escape.

"That must be the housekeeper! I'm coming down." The image in my mind of Mrs. Richardson was a mature woman with a headscarf, apron, and feather duster. Very much in the granny mould but I was completely wrong. Mrs. Richardson was about my age, or slightly younger, well presented in a cotton jersey navy sweatshirt, skinny ripped jeans, and wedge sandals of pewter metallic. Rather attractive with her blonde hair tied back in a ponytail, she had a bubbly personality to match. I told her what we wanted then introduced her to everyone except Amy. She agreed to come in each day from ten until two and do whatever was required. Antonella took to her straight away.

I took Amy up a cup of tea. She was still unpacking and still not in a very communicative mood.

"The security guys want to have a meeting with us all to go over everything. Will you come downstairs?"

"Now?"

"When Rowena and Sandra arrive."

"Sandra? The ghost writer is a woman?"

"Apparently yes. But I've not met her yet."

"Well, lucky you!" I knew where this was going and as Amy was yet to meet the delightful and eye-catching Mrs. Richardson, I didn't dare mention her.

"What does that mean?"

"You and four women in the 'big brother house'! Your jaw was on the floor when we met Rowena." She mimicked her in a sycophantic manner rather unkindly. "Yes, Rowena! No, Rowena, three bags fucking full, Rowena," she said in an affected voice.

"Just listen to yourself, Rob!" I felt this was hurtful and uncalled for.

"Amy, just remember. This book was your idea, not mine." I had not seen her like this before, so I made an exit.

Our two new housemates arrived. They were marshalled in by security men, and introductions made. Amy made a reluctant appearance. I kept my distance, but I could tell by the look on her face that she wasn't happy. Dave outlined several issues, in his words, to make life easy for all of us, but mostly it was common sense. When he had finished, Rowena took over the meeting, much to Amy's annoyance.

"Listen up, chaps! This isn't going to be comfortable, but we have a job to do and that's our priority. When it is all over, we can all go our separate ways and get back to normal. The first item on the agenda is catering. Antonella is on kitchen duty. The second item is housekeeping. We have a lady coming in to clean, I believe?" I wasn't sure if I should raise my hand or not.

"Mrs. Richardson. She's coming in ten till two every day." I felt I had made a valuable contribution.

"What's her first name? I don't particularly like to use surnames with staff. Rank and title are so 'yesterday'"

"I don't know. Sorry. I never thought to ask."

"Never mind, Rob, but remember in future, please. It's all in the detail!" I had messed up and been scolded for it. Even worse, was the smile on Amy's face.

"Third item. Bedroom allocation. I have prepared a spreadsheet. Dave and his team have been given a copy."

"We've already sorted out rooms," Amy said, defiantly. "I've unpacked and I am in the master suite, so I'm not moving!"

Antonella also chipped in.

"Ro! I've unpacked as well. I'm in the room facing the drive."

"My name is Rowena! Let's get everything correct, shall we!"

I wasn't sure if it was a mistake on Antonella's part, or she was winding Rowena up. I would be amazed if Antonella knew how to wind anyone up. Rowena's body language took a confrontational stance. She addressed Amy now, ignoring Antonella.

"No! That's mine. You are down for the front room with Rob."

"Why don't you take that one?" Amy's tone was challenging. Battle lines were being drawn.

"Because the master bedroom has a desk and an en-suite. I need the workspace and I have no intention of queuing for the bathroom!" I could see this going nowhere without resorting to verbal violence. I tried to defuse the inevitable exchange and de-rail the flow.

"You are well informed about the rooms, Rowena?"

"Naturally! I requested a layout from the agents." It was evident that Rowena did nothing unless she was in full possession of the facts first. Amy went on the attack again.

"Sorry, but I am not moving. We are the only couple here, so we should have the largest room. As the only bloke, Rob should be in the room with the en-suite." Amy was adamant, and her position did make practical sense.

Sandra, the ghost writer, had not said anything up until then, but she also attempted to soothe the growing tension.

"I really don't mind where I am. Can I have a copy of your spreadsheet?"

"You are in the second one at the front next to Amy and Robin." Sandra picked up her bags and went to leave, but this was the last straw for Amy.

"I am not moving! So, Ms ghost or whoever you are, you're in the room next to Ms. Bossy here!" Everyone went silent and it was like watching two stags confronting each other for control of the herd. Such an outward challenge to her self-appointed authority was hard for her to take, but Rowena held her corner firmly.

"I must say, you have a very immature attitude for a schoolteacher."

I knew that such a remark would light the fuse. Amy's face was changing colour.

"Besides," continued Rowena, condescendingly. "Your role in this is very minor!" Amy's eyes widened, her voice trembling in anger.

"You fucking bitch! You have the room then! I am out of here!"

"I beg your pardon! How dare you speak....!" Dave jumped in before Rowena could finish her indignant reply. He spoke with authority.

"I'm deeply sorry, ladies and gent, but we are under strict orders. Nobody is leaving while the threat level is on red! You must all resolve the bedroom situation."

There are times in your life when you regret what you have said as much as times when you regret not saying something when the chance presents itself. It happens to me all the time, but on this occasion, I got it right.

"Can I say that I am totally with Amy on this. I am the only man sleeping in the house and I don't want to have to get dressed in the night to have a pee. We are a couple and as that room has a TV, we can spend time together in the evenings. We can easily put the desk in the front room, for you Rowena and if we use the en-suite, then it will be two less for the bathroom anyway!"

Everyone held their breath, waiting for a response from her. She knew it was the obvious solution, but how was she going to back down in front of everyone? It was expertly done with a knowing laugh.

"Rob! You are absolutely right and I defer to your experience and skill as a 'hotel manager.'" She carried on with a calm composure as if nothing had happened.

"I think we are done. I don't have anything else on my list. If we can spend the evening getting to know each other, please? Work starts at eight tomorrow. If you have dietary requirements or particular foodstuffs that you want, please inform Antonella. That also goes for security." She continued barking out her instructions.

"Dave! Your lads can use the toilet facilities at the back of the garage next to the utility room." Dave's professional response left her in no doubt that he was in charge of operations.

"Thank you, Ma-am, but my team will report directly to me. They have been well-briefed on the layout."

As I had defended Amy, I felt that I could now take my bag into the bedroom without any reprisals. She followed me in and slammed the door shut.

"That woman is beyond belief!" Fortunately, I was no longer the target of Amy's frustration. I had taken a bit of a dislike to Rowena myself. I let her be the reviled female in the camp! There was a knock on the door and Antonella came in.

"Isn't she horrible? I can't believe it! She's given me a detailed list of what she wants to eat and when she wants to eat it. I said I would do the cooking. I didn't say I would be a slave!"

"Give her what you cook for everyone else in the morning. I will vouch for your kitchen skills and your bacon sandwiches, which are excellent! Tell her you didn't have the ingredients. The bitch will soon get the message that she can't piss us about!"

"But that's it! There's been a Tesco delivery with everything that she eats. It arrived two hours ago."

"***It's all in the detail, girls***!" I put on her Essex accent and the three of us laughed. Another knock on the door and it was Dave.

"Miss Rottweiler has detailed me to move the desk."

"Ha-ha! *It's all in the detail.*" We even got a smile from Dave.

"We could do with her at boot camp for the lads. Make an excellent colour Sargent!" Dave said as he lifted the desk on its side to get it out of the door. I didn't know what a colour sergeant was, but I could guess.

Chapter 14

The next morning, Sandra and I sat in the study discussing the book. Rowena had breezed in and given out more instructions, which included requesting Amy's help in the kitchen.

"With all these guys to feed, it's far too much for Antonella to be cook. Time is of the essence. If meals are not punctual, we will lose precious time."

I objected strongly, on the basis that Amy was part of the story. She had also lost her job because of what happened and as an English graduate, her input would be valuable. Amy had talked about going home to see her parents at the weekend, but more than anything, she needed my support.

"Two minds recalling all the events will get the book written quicker. I want her with us!" Rowena magnanimously submitted.

"Fair enough. I will organise more kitchen help." With that, she left and I was sure she would.

"*It's all in the fucking detail...*" muttered Amy disdainfully.

"I know she is a bit dictatorial, but you have to admit, she gets things done." When the three of us had our coffee break, we asked Sandra how well she knew Rowena.

"I don't really," Sandra said, munching on a digestive biscuit. We've crossed paths a few times. At a writers event dinner and once we shared a train compartment from Birmingham to London. I know her more by her reputation than anything. I can assure you, whatever else is said about her, she's the best in the business!" Both Amy and I warmed to Sandra straight away.

"What stuff is said about her then?" Amy was curious, wanting to know every personal detail about her foe.

"Gossip, you mean? Very little, really. It was rumoured that she might be gay, but that's just hearsay. She's so driven and focused. It's most likely because she never has time for men! Rowena's never made any advances to me!" We chuckled at that. Sandra continued.

"The lady is extremely competitive and the sort of person who has to excel in everything she does, which, in a way, gives women a bad name. My theory is that she derides men because she is better than them. I don't think our Rowena is a particularly happy lady, but that's my own humble opinion."

"The bitch will get my fist in her gob if she tries to come on to me!" remarked Amy and we all laughed.

"I don't mean to be nosey, Sandra, but why did she ask you to be our ghost writer? I got the impression you had both worked together before."

"No! We haven't, but as I say, she researches everything thoroughly and must have felt that you and I would work well and quickly. I must confess this job has been heaven sent for me. I've been struggling financially for the last few months. The market for a ghost writer seems dead at the moment. I was seriously considering a career change and then this came up. She offered me a contract with such good money. I couldn't refuse."

"That's interesting! Rowena told me she beat you down on your price!"

"No, that's not true! I can assure you. I haven't exactly been inundated with work in the last six months. So, can I ask who is paying me? is it you, Rob?"

"Yes! However, due to recent events, the house is now on somebody else's tab, but I can't say who."

"The publisher?"

"No. We haven't got one as yet."

"Strange! Rowena told me that was all sorted, but never went into much detail about the project. Can I ask who is coughing up for this level of security and why?" Amy stepped in to explain our position and Sandra listened intently.

"As for the book, who knows what's going on? I think we are being used in some way, but Rob is a bit more trusting. A government department employs the security guys but we can't say anymore. It might all become clearer when the book is finished." Sandra took another biscuit.

"Well! Exciting times ahead!"

It was not easy for me to get into a flow of work with Sandra. It was so different from the world I was used to, but she was sympathetic and tried to help or guide me through the process. Sandra wanted me to give her the story as I remembered it so that it could be all rewritten in her words. In the end, she asked me to make chronological notes of events, which I found better. Amy's job was to go through the re-writes of the first few chapters, which I had done. Correcting anything wrong or adding things I had missed. As a teacher with a degree in English, composition and literacy came easily. They both got on with the task in hand, except for me. I found it difficult to concentrate, especially when I could hear things being talked about. When I butted into their discussions, I was told in no uncertain terms, to get on with what I was doing.

Eventually, I was banished to the bedroom. Although there were no distractions, it was not so easy to write long hand perched on a bed. Rowena had almost taken over the dining room with her papers and two computers. She was also constantly on her three mobile phones.

Looking for some inspiration, I went into the kitchen to talk to Antonella and ended up helping her to prepare lunch. A natural habitat for a hotel manager like me. I felt more focused in the afternoon and eventually, I had finished another section which I passed on.

Later, that afternoon I received a call from Penny.

"We have intelligence that the French operatives have now left the area. Hopefully, it might make you all sleep better tonight!"

"Are we going to lose our security?"

"No! Not all of them at the moment, but we might lessen numbers soon."

"Will it be possible to leave the house, then?" I knew Amy wanted to visit her parents and if Rowena returned to London, we might have a more comfortable few days.

"The general feeling in our office is that Rowena Kerry is now a possible target because of her articles, so she must stay. Amy, on the other hand, is only in the picture due to her association with you and what she might have overheard. I will check with Hansen and confirm. So long as she has a security officer with her as an escort." I gave her a brief summary of all the tensions in the house.

"This isn't an easy environment to be in. Rowena is a difficult person to work with, let alone live with! She orders us about like we are some delinquent kids who need discipline!" Penny listened sympathetically.

"Try to cope with it as best you can, Robin!"

"The girls and I like Sandra, but the main friction is between Amy and Rowena. Amy's gone through so much and now she thinks she's lost her job. Is there anything you can do to help?"

"I understand your concerns. I'll assess the situation tomorrow but tell her not to worry. I'm sure she will be going back to her school when this is at an end. I promise I will speak to her employers in the morning."

"Thanks, Penny. It will mean a lot. Do you know what they were up to in Plymouth?"

"The two men are known associates of the AF rather than active members. That's something that we are sure about. A nasty group of mercenaries is the best way to describe them. They also have links to other terrorist groups. What we don't know is whether they were looking for you or they just happened to be interested in something else. At the moment, we've not had any positive intelligence either way. It appears they are heading to Wales. They're not making any efforts to hide their whereabouts, so we can conclude, it might just be a recognisance mission. In these circumstances, we may downgrade you to amber, but as I said, until we know what's going on, the security stays."

I went back into the study and relayed the conversation to Amy, who perked up at the news and wanted to leave immediately. I called Penny again. She eventually agreed that Amy could go on Friday evening. That gave us two full days in the house. Penny also confirmed that one of the officers had been instructed to accompany Amy.

Rowena steadfastly refused to move her things from the dining room table, so we had our dinner on trays in the lounge. Then we were summoned.
"Are we all here? Let's have a quick run through on how everything has gone so far." Big brother house meeting, I thought. I wonder how it will go.

"First, thank you to Antonella. The food has been top draw all day." Antonella beamed, basking in the praise. We gave her a round of applause.

"Antonella. Do we know Mrs. Richardson's first name, yet?"

"No! she answers to Mrs. Richardson." Then Amy started whispering audibly to Antonella.

"There, that's my girl, Anton. Don't let Ms. Bossy stress you!" I could see in her face that Rowena was frustrated by Amy's interjection, but ignored the challenge.

"And is Mrs. Richardson's work satisfactory?"

"Couldn't have done it without her. Do you know how many bacon rolls and cups of tea those security guys go through in one day?" Amy baited Rowena again and started clapping.

"Let's hear it for Mrs. Richardson!"

Rowena disregarded her and continued.

"Good. Does anyone else have any housekeeping issues?" We all looked at each other, but no-one said anything.

"Moving on then. The book." She addressed Sandra directly. "Can you give us a short report, please?" Sandra outlined her approach of getting me to write the facts in chronological order and how she was constructing the story with Amy, whom she praised for the excellent standard of support. Another round of applause went around the room.

Rowena hadn't orchestrated that one, but I couldn't help noticing a peevish look on her face.

"Sandra. Is there anything we can help you with?"

"No. Not really. When I have some of the finished book to show you, I will get everyone to read it and ask for comments but early stages yet."

"Rob? What about you? I noticed you seemed to be wandering aimlessly about the house this morning instead of writing." This comment got my back up.

"I'll tell you why Rowena! It is difficult for me to concentrate in the study with Sandra and Amy as they keep discussing matters out loud. I need to be in a silent space so I can think and gather my thoughts, but the desk which was in our bedroom has been moved to yours. I can't work in the dining room because you have most of the table and with all your telephone conversations, I am again unable to think. Perhaps I could use your bedroom?"

I knew this would rile her as she kept going back to her room to make and receive calls. Her reply was noticeably curt.

"I will organise a desk for you." She noted it down.

"In terms of output, then, how much have you achieved?"

"Quite a lot, in the circumstances. It's far better for me to write things down as I remember them, like a diary. Now that I'm not trying to write the story myself, it's moved on very well. Despite my workplace issues," I added. I was still trying to needle Rowena.

"Good! Well done, team!" she rumbled on about the new articles she had placed in the newspapers and how an MP had started to raise questions in the House of Commons.

"It may be on the radio, so we need to keep an eye on the news." Just before she had a chance to say any more, I got a text from Penny, confirming the latest news. I interrupted Rowena to tell everyone.

"The security threat has been officially downgraded from red to amber, which means we are no longer confined to barracks!" An audible sigh of relief went around the room. I could see Rowena looking uncomfortable as I was stealing her limelight. I carried on deliberately, with orders from the highest level.

"Those of us who are considered main targets are not able to leave just yet. They include Antonella, Rowena and of course, me." Rowena reacted immediately.

"Why am I included and how do you know this?"

"According to my sources, your articles have upset some people in the AF. Possibly, they think you have some inside information. Amy and Sandra can leave this weekend but only with a security officer." I looked over to Dave and he took over.

"That is correct. We will be here in reduced numbers until the situation is resolved, so I still need to know what your movements are going to be, day by day."

"If we can't go anywhere, we may as well continue with our work." Rowena was trying to chair the meeting again.

Sandra put her hand up as if to ask permission from Rowena to speak.

"If you can do without me for the weekend, I need to go home to look after my dog. I'll be back Sunday afternoon. Maybe if we could get a voice recorder for Rob to use? To keep the momentum going until I get back."

"Excellent suggestion! I will get one delivered by tomorrow."

The meeting broke up. Amy and I retired to our room. She switched on the telly and sat on the bed with arms folded.

"I don't want to sit in the lounge with that cow! She's getting to you now, as well, isn't she?" I was just about to reply when there was a knock on the door. It was Antonella.

"Can I join you? There's no TV in my room and Rowena has a politics program on downstairs in the lounge."

"What a surprise," Amy said scornfully.

"'Course you can Anton. We're only watching Eastenders!" It wasn't long before Sandra also knocked on the door and joined us. I did start to feel guilty about Rowena. After all, we were the ones who hired her. I needn't have worried. She was on the phone in the dining room. I don't even think she noticed we were not there.

We all put in a good stint Thursday and Friday. Amy was in better spirits, knowing she was getting away. I had done two more days work on the story, but it was still slow progress for me, particularly getting used to dictating into the gizmo. Friday's house meeting was a little low key. In the end, far shorter than usual so that Amy and Sandra could leave early, which they did about 2 o'clock. Ricky was to chaperone Amy, while Kevin was with Sandra. Rowena spent most of the time recounting issues and managed to get a video of the parliamentary exchange.

Q. "Would the Prime minster like to inform the house about press reports concerning the activities of a French anarchist group in my constituency, which has led to the death of a prominent Devon Solicitor."

A. "In reply, to the honourable gentleman. The case is, as I believe, ongoing, so I am unable to comment, but British Officers in MI6 are keeping me well informed of any developments. As the man in question was not involved in any way, it seems to be a very unfortunate case of mistaken identity. Our sympathy goes out to his family at this time."

Q. "Has the government, at any time, had any contacts with or is in the process of having any contact with this group?"
A. "It is a matter of historical fact, that governments of this country have had support for and have indeed provided funds for the Action Française. I can assure the House that funding ceased in the 1970s when the AF went from being a pressure group with the sole aim of restoring the

monarchy, to a terrorist association with varied aims. As such, we have had no contact since then."

To me, it was amazing that this had come out in such a way. I didn't know how significant these questions in the House of Commons were. The one thing that jumped out was the admission that the government did, in fact, have contact up to and until the nineteen seventy's. Our research showed that it ended during the Second World War.

I had started to get to know Dave, our security guard. I liked the guy and we shared the same sense of humour. I needed to seek out some bloke time as there was often far too much oestrogen in the house for comfort. He never talked about his job. On the Friday evening, we were in the kitchen having a beer together, generally talking about football and sharing a joke or two, when I got a call from Amy's mother.

"Robin! I am sorry to bother you, but do you have any idea when Amy will be with us?" My heart missed several beats.

"What! Surely Amy's with you by now? She left after lunch."

"I have been trying her phone Robin, but it just goes to voicemail. Has she been in touch?"

"Let me try. Maybe there's something wrong with her phone. We have the number of the officer who is accompanying her, so don't worry. I'll call you back." I looked at Dave incredulously. He had got the gist of my conversation but saying it out loud made it real.

"Ricky and Amy haven't arrived in Hertford! Should I call Penny?"

I could tell by his tone that there was an immediate cause for concern.

"Wait. I'll phone our man." Several long minutes passed.

"He's not picking up." Dave was sober in an instant and made another quick call. I heard him mention the word 'code.' He was completely calm and professional as he was trained to be. I, on the other hand, was sinking fast. Horrible thoughts were racing through my head. I let out an involuntary scream. Everyone in the house came to see what was going on. Dave filled them in as I was starting to shake. He poured me a brandy and I became oblivious to what was happening around me.

"Rob! It could be nothing. A breakdown in the car, or maybe they just got lost?" Rowena was trying to be comforting, but I knew something was wrong and that the worst had happened. Everyone looked to Dave for a reassuring comment. None came.

"Rick is a highly trained professional and knows procedures. He would have sounded the alarm if there had been any trouble."

The next few hours were a blur for me. More security officers arrived, but I was only aware of strange faces, whispers and people milling about. A door opened. Then Hansen appeared.

"The local police have been informed and a search for your girlfriend is now priority." I felt a strong arm on my shoulder.

"Robin, my friend. Stay calm. We'll find her. In the meantime, this house is back on red alert!"

"What about her parents?" I asked weakly.

"Our trained officers are with them. Unfortunately, it is now a waiting game. The officer with your girlfriend is one of the best we have." He paused.

"I won't lie to you, Robin. In circumstances like these, where a threat is perceived, procedures are immediately put into place by the officer. Ricky hasn't done so. It could be bad news." I could hardly take in what he was trying to tell me.

"Bad news? What the fuck does that mean?" I was shaking with emotion. I broke down, crying like a small child.

"At the moment, there is only one explanation. He may have been eliminated!" I couldn't listen anymore and went to my room, but that was worse because it was all Amy. Amy's clothes, Amy's things. Amy's smell. The room she had fought to have just a few days before. I ended up a crumpled heap on the landing. Someone came upstairs and helped me into bed. They must have given me a sedative. Blackness and sleep devoured me, swiftly sending me to oblivion.

Chapter 15

I awoke to find Antonella lying beside me fully clothed. As my brain kicked in, the horror of the situation from the night before hit me. I shot up and felt pain throbbing in my head.

"Any news?" Antonella looked at me with red eyes. It was clear she had been sobbing.

"They found the security man last night. His throat had been cut." I closed my eyes. A coldness seeped through my body and anesthetised my limbs. I felt numb. She rubbed my arm in a consoling way.

"But there's no sign of Amy. We can't give up hope. Not yet."

"Have you been here all night?" she nodded. I slowly climbed out of bed and went downstairs. Penny Carter was in the living room, talking to one of the guards. I stumbled in and asked,

"Anything?"

"I am afraid not. We think she may have been taken for ransom. There was no sign of her when the car was found and no evidence of any violence. The only blood on the scene was Ricky's." I was struggling to comprehend that yet another man had been murdered and now my girlfriend was missing. If it was the AF, then I shuddered. I recalled what Antonella had said about their brutality and tried not to imagine what my poor sweet Amy was going through at this very moment.

"Where was the car found?"

"Taunton."

"Taunton? That's only half an hour from here." I was shouting now.

"They must have been watching us, the bastards! How come you didn't know that?" I ran upstairs to get my car keys. I was going out to look for her. Amy needed me now. As I tried to leave, Dave and two other guys held me back, very forcefully. Penny pleaded with me.

"Robin. You can't help! Leave it to the professionals. Please. We have doubled our efforts to protect you and Antonella."

"Why did you say she could go? Why? You said it was OK to leave the house!" I broke down again, sobbing but I was able to pull myself together enough to stop anyone from sedating me again.

The day dragged on endlessly. Sandra returned, I imagine, somewhat unwillingly. Being in a secure house and not knowing why was one thing, but when a house member goes missing, it's quite another. I think it was beginning to scare her. The same could be said for Rowena. All her energy was gone and her phones switched off. She sat on the sofa, looking blank. Despite their antagonistic relationship, I knew that she was genuinely worried about

Amy. She may well have felt rather vulnerable and a little responsible. Her news features had generated attention, not just to us as a group but to her in particular. I suspected she had been used, like all of us, as a conduit to get articles out about the AF and bring them out into the open.

Any thoughts about the book were gone. I had no focus, no concentration. Just deadened in the extreme. Sandra asked Penny if she thought writing the book would take the heat off us.

"Perhaps in the long run. Yes, I do. I don't know how far you have got with Robin's story, but you see, the AF want the documents which are in the missing trunks. Whatever it is, this information has to be brought out into the open, so certain things can be proved, or disproved. I think if they believe they were gone for good, then maybe, they would be happy. Their idea is to destroy them anyway. A book saying what happened might work." Sandra considered her answer and asked,

"What exactly is this information?"

"We may never know that."

"Let's get back to work then." I did feel Penny intended to keep us

busy. Sandra went into the study and started going through my story. I was finding it hard. I could hear my voice on the recorder, in happier times and all I wanted to do was turn back the clock.

Saturday turned into Sunday, which turned into Monday. Penny Carter had gone, but we still had Dave and his lads. They must have been gutted about losing Ricky, a colleague and friend, but they never let on. Pro's to the last. Antonella had relinquished catering duty since we got the news about Amy. Not that any of us were in the right frame of mind to wine and dine. I certainly wasn't. We were joined by two extra women who were detailed to do the catering. They both came and went under security.

Antonella had been a comfort to me during the last few days and I hoped she might well say the same about me. We spent all our time together, reminiscing about Amy and going through what had happened. She blamed herself for the whole escapade, but I couldn't help thinking that it was me who pushed Penny into giving the go-ahead for her to leave. Sandra was now the driving force behind the book and asked me to do some more, but I think she missed Amy's input. I told her to try and get through to Rowena, but she had little success.

Developments on the political front were still keeping up the pace. The French foreign minister had made a speech about government backing of terrorist groups, not mentioning Britain by name, but he made it clear exactly which government he was talking about. Then, there were more press exposures about AF activity on British soil. These had not come from Rowena, so other journalists were now getting involved. The BBC had a slot about the issue in its main news and pressure was mounting for the government to make a statement. However, not even locally in Devon or Somerset, was there any news about a missing or kidnaped woman or the brutal murder of a family man. Our secret friends had suppressed the story, for reasons unknown to me.

It was a lovely late spring morning as we sat in the garden by the ornamental pond, which contained large carp, swimming between white water lilies and hornwort. It was a very peaceful area, so it naturally became a place to console ourselves. Peace was shattered when we heard three cars pull up on the drive. Brakes applied heavily and doors flung open. The urgency in which they arrived was alerting me to some impending and disastrous news.

"This is it. They've found her." I said to Antonella. I stood up.

"You can't know that!" I looked at her.

"Yes! I do."

I watched several men and Penny Carter get out of one of the cars. The entourage walked up to Dave and he gestured over to where we were sitting. I stood frozen to the spot as they rushed over to me.

"Rob! I am so sorry to have to tell you, but we have found a body." The news didn't hit me as hard as her disappearance. It was because I had known all along, so there was no shock. Antonella broke down and openly sobbed. Sandra was walking across the lawn towards us. Like me, she guessed what had happened. I stood emotionless and detached.

"What now?"

"We would like you to identify the body. Do you feel you are up to it?"

"Can we go now? I don't want time to think about it."

"If you are sure?" We left the coolness of the garden and got in one of the black cars. I sat in the back. People were talking, but I didn't hear them. Someone spoke to me. I didn't answer. I felt I was in another dimension. Alive but dead inside. I shut my mind to any further sound. Eventually, I spoke.

"Where are we going?" Penny turned round to address me.

"Bristol."

"Is that where she was found?"

"No. Near Glastonbury." She never got anywhere near her parents. I suddenly realised that this was not just my anguish. Amy's family would be just as devastated.

"Has someone told her parents?"

"Yes, but they couldn't face doing the identification."

"Christ, no. Penny, her father, is not a well man to start with. Dementia or some mental illness, Amy told me. Surely, he will lose the plot after this." I didn't want any more information, so I slumped back into the seat for the rest of the journey.

I had been through a whirlwind of new experiences in the last couple of weeks. Now there was another one to face. I couldn't even begin to focus on how I would cope with identifying a body, let alone the dead body of my girlfriend. I had seen it on TV drama shows so many times, yet here I was, walking through the mortuary. Everything was colourless. It was unreal. The whole process turned out to be such an accurate interpretation, with the white sheet pulled back to reveal an ashen coloured head and shoulders. And then I saw her. Amy, the girl I loved, the woman I wanted to marry. Yet, this wasn't *my* Amy. This was only a corpse with Amy's beautiful face. It was too much to bear. My legs went to jelly and I was on the floor. I lost all control and collapsed into a sobbing rage.

It was a good half hour until I was calm enough to confirm to the policeman who she was. I asked for a few minutes to be alone with her, to say goodbye. I stroked her hair, her white face and reached out to hold her hand. The shock of her coldness made me want to pull away, but I couldn't let go. I grasped it tightly. I kissed her on the lips for the final time and cried my heart out.

I was returned to the secure house at high speed, the whole journey in silence. Sandra and Rowena greeted me at the door, waiting patiently for a sign from me that it was Amy. I guess that they had hung onto a tiny hope that it was mistaken identity. Antonella ran into my arms, sobbing. Sandra also joined us for a group hug and we held each other for some time. Rowena asked me directly.

"Was it her?" I just nodded. Her face showed real pain and emotion as she put her hand up to her mouth.

"I am so, so sorry for you." then she looked at Antonella.

"Both of you."

The mood in the house that evening was sombre and sad. I went to bed that night but found it hard to sleep. I was dreaming about Amy and several times, and my pillow was wet with tears.

The next day I was last up. When I finally made an appearance, Sandra had got Rowena working on the book with her. I saw them busy in the study. I grabbed a coffee and went to talk to Antonella, who was in the garden gazing into the pond.

"You OK?" I asked.

"Not really. You? Did you manage to catch any sleep?"

"Some, not much."

"What was she like? You know when you saw her?" I thought about what I had seen.

"At peace, really. Tranquil. Weird. Like she had been turned to stone, but the spirit of Amy was gone. Does that make sense?" She didn't ask me for details of how Amy died thankfully. I wouldn't have been able to describe the gaping wound in the back of her head.

"I only wished I had known her longer."

"Amy was a lovely person and very kind. She adored the kids she worked with."

"I'd like to go with you to the funeral. Do you know when that might be?"

"Fuck knows! We haven't buried your grandmother yet!" I stood for a while watching the fish.

"What you going to do?" Antonella said in a soft voice.

"Finish the book and get out of here. Maybe go abroad. I don't know. Anything to move on from this nightmare!"

"What about you?"

"Me? No plans. Before Amy's d.....I mean before... I just wanted the past to end until I was rid of this crap. Now I just don't know."

"Antonella? Do you think there is something in this King of France business? You being his direct descendant, I mean?"

"I don't know. I guess so. Grandmother was convinced. My mother was so frightened of it all, she tried hard to keep me shielded or protected even." As I watched the fish swimming about, I felt hungry and couldn't think of the last time I had eaten.

"Rob! Have you had breakfast?"

"No. but it's after one, so I guess lunch will be ready soon." As we walked back into the house, she took my hand and squeezed it. I knew she felt my pain and her action was consoling.

In the next couple of days, I resumed work on the book, which was good timing as Sandra had nearly caught me up. It also stopped me feeling so maudlin. Antonella returned to the kitchen and we got rid of the two ladies acting as temps. Penny came every day and gave us all strict instructions not to say anything to anyone. On the third day, she wanted to have a word with both me and Antonella.

"We have an idea that might help you. At this stage, I must stress that it is just an idea, but we want you to give it some serious thought. There has been a news blackout about Amy and for a good reason. We are certain that the two individuals who we were tracking were responsible. However, they've given us the slip and we don't have any information on their whereabouts. You might have spotted there is a political storm growing between us and France. The French believe we are helping the AF, which is completely untrue." She went on to explain the plan.

"If we release the identity of the female victim as you, Antonella, it will have several effects. Firstly, the AF might think they have eliminated the target that they were after. Secondly, we can then release the identity of the two men, so the chances of their capture are much greater. Thirdly, the government can start asking questions. We can ask the French why known terrorists are allowed to cross over here and commit murder. If you take Amy's identity, we can provide all the necessary paperwork and the world will think that you died."

"You've got to be kidding, right?" I was lost for words at such an outlandish, absurd and almost sacrilegious proposal. Antonella spoke first.

"It would be a bit ghoulish, being Amy," said Antonella, tentatively.

"What about Amy's parents? Won't they be allowed to bury their daughter?"

"They will, of course."

"How?"

"Let's not go into details just yet. They will be party to this plan, but I want you to think about it first and talk it over." I was quite incensed.

"I don't think there is much to talk about. For God's sake, Amy was my girlfriend. Am I now supposed to be in a relationship with Antonella? Seriously?" I felt very uneasy about all of it.

The mounting political storm was now dominating the news coverage. It appeared that the AF had or still do have offices in London. The Times had published a list of terrorist or anarchist groups who were active on British soil. The Guardian had a story about a known AF member who had been found entering the country with a large quantity of drugs. The culprit was not prosecuted as it was deemed not in the public interest.

It all made the Prime Minister look bad, after stating that there had been no contact since the 1970s. The opposition was having a field day, saying he had lost the plot and the government didn't know what was going on. But it was countered by the Prime Minister making a speech about how the French secret services were surreptitiously operating out of London, under the cover of anarchist groups. This was in direct contravention of treaties and agreements concerning inter-state cooperation.

I did wonder where they were getting their information from. For so long, I had believed that Hansen and the intelligence services were behind everything, they were orchestrating every move. Yet how could that be true? Was it simply all about Hansen's department wanting the UK to be rid of these people whom he perceived as problematic? In many ways, it made sense and yet that meant they might have had a hand in Amy's murder. Then there was this macabre idea for Antonella to take Amy's identity. Who would be the main beneficiary of that? I thought of a hundred reasons why it would be impractical. None more so than my relationship with her. I had just lost, in tragic circumstances, the first and only woman who I could say I truly loved.

I was in mourning and I didn't know how to deal with my grief. I kept all these thoughts locked away in my mind and got on with my recordings. It was easier to block it out than brood over it all. Mrs. Richardson had been enlisted to be a reader in between her domestic duties. We also now called her Sarah. She had fitted well into our little group from the outset but now Sarah had got to know us, she was becoming indispensable. No wonder Antonella had warmed to her.

Sarah was a single mother whose life, she told us, had been quite stagnant and unfulfilling. With her new role, she was revelling in the feeling of being valued as well as being part of some adventure to catch bad guys. Sarah had a wicked sense of humour and a cackle of a laugh, which was never unnoticed. Having her around the house lifted everyone's spirits far better than the incessant links to bereavement websites, which Penny kept sending me.

Sarah asked if she could stay in the house with us during the half-term break. Her young son was going to stay with his father for the week. We had started up our evening house meetings again, now chaired by Sandra and the thorny issue of beds was back on the agenda.

"Why doesn't Antonella move in with someone else into Rob's room and Rob, you do a swap?"

"I'll move into any room." I offered not caring enough to be bothered.

"I don't share bedrooms," commented Rowena. "It's bad enough having to share a bathroom."

Antonella butted in.

"I don't mind sharing a room, but I'm not comfortable with sharing a double bed with another girl." She was recalling the gossip that Rowena might be gay.

"Sarah? Do you mind sharing a bed with one of **us**?" asked Sandra.

"I'd much rather share with Kev!" We laughed at her reply, but clearly, Rowena was not amused.

"I would have thought anybody in your circumstances, Sarah, would think twice about getting involved with a man!" Rowena snapped at her, sarcastically.

"Really! And I am rather surprised that **you** haven't jumped at the chance of sharing a bed with a woman!" Sarah responded with her own cutting remark, obviously having heard the rumours surrounding Rowena's sexuality.

"I beg your pardon! What exactly do you mean by that?"

I tried to calm things down by offering an alternative. I could see that Rowena was fuming.

"We can change the double bed for two singles. It's not a big job and there's plenty of extra bedding available in the landing cupboard." No-one disagreed with me.

"Perfect solution, ladies. I was a hotel manager in my previous life, after all!"

The next day I had reached the point in the book when Amy disappeared, and the past met up with the present.

"Sandra. I've gone as far as I can. Will you do the next section? It includes what happened to Amy. I would find that far too difficult."

"That's fine, Rob, I understand. I'll take over the story now. I have an outline of the ending from Penny Carter."

"What?"

"She gave me a list of points to include."

"Can I see it?"

"Sure." There it was. The ending. The deceitful lie. That Antonella had died and my girlfriend, Amy, was still alive. There were other various items under a long list of changes, but in my present state of mind, I couldn't get my head around any of it.

I sought out Antonella, to talk about the 'switching plan,' as we had nicknamed it. She was in the garden by the pond, reading.

"I don't have a problem with it. I like it. I can see how it could make things easier for me, but I know you don't."

"Why?"

"Why do I like it, or why do I know that you don't?"

"Both."

Antonella looked at me, with her big doe eyes. She walked over and planted a big, lingering kiss right on my lips.

"That's why! I will never be your Amy and I don't want to be, but I..." she hesitated. I guessed what was coming. Amy had warned me.

"I want to be rid of my history. I'm so tired of all this bullshit, but it just keeps on following me." I didn't often hear her swear and in a way, I could see how emotionally draining it must be for her. She persisted with this revealing speech.

"I would like to be your Antonella, though." Was she declaring her love for me? I was confused for all sorts of reasons.

"Antonella, please don't get the idea I am some kind of catch. All I have in the world is an eight-year-old car and some cash in the bank, which appears to be diminishing rapidly." She attempted to lighten the tone of our discussion.

"I don't care, but I think you will be a published writer sometime soon."

"Bollocks! Sandra is the writer, not me. You could have outlined the story in the same way that I have, if not better. To be honest, with all the changes that Penny Carter wants to make, it hardly seems my story at all." I skilfully steered the conversation away from the theme of love. She seemed preoccupied.

"You aren't OK with me taking over Amy's identity, are you?" I shrugged my shoulders.

"It's your call!"

"Not fair, Mr. Ashurst! You have to tell me or convince me!" she teased.

"Well. Amy's parents for one." She nodded in agreement.

"It's an awful thing to ask of them, isn't it?"

It's a complication, but on the other hand, her dad is away with the fairies and I gather from Penny that her mother is fine with the idea."

I came up with all sorts of other crap, but in truth, I couldn't think of another genuine reason why Antonella should not become Amy. Eventually, I said so. The physical resemblance between the two girls was clear from the start, which is most likely what gave Penny the idea in the first place.

As we stood together, I could feel something happening. I knew exactly what she wanted from me. I couldn't stop myself from giving it,

in exchange for much-needed comfort to heal the pain I was suffering. Antonella took a step nearer and touched my arm. A surge of sexual heat went through my body. In an instant, I grabbed her, our bodies were touching and we held each other in a long lingering embrace. I closed my eyes. My emotional wounds were bathed in the warmth of close, physical contact. I stroked her hair.

"It means that much to you, does it?"

"Yes, it does, Rob. A new life. A new identity. A new start. The only downside is that I'm going to be shackled to you!" Her cheeky laugh made me realise it was just a joke.

"I need some time, Antonella. I can't rush into this… with you."

"I know, Rob, I know." She put her fingers over my mouth to stop me speaking.

"Amy was a special person for me too. So, phone Penny and get it sorted! I am sick of it here. Look at my hands. They've been worked to the bone!" I laughed and kissed her affectionately on the cheek.

"The problem I am going to have is calling you, Amy!"

"That will take some getting used to. For both of us."

"Can we find some other name? Sorry, but I don't think I can do it!"

"Rob, you're right. I would find that difficult too."

Chapter 16

It took me a while to feel strong enough to speak to Penny about the switching plan. I called her mobile.

"We've decided to do what you suggested and change Antonella's identity, but we do have a question. Several, in fact."

"I'll try and answer them!" I clicked on my voice recorder. A lack of trust made me feel I needed to record what was discussed.

"I'm concerned about Amy's parents. Surely they will want to bury their daughter and have a funeral?" It was such a bizarre subject to be talking about, but Penny was very 'matter of fact' in her reply.

"I appreciate your concerns, but I have spoken to them. The family is happy to have a funeral with no inscription on the headstone and a service without her name being mentioned. It will be something along the lines of '*loving daughter and brother.*' Fortunately, they don't have a large family. I've given them a brief summary of what occurred but, as yet, not explained why it happened. Her mother believes it will be a quicker way for her daughter's killer to be brought to justice." At once, it was clear how Penny had sold it to them.

"There is no point at the moment in telling them the full story and as you know, we don't have all the answers ourselves. One more thing. They have expressed their wish **not** to meet you."

"Really?" I felt disappointed. "But couldn't that be difficult in the circumstances. Penny, I have to go to the funeral. She was my girlfriend!"

"Robin! Rest assured, they know you didn't abduct or murder her. I have taken great pains to convince them that you are another innocent victim."

"What about Amy's house? What will happen to that?"

"To be discussed at a later date. Her parents told me that they don't want it, so it may go up for sale. The official story we'll put out is that Amy resigns from her job, then pursues another career. We will arrange all the documents needed, passport, driving licence and birth certificate."

"Why don't I just take on Ricky's identity?"

"Simply because you were never the number one target. It was only what you might have learned that made you vulnerable. It would be much easier if you slipped back into your old life with your previous girlfriend." She really had it all worked out. Out of the blue, I slipped in an extra request.

"Penny. Can you sell me The Limes at a knockdown price?" Penny was too highly trained ever to be taken off guard.
"An interesting idea and I must say it's a particularly good one. I will discuss it with Hansen and let you know. I am sure something can be arranged."

"Thanks. When will the heat be off here?"

"I guess with the entire political storm brewing, I can see a matter of days, but watch the six o'clock news. Anything else?"

"No, I don't think so. But I am going to have a problem calling Antonella, '*Amy*.'"

"I can see that it might be difficult. May I suggest you choose a nickname that you both like."

I went to find Antonella. She was curious. "What did Penny say?"

"That we should think of a nickname for you."

"Is that all she said?"

"No. There was other stuff, but I'll tell you later. We've got to keep an eye on the news tonight."

After no more than about twenty minutes, something unexpected happened. Dave came in and asked Rowena to pack and get ready to leave. He had received instructions that a car would be sent in thirty minutes. Sarah was also sent home.

"Go? Where to Dave?" Rowena asked nervously.

"Home. We feel we can protect you better there." He was following orders. That much was clear. That left only three of us in the house. Events were moving quickly. Discussions about sharing rooms were no longer needed.

We sat around and waited for the news. On News24, the breaking story unfolded.

'Two bodies have just been discovered. One, a member of the security services and the other, a girl in her late twenties, called Antonella Walford. Miss Walford had no other living family members, but her death was related to the still unresolved death of Gwendolyn Aguirre, in Torbay. Police investigators are trying to piece together events leading up to the double murder and looking for any links.'

The program rolled on. Antonella sat aghast listening to the details given of her own life and death.

"How surreal! Antonella, will you go to your own funeral?" asked Sandra. It made us think about the wider picture. Antonella didn't answer.

"Sandra? Have you got any connections with the security services, or did Rowena pick you?"

She looked slightly surprised at my question.

"No. I haven't, but now you mentioned it, I was asked to sign the official secrets act by Penny Carter the other day. Didn't think much of it at the time. Although, I guess Antonella's change of identity is now classified as a state secret. Why do you ask?"

"After all that's happened, I am not sure anymore who our friends are, or which ones might be enemies." She looked quite hurt, so I qualified my rather harsh remark.

"I hope you are and will be for a long time, a friend to me, to us!"

Sandra smiled. "My feelings also. I knew nothing about any of this until I got an email from Rowena asking me if I wanted any work. As I said before, I took the job because I was skint." She added. "Like you, I'm still not sure what I've got mixed up in."

The news rumbled on. There were reports that arrests had been made regarding the Glastonbury deaths, but details of the culprits were vague. The now open wrath between the French and British governments was also well featured. The German chancellor had asked for a face to face meeting of the two sides and was trying to appease the situation. Several EU leaders had made speeches about European harmony and how two great nations should be able to sort this out amicably. Some homes belonging to British ex-pats in France had been attacked and there was a mini exodus from the country. The TV reporter was trying to simplify the story for the benefit of the viewers.

'*The French are upset about British involvement in what they see as terrorist activities and want an explanation. On the other hand, the British are unhappy about French Intelligence officers breaking laws in the UK.'*

The three of us lounged about in the house with no particular purpose until Dave joined us.

"Any chance of some coffee and sandwiches for me and the three lads outside?"

"I'll do it. It will give me some purpose. Anyone else want anything?" asked Antonella. Our hands went up with various orders. Sandra disappeared into the study and returned with a red folder. She handed it to me.

"Rowena didn't want me to give this to you yet. She said it should go to Intelligence first, but I want you to read it. It's not quite finished, there are still some changes to be made but read it anyway."

"Sandra, do you think Rowena works for the secret service?"

"You mean like a double agent? A spy? Surely not." From being dismissive, she then reconsidered my question. "You make it sound like there is a 'them' and an 'us.'"

"I think there is. Don't you?"

"This is how I see it. From writing the book and listening to the news reports, French intelligence officers are running around after British intelligence officers and vice versa. This is all causing such a stink. Whatever evidence the old lady had or could have had, is ancient history. What possible implications could it have in today's world? It's all rubbish."

"Exactly! How is it all relevant now? Are they just worried about the unknown?"

"Yes! They must be."

"Rob. I'm no expert, but I think both sides are making a fuss about nothing to justify their existence. It is all such a disgrace, particularly when innocent people get killed." I nodded in agreement with her and went in search of a quiet place.

I opened the folder and started to read. I had to hand it to Sandra. She had made the whole story come alive. I was interrupted by my mobile ringing. It was Penny with a barrage of information.

"Just thought I would let you know. It's all going to plan. We captured four AF operators last night after the story broke. They were already under surveillance. Two others have vanished into thin air, so we feel that they may have left the country. Dave has instructions to scale down security to green. You can stay in the house as long as you want, but the three of you will be on your own in a couple of days. Finally, the new identity papers for Antonella as Amy will be with you in forty-eight hours."

"This has all moved on extremely fast. How can you be so sure they were the only perpetrators?"

"These events often do. I think the pressure from EU governments and the high-profile political situation meant that we needed to finalize things quickly. Anyone still operating will have gone to ground." I wasn't quite sure what she was talking about, but the news was encouraging. Nothing she said, however, convinced me that the secret service had not been involved in Amy's death in some way.

"And Rowena?"

"I can't reveal too much, but I can tell you this. Please keep this between yourselves. We have thought for some time now that Rowena Kerry may have been working for the AF. She certainly had strong contacts with them and has been under observation. In our view, the lady was always too well informed. For the moment, she is being detained and helping us with inquiries!" Again, my thoughts were mixed. Penny only told me things that might benefit the intelligence service.

"Jesus! That's a surprise! She genuinely looked concerned when Amy went missing, though."

"I don't doubt that was real, but Rowena was playing a serious game by poking the tiger, so to speak. Death and murder were just words to her, but when people she knew got hurt, she realised that the AF were not just idealists but extremely dangerous indeed. Anyway, changing the subject. Hansen has suggested waiting a few months for all this to die down and then we can talk about a deal on The Limes."

It was somewhat ironic that Amy had wanted nothing to do with the hotel business, but Antonella or the new Amy positively revelled in preparing food and planning menus. We would certainly make a good team, but I had to be sure it was what I wanted for the future.

"OK. Fair enough. The book is finished now. Rowena had lined up a publisher for us, but she never gave us a name. What do you think we should do?" Penny was strangely dismissive.

"No need to publish it now. Just keep it as an account for yourself. The AF were interested in Antonella Walford. If there was any evidence to her lineage, then it's all rather irrelevant with her death. As much as they preach anarchy, they want to keep the status quo."

I wasn't sure that it was true, but I didn't comment.

"Right. Thanks." The line went dead.

I recounted a shorter version of the call to Sandra and Antonella over supper. My supposedly new girlfriend had produced a platter of cheeses, cold meats, fresh bread, pate, dips, and very nice pastries. All washed down with a bottle of red wine and some beers. Dave came to join us and confirmed my news about downgrading the current security level. The other guys were to go in the morning, but he would stay an extra night. I never said anything to the girls about Rowena.

"Sandra? Do you have any contacts in the publishing world?"

"Nothing like Rowena. Why do you ask?" I thought for a while, then I said,

"Let's go and feed the fish." With my finger at my mouth, we went outside to sit by the pond. I threw the carp some leftovers.

"I don't know if the house is bugged or not, but it's strange that certain people always know what's going on, don't you think?" Sandra looked puzzled, so I told her about

Rowena. She was stunned. I asked her to remove Penny's list of amendments from the book.

"Is that wise?" she asked.

"For Amy's sake, I want to publish something which contains nothing less than the truth, including the way MI6 have behaved, by just using us all. The spooks want us to drop the book now as they say it serves no purpose."

"I can't believe it! Why would they do this? Have we done all this work for nothing? Rob, I am with you on this, I didn't know Amy that well. I was only with her for a few days, but she didn't deserve what happened to her." I felt relieved. I had a trustworthy ally in Sandra, albeit an anxious one.

"Will we be in danger, do you think? Stirring up the hornet's nest again?"

With many reservations and unanswered questions, we went back into the house.

My suspicions about surveillance may well have been unfounded, but we continued to visit the fishpond if we wanted to talk things over in private. It didn't go unnoticed by Dave. I tried to justify it by telling him we felt cooped up in the house and needed some fresh air. It was plausible enough. Dave had become more involved with the three of us during the last couple of days. He felt he was almost off duty and was quite entertaining with some of his diplomatic protection tales. Things were coming to an end. We started packing up. Sandra was returning to London and accepted a lift from Dave and Antonella's documents arrived as promised. On our last evening together, the four of us went back to the pub. It was supposed to be a name-changing celebration, but things were all still too raw for any merriment. The evening was pleasant enough and we discussed a nickname for Antonella.

Sandra thought that we should choose a name which began with an A, but we couldn't think of anything suitable. I came up with 'sprout,' after a much-loved dog I had when I was a child, though Antonella robustly refused to answer to a name of a vegetable. Her middle name was Costanza, after her mother, which was far too much of a mouthful. We ended up going with Dave's suggestion of 'Ella.' It was going to take a while for it to sound familiar, but it was better than using 'Amy.' Our relationship was still undefined, so we slept in separate bedrooms. To be fair to her, I had told her that I needed time. A complicated relationship was the last thing I needed.

Finding accommodation was now a priority. We had just less than three weeks to make plans before we were homeless. Sandra had said she would return from London in a few days after she had made some enquiries about a publisher and had given the first draft to friends for opinions. We saw Dave and Sandra off after one of Ella's full English breakfasts. The good thing in swapping Antonella for Ella was that it brought no deterioration in the quality of the food from the kitchen. We now had three days entirely on our own with no distractions and no-one else about. I felt it crucial that I kept myself occupied, mentally and physically to prevent any brooding. Perhaps a trip somewhere was a good idea. I passed on my thoughts to Ella, after gestures again to rendezvous at the fishpond. We pondered about where we could go.

"Why don't we go and retrieve the trunks from South Wales? When we get back, we can meet up with Sandra and finalise the book properly."

"I must admit, it would be nice to be out of here for a couple of nights," Ella said, thoughtfully but she had some reservations.

"Maybe it's too soon? I know nothing bad has happened for a week or so and we don't seem to be in any danger now, but the last thing we want is for it all to kick off again."

"Who knows? Look, it's a risk I'm willing to take. I can't live a lie, Ella. I need to find out why Amy and all those other people died. For her sake, I want to know who is pulling our strings, so I am not looking over my shoulder for the rest of my life." She repeated my words, loudly and forcefully.

"Looking over your shoulder! Welcome to my world! Don't you think I don't know how that feels? I've been doing it all my life."

"Exactly! That's my point. Don't you want to be free of it?"

"I don't know any different. Even as a young girl, my mother made me believe that what grandmother knew was dangerous and had to be hidden. Who knows what will jump out of 'Pandora's Box?'"

"Whatever it is, has just got to stop before anyone else gets hurt. Put your life forward fifteen years. Say we are still together, we have children, perhaps a boy and a girl. Then a new generation of the AF decides they want to resurrect this shit because questions were not answered here and now. They are such ruthless bastards they might just work out our ruse and come looking for us. Our children would always be at risk!"

"I understand what you are saying, Rob, but it might not be our kids or us. None of us can predict the future!" I wasn't sure where she was going with that comment.

"I agree. We can't, but surely the same argument holds if you have a family with any bloke, doesn't it?" I felt her reticence, both to open the boxes and to talk about the future, so it seemed best to give her time to mull it over. I started walking back into the house. She made the decision far quicker than I expected. She called me back.

"Rob. OK. You're right. I understand what you are saying, but first, let's have a couple of days away from here and behave like ordinary people. Then we collect the boxes."

With a weekend bag each, we locked up and were soon on the road north.

"Any places you want to visit? We've got nothing booked."

"I really don't know this part of the world at all, but the last time we went this way, we passed a big city. Can we stay there? People, shops, noise and possibly some nightlife. That's what I was thinking of, Rob." I looked at her in amazement.

"Nightlife? That doesn't sound like you?"

"I'm Ella now! The old Antonella has gone!"

"I think you mean Cardiff."

We were like two kids skiving off from school, heading for an adventure. Finding accommodation on a Saturday night wasn't so easy without prior booking because there was an International rugby game on at the city stadium, but eventually, we had some success. As it happened, they only had one room available, which got us around the tricky subject of sleeping arrangements. We spent some hours wandering around the city centre shops. It was a surreal and new experience for both of us, but very enjoyable. We tried on jeans, jackets, and new tops. I waited for her to come out of the fitting rooms and expressed my opinion as any boyfriend would. If I conveyed my approval, she made a purchase. Our retail therapy was beneficial as it kept us from talking about difficult issues and made a nice change. I felt as comfortable in her company as she appeared to be in mine.

In the evening, we walked around the city until we came across a restaurant, which appealed to both of us, then headed back to the hotel and had a few drinks in the bar.

As I sipped on my Irish whisky, Ella sitting beside me with her head on my shoulder, I felt at peace for the first time in ages. Ella was not as demanding as Amy on a weekend away. Amy was an organiser, a planner. Hotels, restaurants and tourist attractions booked well in advance. I preferred to be less organised and more spontaneous. I hated to admit to myself that Ella and I were more compatible. Her unworldliness and innocence surfaced every so often, which was extremely endearing. That night we shared a bed for the first time, but that was all. No kissing. No lovemaking. Just two bodies holding each other for comfort.

Sunday was another lazy day. We walked around the medieval castle, right in the city centre, restored in the eighteenth century into a Victorian gothic pleasure palace. Nearby, we stumbled on a traditional oak-panelled pub serving up classic pies and cask ales. After a heart-warming pie and chips lunch, we took a stroll along the front at Cardiff Bay. Amy had often talked about this place and its connection with Roald Dahl, her favourite children's author. The old Cardiff docklands had been completely redeveloped into a vibrant waterfront centre with a mix of attractions, entertainments, and events. As we walked around the Norwegian Church Arts Centre, I felt Amy's presence and not in a good way. Retribution for spending the night with another woman? Her spirit was with me.

We had decided to pick up the trunks after breakfast on Monday and return to the house before Sandra got back.

This gave us time to have a grand opening and see what was inside. There had been no word from Sandra, but we had a loose arrangement that she would be back at the house Monday afternoon. We left Cardiff and headed west.

"Tell me again? Why are we going back to Amy's mother's holiday cottage? I thought you'd hidden them somewhere else?"

"When I got back, the police had surrounded the house. Don't you remember? I didn't want them to find the keys on me, so I threw them over a hedge. The fob has the key to my storage unit and also the door code for the large gate to get in."

"OK. Yes, I get it."

"I never let on to Penny or Hansen that I knew where the trunks were. It would have given the game away if they'd discovered I had a key to a lock-up!" Ella was in a jovial mood.

"So, in the meantime, the keys could have been found, the stuff collected or eaten by a cow or whatever?" Ella was looking for problems, so I playfully defended my actions.

"What else could I have done? With a split-second decision before I had an automatic weapon shoved up my arse! Anyway, what do you mean, 'eaten by a cow'? They don't eat keys."

"More than possible, isn't it? Key in grass, cow not so clever. Cow eats grass and key. How on earth are we going to find a key in a field of cows?"

"I don't even know if it is a field of cows!"

"That makes it worse!"

"Meaning?"

"Farmer comes along with his tractor ploughing his field. How can he spot a key from high up in his big shiny tractor? He can't so he ploughs it deeper into the earth, only to be found by a man with metal detector a hundred years later!" This was a ridiculously hypothetical conversation, but it made us both smile. Then she said.

"What about the birds?"

"Birds?"

"Yes! Have you thought about birds? One comes along. Flap, flap, flap. Sees something shiny and picks it up. Flap, flap. Back to the nest!"

"Birds don't do that!"

"Course they do! Magpies are renowned for it!"

"There are no magpies in Wales." I retorted with authority.

"Why?"

"They can't speak Welsh!" Ella burst into laughter.

"Right! So, magpies flying along flap, flap. Head magpie says, 'that's as far as we go chaps! Over there is Wales! Everybody turn left at the next pylon!'"

"OK! Maybe it wasn't such a good idea but at the time, but I had guns pointing at me and one second to come up with an idea to lose the key. So, flap, flap to you!"

"A cow could have pooped on it!"

"Ella!! Will you stop being so bloody frustrating. Look! If we can't find the key, we'll have to think again, won't we? That's as maybe!"

"What does that mean?"

"What?"

"What you just said. 'That's as maybe.' Does it mean something or nothing?"

"It means possibly cows, possibly magpies!" We both burst into laughter.

In the end, we spent ages looking for the cottage. I couldn't remember the way and we didn't have the full address. Ella wasn't able to add anything in the way of help, because, in her words, 'she didn't exist then.' When we finally seemed on the right track, it all came back to me. The field was full of cows as she had predicted. I had to find the exact point of entry in the hedge, which wasn't easy unless we re-enacted the scene, so I parked the car exactly where Amy's mini had been parked and got out ready to throw my keys.

"Rob, you dummy! What are you doing? What if we lose those keys as well?"

"We won't so long as you keep an eye on where they land and don't call me 'dummy' or I'll call you 'sprout.' You go over the other side and wait."

"Why on earth would anyone call a poor dog, sprout! You must have been a horrid little boy!"

"I like sprouts! Anyway, pay attention! After three! One, two, three." I tossed them over in the same fashion as I had done with the previous bunch.

"Yes! I've got your car keys. Thank god! No sign of anything else, though."

"I'll try again?" There was a pause as Ella grovelled about in the field.

"Wait! There's something here, in the grass. My God! It's here! I've got it!" Her head popped up over the hedge and she was waving the key fob.

"I said it would work!"

"That was lucky! It was only when I bent down to pick up the car keys that I spotted the blue and yellow stripes on the tag, but it was much nearer the bottom of the hedge."

"We have them. That's the main thing!"

Ella emerged from the gate leading into the field, with very muddy trainers. We both looked at them at the same time.

"And these were my new ones! Your idea, dummy!"
As we got back into the car, we spotted two magpies perched on a gate. We looked at each other and giggled. It was the first time I had a proper laugh since Amy disappeared.

"Flap, Flap!" I said.

We drove onto the storage unit. Lines of yellow-painted cubicles in rows. Security lights came on when we got near and went off as soon as we were past. We opened up and looked at the trunks. How could such beautifully decorative brass-bound leather trunks have the potential to cause such unforeseen problems and release evil and chaos into the world? We loaded them onto my sack barrow and retraced our steps along the corridors. Just as we were leaving the depot, my phone rang. It was Penny Carter! Suddenly the thought that we might have been followed burst into my head and I started looking round, expecting Hansen and a crack team of marksmen to jump out at us.

"Yes?" I said tentatively.

"Are you alright, Robin? You sound worried!" She didn't wait for an answer.

"I just thought I would let you know that Amy's funeral is on Thursday, in Hertford. I have been trying to call you at the house, but there was no reply. Where are you both?" The news hit me like a force ten gale. I struggled to speak and handed the phone to Ella.

"Hello, Penny. It's Ella! Ella is my new name!"

"I see! Good idea." Penny gave Ella the details as I just sat on a stack of pallets. I could hear her explaining that we fancied a change of scene from the house, but she didn't say where. Ella told Penny that we were house hunting. I took my loaded barrow and went to put everything into the car. I was more composed when we got into my Toyota.

"What else does Ms. Moneypenny have to say?"

"Who is Ms. Moneypenny? Rob, are you OK? You've gone white!"

"My God, Ella. Don't tell me you have never watched James Bond? I am fine. It just hit me that's all. You were on the phone for ages!"

"Penny told me about the funeral arrangements and said that the Goochs' would prefer it if you didn't go. They are not going to stop you, but they feel you got her involved in something which cost her, her life!"

"That's bloody unfair!"

"She's going to text you the details. If you insist on going." I felt the emotion welling up again, so we drove in silence for some time.

"Can you call Sandra and tell her that we are not going to be back until dark. She won't have a key to the house." As I was just about to tell her how to find a contact number, Ella picked up my mobile, located the number and made the call with a swiftness of speed which surprised me, for someone who didn't use a mobile.

"Sandra? Hi! It's Ella!" They started with pleasantries and then discussed arrangements. Sandra eventually decided that she would come by train the following day.

"She wants us to pick her up from Exeter station about three in the afternoon, said Ella. "That OK?"

"Yes. Why isn't she driving?"

"She's bringing her dog and apparently can't drive with the dog in the car."

"I wonder what the dog is called!" I mused.

"Who cares so long as it's not 'sprout'?"

"Tell me what else Penny Carter said."

"Arrangements for my grandmother's funeral. Her body can now be released, so I told her to do it in Torquay. Then, stuff about the estate, which is extremely complicated, as it is mostly held in Switzerland. Penny's going to put me in touch with someone who can help finalise everything and work with the Swiss authorities. All her assets should come to me, but I've got to prove the link. I have a passport in my name, but I'm not sure about my birth certificate. Penny says they want to muddy the path between Antonella and Amy, so we can't create a financial paper trail and it all might take some time. She also wanted to know what I intend to do with grandmother's flat in London."

"Did you go there much?"

"No, not really. I never thought it was hers if I thought about it at all." Ella seemed a touch edgy with the conversation and oblivious to suddenly becoming a woman of property.

"Ella! A London flat and a house in Switzerland? You are going to be a wealthy lady!" She didn't want to discuss it, so she changed the subject.

"Penny also wanted to talk to you about The Limes. What's that about?"

"Just an idea. I need to think about getting a job and since I've never done anything except hospitality, it crossed my mind to buy the old place. But…oh, I don't know, it never really made any money and it could certainly do with a refurb. I've severely dipped into my funds, so maybe the whole idea is a bit of a non-starter."

"Rob! That's a lovely idea. We would make such a good team. I'll run the kitchen and you do front of house!"

"Seriously?"

"Yes. Why not? It's a beautiful spot and we don't have anywhere else to live at the moment." It did get me pondering about the whole idea again.

"Maybe. I was thinking of changing the name of the hotel from The Limes to 'The Amy.'

She reached over and touched my arm.

"Give that a bit more thought."

Chapter 17

It was getting dark when we got back to the house and everything was just as we left it. Life was strange. The news about Ella's potential inheritance and the idea that we could run The Limes together, occupied my thoughts. The only uncertainty troubling me was whether to go ahead and publish the book.

I had felt all along that the intelligence services were using me for their own ends. I figured the book would expose them as manipulating and exploiting people's lives. That's the outcome I wanted. But now, I had serious reservations. Did I have the fight in me to take on such a powerful opponent as the British secret service? Was it a battle worth fighting? All these doubts were flowing through my brain as I stared at the two trunks on the table. Ella came into the dining room, holding the keys.

"Wait! I want to say something. Are we ready for this? We don't know which genie will come out of the bottle. We can finish this adventure now by destroying them. Then we can get on with the rest of our lives."

"Destroy them! How?"

"I'll go and dump them in the sea. I don't know! If they are opened up, it might bring down an almighty shit storm on our heads. Then, how much help are our 'so-called friends' going to be?" Ella stared at me in disbelief.

"You've changed your tune!"

"I know." I felt my voice quivering with indecision.

"I don't know if we are doing the right thing, Ella. All along we have dealt with the unknown but…" I never got a chance to finish my sentence. Ella was indignant and cross. She raised her voice.

"Rob, No! You cannot destroy this stuff! That's crazy! And I have a right to say what happens now. You said that all this has to end. Remember? It could all come back to haunt us in the next fifteen, twenty years. Well, I am not going to spend the rest of my life, wondering what this was all about. The answer is here on the table, so just open these stupid boxes, will you?" There was no arguing with her.

I took the keys hesitatingly. I tried the first key, then the second. Neither fitted the lock, but the third did. I could feel the metal bolts sliding across the gate. Then I opened the second lock. It moved freely too.

"I would swear that these locks have been opened recently, Ella!" I fumbled again with the keys and eventually found the correct key for the third lock. The suspense was nerve-racking as the levers slid effortlessly. Slowly, I opened the worn leather lid and looked inside. It was packed with brown files, all neatly labelled with handwritten names. The top file was marked 'Antonella.' The next one had the name of her parents emblazed across the corner. Ella took it and went to sit on the sofa to study the contents. I sifted through the first file.

There were official documents, birth and death certificates. Dossiers of press cuttings and reports which looked very official, but unfortunately, they were all in French.

"I think we are going to need a translator?" Ella was so engrossed in what she was reading.

"What's it about?"

"It's a police report on my parents' car crash."

"Can you understand it?"

"More or less. My French used to be better than my English, although I'm a bit rusty now."

I went back to emptying the box. The last and biggest file was named LP. I put the documents in date order, which seemed a useful exercise and then turned my attention to the second box. This one had four locks. Two in the front and the others at the top. They were all somewhat corroded, so I spent some time with a screwdriver, fiddling about. I opened one but found the others difficult. Ella was still engrossed in her parents' file. The second lock let go eventually, but I had to use pliers. The last thing I wanted to do was break a key, so I proceeded with care. Unlike the document box, which was well used, this one did not appear to have been opened for years. The last two locks seemed to be stuck fast, so I went out to buy some lubricating oil from the nearest petrol station. I also felt that I needed some air.

Ella was too absorbed in the papers to notice what I was doing. Her concentration didn't even break when I came back armed with two portions of fish and chips. A liberal soaking of penetrating fluid, and what felt like endless jerks and jiggles, the keys moved the bolts very slightly. In the end, I had all four locks opened, but the top was still firm. I oiled the hinges and then had to pry the lid open bit by bit. I had spent about three hours doing this with little success. It was getting late. Ella's supper was now cold on the plate and she had perhaps only eaten two or three chips.

"Ella, you haven't said anything for ages. Are you going to tell me what so fascinating?"

"Sorry, Rob!" She looked up and apologised. "This report into my parents' death is taking me ages to translate. How the old lady got hold of it, I don't know, but the initial report says the accident was very suspicious. Apparently, sometime later, a witness came forward, a Claude Duvall, who says he saw the car going extremely fast and being driven recklessly."

"So? What's the significance of that then?" I asked.

It's strange because Claude Duvall is like John Smith in England. It's a common name. Then there's other stuff here that doesn't make sense. Every time the police thought they'd cracked the case, someone came forward with conflicting evidence. Like here, hang on..." She rifled through the papers until she found what she was looking for.

"Here it is! The initial report says that the police thought the brakes had been tampered with. Then a garage mechanic came forward and made a statement saying that he sent a letter to my father a month earlier, telling him that his brakes were in a dangerous condition. There is a copy of the letter on file. Why would he do that?"

"If it wasn't all bogus, you mean?" She was coming to the conclusion that her parents' death might not have been an accident.

"Suspicious or what? I also looked at some of the other files while you were out. There's loads of stuff on the son of Louis and Marianne. Everything from his school report to his business accounts. He was a wealthy man and had five kids. He lived his whole life in Milan. Most of the documents are in another language but not in an Italian that I can understand very easily. Could be some form of Lombardi dialect." She put the file down and grabbed a piece of cold fish from the newspaper. I was still struggling to open the other chest.

"Looks like you are having trouble?" she said, now giving my efforts some attention.

"Do you think you can get it open?"

"It's nearly there! This one hasn't been unlocked for years or even decades at a guess!" I gave one more yank and suddenly, the lid came free.

It was like looking at a pirate's chest, full of artefacts and carved wood, jewellery caskets. It explained what had been clanking around. Lying on the top was a threadbare velvet bag, tied with discoloured ribbon, which almost disintegrated as I undid the bow. It revealed a diamond and pearl pendant shaped like a four-leaved clover, two gold rings, one with a big jade stone and the other encrusted with diamonds and a ruby. Ella and I looked at each other in amazement. There were more ancient documents, all neatly rolled and tied together. Underneath their protective covering of frayed linen cloth was the most exquisite trinket box, made from gilded and painted wood, inlaid with mother of pearl, agate and tortoiseshell. I unfastened the tiny brass catches carefully and lifted the delicately hinged lid. There were several gemstones in the box, but one piece caught my eye immediately. A striking large, steely blue stone. Astounded, Ella picked up the blue jewel.

"My goodness! Could it really be 'The French Blue'?" This unguarded comment seemed a little out of character for her.

"The French what? You know about this stuff then, Ella?" I think she had let something out of the bag, but she backtracked so quickly, I hardly noticed it.

"Only by legend. Most kids schooled in France know about the curse of the French blue diamond." She explained.

"It was a spectacular gemstone which belonged to Louis XIV and then passed down to other kings of France. During the revolution, most of the French royal crown jewels were stolen. Some pieces showed up years later, but the French blue was never seen again. Many people thought that it had been re-cut into much smaller stones."

I thought she had told me she went to an Italian school, not French, but I didn't press her as I was so intrigued by the story and the contents of the second box.

"What was the curse?" I asked, with intrigue.

"I only know that it was supposed to bring misfortune and tragedy to whoever owned it, like Marie-Antoinette, who was guillotined. I can't remember the details."

"Do you swear you've never seen any of this before?" I was not sure why I even asked her that question. From the look on her face, the booty was just as much a surprise to her as to me.

"No, of course not." Ella shot me a hostile glance.

"I'm as stunned as you! I can't believe my grandmother was carrying all this around with her. It's remarkable."

"That's an understatement! But where did she get it all from? It proves what was said all along, doesn't it? Jesus! What are we going to do now?" I was in shock.

We communicated little after that. Both lost in thought. Ella reverted to her own bedroom for the night, which was probably the best thing. I couldn't concentrate on anything except the cache we had discovered and I guess she wanted to be alone to think about her past.

It was the first day of May, usually the prettiest week of the year, with all of the beautiful colours in the garden and the freshness that only spring can bring. I was outside at the fishpond, gazing aimlessly at the ornamental carp when Antonella came to join me holding two mugs of coffee.

"I love this spot."

"Course! Me too!" She handed me a large beaker.

"What's your feeling about the book now, Antonella?"
That was the first time I had made a slip up with her name.

"Antonella?" She looked cross.

"**Ella!** Sorry!"

"This is about a lot more than my name, Rob. The jewels, the documents, the files are not just my past. They are my present and my future. They belong to Antonella and as long as no one else knows they exist, I can never be Ella." It made sense. She begged me to carry on with the book, to tell the story and tell the world.

"So, what do we do with the collection of jewels?" I felt we needed to talk about the treasure we had just uncovered.

"It's part of history and should be preserved in a museum!"

"You are very firm in your convictions, Ella!"

"Be real! What else can I do with them? Wear them!!"

"You'd get a lot of money if you sell the collection at an auction!"

"No! Definitely not."

"What do you want out of life, then?"

"A beautiful home, maybe a family? I just want 'normal.' I'm not particularly ambitious. Like I said before. To live my life, not looking over my shoulder."

"We'd better go now if we are going to meet Sandra's train." She nodded and went in to grab her bag and coat. As we walked to the car, she reached out to hold my hand.

Exeter must have had such a grand railway station in its day. The large 'G.W.R.' plaque still remained high on the façade of the building as evidence that it was constructed in an era to symbolize the zenith of the Great Western Railway's opulence. Sadly, it looked to have had a make-over in the seventy's or eighty's and the result was a complete act of vandalism to one of Brunel's most elegant designs. Sandra's train arrived on time. She appeared from the carriage with Scott, a rather yappy black Scottie dog. I suppose he was just annoyed at the change to his routine, but Scott was a rather grumpy lad.

"Nice to see you both! Have you had a relaxing time together?" My fears over bugs and listening devices had abated. I had concluded that hell would have descended upon us if they had been listening in while we opened the trunks. We walked to the car park together, chatting nonstop.

"Shall I tell her, or will you, Ella?"

"Tell me what? Come on, guys! Tell!

"We opened the cases!"

"What!!! And?"

"Prepare to be amazed!" As we drove back to our rental house through the Devon lanes, the topic of conversation revolved around the contents we had unearthed. I don't think Sandra could quite believe what we were telling her.

"Jesus! This is so much over my head! You guys have uncovered some crucial documents, but the big question is, what are you going to do with everything you have found?"

"Give it back to France or donate it all to a museum?" Ella announced.

"That's very noble and honest of you both."

"Not before, we have our story published. A book launch with the publicity surrounding the donation of these documents and treasure. Wouldn't that give us an edge that other authors can't match? What do you think, Sandra?"

"Quite frankly, it will be the launch of all time, but it will need to be professionally managed. The only problem I can see is that you might need it all verified and endorsed by experts first."

"Possibly, but I wonder if it would be better kept under wraps until the day. Sandra, people have died for this. In particular, one person close to me. They can do all the authenticating all they like when the book comes out."

We couldn't wait to show Sandra all the documents and booty after returning to the house. Our discussions about the best way forward went on well into the evening.

"Ironically, if the experts can't validate the documents, then the book is merely fiction. However, if it all proves to be genuine, it could make us…."

Sandra butted in.

"Yes! I get it! Winners, either way!" Although she still sounded a little doubtful. "Where on earth are you going to keep this lot?"

"I have a place in mind!"

Sandra raised her eyebrows. Maybe she was coming around to my idea, or perhaps she just thought I was mad. Ella explained our reasons to Sandra about why we wanted to go public, better than I could and, in fact, put up a compelling argument about not wanting a life in the shadows. "Do you remember me showing you my family tree with all those historical names? Let's look at it again." She opened her handbag and pulled out a folded piece of paper.

"Here's Louis Philippe and the line down to his son Leopold. The new documents we have now show he was not illegitimate, as historians believed. I found a marriage certificate. They provide the key to the story in that, and more importantly, this changes history. Louis Philippe died in 1850, which was a healthy age of seventy- seven, for the times he lived in. Leopold was sixty- eight when he died, which shows as a family group, we could expect to have a long-life expectancy. There are a further six generations before me but look at the ages when most of them died. My mother was thirty- four and my father was thirty-six. No-one else made it past forty except for my grandmother,

Gwendolyn Aguirre, somehow, was a special case and the only one in seven generations who didn't succumb to some form of misfortune. These documents prove it all!" Ella was busy thrusting papers onto the table and carried on, her voice getting more emotional.

"The killing has to stop now! Publishing the book will do that!"

Sandra got up and tried to calm her down.

"I really want to believe you're right!" She clasped her hands over her face and sighed. OK! You've convinced me. I am with you! It's just so daunting. This is the biggest thing that's ever come into my life and probably ever will!"

"Good! Same here, Sandra. We are all in unknown territory. How did you get on finding a publisher?"

"Not very well, to be honest, Robin. I don't have the connections that Rowena has, but I have found the name the man she was speaking to."

"Well! That's a starting point. I'll call them for an appointment. Any news on how the book was received?"

"My readers took to it well enough, but we need to re-write some chunks. If I've got it correct, you want to include the collusion between British and French intelligence in covering up the story?"

"Certainly, but we still have some unanswered questions, though. Why would something which happened in 1790 have such an impact today?" Sandra's comments about intelligence services were making me think back to The Limes.

"I guess we can assume that the guys in the hotel were just criminals and only after the loot, as Hansen said. After all, he does head up the International Crimes department. As for this AF business, well, that is harder to prove one way or the other. He did tell me that Madame Aguirre had sensitive information about the AF. Yet, if she did have some names of the terrorists, where are they? We haven't found anything with any reference to the AF. Could that be a smokescreen? The descendants of the Bourbon and Orleans families are still alive, so maybe they could be affected by all of this? I feel that there is some high-up diplomatic influence involved. Who knows?" I added that we had to make educated guesses to questions which we did not know the answers to. We all went quiet until Sandra broke the silence of our reflective mood quite unintentionally and rather humorously.

"Have you got any dog food?" I shot a smiling glance over to Ella.

"Sandra? Does that mean what I think it means?"

"Yes! I'm staying!" We all jumped around like silly kids, which made Scott bark extremely loudly, jumping up at us.

Our first task was to photocopy every document using the printer we had already bought. It was a mammoth task and extremely painstaking, but we felt it was better to work with copies. The originals were carefully put back into the trunks and by early evening, we were finished. I left the house to deposit them for the second time. But first, disguising them as general household belongings by putting them in cardboard packing boxes and taping them up with black duct tape. I had considered where I was going to hide them again and in conclusion, I felt that they would be best back in Tenby, even if it did require a six-hour round trip. Ella was desperate to come with me, not knowing I was returning to Wales, but I wanted some time alone and a long drive would provide that. If anyone came looking, they would assume I had stored everything in Devon. Always an eye for economy, I had paid six months storage in Tenby without attracting any suspicion. I kept the location to myself and slipped out for the day.

With the trunks secretly stashed away, I could now focus on other things. The name which Sandra had given to me as a possible contact in the publishing world, was a Mr. David Price of P&I Publishers. He was the chap who, Rowena had indicated to both of us, was all set to go to print. Getting through to Mr. Price was another matter. I found it impossible to induce a response from his voice mail. My calls were never returned; neither were my e-mails. It was all very disheartening. Sandra thought we would be better finding a literary agent who would look at the book and pass it on if it was of any interest, but I felt that even more time would be lost. I was determined to visit his offices and stage a sit-in until he saw me. The following day was a good time since it was the day of Amy's funeral, in Hertfordshire. After what Penny had said to me, there was every chance I would be an unwelcome guest, so I planned to stand back at a discreet distance. Afterwards, I could visit the Price office. Both Sandra and Ella thought I was wasting my time with Price. Neither could they understand why I was going to the funeral. Ella did not want to come with me, which was understandable. The horror of Amy's death would be relived and emotions would be running high by all family members.

The pending trip to Hertfordshire made me think of Amy's house. I stopped as I passed by to have a look, out of morbid curiosity. Her quaint little cottage was as untouched as the day we departed on our way to our rented hideaway. Sadness filled my heart. I told the Polish lady next door that Amy had a new job in London and had moved quickly. I wasn't sure she believed me as she talked about the goings-on at the school.

It was apparent that no-one had been there, not even Amy's family. Her stuff was everywhere. The Roald Dahl storybooks that she loved to read to the kids at school. A graduation picture of Amy in her gown, standing beside proud parents. Her most treasured item, a cricket bat, signed by all the England team. Also, some mounted photographs of her with famous players. The next photo on the wall filled me with tears. It was a picture of the two of us at the Devon and Exeter races, several months earlier, before…. I recalled the day so well and how happy we looked together… As I remembered her face, her smell, her voice, my heart ached. I kissed her in the photo, put it in my pocket as a keepsake and left.

I had too much on my mind to delve deeply into all the current media coverage, but, on the political front, the news stories appeared to have moved on. The diplomatic crisis had been averted, which the press claimed was due to the efforts of the German Chancellor. Who knows what was happening behind the scenes, but the senior political leaders had stopped baiting each other in public.

I had left the house early Thursday morning before anyone else was up. Although, I couldn't sneak out past Scott without him barking. I was finding it hard to warm to Mr. Grumpy as I had now named him. I messaged Penny asking for up to date funeral details and yet again, in her text back to me, she advised me not to go. With this in mind, I arrived early at the church as I didn't want to be seen by Amy's parents. I had once met Amy's brother Karl, a guy I really liked from the first, but Amy had kept me at a distance from her mother and father. Something in my subconscious was pressing me to be part of this poignant farewell ceremony, even though I knew that I would find the emotional impact hard to deal with. Ella was right, telling me to keep away. Why had I not listened to her?

I planned to linger at the back of the church, then stand at a respectable distance as the coffin was being interned. I managed to get inside unnoticed, so I stood behind a large stone pillar, pretending to read a plaque on the wall and trying not to look suspicious. What my position didn't do, was conceal me from the mourners at the front, which included Amy's brother.

"Rob? I thought it was you!" It took me by surprise.

"Hello, Karl."

"I'm glad you came, mate."

"Thanks. That means a lot since …." my emotions were starting to get the better of me and I couldn't finish the sentence.

"Let me introduce you to my mother and father."

"Sorry, no. I can't." Panic was starting to set in. I assumed they would be hostile to me and I did not want an awkward scene, but Karl was insistent.

"Just come and talk to them."

"It could be awkward. I don't know what to say. Do they blame me for what happened?"

"No, they don't, not at all, but they would like to meet you. Come and sit with us at the front." Karl took my arm and we walked down to greet Amy's parents. Her father looked glazed and confused, but her mother received me with a smile. I felt such a massive sigh of relief, I nearly choked.

"I am Grace and this is Gordon. The two G's!" It must have been an old joke. I was unable to say much as the coffin was on its way.

The ceremony and the committal were very moving. Karl delivered the eulogy with due sensitivity under the circumstances. By the end of the service, I was so glad I had been present. They invited me back to the house, a request I felt I could not ignore, so I followed on. Amy had always led me to believe her parents would not like me or have a 'not good enough for our daughter attitude.' I found interaction with the father slightly difficult, but Karl explained that he wasn't well and that there were some psychological issues developing.

Her mother, on the other hand, was lovely. She made me welcome and was genuinely pleased to meet me. It was strange that Penny had led me to believe otherwise. It crossed my mind to say something about it the next time I spoke to her. Amy and her mother were far closer than I had thought. I must have been a major topic of conversation as she knew all about our plans. We kept the discussion to happier times and practical issues. I felt unable to discuss what happened or why.

"What will you do with Amy's house?" I asked.

"Her father and I would rather you take it."

"There are too many painful memories, Grace. I don't think I could live there. Have you thought about what you will do with Amy's things?"

"Could you deal with that for us, dear? We don't even have a key to the house and Gordon doesn't travel well these days."

"If you want to sell it, I can speak to an agent for you."

"Are you sure? You can stay there until you find somewhere else?" At that point, Karl joined us.

"Mother! Rob does not want to live in the house." He turned to me.

"It would be a great help, Rob if you can clear it out. It's too much for mum to do and too far."

"Of course, but I could do with some advice on what to keep and what not to keep." Grace nodded and appealed to Karl.

"Yes, of course. Give me a day or so and I'll arrange a time when I can pop down and help you."

We chatted on for some time. It was clear that the whole proceedings were a strain on Grace, so I made my excuses and left.

I felt quite drained, on my return to the car, but I called Mr. Price, only to be blocked yet again by some office receptionist. I felt angry that some petty employee was hindering me. I changed my tone to one of insistency.

"You are very obstructive, which does not reflect well on your company. Mr. Price is expecting my call. It has all been arranged through Rowena Kerry. If you don't put me through, I'll come to your office and make a nuisance of myself until he agrees to see me!" My attack had its reward, as the receptionist replied.

"Just one moment, please." I was put on hold to listen to some dreary music. It took some time, but finally, I heard a man's voice.

"This is Mr. Price. What can I do for you?"

"I was given your name by Rowena Kerry. She said that you were going to publish my book, but Rowena is now indisposed and I still have a book to publish. Can we please meet to discuss it?"

"Mr. Ashurst. I feel you have been somewhat misled. To say that we were going to publish your book is completely untrue. I've never heard of you. I know Ms. Kerry on a purely social level. We last met at a party where she did indeed speak to me about an idea for a book she was involved in. Ms. Kerry is an investigative journalist and as such, she is not someone with whom my company would normally collaborate. However, she claimed that she was going to have a serialisation deal with a national broadsheet, so in those vague terms, we expressed an interest in looking to publish. That is all. I believe the book has yet to be written." I was dismayed at this response, but beneath his pompous tone, I felt he was honest with me.

"I see. I'm sorry. As you say, I have been misinformed and quite frankly, I have been led up the proverbial garden path." Mr. Price was rather more interested in Rowena's whereabouts than expressing any sympathy for my predicament.

"You say she is indisposed? Can you explain further? Rumours about her are rife in the publishing world."

"She was arrested and is currently being held by the police. I've not been able to contact her since."

"Really! Well, that is news! I must say no-one has heard from her for a few weeks."

"I am the writer of the book, which is now finished. I'm sure it just needs some finishing touches so I would like some advice. Is there any chance you might take a look at it?" I was pleading with him, but I was desperate.

"Have you had anything previously published?"

"No, nothing."

"I am sorry, but we generally don't look at new authors." The conversation was going no-where but I felt a note of sympathy in his voice.

"You could try self-publishing? Many new authors now go down that route."

"Thanks anyway."

I felt somewhat silly and embarrassed. I had been lied to, so much in the last month that my bullshit radar should have been on red alert. I had taken everything Rowena said as gospel truth. It brought back to mind the spats between Amy and Rowena in the last few days that they had known each other. Heading back to Devon, I had, as usual, much to think about.

Chapter 18

I was really out of my comfort zone with all this talk of self-publishing. Sandra and Ella were positive about the whole notion, but I had my doubts about the sanity of the plan. The costs of self-publishing could easily swallow up the rest of the money I had and more, so I needed some reassurance.

"Tell me again, how would it work, Sandra?"

"In simple terms, we get 2000 copies printed, then organise a big press launch where we present to the world what we have. Documents and the jewels. Then we publish on several retail platforms, Amazon Kindle, Kobo, Book burb etc."

"Yes, I get that. I'm concerned about funds, though. My bank account is getting low. How long will it take to get the book printed? Won't some big launch cost plenty?"

Both Sandra and Ella understand my financial worries.

"Rob, how much have you got in the bank?" Ella asked.

"About half what I started with, which is around twelve thousand pounds, but I owe Sandra four on the basis of our agreement, so that only leaves us with eight. We can't do it on that, can we?"

"Come on, Rob! Where there is a will, there is a way," said Sandra. Ella added

"We haven't come this far to give up now!"

Sandra thought for a few minutes and then spoke.

"Look! I am happy to waive the four grand fee until we have funds to cover it from book sales. If they don't come in, then I've worked for nothing. Not a new experience for me! That's how strongly I feel we have a best seller here. If I had any money to throw into the pot, I would."

"That's kind of you, Sandra, but the printing? That could be about five thousand, and then there is the publicity. A launch would be five to ten, at least. Wouldn't it!"

"We don't need to promote the book until after the launch and if the presentation goes well, we can make a big noise. We might even get a deal with a publisher."

"Yes! Ok, but how do we go about making this 'big noise!"

We all spent the next two whole days discussing the same financial points over and over. 'We have come this far!' was said so often, I took it up as a catchphrase which made us all laugh. The short-term rental on the house was also starting to bother me. Even if we could extend the rental period, I couldn't afford it. We desperately needed some cash and some inspiration. Surprisingly, both came from Ella.

"The flat in London." She said as she handed me a coffee one morning.

"The what?"

"Grandmother's London flat!"

"Yes? What about it?" I had no idea what she was getting at.

"We could move in and live there. It's big enough!" Sandra's ears pricked up. She had been hard at work on an array of papers with two laptops open.

"Where is this flat, exactly?"

"It's near Hyde Park. I think."

"Wow, that's posh! My flat is more like just a studio and it's in Kilburn. There's hardly enough space for Scot and me."

"Ella! Do you know for sure where it is?" I asked.

"I can't remember the address exactly. I think the name of the road begins with 'B.' I spent three days there with my grandmother before we came down to Devon." Just as we were all beginning to feel excited, I suddenly remembered that we would need keys to get in. I felt deflated again.

"But the keys? You don't have them, do you?"

"God! Men! What is it with them?" Ella smiled at me, teasingly.

"The bunch of keys we have to open the trunks?"

"Ella, that's a stroke of genius! To think I considered you dim-witted when I first met you!"

"You're the dummy and it's well documented in the book how simple you thought I was! I could sue you for defamation of character!"

Sandra interjected our banter. She was curious about the layout.

"So how many bedrooms has it got?"

Ella started to think about it and closed her eyes to recall the rooms.

"It's Flat three on the first floor. So, you go in and there are two doors on the left and …"

"Yes, yes, you don't need to give us a running commentary. How many bedrooms, 'sprout'?"

"Look! Don't call me sprout! Be quiet! I need to visualise it." She closed her eyes again.

"Turn right into the lounge, which faces the road, left into the kitchen, which is small or long and thin. Galley style. Down the hall.   One bedroom on the right and one on the left. There's also a small room full of junk opposite the bathroom at the end of the hall. How many is that? Yes, three then. I guess. It's very old fashioned. I do remember an old piano in the lounge."

"A piano! I'm sure that will come in handy then!" I remarked sarcastically.

"Do either of you two play?"

"I know I am the resident kook here, but actually Rob, yes, I do play!"

"Really! You are full of surprises! What a clever 'sprout' you are!"

Ella had a finger to her lips, hiding a wicked smile.

Sandra interrupted our banter to keep the conversation on track.

"Can I bring Scott?" Neither of us answered, so Sandra took off her glasses and put down her pen.

"What's the game plan then?" she asked in a more serious tone. We both gave each other a knowing look. After several moments, I spoke first.

"This is the way I see it. Since we've had the book idea, it has been a bloody mad rush, which has put pressure on all of us. We saw it as a way to rid ourselves of a bunch of psycho-nutters and for what-ever reason, Rowena put a tight cut-off date on everything. She had her own agenda. This flat idea gives us time to pull back a bit and finish the book properly without the pressure of a deadline. We can work on trying to get the publicity we need to promote it, with our budget restraints. It doesn't matter if we go public in six months or a year. If we're based in London on a road beginning with 'B,' we might even be well placed to make some useful contacts in the publishing world or in the media. Do you agree, Sandra?"

"Potentially yes. I don't disagree with anything you've said. From my point of view, I want to know the basics. I won't go anywhere without Scott, so I hope that's not a problem. Also, how much rent would you want from me?" Ella answered her.

"Nothing. There are three of us in this. We'll all work at whatever is needed until we launch. We will all live in the flat and yes, Scott as well! I like dogs even if Rob doesn't! At best, we make some money out of this, so you get your fee and Rob gets his money back. If there is anything left, we split it three ways. And if the book doesn't sell, then Rob is out of pocket and we've all worked for nothing." I marvelled at how the shy, unworldly girl I had first met, had become such a commercially aware and confident young woman of means. After a pause, she added, "After all, the flat will be costing us nothing except bills."

"Fine by me," said Sandra.

"And me. When do we move in?"

"From what I can remember, it will need cleaning and tidying up. Not like here!" said Ella.

The flat was on a charming and typical Georgian avenue just off the Bayswater Road W2. Sandra wasn't wrong when she said 'posh!' Similar apartments in the row were fetching between one and a half to two million. Ella and I arrived first to make arrangements and to do some clearing up. We all felt Sandra's time was best spent working on the book and trying to find a modest printing company that could offer us a reasonable deal. The level of clutter inside the apartment was immense and had obviously accumulated over a long period. A musty smell from being uninhabited permeated the rooms.

The décor was very 1950's, likewise the furniture. I was happy to spend some time boxing things up and getting them out of the flat, to be sorted later. I found another lock-up self-storage depot nearby. Several trips later, we were starting to make some headway clearing out the paraphernalia.

From the bedroom, I shouted to Ella, who was scrubbing down the kitchen worksurfaces.

"Come in here and look at this?" I showed her a pendant necklace, with a pear-shaped green jewel surrounded by what looked like diamonds. It had matching earrings and was in an oval presentation case of red satin.

"Wow! Where did you find that?"

"It was in the drawer of that antique desk. Do you think it might be valuable?"

"Maybe! I don't know much about antique jewellery, but why don't we see if it is worth anything. Anything to help the bank balance!"

I thought this was such a great idea, that on the third day in London, after my return from the lock-up with my daily delivery of boxes, I stopped at Christie's Auction House in King Street. I took the necklace, some Worcester porcelain, and a bronze statue of a gun dog with game in its mouth. The only thing that made me take it was that it had a name on the base. I left the items with a representative who told me that I would receive a valuation in due course.

The apartment, now known by all of us as 'number 3', was suitably tidied, cleaned, aired and ready. Sandra and Scott moved in. She had been giving us daily progress reports and felt that our book was finally coming together. She had also found a company to print and bind 2500 copies. I knew Sandra had our best interests at heart. I was impressed with the way she handled things, quietly and efficiently and nothing like as despotically or confrontational as Rowena. The other thing on my mind was my relationship with Ella. Since we had returned from our little holiday, we had slept in separate bedrooms. I wasn't ready for a physical relationship. It was far too soon. Ella was giving me space, giving me time. I felt we need to talk about it, but neither of us wanted to be the first to broach the subject of intimacy.

I let the two girls settle in together and I went back to Devon. I had a few jobs that needed my attention. The most pressing was emptying Amy's cottage. I also wanted to carry on with some more research without telling the girls. Mr. and Mrs. Saul had taken up residence in their own home again, so I spent a couple of nights in a hotel managed by an old friend, Tom. I cleared out all Amy's stuff from the cottage and found a local agent to handle the sale. I also paid a quick visit to The Limes to see how I felt about going back to manage it as owner. As I drove the now familiar M5/ M4 route, I pondered on my future plans.

I needed a jewellery expert who could authenticate the items and match them to their maker. On the other hand, the book needed to be ready to publish as it was apparent that any exposure would alert Penny and Hansen to the fact that I had told them a load of bollocks. I did have the idea the sky would fall in on us again, but this time I would be ready. Events took an unusual turn as I was unloading the last of Amy's personal belongings to Karl when my phone rang.

"Mr. Ashurst?"

"Yes! Speaking."

"Good morning. This is Christie's auctioneers. My name is Derwent and I am one of the managers. I believe you left some items with us for appraisal. May I ask, sir? Are you the owner?"

"No. They belong to a friend. Her grandmother died and we have been clearing out her property."

"I see. Would it be possible for you both to come into our office here as we would like to discuss the situation?"

"What situation? We want to know if they are of any value."

"I would prefer not to discuss this matter on the phone. Could you possibly call into our offices?"

"Yes, OK. What time?"

"Would 10.30 tomorrow morning suit you?"

"Who do I ask for again?"

"Derwent. Mr. Charles Derwent. Goodbye, Sir, until tomorrow."

The line went dead. His use of the word 'situation' made me feel a touch nervous. It also seemed rather odd that someone, so high up in Christie's, would phone me.

When I arrived back at the flat, I relayed Mr. Derwent's conversation to my housemates. It created more debate.

"We need to talk about the ownership of these items from Ella's grandmother," Sandra said, over a take-away pizza and bottle of wine.

"In what sense?" I asked.

"I assume Ella, that you have not been contacted by anyone about when your grandmother's estate might be settled?"

"No, not really. Penny told Rob and me that it could take a while and was proving difficult."

"So, what I'm asking, is all this stuff yours to sell then? Legally, I mean. You've changed identity, so how can you prove any of it is yours? How, on earth, did the old lady keep this flat away from the AF?" Ella didn't know the answer, so I tried to give some sort of explanation.

"If they knew she had all this stuff, then surely her flat would have been searched." I tried to make a joke about it.

"Listen, if you'd seen the state of it when we first arrived, you would have thought it **had** been ransacked!" Ella smiled in agreement.

"To be honest, Sandra, I've come to the conclusion that we will never have all the answers. The infamous AF office is within walking distance from here, which surely can't be a coincidence. We may learn more tomorrow when we see Mr. Derwent. Don't valuable pieces have some provenance or something?" Sandra nodded in agreement but then she thought of something else.

"Rob. Another question for you then. At the end of the book, do we tell the world about the identity swap? As Ella said, it ends the horror of six generations. Won't the book change it all back, though?" At this point, Ella jumped in with her thoughts.

"That's what I want, Sandra. I have given it a lot of thought in the last few days. I don't want to be Amy and it's not fair to her memory, her family. I want to live as Antonella, so the idea of the book is to tell the world. When the truth comes out and all the treasure is returned, I won't be a threat any longer, to anyone. I'll have nothing that any person might want to steal and murder for. Rob says we have a lot of unanswered questions. He's right, but surely the most important one is why all this matters and to whom."

"Just as I was getting used to calling you, Ella!" I tried for the second time to lighten the mood, but as with my first attempt, it failed.

Any issue over sleeping arrangements was settled when Sandra said she was leaving to go home.

"Why? I thought you were staying here."

"There's a smell of damp in that back room and it is not good for my lungs. I suffer from asthma, so if you don't mind, I'll stay in Kilburn. I've arranged for a contractor to find the source of the damp, then treat the wall. I don't understand why we would have any damp as we are on the first floor, but it's very unpleasant. When it's sorted, I'll move my stuff in. Didn't you both think it was quiet without Scott barking?" We all laughed.

First to arrive in the morning, were two middle-aged men in white boiler suits. Very unlikely builders, they appeared too, one short and one fat. But with great efficiency, they fixed a leaking downpipe, which was the root cause of the damp, then repaired the wall. By the time Sandra returned, her room was looked and smelled clean and fresh. Ella and I headed off to our appointment with Mr. Derwent.

Christie's Auction house was very much in keeping with the status held as the world's oldest fine art auctioneers. A cavernous entrance, richly decorated with paintings on the walls, some classical and others more contemporary. Rows of modern executive desks, stood in a long line upon a luxurious burgundy carpeted floor, each with gold tabletop signs depicting their position or speciality. Nothing so vulgar as an overhead noticeboard or any advertisements here. My eyes ran down the line, but I couldn't see anything applicable to me. As I was still looking for an appropriate class of antiquities, I was greeted by a smart gent in a slim-fitting navy suit, clutching a clipboard. He introduced himself as Edward, Mr. Derwent's personal assistant and shook my hand with a rather weak handshake. Edward was a well-groomed young man, slightly effeminate in his manner but extremely courteous. He took my name, checked his notes and welcomed us in the style that one could only assume Christie's reserved for their most wealthy and discerning clients. We were ushered to be seated on a very sumptuously green leather chesterfield sofa.

After no more than five minutes, we were guided by the ever-attentive Edward into a large office with a gold nameplate on the door. A tall imposing and authoritative man wearing an impeccably tailored, Saville Row pinstripe suit walked towards me to shake hands. Mr. Derwent introduced himself as General Manager. On the phone, I hadn't realised how senior a figure he was, but now it was evident by the way the staff gave him such reverence, that he was the top man. A woman was also in the office, looking out of the window. My sense of decorum quite failed me when I saw the woman turn to face us. It was Penny Carter. I inadvertently pulled my hand away, my voice raised.

"What the heck are you doing here?" I asked in amazement. Mr. Derwent just stood and observed this verbal exchange, still with his hand out firmly to shake mine. Edward's startled gaze went from me to Penny and then to his boss. Penny tried to reply, but before she could say anything, I interrupted.

"How the hell did you know we were here? Let me guess… you have us under surveillance?" I was so angry.

"No! Robin, let me speak. I have a question for you! Where did you get the necklace from?" I was seething with rage, but I knew my best defence was to go on the attack.

"If you've had us watched, do you need to ask?" Penny folded her arms as if she were dealing with a naughty child.

"Just answer the question, Robin!"

"We had to move from the rented house as I'm sure you know. Ella came up with the idea of staying at her grandmother's flat to save money. While we were clearing up, we found a few items that we thought we could sell to raise some cash. I have no job, as you know, so my funds are going down rapidly. Ella has no access to funds until the Swiss business is settled, so needs must. That's the long and short of it. Now tell me why you're here?" My tone was stern and left Penny in no doubt that I was thoroughly pissed off.

"Robin, Antonella. It's not what it appears." Her voice softened as she explained.

"Every five to ten years, a crucial and significant item of French royal jewellery appears on the market. This has been happening now for the past forty years. Mr. Derwent, with his specialist knowledge of antique French jewellery, very kindly notifies us." Mr. Derwent nodded in agreement. Penny continued.

"These pieces are of extreme historical importance because, as I am sure you both know, most of the French crown jewels disappeared after the revolution. Despite investigations and inquiries by the French and us, we have never been able to track down the source. They have remained anonymous until now!" She paused and then looked directly at each of us, in turn.

"However, thanks to you, we now know the true identity of the seller!" Ella and I glanced at each other, but neither of us had a clue what she was talking about.

"Mr. Derwent called us this week to say that another piece of French pre-revolution, royal jewellery had surfaced. The identity of the seller is a man already known to us, as the chap who hid some chests in a store in his Devon hotel, goods which then mysteriously disappeared, only later admitting he took them. He then claimed he had disposed of them in a place… what were his words… '*where they can't be found*!' **Do you see where I am going with this?**" Her voice got sharper and louder. I was aware of her eyes staring coldly first at Ella, then me.

It was clear she was now convinced that there was a lot more jewellery and that I knew where it was. I had to think quickly, should I come clean or not? I stared back at her and pleaded complete ignorance of anything to do with historical treasures of the state. I acted as if I couldn't believe what she was accusing me of. Her attention turned to Ella.

"Do you have anything to add?" Ella reverted into her role as a slow-witted innocent girl. She shrugged her shoulders, pulling me close to her by the arm. I challenged Penny.

"Penny, come on! Look! I told you the truth. The chests are gone. We only chanced on these things when we tidied up the flat, so I brought them here. There was nothing else. Trust me! You're more than welcome to take a look round the flat!" Penny smiled knowingly.

"Thank you. That is precisely what is happening at this moment, Robin. A specialist search team is there now." She paused for a moment.

"You are very plausible, Robin, but why didn't you come to us with this?" The lies came quite easily to me now and I knew she had no choice but to believe me.

"Because I'm not an antiques expert! I've spent my life in hospitality. I had no idea what these things were! Our motivation was solely to raise some funds. I brought some porcelain and a signed bronze. Had to be worth a few hundred quid."

"And how did you get into the flat?" Yet again, I fought off her interrogation by being confrontational. I surprised myself with such an ability for deception.

"Are you suggesting we broke in? How dare you? Antonella knew where the spare key was hidden." The lies just flowed. "She'd stayed in London for a few days with her grandmother before they both went to Devon."

"Did she? That's interesting!" Penny didn't elaborate on that point.

"I understand that your ghost writer, Sandra Pegg, is at the flat. What is she doing there?"

"Sandra is moving in with us and why not? We've all spent so much time on the book, we've decided to publish it ourselves, but I assure you that it will be a book of fiction. I want to dedicate it to Amy and perhaps make some money out of this…. this experience so that I can buy The Limes." My voice wavered with emotion. Penny looked slightly exasperated but did not challenge me again. Ella spoke for the first time.

"We believe that these things are mine. They belonged to my grandmother, so surely they are my inheritance?" Penny put her head on one side and frowned.

"It is not as easy as that, my dear. Firstly, the jewellery can be classified as 'state treasure' and rightfully belongs to France. The other items are not yours yet. Legally, they form part of your grandmother's estate and, as such, should not be sold until the whole matter is settled." Ella looked so crestfallen that Penny had a rethink.

"However, if Mr. Derwent here is happy to sell them, then maybe I can allow it. But not the jewellery." Mr. Derwent nodded and spoke for the first time, referring to papers in his hand, swiftly passed to him by Edward.

"Our valuation is that the bronze should sell in the region of eight to ten thousand pounds and the four items of Royal Worcester might make around five thousand, less commission, of course. Do you wish to proceed, Madam?"

"Yes," said Ella. Penny continued.

"That leaves us with the pendant. The French government will pay a finder's fee if it is donated. The last items of similar importance fetched about two million euros if I remember correctly. A tidy sum with which you could both purchase the Limes, renovate it and reimburse HM Government for your grandmother's funeral and other expenses we have incurred leading from your actions. Still leaving you with a million or so!" She looked at Mr. Derwent and asked him if she could speak to us in private. I was still reeling from the high numbers bandied about by Penny and Mr. Derwent.

"Certainly, Ms. Carter. I will organise some refreshments for you all. You two look as if you might need something!" he said, looking at us. All I could mumble was, "Did I hear that correctly? Two million?" He nodded to me, then bowed his head in deference to Penny and left the room. Edward meekly following on behind.

"You have been through a lot, so I am willing to help. However, there are conditions attached." Her manner was stern, but she was offering terms.

"Firstly, you both sign an official and legally binding non-disclosure agreement. Secondly, there is no publicity. The donation will be anonymous. Thirdly, there is no book. Condition number four is that in the future, if anything, however small, turns up, you bring it straight to us. And finally,…." she hesitated.

"Finally, you marry and live happily ever after as Mr & Mrs. Ashurst." We breathed a sigh of relief.

"You too are very suited. Now, do we have a deal?"

"How long do we have to think about it?"

"Until the tea arrives!" replied Penny with a touch of sarcasm.

"OK. I'll give you five minutes." With that, she got up and left us. We were on our own in this splendid office. Ella went to look out of the window, I sat down on a chaise longue with my head in my hands. Neither of us spoke for a minute or two.

"What you think, Ella?"

"The first - no problem. I don't mind signing something. The second - no publicity? That's ok too but no book? That's a shame. We will have to give Sandra something, though, so she can keep Scott in doggy biscuits. The fourth? – we'll have to lie about that, won't we? We know where the trunks are. The last one? Marry you? Hmmm. I'd have to think about that!" I was smiling when a young girl entered carrying a silver tray of Royal Albert cups, saucers and a teapot. Followed by Penny, of course. The girl put the tray down on the leather-topped desk and left. Penny poured out the tea. She gave one cup to me and the other to Ella, then returned to sit on the antique mahogany swivel chair behind the desk and put her hands together, in front of her mouth, elbows on the edge.

"Well?" She asked. "Do we have an agreement?" I chose my words carefully and gave her something first, which was often a useful ploy in negotiations, as I had previously discovered.

"When we cleared the flat, it was in a real mess. I took loads of stuff to a lock-up self-storage unit. We just threw it all into boxes and planned to go through it all later. Here are the keys to the unit. It's just behind the Queens Park Rangers football ground. Cubical 143 or 134, registered in the name of Noel Greenwood." Penny knew we were being co-operative, so I tried to get something in return.

"We accept all your terms except the one about the book. I would still like to get it published because we've put in so much work. It's almost finished. As I said, Amy died for a reason which you know more about than we do. I want to dedicate my book to her memory." Penny was thoughtful for a moment as she considered her reply.

"We would have to read the book first. We have to approve the content. It's the only way we could agree to publication and if…." I jumped in quickly and interrupted her.

"That's fine by me. I have no intention of divulging any state secrets."

"Is that all right with you, Antonella?"

"It is Ella now. Yes, it's all OK with me except…. do I really have to marry him? That could well be a life sentence, and he snores like a pig!" A smile came over Penny's face as she got up to go.

"Too much information, thank you! Anyway, I have much to do, so I will be in touch shortly with papers for you to sign." As she opened the door, Penny turned around to face us.

"By the way, who is Noel Greenwood?"

"Goalkeeper for Queens Park Rangers!"

"Right! If those trunks ever turn up, I will throw you both in prison for an exceedingly long time!" On that severe note, she left the office.

"Shit! That was a threat, wasn't it?"

"It certainly was! Lucky, I recorded it then!" I took Rowena's voice recorder out from inside my jacket pocket. Ella stared at me.

"You crafty bugger! What made you think of doing that?"

"Insurance, my sweet girl."

Chapter 19

"Rob, there are some men here ransacking the flat!" Sandra's voice was frantic on the phone.

"We know Sandra. Don't worry. It's the security services."

"You know about it? What do they want?"

"Can't talk now. Tell them you need to pop out for something and meet us both at that Italian coffee shop around the corner in twenty minutes." Ella pulled at my arm.

"I need more than a latte macchiato Rob. Tell her to meet us at The George, the pub opposite the Indian restaurant."

Sitting at a corner table with a bottle of wine and three glasses, we replayed the recording to Sandra from the voice recorder and tried to make sense of it all. There was no doubt that Madame Aguirre had been selling off pieces of jewellery from the chest to fund her life and campaign. We assumed that she was going to sell the pendant next, which just happened to be the item I picked up. Sandra commented on my quick thinking.

"You did well to get Penny to agree to the book. Just hope we don't have to re-write it again," she asked. I shook my head.

"Not completely. We have two books. We submit one to the spooks and the other, we sell at the launch!" Ella protested vehemently.

"No! For God's sake, Rob. No! Did you miss that bit about doing time in prison?" I dismissed her objections.

"Threats! Just idle threats. If the book sells, there is no way they can put us away."

"How do you make that out. Explain?"

"Before we go to prison, we'd have to appear in court so we can say what we like. I've got several recordings that prove our story is true. And, more crucially, we'll have donated so many French royal jewels back to France that if the British government prosecutes us, the French will have something to say about it!"

"You don't know that for sure!"

"No, I don't, but it's worth a try?" Ella raised her eyebrows, which made me feel much less confident about my convictions.

"Speaking about a prison sentence.... I have to marry Ella!" I felt my arm being pinched playfully by Ella. Despite my attempts to be convincing and humorous at the same time, I felt the girls didn't quite agree with me. I wondered if we were being careful enough covering our tracks.

"Just a thought, Sandra! Were there any photocopies lying around the apartment when it was searched?"

"No! They're all in a box file, well hidden in my wardrobe at Kilburn."

"That's a relief!" It crossed my mind that the game might be up, but the wine dulled my anxiety, leaving me mellow and calm. After several bottles, we were all quite intoxicated and feeling very blissfully detached from the gravity of our situation. We left the pub giggling, but we were harshly reminded of it when we saw a policeman at the door.

"Sorry, Sir, Ladies. I have orders not to let you in!"

"What?"

"I have instructions that you are to go to The Russell Hotel on Bedford Street for a meeting."

"Meeting? What fucking meeting?" My calm resolve was gone in an instant as I wondered if we might have been rumbled.

"I am not at liberty to say and kindly moderate your language, Sir!"

"Sod off! I am not going anywhere. This is our flat." I tried to sidestep him, the wine giving me the courage to show belligerence towards a uniformed officer of the law, but he obstructed me with his hand rather forcefully. He started speaking into his personal radio unit. Sandra whispered to Ella,

"Rob can be very masterful, can't he?"

"Only when he's pissed!" replied Ella. They both laughed. The policeman's mobile now rang, from inside his pocket. He took the call and spoke to me directly.

"Excuse me, Sir, but I have a Ms. Carter on the phone wishing to speak to you?" I sighed and grabbed the phone very discourteously.

"Robin?" Penny's voice boomed into my ear, causing pain across my temples. "Where are you both? I have been trying to call you for ages!"

"Sorry. We went to the pub because the flat is crawling with 'the old bill'!" She ignored my weak sarcasm.

"I am at The Russell Hotel. We have the papers here for you and Ella to sign. Sandra needs to come too. My investigation team hasn't finished yet, so I've booked rooms here for all of you tonight. Please come immediately as I have spent so much time on this today?"

"I can't drive. I've had far too much to drink."

"Get a cab then. See you in ten minutes." Penny said, with frustration in her voice. The line went dead.

We ended up spending two nights in the hotel before we were allowed back to the flat. In that time, we had endless interviews with faceless civil servants from various departments going through the deal Penny had outlined. We became weary from signing papers and documents. For Ella and me, it seemed like we were under house arrest, but luckily for Sandra, she was free to go about her business. She stayed at her flat in Kilburn and not at the hotel, as dogs were not allowed in hotel bedrooms. The other consequence was that again, it sidestepped the bedroom issue. Penny had booked two rooms. One for Sandra and one for Ella and me. Sandra didn't need hers, so we had one each.

I had always considered the British legal system to be slow and archaic. It is honourable and can generally be trusted, yet the speed with which these people got things done lawfully was quite amazing. Documents were swiftly drawn up giving us title to own The Limes. The London flat was miraculously transferred into the name of Ella Gooch. There was nothing that Penny Carter and her team could not achieve. The only legal document she could not present us with was a marriage certificate, although I felt she was putting a lot of pressure on us both to do the deed. Why this was so important, was an issue we puzzled over. In those forty-eight hours, I had a sense of foreboding that we were being paid off to keep quiet. Then we would be discarded, put back into the shadows to run a hotel in Devon, well out of the way. I kept trying to convince myself that this was probably best for our future.

Going back to the flat was disconcerting yet strangely familiar. It reminded me of the turmoil I had encountered at Amy's cottage. The police had been extremely zealous in their search. Floorboards taken up, cupboards ripped off the walls. A team of workmen was laying new carpets and re-plastering some internal walls, including the back-bedroom, which I thought strange. Feeling battered and bruised, we needed a distraction. To take our mind off our ordeal, we decided to focus on The Limes. Now, my online searches were more about hotel interiors and not French history. Ella and I spent hours in the pub talking about plans to renovate the hotel. One afternoon, Sandra called to say she would meet up with us in a local pub.

"Here it is, Rob! The book! Your story!" She handed me a flash drive.

"This is the original. The book for the spooks isn't quite ready yet. Maybe another week or so? I think we have a best seller and I'm really proud to be a part of what you have both achieved."

"Let's drink to that!" We held up our glasses.

"A toast to us! What will you do now, Sandra?"

"She can help me choose a wedding dress!" Ella interrupted.

Both girls gave out a squeal, which made some of the pub-goers turn around and look. We ordered champagne to celebrate.

"Sandra, you know you can live in the flat?" offered Ella. Rob and I will be in Devon.

"Thanks, but it's a bit too posh an area for me. I'll think about it."

"On a more serious note, how about we pay you the agreed fee with a bonus?"

"Ok," said Sandra.

"Whatever you think best. I've got two new friends for life and that's how I want it to stay."

"You will be coming down to see us in Devon, won't you? There will be plenty of work for you to do!"

"Very tempting, I must say, but I am a big city girl. Just keep a room aired for me and I'll visit as often as I can. This hotel thing sounds cool. You two will be good at running the place." She touched her chest and patted it. "You know my heart is here. Changing the subject again. You guys fixed a date yet?"

"No. Penny wants us to get married asap, but we'll do it in our own time. Won't we, Rob?" Ella took my arm affectionately.

"Why do you think the marriage thing so important to the secret service?" asked Sandra.

"Christ knows! We guess it's part of the payoff which links us together and puts us in Devon. Well out of the way. It's the only thing we can think of.

"Well, its good news to hear. Anyway, how much is my bonus?" she asked, rubbing her hands together. I smiled.

"I'll go and get some more drinks. I'll let Ella tell you." I went off to the bar leaving the two girls to have a private chat.

"And the plan now?" asked Sandra.

"Rob's going down to The Limes tomorrow, to check it over and see what state it's in. I'm having a day shopping. Do you want to come with me?"

"Count me in. I never say no to retail therapy! So, you will be Ella Ashurst after you get married? How do you feel about that?"

"Confused! I'm still getting used to being Ella Gooch. What is a Gooch anyway? It sounds like a species of fish!" Sandra burst into fits of laughter

"What's so funny?"

"You really don't know what it means?"

"No! Why what is it?"

"It's slang for the area of a man's body between his balls and his bum hole." They both fell about sniggering.

My trip back to The Limes was constructive yet depressing. I felt melancholy at the thought about the work that needed to be done. I should not have come alone. The place looked woefully neglected and this was a time of year when, under normal circumstances, it would be buzzing, and I would be rushed off my feet. I knew the hotel so well, not only as my home but also as a place of work, for the last four years. Yet now I saw it through different eyes. I was the owner and here was a business that needed attention. It was like the 'Marie Celeste! The place hadn't been cleaned. The kitchens were filthy, pots and dishes left in the sink. Mould was growing on crockery left unwashed on one of the serving stations. The door to the store cupboard was open, but there were cobwebs everywhere and I could see mouse droppings on the shelves. I wandered into the bar and it was much the same, a thin layer of dust covered the bottles and glasses. Surprising, as I felt sure I had seen a cleaning company van arrive last time I was here.

I didn't care. I wrote in the dust, 'Can I be bothered?' It summed up my mood. I didn't want to see any more, so I left the hotel and walked into the village. My spirits lifted when I saw a familiar face walking towards me. It was George Webster, pushing who I discovered to be, his granddaughter in a buggy.

"Hello, George! Who is this?"

"You remember my daughter? Well, she had a little girl. This is Leah. How the devil are you, my boy? Last I heard you were a wanted man. Abduction, wasn't it?" I lowered my head.

"Yes. That was all a load of bollocks, as you well know George!"

"Thought so. All to do with that business at The Limes, wasn't it? I never really knew what was going on. As soon as the security services got involved, we were out of the picture."

"It was all some trap to catch some big-time villains!"

"So, you didn't really have terrorists staying then?"

"No, George. I was in the dark just like you. I didn't know very much at the time and now I don't want to."

"How's that girl of yours, the schoolteacher from down the coast. What was her name again? Amy?" I paused because I knew I had to say those awful words, but I couldn't tell him what really happened.

"She died." My news obviously shook him.

"What!!! Oh, my God! I am so sorry. I hadn't heard! Oh, Jesus, son! I know you were sweet on her." George was genuinely upset, and he was never a man to hide his feelings.

"How did it happen?"

"Car accident. She was on her way to see her parents."

"Life can be such a shit and you, my boy, have had your share of that just lately."

"I know, but on a brighter note, I have decided to look to the future. George, I've bought The Limes from Mulhenny." He was visibly surprised and pleased.

"That is good news! You will get far more local trade if you own the old place. They didn't take to the owner, him being foreign and aloof. They always liked you 'cos you involved yourself with the locals. Not like high and mighty Mulhenny. When are you opening again?"

"Not this summer. I'm going to do a total refurb and the roof needs some repair work as well." George nodded in agreement. The obvious question must have popped into his mind. He was a copper, after all.

"That will cost a packet, my boy. You come into some money?"

"That's my next piece of news. I've had an inheritance, George. Got some cash under my belt now. Hansen wants out, so he gave me a really good deal. He's agreed to stage payments on the property. I'll probably get a mortgage to help with cash flow, initially."

"I'm pleased for you. Everybody around here will be excited about the news!" George must have assumed the cash came from my father as he changed the subject.

"Didn't your Dad live in Africa or somewhere?" He scratched his head, trying to remember my family history. I just nodded as I didn't want to say too much, but I realized that the first thing on the mind of the natives would be where I got the funds. The two subjects that always fuelled local gossip was who was sleeping with who, or where did the money come from.

"I also have a backer, you know. A partner who wants to come in with me. Someone the bank recommended. A professional woman who's going to help me run it. Loads of experience in hotels."

They are a very conservative bunch in south Devon. I could see it all being the next tittle-tattle in the pubs, shops and hairdressers in the town. They wouldn't be too impressed if I got married within a month of my girlfriend's death, so I kept that to myself. On reflection, I was still uneasy about the marriage thing myself. Not about having a relationship with Ella but being pushed into matrimony. George was genuinely interested in my news and I knew that as the local policeman, he was the best person to spread the rumours. It was good to see him though, he made me feel welcome and our chance meeting made me believe this was the place where I belonged.

My trip back to London, however, didn't rid me of some uneasy feelings. I wondered if I had the business head to make this venture into a success. Working for someone else was quite different from being your own boss. Spending large amounts of money on The Limes was going to be a struggle, simply because I wasn't used to spending money on anything. It went against the grain for someone like me who had always lived on leftovers. I was joining the M4 at Bristol, mulling over all my insecurities when I got a call from the flat.

"Rob! Something unnerving going on. Sandra's here in a right state. She thinks someone's been in her flat. Scott has been drugged and is very poorly. He's with the vet. She's so upset and worried about him and she thinks she's being followed. I am not sure if our flat isn't being watched as well." Ella sounded quite freaked out.

"Ella! I'm about two hours away. Stay put and lock all the doors. Does she have the photocopies?"

"Yes, she's got them with her. Why?"

"I'll phone Penny and see if this has anything to do with the security services." I knew she would confirm or deny if they were involved. I explained to Penny what had happened.

"OK, Robin. Leave it with me. I'll check it out." I could tell she was just about to hang up. Then, an idea or flash of inspiration came to me.

"Penny, before you go. I've got something for you that you might be interested in?" She took the bait.

"What is it?"

"I went to The Limes today to check things out and I found some papers."

"What sort of papers?"

"Photocopies really, of old documents in a brown envelope. I don't know what they are. It's all in French."

"Impossible! We went through that place with a fine-tooth comb!" This was the crunch if she believed me or not. "Where were they?"

"In the safe, but I've never seen them there before."

"Who had keys to the safe?"

"Only me and Hansen. No-one else."

"So how did they get there?"

"I've no idea, Penny." I didn't want to spell it out too much. A good liar can mislead someone into absorbing information until they reach their own conclusion, which is precisely the subliminal one you are leading them to. At that point, a police car overtook me with blue lights flashing.

"Shit! Penny, I've got to go. I'm being pulled over by the police. They've seen me using my mobile phone."

"Robin! Wait! This is important!"

"So is this. I have a copper, I mean err… policeman tapping on my window."

"Let me speak to him. Pass him the phone!" I lowered the window and handed him the phone saying, "It's for you!" feeling quite ridiculous. He wasn't impressed but took the call. Whatever she said made him return to his car, radio in, then he came back to me a few minutes later.

"On your way, Sir." He handed my phone back. Penny had gone, but it still amazed me what power these people had. After about ten minutes, she rang back as I knew she would. I was pressed again about what I found in the safe. This time, I suggested that perhaps someone had put the papers there when Madame Aguirre had arrived. Nothing else was mentioned about the break-in at Sandra's, so I figured it was her people. I was under strict instructions to meet her at The Russell Hotel on my return to London and I was to call when I was thirty minutes away. Then I phoned Ella and told her to meet me outside the Bayswater tube station with an envelope containing the photocopies. If the flat were being watched, I couldn't risk going there first.

"The back window of my car will be open. When I stop at the traffic lights outside the station, throw the envelope onto the back seat. You got that?" It all went to plan except it was Sandra who did the drop-off.

I arrived at The Russell Hotel with the envelope, feeling anxious. I knew I would be under interrogation. Hansen was waiting for me and didn't waste any time.

"Robin! Let's sit down and talk about your story concerning some papers in the safe! You see, my men checked the office at the time and I can assure you that there were no papers in there!"

"Here's the envelope. All photocopies of old documents." Penny took it from me.

"They obviously got missed. I didn't know of their existence either. I've never seen anything like these before. The envelope was at the back of that little shelf under the cash box." His mouth twisted into a scorn. I was gambling on the fact that Hansen didn't know the layout of the office at The Limes, let alone the safe.

"Well, who the fuck put them in there?" It was unlike Hansen to swear in front of Penny.

"Not me! Why would I make up a story like that? I could have put them in a bin, but I've brought them to you. I found them this morning and I called Penny immediately!" Hansen stared at me, not quite believing what I was saying, but he couldn't prove I was lying or even think of a reason why I would. If my plan worked, it could take the heat off us. Ultimately, all they wanted to know was what Madam Aguirre had and this provided the evidence. Penny Carter opened the envelope and had a look.

"These copies look newly made!" She handed some of the papers to Hansen. It was an accusation, but I was on the offensive now.

"They would be, wouldn't they? If she came to The Limes to meet a buyer and wanted to prove that she had the 'goods,' surely she would have shown him copies first. It's insurance, isn't it" It all made sense, but did Hansen buy it? Before he had time to find a flaw in my story, I changed the subject.

"Anyway, what about this break-in? Sandra Pegg says her flat's been searched."

"Not by us," he replied coldly. He was more interested in the photocopies. That was confirmation that someone other than the Intelligence Service was watching us. Hansen let me go saying he would be in touch.

I returned to the flat and told the girls what had happened.

"Rob, you are so cunning! You should be in Intelligence."

"Funny you should say that Sandra. Hansen once told me the very same thing. I reckon I would be quite a good spy. I'm shrewd, cunning and I lie extremely well". I put on my best James Bond accent and grabbed Ella's waist. *"Will you come undercover with me, Miss Moneypenny?"*

"Yes, please, 007! Would you like something to eat first? There's a casserole in the oven."

Over supper, we talked about my meeting with Hansen.

"I reckon we will know within twenty-four hours if they've swallowed it. If they come to arrest me, then my plan didn't work."

"That's not very reassuring," Ella said. "Tell me something else. How you are going to get the rest of the stuff to them without letting on that you've lied all along."

"I'm still working on that one! Feel free to make suggestions."

Sandra disappeared to call the vet. We knew how worried she was about Scott.

"No change. Apparently, some form of toxic shock. No evidence of poison." We sat and watched a film together, but it was a half-hearted attempt to distract ourselves from our private thoughts and worries.

Chapter 20

We didn't have any visitors the next day or the one after that. Intelligence kept in touch with us about various minor things, but their calls were less frequent. We were nudged again about getting married. I still kept to the line that it was too soon after Amy. I knew that excuse wouldn't last forever. Scott never did pick up, so Sandra made the tough decision to have him put down. She moved in with us during this emotional time. I had never known anyone as close to a pet as Sandra was to Scott. Although Ella and I talked about getting her another dog, she made it clear she didn't want one until Scott was out of her system.

During the next few weeks, we started to feel that our nightmare or adventure; however, we saw it, was coming to an end. We turned our attention to the renovations of The Limes. We discussed ideas with various interior design companies. It was sort of exciting, but at the same time, I felt my heart wasn't totally in the project. I had money in the bank, but this was quite by accident, making me feel like a fraud. The bronze sold at Christie's for twelve thousand pounds. Money gave us time and options. I got the key to the lock-up back from Penny, so I made a concerted effort to go and sort out the rest of the stuff. I found other items to sell. Even Sandra got involved and set up an online shop, which provided a nice flow of work to keep her busy. The late spring had turned into summer with children now off school for the holidays. London during midsummer is a great place to be. With plenty of distractions, we tended to spend time enjoying sunny days in Hyde Park. We looked over our quotes, our books of samples, paint charts and colour swatches but there wasn't much being done. The problem was that we were all too comfortable. One morning, over our usual breakfast for three, Ella made an announcement.

"I think we should get married at the end of the month!" It took me by surprise as much as Sandra. The bedroom situation still being unresolved. Sandra had taken the once unusable back room and we still didn't share. I felt confused. Ella's sense of humour and her kind, easy-going nature were fantastic, but we seemed to be inexplicably thrown together by events, as well as by pressure from other external sources. Was that a good enough reason to spend the rest of our lives together? Did I love her? I wasn't sure.

All previous girlfriends, even Amy, had needed to fit around my work. With very unsociable hours in the hotel business, this meant they were generally not long-lasting affairs. Spending all day, every day in each other's company, was a new experience for me.

"That's great. Can I help with arrangements?" Sandra was delighted at the news. I deliberately changed the subject and ignored the comment entirely, which did not go unnoticed by either of them.

"Sandra, have you heard anything from Rowena?" I didn't want to discuss a wedding. I felt we had too many issues to sort out first. Ella gave me a black look and flounced off, to make it known that she was not impressed with my attitude. Sandra looked a bit uncomfortable for the first time.

"No. Gone to ground. No-one has heard from her since she left our house and her phone has been switched off." She paused and then added, "Everything ok with you two?"

"Not really no. Any advice?

"I think she's waiting for you to make the first move."

"That's not how I see it."

"Maybe you should try and see it differently then?" I changed the subject when she raised an eyebrow at me.

"I heard Intelligence was questioning Rowena, but surely she isn't still detained at Her Majesty's pleasure?"

Sandra shrugged her shoulders.

"No idea, Rob. I never liked the bossy cow, but I don't wish her any harm."

An internet search on Rowena Kerry produced little. Neither her web site, blog, or Twitter account had been updated in the last three months. I kept scrolling down the articles she had written. She had undoubtedly been a busy lady. Then something caught my eye. Her name came up on a listing from a law pages website but nothing more. Only her name, the time, and date of the proceedings, which appeared to be a closed session. I showed it to Sandra.

"This doesn't look good. Do you think she's in trouble?"

"No idea, but I'll check it out."

"Check what out? Ella walked back in the kitchen to see Sandra and me huddled over the laptop.

"We think Rowena is still being held!" Ella did not seem surprised.

"Do you remember when we were at the Saul's house and Rowena suddenly changed. Just sat around thinking and not contributing anything."

"Now you mention it, yes, you're right. She did seem frightened, but I thought it was about what happened to Amy. Maybe she was scared for herself?" Then I thought of something else.

"Don't you think it was odd that Penny gave us her name as a contact, yet Rowena had never heard of Penny. I wonder if they were trying to flush her out too?"

"You mean like giving her enough rope to hang herself? Well, she created all that uproar in the press, which started a diplomatic incident!" We considered the implications.

"Makes sense. What if they thought she was an insider working for the AF?"

"Or inadvertently being used by them?" Sandra added.

"Didn't like the lady, but never thought she was a spy."

"It does explain why intelligence was happy about the book and now they aren't. Come to think of it, that publisher bloke didn't know much either."

"I'll have a dig around. Contact some people I know." Sandra offered. Ella interrupted her.

"Why does it matter to us? Who cares what side she was on."

"Ella, that's a little heartless! It doesn't matter, but it would be nice to know. We have been dicked about so much. There must be a connection." Ella shrugged her shoulders. There was nothing more to say. We didn't know what or if anything had happened to Rowena or why. We turned our attention back to the subject of décor, colours and designs for The Limes. It seemed to be less controversial than discussing Rowena.

"I've just received a brochure from a hotel refurbishment company. I like the look of what they do. Rob, have you decided on the general theme yet?" Ella was trying to inspire some enthusiasm from me.

"I think we should go with classical."

"By classical, you mean old fashioned, old style and out of date!"

"No, not old fashioned, but I don't feel The Limes suits an ultra-modern minimalist scheme, like the one you want. It may go down well here in London but not in Devon! I think I know my own clientele!"

"Can I say something?" Sandra attempted to defuse the situation before it got too heated.

"Look, I don't know much about hotels in Devon, but if we all had a weekend away, then I could give an opinion. I promise to give an impartial view!" This was a very acceptable solution.

"This weekend?" Ella asked. Sandra and I nodded in agreement.

Ella was determined to get her way on some of the decisions still to be made and tried to get Sandra on her side.

"Sandra, what do you think of Rob's idea to change the name of the hotel to The Amy?" Sandra looked over to me and apologised in advance for giving her honest opinion and taking sides with Ella.

"I think it's a bad idea, Rob. I don't mean any disrespect to Amy, but how can you move on if you answer the phone every day with 'Good morning! 'The Amy Hotel!' Even the sign outside will always remind you. Find another way to make some tribute to Amy, but please, leave the name as The Limes." I knew she was right. I valued her opinion and thought for a moment before agreeing.

"Ok, ladies. I'm outvoted. The name stays!" I took it upon myself to book accommodation at The Regent, the local hotel in the next town without telling the girls. I saw it as an opportunity to resolve the bedroom issues. If I only booked two rooms, Ella would either want to share it with Sandra or me.

Our weekend away coincided with some event in the Bristol area. Traffic was heavy and we didn't arrive at our destination until around five. Ella was surprised as we pulled up in the car park.

"I thought we were staying at The Limes?"

"This will be more comfortable. There's no food at The Limes or any rooms made up."

"Looks nice!" remarked Sandra.

"Sandra! Clearly, you have not been away with Mr. Hotel Inspector here. He will go on and on about the cleanliness, the quality and the level of service!"

"If you're going to be a 'sprout' about it, then I will take you to The Limes and you can sleep in a dirty room!" We both exchanged a smile and we went to check-in. I was recognised by the manager Tom, an old friend, who came over to speak to us.

"Rob, mate! I thought it was you! Heard it on the grapevine that you bought The Limes. How the hell can that be true?" My gossip channel via Sargent Webster was working better than I'd hoped. I left the girls to go and check in while I told Tom all my news and gave him an outline of our plans. We chatted a while then I suggested we met up later in the bar for a drink. I had another idea, as Tom would be an ideal manager if we could make The

Limes earn enough. I ran swiftly up the stairs to the second floor. The next few minutes were going to be defining moments in my relationship with Ella. She was waiting alone outside one of the bedrooms.

"Rob! Why are there only two rooms?"

That's all I booked!" I opened the door and grabbed her arm so that we could go in together.

"And it's a king-size bed!"

"I want to talk about this marriage thing and get some practice in!! Where better than a nice sexy hotel bedroom?" She looked at me with those big doe eyes of hers.

"Why didn't you say? I can't do anything this weekend." I was deflated and a little confused.

"Let's see what happens. One step at a time." She came over to me and planted a big lingering kiss on my lips.

"No. You don't understand. It's exactly five months since that fateful night when we walked around the headland to escape!" It took a while for the penny to drop, but when it did, we embraced and kissed again. Ella got changed in the bathroom, but I walked about naked to show her it didn't matter.

We took Sandra to show her The Limes in the glowing, evening summer sun and then again in the morning. Every time I went back to my old hotel, I felt more motivated to undertake the renovations and make a go of the business.

Sandra was genuinely impressed with the old-style grandeur of the building and captivated by its cliff-top position overlooking the bay. She immediately understood why this hotel was such an important part of my life. Her enthusiasm to discuss ideas was infectious. We were finally coming up with a vision that we all agreed on.

That evening over dinner, Sandra got a text from someone who said Rowena had been charged with an espionage offence. There was something not right going on, but I couldn't put my finger on it until I was in bed that night. I suddenly woke up in a cold sweat. Rowena was still in custody, but worse than that, she must have known that I lied to the spooks about where the trunks were.

"Ella, Ella, wake up!" I switched the bedside light on. Ella stirred from a deep sleep.

"Jesus, Rob! What is it?"

"I've just had a thought! Rowena knew our secret about the trunks!"

"Did she? How? Did you tell her? You didn't tell Dave or the security guards. If she did know, she couldn't have said anything; otherwise, you would have been arrested by now. Go back to sleep and we will talk about it in the morning." I couldn't switch off. I lay there, feeling anxious. My mind was racing.

Over breakfast, we discussed it again with Sandra.

"Are you absolutely positive that you told her you had the trunks, Rob?"

"I don't know. I've told so many lies now. I can't remember who I have told the truth to!"

Both Sandra and Ella felt that it was unlikely that Rowena knew for sure, even if she had suspected. It made me feel easier.

To take my mind off all this hypothetical supposition, we returned to The Limes and sketched out some plans of the ground floor. We liked the idea of adding a conservatory to the dining room, where guests could have a coffee overlooking the garden and taking in the views of the harbour. We enjoyed discussing our schemes over a fresh fish supper and my terrors of the night before had departed. That evening Ella initiated some petting in bed, so I was happy with our conjugal progress, albeit unfinished. After breakfast the next morning, I left the girls together and went to check over Amy's old house in response to a request from Karl. It had not sold and he felt it needed to be checked out.

Turning up at the railway cottage again was strange. It felt like my life from another era. So much had happened in such a short time. I discovered a broken window in a small panel of glass in the back door. The broken debris was on the inside, but the door was still locked. I put it down to kids. I called Dean, my fisherman friend. I knew his brother was an odd job man. Quite predictably, Dean knew all about my plans for The Limes and wanted to know when I was back. He would get his brother to sort out the window tidy up the garden. I called Karl and explained everything and what I had done. He thanked me and asked me to meet up with him as soon as I got back to London. It sounded urgent, but he wouldn't say why. We arranged a rendezvous at a pub.

The following evening, I arrived at the pub a little early. It was a brewery chain, where all the food arrives in a lorry and gets plated up in the kitchens. Not a usual hangout for a hotel man like myself, but I ordered a pint of Guinness. Karl came in five minutes later and joined me at the bar.

He looked flustered. It was evident that Karl wasn't interested in any chit chat or pleasantries.

"What's up, mate?"

"Two things, Rob and I don't know who to talk to." His anxiety unnerved me, but I was keen to assist.

"Fire away. I'll help if I can."

"It's my mother. She's starting to give up on life. Mum can't seem to get over the loss of Amy. Dad's getting worse so quickly. Thankfully, he doesn't understand what's happening, but she's been talking about ending it all for both of them. Would you speak to her?"

"Oh, my God! That's terrible! Of course, I will try, but I don't know her. I've only ever met your folks at the funeral. Maybe it's a doctor she needs. To give her something for depression?"

"Look, I'm not trying to put you in an awkward situation, Rob, but there's so much we don't know. Maybe you can come up with some answers? You were together during the weeks before she died."

I felt extremely uncomfortable. The family needed closure, but how much could I tell him? I was trying to think of an explanation as Karl carried on talking.

"You see, Amy believe it or not, was a rebel. My folks were on the old-fashioned side. Dad was a control freak, so mother did as she was told. But it was their middle-class values of morality and respectability, which Amy hated. Dad wanted to dominate her, so it put a distance between them to the point where they didn't know her. Their view of Amy was that she was only interested in sex and drugs and being a party girl." I couldn't believe what I was hearing and protested vehemently.

"Amy? Sex and drugs? No way, Karl. How could they think that? That's certainly not the Amy I knew! She was a very respectable schoolteacher. She did everything properly and with decorum. It was four dates until I got a kiss, then a month before she would let me stay the night." Now it was his turn to look incredulous.

"Jesus Christ! Really! After she left college, they never visited her in Devon. Dad felt she was lost to them. Amy and I have never been close, so I didn't have very much to do with her either."

I took in everything Karl was saying while trying to remember anything that Amy had told me about her upbringing, which was very little. I couldn't think of one single thing.

"I always thought she didn't want me to meet her parents because I wasn't good enough!" Karl smiled and shook his head.

"You couldn't be more wrong! It was because they never knew about you. It wasn't Amy's fault that dad was a bastard, but since his illness, things have changed. It's only now that my mum's views are coming to the fore. I found out that she wanted to make peace with Amy." Karl's voice faltered with emotion.

"Mum was going to get in touch with her, to talk. You know, try to reconcile their differences. But before she did, we heard the news. Amy was dead. If you can do anything to help? Tell her about the Amy you knew. It might help ease her pain."

"God, yes! I'll do anything!" I fiddled with the flash drive in my pocket.

"Rob, Tell me something? Do you know what she was doing in Taunton?" I gulped.

"She was on her way to see your mum and dad." Karl's expression was full of pain.

"What? Oh, shit!" Neither of us spoke for a moment as we both tried to take in this new information about Amy.

"Can I ask another question? Why was she with this other bloke in the car if you were her boyfriend? That detective woman, Mrs. Carter, never really told us much at all." It was clear he had no idea about Penny Carter's real rank.

"It's not what you think. They just happened to share a lift. I can't say any more than that." The look on his face made me realise he deserved to know more.

"Karl, this is awkward for me and might sound far-fetched, but I have to take advice about what I can and can't say." Karl looked confused.

"Advice? From who, Rob? I don't understand. What sort of stuff was Amy mixed up in? Was it something illegal?" I could see his mind imagining the worst kind of activity that his sister could have been up too. I had to give him the truth.

"No, not exactly illegal. But she and I were involved in something which was not instigated by us, in any way. We were both innocent bystanders. You must believe that!" In a moment's madness, I took the flash drive out of my pocket and showed it to him.

"Read this but do not, I repeat, do not copy it or save it." Karl looked at me bewildered, as I passed him the flash drive.

"I want it back when you've looked at it. It contains a manuscript which I have written. It explains everything. From a fateful spring night four months ago. Certain people, who I am not in a position to argue with, have expressed a wish that I do not make this common knowledge." Now he looked even more baffled.

"When you read it, you will understand. That's all I can say."

"My God. It sounds heavy!"

"It is and it's all true. Have no doubt in your mind, however unbelievable it may seem, that any of it is fiction." At that point, we both ordered a double whisky from the bar.

"What was the second issue you wanted to discuss with me, Karl?"

"Sorry, Rob. I can't remember now. I'm so intrigued to read this." I did, however, warn him that there were some unpleasant bits concerning Amy, which I asked him not to mention to his mother.

"OK, I promise." As he sipped on his drink, he recalled the other thing he wanted to tell me.

"Oh, yes. I know what it was. A guy was asking about Amy last week, a reporter chap. I said you were more in the picture, so I told him that I would talk to you first before I gave him your number."

"Thank fuck! What was his name?"

"Hollis!"

"Karl! When you read the book, you will understand why I can't speak to anyone." He didn't press me anymore for information, so we chatted about my plans for The Limes. When I left the pub, I had a such a sense of foreboding about what I had just done. I caught the train back into town and then the tube to Hyde Park, so I had time to reflect.

I opened the door to the living room to see Ella and Sandra sitting together watching TV, which provided a sense of normality after my emotionally heavy evening with Karl. They were keen to know about what Amy's brother had wanted. I briefly outlined the concerns he had for his mother's state of health and that he mentioned a reporter called Hollis poking about. I certainly didn't tell them I had given him the flash drive. On a much lighter note, Ella wanted to talk about the sleeping arrangements.

"Look, I have been thinking. Your bedroom is such a stinky bloke pit, while mine is a girly paradise. How about if I make some space and sort stuff out tomorrow, you move in with me?"

"That's nice. Great!" I quickly shot a look at Sandra in appreciation. I knew she had been speaking to her about moving our relationship on.

The next day Ella barged into my room fairly early. She started by measuring the bed and then making notes about the furniture.

"I hope you don't have any plans for today. I'd like you to move some stuff. Can you start with that picture?" she remarked, pointing to the one above my bed. I can't say I had taken much interest in it, except that it had a pig standing upright on its back legs in one corner and some kind of boat in the sky.

"I'm at your disposal, my love. Be gentle with me!" She raised an eyebrow as she opened the curtains. I got out of bed. She took my nakedness for granted now and seemed much more at ease with it. I knew she liked what she saw. I put on a pair of tracksuit bottoms and went to make a coffee. My phone rang and it was Karl. He sounded agitated.

"Are you busy, mate? Can we meet up this morning?" I wondered what had happened to prompt this sense of urgency. We agreed on a rendezvous at the Westfield Centre in Shepherds Bush.

"Starbucks, the one on the ground floor. Say in an hour?" I put down my mug of freshly made coffee.

"An hour? Sure. What's happened?"

"I've been up all night reading your book. We need to talk."

"OK! See you in an hour then?" I felt slightly unnerved by this request for some emergency meet-up, but it did provide me with an excuse to go out and miss the furniture relocation exercise. I went into the bedroom where Ella was emptying some drawers onto the bed. I quickly changed into jeans and a sweatshirt and grabbed my wallet. She stared at me.

"Where are you going?"

"Sorry, Ella. Something has come up."

"But you said that we were……" I blew her a kiss as I left the bedroom.

I took the tube as I didn't want the hassle of parking, but still managed to get there some twenty minutes early. To my surprise, Karl had already arrived, as I spotted him in the queue. He looked around and smiled when he saw me. I gestured across the room to him to get me a coffee. He was already talking quickly as he put down the tray of cups.

"I have to say that I've been blown away by this. It's incredulous! Firstly, by the story and secondly, the stuff about Amy. Once I started reading, I couldn't stop. I've been up all night. I'm supposed to be at work now, but I've called in sick." He was rattling on ten to the dozen.

"So now, do you understand? Official Secrets Act and all that shit?"

"Yes, I do. But Jesus, this story must be told, for all kinds of reasons. For Amy, for the truth! It goes up to the point when you got The Limes. What happened after that?"

"They have paid for our silence. We were warned off, not physically, but intimidated. These guys are serious!"

"I get that. It says so in the book. You have to publish this."

"Not that easy. It's the 'how to publish without committing treason,' that we are working on Karl!"

"You'll find a way then?" Karl was getting animated. He looked around Starbucks to see if anyone was watching us.

"I can't believe that you and my sister got mixed up in all this secret service, spy stuff by accident. Have you got to grips with what it's all about?"

"Karl, I don't think we'll ever know the whole story, but with all the information and research I've done, it leads me to only one conclusion."

"What?"

"If I tell you my theory, it goes no further than this coffee shop?"

"Yes, of course!" I hesitated and moved closer to him so that no-one could eavesdrop.

"The French intelligence agency has been getting up to some unsavoury clandestine things. Political murders, shit like that, bankrupting some business leaders who they didn't like. Supposedly, France is a civilised country, above all these things, so this was all done under the name of Action Française. The AF, historically, was a group wanting to restore the French monarchy. My theory is that the AF died out between the two world wars, maybe 1930's. It was replaced by a new, more modern AF, based in the UK and operating out of London. British intelligence has had enough. Wants to get rid of them but is in a potentially difficult situation, diplomatically speaking. They can't just go and arrest them, can they? To do so, out in the open would cause a political storm."

Karl was listening intently to my hypothesis.

"Madame Aguirre and her family were a target for the original AF. She had conflicting evidence about the French line of succession. There was a rumour that she had a lot of treasure, which, over the decades, she had been slowly selling off. That made the old lady a target for international criminals as well. I am convinced it was those bastards who raped Antonella and maybe killed her parents. MI6 tried to spring a trap to rid the UK of what they thought of as rogue French intelligence personal, but it went wrong as the old bird died at very much the wrong time."

"Bloody hell! What a story!"

"Problem is. I've not one shred of evidence for any of this."

"Who's behind it all then? The French Government?"

"Most likely, they knew nothing. I think it was like I say, 'rogue elements' within the French intelligence community who believed they could dictate events, for their own purposes. Who knows why, but that's not the issue. When the political storm blew up, the French had to look internally at themselves, and heads have rolled. How could France admit to the world that things like this had been going on in a democracy such as theirs. They had to get the British to cover it all up. Four people died, all because of mistaken identity. A very unlucky solicitor in Devon was killed by criminals, likewise the Swiss lawyer. Amy and her bodyguard were ambushed by French intelligence, operating as the AF. They thought it was Antonella and me and believed we had all her grandmother's documents. They were seriously scared that these documents would expose their true identities so that they couldn't take that risk. What they didn't know was that it was all bollocks. It was a lie spread by MI6 as part of the initial trap! The fucking irony, of course, is that it wasn't Antonella and me in the car that night." He lowered his eyes and I could see the pain he felt, remembering his sister's death.

"Do you know anything about the others who were murdered?" Karl asked.

"I knew nothing about Davis and we never got to meet the Swiss lawyer, but I did know the bodyguard. He was a nice guy. He was a diplomatic protection officer who fell in the line of duty, which is all his family will know and need to know." Karl went quiet and then said, "I'm struggling to take all this in, mate! Can you tell me something about this girl who took my sister's identity? Are you married yet?"

"No!" I reassured him. "We live in the same flat. I really don't know why our marriage is part of the deal. It can only be because they want us tied together in some way. But can I assure you that I was in love with your sister and as such, marriage for me is far too soon. In time I guess we will. I like her very much, Karl. That's all I can say. I'll invite you to the wedding when it happens." He didn't seem convinced, but he respectfully changed the subject.

"And this Rowena woman? Who was she, then?" he asked.

"Ms. Kerry was certainly not who we thought she was. Personally, I think the lady was in the employ of French intelligence/ AKA the AF to stir things up."

"As a story, it is a fantastic read! If you can't say it's true, can you call it fiction? Can't you write some more chapters up until what you have just told me?" I finished off my macchiato and considered options.

"Karl, I really don't know where we stand with it, to be honest. What do I know about getting a book published? I'm hardly JK Rowling! I'm an unknown author who is not a celebrity. I've got no chance." I explained that we had looked into self- publishing as an option.

"I might be able to help with that. My other half works as a publisher's agent. Did you ever meet Bridget? Do I have your permission to show the book to her?" I hesitated. This whole meeting had gone in a completely different direction to what I had intended.

"OK." I heard myself agreeing to this.

"Rob! I want to ask you a favour, though. Is there any chance we can print some bits of this which we can give to my mother? There's quite a lot in the story, which is about Amy. It will give back my mum, the daughter she always wanted." Yet, again. I agreed. On my way home, I was beginning to regret some of the decisions I had made. I started to feel that I should have consulted the girls.

Chapter 21

A few days passed and I was in a reflective mood. We were both sleeping in my room. I couldn't say anything after all the trouble Ella had gone to make it nice. She was starting to walk around our bedroom in her underwear. I didn't rush her. I understood that Ella had a complex body image issue and I knew she was trying to overcome her insecurities. As a bloke, I found her very physically attractive. She had a sexy body, and I always got aroused when I watched her get undressed. I ached to pin her down on the bed and make love, but then I would think of Amy and felt disloyal.

The girls picked up on my maudlin mood. Over a spicy supper of chili con carni washed down with a bottle or two of red wine, they both prised out of me the reason why. It was quite a relief to come clean about my meeting with Karl and his idea of publishing the story as a fictional one. They listened intently. Ella spoke first.

"What about the spooks? I don't fancy twenty years inside." Ella turned to Sandra.

"What are your thoughts?"

"I am with Rob and Karl on this one. I want to publish the book as it is by far the best story I have ever worked on, or ever will. It is also the composition I feel proudest of. I believe the story must be told. Ella, you've not read it, have you?"

"I don't need to. I know what happens, don't I?"

"Ella, please read it." We were both looked at her intently.

"Just get the stupid thing published!" I couldn't understand her stroppy attitude, so I held my ground.

"Not before you have read it!"

"For God's sake, why?" She was refusing, so I paused to choose my words carefully,

"If you just go along with the majority, you will not get the benefits."

"Benefits? What are you on about? You get to have a memorial for your dead girlfriend. Sandra gets her name in lights as the writer. Exactly, what benefits I get?" Her voice was agitated. I couldn't understand her reluctance, but Sandra stepped in to argue the case.

"Ella, yours are far greater. You will escape from the trauma that haunts your life, an unhappy childhood living under fear, the ghosts of your murdered parents and the horror of your brutal rape!" Ella felt the full force of suppressed emotion awakening in her body, touching every nerve. She looked at us, tearfully. Sandra and I couldn't push her anymore. She was at breaking point. We comforted her with a group hug.

Surprisingly, that evening, Ella started reading the book.

"I didn't realise you are an only child, Rob! That figures!" I looked up from my laptop.

"Meaning what exactly?"

"They can often be very self-centred."

"So are you. An only child, I mean."

"Different circumstances. I was brought up by my grandmother, so it doesn't count."

"I fail to see why. If you don't have any brothers or sisters, you are an only child!"

We kept having this sort of interruption every time she learned something new about me, but after two days, she said, "OK. You've convinced me," just as a call came in from Karl.

"Rob! Any chance you can go and see mother anytime soon. She's getting worse."

"I'll visit first thing, but I am no therapist, so it is going to be a long shot. Have you got professional people involved or Social Services?"

"Yes. They've sorted out respite care and placed dad in a home for a month. Listen, the other thing I wanted to tell you is that Bridget can place the book. She's read some of it and thought it was very commercial. Bridge' wants to meet with you and a publisher, but she needs the full script." This was indeed excellent news.

"We have added to it, but we could do with another couple of weeks to get it finalised." Karl felt that would be ok.

"If I go to see your mother tomorrow morning, will you be there?"

"No. Try going alone." I wasn't sure why he wanted me to go on my own, but the way he had described his mothers' state of mind, I certainly wasn't looking forward to the task. I drove over to her house the next morning.

"Mrs. Gooch?"

"Robin, I didn't expect you so early. Surely you have not come all the way from Devon?"

"I have a flat in London now. I am glad Karl told you that I was coming. He's worried about you." She was more lucid than Karl led me to believe.

"Would you like some tea?"

"Yes, that would be nice." She ushered me into a neat and well-ordered lounge, less fussy than I had expected for a lady of her generation. Mrs. Gooch ambled off to make a pot. I wondered if she was as uneasy about this meeting as I was. What was more disconcerting was the fact that the room had become a shrine to Amy, which somewhat pulled at my emotions. Little evidence of Karl, which I found strange, but then wondered if this wasn't always the case with Mr. Gooch's ongoing dementia. Karl said his mother was trying to get Amy back in her life when she died, but this was somewhat ghoulish. The funeral had given me an element of closure. Since then, being so occupied with my own problems, I had little time to brood. Amy's mother returned carrying a tray with china cups and saucers, a big teapot and some slices of a homemade lemon cake. Mrs. Gooch was not a' teabag dunked in a mug kind of a lady.' I felt uncomfortable and didn't know how to approach things.

"I.. err.. have a book. Well, I mean that I've written a book and thought you might like to read it." I could see so much of Amy in the lady. It was such a shame that we had not met in happier times. Mrs. Gooch did not even look up as she poured out the tea using a tea strainer.

"I'm afraid I do not read books anymore. I find I do not have the concentration." She handed me a cup and proceeded to add a teaspoon of sugar. I gestured her to stop after two. I tried again to engage with her.

"You see, Mrs. Gooch. I started to write this book while I was working at my hotel in Devon when strange things started happening. It was just a diary at first, but now I have finished it and I want to get it published. There is quite a lot in it about your daughter. It covers the last two months of her life, so I didn't want to publish something without you reading it first. Or, I won't go ahead if you are expressly against the idea." She sat and listened but remained quiet.

"Anyway, it's about our lives together, our plans and things about that fateful night. It might help to understand why she died."

"I see." She didn't say anything more for a few moments. She crossed her hands and rubbed them. I tried again. "Would you like to see the book?" I took it out of my bag. It was a printed off copy on A4 paper, which I handed to her.

"It might not be the final copy as it is still work in progress."

Mrs. Gooch didn't take it from me, so I put it down on the walnut coffee table.

"Would you like some more tea?" She picked up the teapot. I was determined that I would have one more attempt before giving this up.

"No, thank you. I loved your daughter, Mrs. Gooch. We were going to get married!"

"You were? That surprises me!"

"Can I read you some parts of the book?"

"No. You say it is about the last few weeks of my daughter's life?"

"Yes. I can only tell you that we accidentally got mixed up in something dangerous and sinister. It cost Amy her life and I will regret it forever."

We made small talk, mainly about Devon and her family. She opened up a little with me. It was clear that she had so many regrets of her own, which the poor woman needed to come to terms with as well as the death of her daughter.

"Robin, I was never allowed to bring up my children as I wanted. My husband was very controlling. I should have left him and nearly did many times, but people of my generation didn't do that. So much time has been lost now. It's impossible to put right any mistakes. All too late." She wiped away a tear from her eye.

"Maybe not with Amy but you still have Karl and his wife?" She turned and looked at me.

"You are very kind, Robin to say that, but I'm not sure he wants it."

"On the contrary, Mrs. Gooch, your son, wants nothing more than a close relationship."

"Do you think so?" I nodded and went over to her to take her hand in reassurance. "Please come again and.. call me Grace."

I wasn't sure if she would ever read the book, but Mrs. Gooch told me that she had enjoyed our chat. She was delicate, fragile, grieving for the loss of Amy and intimacy with her son, which she never had but needed now. She certainly wasn't the lady on the brink of suicide as I thought she might have been.

Back at the flat, I couldn't shake off a feeling of sluggishness. We had decided to put The Limes into the hands of a professional renovation company. After presenting us with various options on style, colours, furniture, kitchen and bar equipment, they agreed to project-manage the entire refurb, liaise with suppliers and tradespeople from start to finish. Their fee was high but not excessive, so it seemed a perfect solution. 'Top Notch' was a bit of a crass name for an interior design company, but Jason, our dedicated project manager and his team, were undoubtedly coming up with some innovative designs and ideas which we liked. Ella was more interested in plans for the new kitchen. She had read the book but had made no further comments. According to Sandra, she was now re-reading it, with an eye to the detail and had picked out many points to go through with me. Sandra was working on the ending but couldn't get on if I didn't give her a basic plan to work from. As I had no concept of a basic plan, we held off until we met up with Bridget's publisher.

The days passed, my focus was straying from the work in hand. Ella's frustration with my indolence was starting to show.

"You rescuing anyone else from the brink of suicide this week, Rob?" Her sarcasm was mildly irritating. She wafted some papers at me.

"Top Notch want decisions and I have a list of things from the book, which are actually, factually wrong!" She announced rather petulantly. "I am not your secretary! I thought we were making all these decisions together, but you seem pre-occupied, Rob." She was right. I had been speaking to Karl about another visit to see Grace.

"I know, sorry. I owe it to Amy." Wearily, I turned my attention to other matters. "OK. What's first?"

Sandra and Ella started talking at the same time. I covered my ears with my hands. "One at a time!" Sandra jumped in first.

"Rob? If you can go through Ella's points, then I can start re-working them." Then Ella.

"I want you to look at these plans for the restaurant layout and tell me the one you like best."

"Ladies!! I can only do one thing at a time!" Both of them threw cushions at me. As each day came to an end, our combined efforts were paying dividends. We felt we had achieved something, however small, towards our objectives. Endless decisions were made, from kitchen appliances to the wallpaper in the 'snug' or the tiles in the bathrooms. We were making progress.

Finally, I finished the last chapter with Sandra, and for the first time, it went into the future, as I had taken the story up to the book launch. Ella had been to see Jason at Top Notch to discuss the figures. She returned, pleased with her efforts.

"OK, Rob, take a deep breath!" she remarked, waving a blue leather-bound file at me. "The final cost of the refurb is £168,000! Do you want to see the breakdown?"

"Do I need to? I guess you've been through it all with Jason?"

"Their finance department prepared the costings, which Jason explained to me. Complete re-decoration of the guest bedrooms, new bathrooms, fittings, furniture. Also, the owner's suite." She was pulling out pieces of paper from the file.

"Re-styled kitchen with all new appliances to a state of the art specification. Two new walk-in fridges and installation of an air-con and air purification unit. Something to take away bad smells, apparently?" I smiled. She continued, "Restaurant, lobby and lounge all redecorated with new furniture and carpets. Re-fit of the bar and area re-worked to include a cocktail bar. Some work needed on the roof and a complete external paint job, which will include the iron balustrades." She glanced up to see my reaction.

"Do we need a cocktail bar? This Devon not London. Ella. If we are too flash, it will put off the locals." She looked like she wanted to argue the point.

"Just an observation. I did run the hotel before!" I changed direction quickly. What's the time scale for all of this?" I asked. Ella looked at the file again.

"Six months maximum. Ok. I will tell them to cut the cocktail bar. They wanted three stage payments with a third upfront, a third after three months and the balance on hand over." I nodded, mulling over the terms.

"You will be pleased to know that I negotiated £165,000 as per the schedule and capped at that figure. Nothing over that unless we add any extras as we go along!"

"Did Jason agree?"

"Yes! He'll have the contract drawn up this week! Rob, I know it's a lot of money, but Top Notch's fee was 20% cheaper than the two other companies' I've been talking to."

"You've done an excellent job, Ella! Quite the businesswoman!" She smiled at me and blew a kiss. Not for the first time, did I see a side to her that had previously remained concealed. How could I ever have thought of her as dim and naïve?

Karl's wife, Bridget, was true to her word and arranged a meeting with a publisher called Hudsons. The office was on the sixth floor of a modern block. Theirs was not the only company based in this massive building, so actually finding the correct entrance was not easy. The sign outside was no bigger than a postcard, which made me feel they discouraged visitors. Inside was simple and open plan, but there was a used feel about the place. It consisted of two rows of desks and two rows of office staff sitting intently looking at computer screens. We were shown into a rather stark boardroom with high windows and half-drawn black blinds. There were many framed signed book covers on the walls, a tribute to their success as publishers, I guess. Hudson's had been given the finished script the week before, so I hoped that we could make an impression on them to publish our story.

The two principal inquisitors, a tall, middle-aged man in a grey suit whose name I didn't catch and his younger sidekick Pete. It was the younger man who did all the speaking. To help us, we had Bridget and Sandra. Bridget took the lead in introducing the book. I came in with occasional points. Ella said nothing. Then there were questions, fired off like a round of bullets and quite intimidating. The grilling stopped for a short coffee break. We were shown into what they referred to as a canteen, but in reality, it was a room with a coffee maker and a vending machine for snacks. After the interlude, we all gathered again in the same boardroom. The interrogation resumed. Ella only spoke when she was asked a direct question. By mid-day, I was feeling the exhaustion of being mentally stripped bare. Mr grey suit reached his conclusion. He put his hands together as if in prayer and waited several moments before he spoke.

"Very well. I think we have heard enough. I must tell you that our first consideration is whether the book is commercially viable. We turn down work from some extremely talented authors merely because of the marketability of the subject. However, if we thought the book did not have some potential, you would not be sitting around this table. So, it comes down to the author and as you are an unknown writer, it will take a lot of work and effort to promote you. How much time do you have? I understand you are currently working on a hotel project, are you not?" He looked me squarely in the eyes. I tried to impress him with my sense of purpose and commitment.

"That's right. We are about to sign the contract for a complete refurbishment and the time scale for the work is six months. I suppose realistically, we are aiming to re-open The Limes eight months from now. Ella will be working with the project manager, not me, so I have six to eight months in which to give one hundred percent to the book." The man showed no facial expression.

"Mr. Ashurst. Is this a one-hit wonder, or are you looking to become a published writer?" I didn't know how to answer this. I felt that the truth might be more convincing.

"I want our story to be read, as simple as that. As for the future, who knows!" Again, he gave nothing away. He just stared at me.

"I have to tell you there will be much promotional work. Radio interviews, book signings. How do you feel about public speaking?" Ella jumped in for the first time,

"What! Mr. Bullshit here could sell Eskimo's to the fridges!" I don't think she meant to get the words the wrong way around, but everyone laughed, which broke the tense atmosphere somewhat. I think it got the point across far better than I could have done. We shook hands and left. It was such a relief to get some air.

"God! I need a drink after that! How do you think it went?"

"Rob, what made you say that bit about just wanting to be read?"

"Christ knows, Ella. What else could I say? Anyway, I've never known you to be so quiet," Bridget interrupted us.

"Rob, Ella! I must go. The fact that it went on so long is an excellent sign. By the way, Karl messaged me while we were in the meeting. He says to tell you that Grace wants to see you."

"Thanks, I'll pop round."

"Thanks for everything, Bridget," Ella said.

Bridget gave us a peck on the cheek and walked away to her car. Ella watched her.

"She's pregnant!" remarked Ella, when she was out of earshot, then after a pause added "Lucky cow!"

"How on earth do you know that?"

"From the way she walks! It's obvious."

Yet another of Ella's contradictions surfaced. There had been a backward step in the bedroom. No longer did she walk about in just bra and knickers. She preferred to get dressed and undressed in the bathroom. No cuddles in bed either, even though we were sharing a room. She gave no affection anymore and I had no idea why. I decided we should have a romantic weekend away together alone, to work on the physical side of our relationship.

After our third-degree interrogation at Hudson's, we were all mentally exhausted. We returned to the flat with a takeaway curry and lounged around watching the telly. The following day was the same. We discussed it over and over, but it all hinged on the publishers. I felt we had done our best and we were now in the hands of fate. I popped around to see Grace and received a warm welcome. A ritual pot of tea and slice of cake before she started to discuss anything.

"Robin. I have to say that I couldn't see the point of leaving me your book, but as I started to read, I got engrossed. The bits about Amy. Are they all true? It would be cruel to deceive me."

"Yes, Grace. Every word is true. What she said to me or what we did."

"It's too late for Gordon, but now I know her true feelings for us. You don't know how much comfort that gives me."

"Grace, I always got the impression that she had a problem with the relationship she had with her dad rather than you.

Amy always spoke of you with affection. Please believe that." Grace looked pensive and sad.

"My husband was a fool. He could never see the wood for the trees. In some way, she was very like him. That's what caused their personality clash."

"You have a fine son and a lovely daughter in law. You never know, but I think they're going to need your help sooner rather than later." She was clearly puzzled by my remark. I decided to retract my comment a little, wondering why on earth I had even mentioned that Bridget might be pregnant. The only evidence for this was Ella's assessment of how she was walking. I made my excuses and left. A text came in from Sandra, which read 'get back here asap.'

I heard the whopping and whistling as I entered the apartment.

"It's a YES!"

"Oh my God!" were the only coherent words I could come up with. I was weak at the knees. I wanted to know the details, but I couldn't comprehend what was going on.

"We have a meeting tomorrow and we are going to be introduced to our account manager who will take us through the process!" Sandra was so excited. Ella stood on the sofa in her pyjamas, her hands were over her cheeks. No-one remembered to ask about Grace, but I felt proud that all our efforts with the book had benefited someone.

Over the next few days, there were many meetings with Hudsons and endless discussions about amendments, layout, cover designs, number of copies, marketing. It was easier to go with the flow, nod in agreement now and then. I let Sandra deal with most of it except the launch. I was focusing my full attention on that.

"Can anyone come?" I asked.

"No. It's invitation only, but we invite the usual sprinkling of literary figures, book buyers, reviewers. Why do you ask?"

"Will you invite anyone from the national press?"

"No."

"I want you to invite them. I have a surprise."

"What surprise would that be?" Charles had been assigned to us as our development editor. I hadn't taken to the fellow, but Sandra got on well with him. The problem was that we came from different worlds. Charles was an academic, a bookworm, an English literature graduate from Manchester University, whereas I had no qualifications, just life experiences as a hotel worker. He also had an annoying habit of saying, *'what do you mean exactly?'* but only to me as if he found it difficult to understand what I said. Ella thought he brought out my inferiority complex. I carried on trying to be forceful.

"I don't want to say what I have in mind, but it's going to make a big splash and it will hit the press. Surely that's got to be good for the book?" I kept up the pressure. "I have something which will cause a storm!"

Charles interrupted me. He was not a man who liked surprises and I could see the irritation showing on his face.

"What do you mean exactly, Mr. Ashurst?" The more he kept using the Mr. Ashurst in such a condescending tone, the more he pissed me off. Ella commented on my hostile body language and suggested I should be less confrontational with him. However, when his response to me confirmed that he considered me a complete amateur, I felt quite infuriated.

"I am not willing to sanction any further expenditure on this project until I know what you are thinking of doing. We are a professional publishing company. We have successfully launched and published many books without pulling any rabbits out of a hat!" Pompous twat, I thought. I nearly walked out but thought better of it as Ella glared at me. I tried to share my idea with him.

"Look, Charles. I will tell you everything, but I want an undertaking that you will say nothing, not even to your colleagues about what I have got to say. Because if you do, I will walk away from this!"

"I think that is something we are more likely to do than you! However, I'll make an assessment first, based on what you tell me!" Charles was becoming aggravated, but he must have seen a look of determination on my face that could not be ignored.

"Go on…. I'm listening!" It was all I could do not to slap him in the face. I simmered down as I caught another, harsher glare from Ella. Before I could explain, Charles spoke again slowly.

"You don't like me, do you. Mr. Ashurst?"

"Frankly, no! I consider you a pretentious 'wanker,' but that doesn't mean we can't work together, just so long as you come down from that cloud of arrogance that you're sitting on." He smiled cautiously.

"Well, that's cleared the air. Personal insults are so negative, don't you think? Anyway, please explain what you have in mind."

"It is like this. You've read the book and you know there is some truth in what we've written. The old lady in the hotel, the incident when we were arrested?"

"Truth?" Charles looked intrigued and moved in closer to hear my discourse. I lowered my voice.

"I said that I disposed of the chests. Put them somewhere where they could never be found." Charles raised his eyebrows in expectation.

"That's not exactly true. They are hidden in a location known only to me. I want to announce this at the launch and I want the state treasures returned to France."

Charles looked dumbstruck and fired a series of questions at me like bullets.

"Are you serious? You have the diamonds? Really? And no-one else knows? Why at the launch? Why didn't you say anything before?" I said nothing to give him time to consider my revelation. He scratched his head.

"Look, Mr. Ashurst. What you gave us was a particularly good commercial story. What you want to do now has nothing to do with the launch of a book of fiction. It will overshadow the launch and then there are the legal issues." I pursued my point.

"Yes, but it's how the book ends. I want to do in reality, exactly what I say, in the last few pages." Charles was getting irritated.

"I know what it says in the book. But it's complete madness to go ahead in this way. I can't let you do this. The implications, the repercussions. No, no, no!" He was violently shaking his head.

"I had my doubts about this book right from the start. My colleagues convinced me that any legitimacy would come out when people started to read it themselves and as such, it would generate its own publicity. It's now evident that there is far more truth in it than fiction. Believe me, telling the world that the book is true from the start, will be an absolute disaster. Do you know how many injunctions will be taken out to gag us? And from very high up! We are publishers, Mr. Ashurst, not gunslingers!" The air was thick with tension on both sides.

"Sorry, Charles. I am determined to do this!" He looked utterly exasperated with me. He tried to regain a sense of calm.

"Mr. Ashurst, let me tell you something. I never disclose this to our novice writers, but we have a panel of 'pre-readers.' Literary specialists in the field, other authors, professors of English, you understand? They read the scripts we send them and give us their opinion. Your book got such a high score, we gave it to another set of readers and the mark was the same. Your story will sell on its own. The world of publishing, Mr. Ashurst, is hugely competitive, ruthless, and greedy. We all want to discover the next JK Rowling! I will not jeopardise that ambition for some fanciful idea of yours! If you do this, it will not be with Hudson's blessing, I can assure you!" He stood up and walked out of the room. His attitude maddened me. Who the hell did he think he was? As far as I was concerned, the man was just an employee.

"Well done, Rob! We've just lost our publisher!" Ella's lack of support on this was yet another blow. I was fuming. I had to simmer down before I said something to her, which I could possibly regret.

"Ella, I can remember a time not so long ago when you had no interest in the book whatsoever. I'm not sure why you feel so strongly now. I thought you would jump at the chance of a big reveal?"

"I think Charles is right!" Sandra too, nodded in agreement. It got me thinking that I might be wrong, but as one who doesn't find it easy to admit when they are, I had to get away from the whole circus that had built up and collect my thoughts.

"Ella! Pack a bag. We are going away for a long weekend. Will you hold the fort, Sandra?"

"Yes, sure." Sandra looked surprised at the hasty travel arrangements. "Are you going anywhere nice?"

"Tenby." Ella stopped what she was doing. "Wales? Why there?"

"No reason. Just the first place that came to mind. We visited before and never really got to see much of it. Don't think any magpies will pester us!" Sandra looked confused, but Ella remembered the story and smiled her coquettish smile.

"You are up to something!" Ella said accusingly.

"Ella! do you want to come or not?"

"Of course, I do. Where are we staying? Nice big posh hotel or cosy pub?"

"Pub!"

"I will only come on one condition." She spoke firmly. "You call Charles. Apologise and tell him that on reflection, you now feel he was correct. Get him to re-schedule the next meeting after the weekend." I looked her in the eye and got the message that she meant business.

"Ok, it's a deal!" I picked up my phone and spent a few minutes on a hotel booking site. Then I made a call to Charles at the publishers and humbly mumbled an apology. Within the hour, we were off.

By the time we arrived at The Red Lion, on the outskirts of the town, the red sun was beginning its final descent towards the horizon. From the outside, it was not the old English pub I had envisaged but a larger, more modern, featureless building. The restaurant was Italian, which appeared to be the focus of the business. More of an eating place with a few bedrooms. The four-hour drive, the emotions of the day, plus the lateness of the hour had made us tired.

We were shown to our room which was outside, in a former outbuilding separate from the pub. It was spacious, decorated in sea-scape colours of turquoise and blue with a king-size bed in the centre and oak wood furniture on a laminate dark stained floor. One wall was stencilled with butterflies, while above the bed, there was an inscription, a quote about the tranquillity of the sea written in flowery script. The en-suite was luxuriously appointed with a roll-top bath, a deluge walk-in shower and a proliferation of fluffy cream towels of all sizes.

Ella had been pensive on the way down and didn't seem to want to talk much, but now her mood lightened and she was pleased with the room. She kicked off her shoes and bounced on the bed.

"Well, Mr. Hotel inspector, what's your opinion?"

"It will do for its purpose!"

"Oh! What devious plan do you have then?"

"You know me, Ella. I am a guy who does things on the spur of the moment!"

"Hah!!! That's true. After today's performance, I feel that sometimes, you fail to think things through at all."

"OK, sprout, I was wrong. Is that what you want me to say? Anyway, I don't want to keep going over it. We needed some time out." Ella concurred with a hand gesture she used when she agreed with something.

"C'mon, let's go eat!"

The young chap who dealt with us was very pleasant but said he could not find us a table for at least another thirty minutes. He asked us to sit at the bar and have a complimentary drink. We chatted about the meeting at Hudson's and how I had probably done the right thing in apologising to Charles.

"I still think he's a pretentious twat!" I commented, a large glass of red wine in hand.

"Don't disagree, but we have to work with twats at times if it suits our purpose and not let them get under our skin." At that point, we were offered a table.

"Oh!!! Wise one so young!" I put my hands together in prayer pose and pretended to bow down to her. She raised an eyebrow at me as we took our seats. A waiter lit the candle on our table and took our order. We chatted easily through our salami platter, spinach and ricotta ravioli, finished off with a tiramisu and a glass of limoncello each. We retired to the room full and tired.

Friday was dull and damp with a few torrential showers. We spent the morning walking along the promenade looking out to sea, playing on amusement machines, and dipping into shops when the rain got too heavy. We treated ourselves to some new clothes and had such a giggle when we were both using a fitting room at the same time. Ella was attempting to try on a denim skirt, but in the middle of proceedings, I pulled her to me and we kissed. The skirt fell to the floor as she let my hands feel around the contours of her body.

"Shall we go back to our room?" she said in a soft voice.

We almost ran back to the car in anticipation of what was going to happen. The traffic appeared to be holding us up deliberately as if people knew what we were up too. Ella slid her hand down the inside of my thigh, then let it linger as if I didn't need any encouragement. Once back in our room, we were naked within seconds. Her body was even more perfectly proportioned than I had ever thought, her skin soft and sweet-smelling. I held her away from me, so my senses could absorb the delight of her contours. We made love twice that afternoon with a long soak in the tub in between. The last time I had sex was with Amy around seven months before when things weren't going well between us. This was a quite different experience for me. I lay back in the luxurious bed with a smile on my face and dozed. Ella nestled in my arms.

The whole weekend was the perfect combination of passion. Eating, sleeping, talking, laughing, kissing, touching, feeling, arousing. Our lust for each other was deep and hungry yet loving and sensual. All of the horrors from the past six months were gone. We talked for ages about books we had read, music we liked and films we had watched. It had been a beautiful weekend, but as we pulled into the self-storage depot on Monday morning, Ella gave me a sideways glance. "Back here? I knew you had other ideas, as well!"

"You've been thinking about it too, have you!" I said it out loud but wished I hadn't, so I added, "Just thought we should collect the stuff."

"I always wondered where you had put the trunks, you were gone for so long, but I never guessed it was back here. What's the plan?"

"Give the jewels back to France at the book launch. You've read the book, so you know what happens!"

"Rob! After everything we said. I can't believe you still think that is a good idea."

"Don't you?" My stubborn side was coming out. She shook her head.

"No. I don't. Neither does Sandra. Neither does Charles. People will think it's all a stunt. After all, they have only your word the treasure is genuine. The authenticity issue will get in the way of your launch."

I considered it for a minute.

"What do you think is the best thing to do then?"

"What are the options? Leave it all here, give it to Hansen or knock on the door of the French embassy and hand it all over."

"But, it's the publicity that we are looking for, surely?"

"Why? The book will sell as a book of fiction and you will be a successful published author. Even if it doesn't, we still have The Limes to run and you'll have your shrine to Amy. Doing it your way, you will piss off intelligence and then they might well come down heavy on us. Remember! This will prove the book is fact, not fiction." Her argument was convincing and winning me over.

"Not at all dim-witted, are you? "I smiled at her.

"Rob, listen! This treasure is cursed, it will always bring trouble. I wish I didn't know we still had it. Leave it where it is and let's go sell your book." I couldn't argue with her. She was right. I paid for another three months' storage and we headed back to London.

Chapter 22

"So, tell me, honestly. What do you really think?" She stood in front of me, wearing nothing but a G-string.

"About what?"

"You know what! Ella was in one of her mischievous moods I could tell and appeared to be incredibly pleased with life.

"No, I don't. Give me a clue?"

"Boobs! Or, in my case, fried eggs! They're too small, aren't they? Obviously, you think them hideous because you've never said anything."

"Ella! Your body is one of beauty and perfection."

"Don't be smarmy!"

"You did ask!" Progress had been made.

We had a lot to catch up on when we arrived back in London. Sandra had made numerous appointments for me with various professionals. A make-over stylist, a barber, and a specialist coach to practise handling media interviews. I was unfamiliar with personal grooming terminology.

"What's she making over exactly?"

"You! She will do your hair, give you a facial and make you look trendy with a new wardrobe. You will need at least three suits."

"I like the way I look!" I protested as if it were an affront to my masculinity. Ella thought this was a great way to get back at me.

"Come on Rob. You always look like an off-duty hotel waiter!"

"No, I don't! I take pride in my appearance!" Ella was laughing out loud now, so much that she couldn't speak. I grabbed hold of her and we had a pretend fight. Sandra watched us, smiling.

"Looks like Tenby did you both good!" I kissed Ella and she kissed me back, very affectionately. Then she remembered something.

"Rob? Do you need the car tomorrow?"

"No, I don't think so. Why?"

"I am at a loose end while you are being done up. I've been thinking for ages that I would like to go back to Burnside. I'll stay overnight. I want to say goodbye properly to my old friends, who formed part of my life for so long. I've got some stuff there, which I need to pick up." It was the first time Ella had ventured to do anything at all on her own, which surprised me. I would not deny her anything after such a weekend of beautiful sex.

"Yes, darling. I completely understand. I'll use the tube."

That night Ella took me to bed early, unusually early. She was very much a night owl, always coming to bed after me. I was never sure what she was up to as it was not watching the TV. She embraced me as I entered the room, slowly removed my clothes, then treated me to a tantalising striptease. Her body image issue had vanished into thin air and all her inhibitions were gone. Making love that night reached a level of intensity I had never experienced before. Our intertwined bodies became one as we devoured each other in desire and lust.

As the early sunlight hit the window, I felt my lips touched by her soft kiss. I opened my eyes and there she was, sitting on the bed, fully dressed.

"Go back to sleep," she whispered. "It's still early, but I want to get off before the traffic gets bad." Ella smiled at me and I thought I saw a tear in her eye.

"You're crying? What's up?" She picked up a tissue and wiped her eye.

"No. It's some new mascara. I must have got some in my eye!" She got up and the door closed behind her. Ella was gone. My head sank back into the pillow, her lingering perfume gently filling my nostrils. I basked in a warm afterglow. With a happy heart, I felt things were getting back to normal even if it was a different life for me.

The make-over was rather enjoyable. I was utterly pampered for the entire day. My face was cleansed, exfoliated, and moisturised. A hair technician re-styled me and a clothes stylist chose several outfits for me to try on. Ralph Lauren oxford shirts in two colours and a pair of stretch cotton chinos. The look was completed with a Ted Baker bomber jacket and new brogues. The voice coach spent several hours working on my 'public persona'.

When I returned home, I felt like I had been reinvented both inside and outside, and it was quite a liberating feeling. I wanted to show off my new look to someone, but the flat was empty. Sandra was out with friends and I missed Ella. However, I opened a bottle of wine and decided to toast my new reflection in the mirror. Just as I was drinking my third glass, scrolling through random posts on my tablet, an email popped into my inbox. It was from Ella. How strange. I had no idea she even had an email address. I was curious. *'Hello Rob'*

Why were my hands shaking? I read the words slowly and deliberately.

'I owe you so much I can't think where to start. I know this will hurt you. All I have, in return, is an explanation. The theory you put forward to Karl, in the book, is exactly right. You have more or less, worked it out.

There was one joker in the pack which you didn't know about. I am so sorry, but that was me. Everything I told you was true except my relationship with Madame Aguirre, who wasn't, in fact, my grandmother. She was the leader of our cause. Being ill, she knew there had to be a change of governance. I was the chosen replacement because I hold the only true linage to the royal bloodline of France. This caused some dissatisfaction with some members, mainly due to my age. I had to find out who they were so the succession could go through, only then would I have total control.

You suspected there were rogue elements inside the French intelligence service and the French government. These are, in fact, our undercover legionnaires who are fighting our cause. Your assumption that Amy was killed due to mistaken identity was also correct. If it gives you any comfort at all, the perpetrators were executed and disposed of, so her killers found justice.

For your own safety, you do not need to know any more about our group or even my real name, but only that I was born into this. It has always been my true destiny, never more so than now.

I have to avenge the death of my parents or die myself. It is not arrogant of me to say you will not understand. Rowena got too close to working out who I was. British Intelligence was using her as she had contacts with our group. I had to get her detained, through our connections inside MI6. I am sorry that you have been so involved. You took the trunks and hid them so well for so long. That's why I had to keep myself close to you. You are a great guy and the whole adventure for me has been astonishing.

Tenby and last night was something special. It will always live in my heart. In another life, we would be happy together. The Limes is yours, but the flat will be sold in due course. You were also right about Madame Aguirre getting that item of jewellery out ready to sell to raise funds, but I am so glad that you have profited. I have emptied the lock-up in Wales and I am sorry about your beloved car. It has been crushed. I know you have enough money to buy a nice new one, which is more suitable for a hotel owner.

I hope the book goes well. You deserve everything in life, which is good. Please say goodbye to Sandra. Like you, she was who she said she was.

It saddens me to say farewell

Ella.'

I was absolutely stunned and couldn't take it in. It must be a joke. I read it again out loud, trying to convince myself it was a mistake. In my imagination, I could hear Hansen's words. *'She is an actress and a very good one.'* No, no, this is wrong. Ella wouldn't lie to me. She went back to visit her friends at Burnside today. I looked up the telephone number and with trembling hands, gave them a call.

"Hello, Burnside," said a voice that was far too cheerful for my present mood.

"I'd like to speak to Antonella Walford."

"Who? Sorry, we don't have anyone by that name here. Are you sure it's Walford?"

"A woman about mid-twenty. Shoulder length hair, brown eyes, 5ft two-ish. She was there for a few years and left a few months ago. She was coming back today to get some of her belongings. Or maybe she worked in the kitchens?"

"I think you are mistaken. We have never had anybody matching that description and I don't recognise the name. I've worked here for the past five years. All our residents cook for themselves, so we don't have a cook." I heard myself mutter some feeble apology. I just looked at the computer as the battery went flat. The email disappeared from the screen. At that point, I completely lost it.

Sandra came in sometime later and found me, sobbing my heart out on the floor. She ran to me and I could vaguely hear her concerned voice shouting my name. Her face was a blur. I was wrecked and incoherent after drinking almost a full bottle of scotch. I managed to show her the cause of my distress after several cups of black coffee. All I kept hearing from her was, "Oh my God!" The impact on both of us was immense.

"I can't believe it! Jesus, what a mess! We've got to phone Penny **now** and tell her so that you're not implicated. I am so sorry!"

"Fucking lying, bitch!" was the best I could come up with. Sandra retrieved my phone from my pocket and started going through the contacts. In my drunken state, I didn't know who she was calling and didn't care. I was feeling ill. My head was throbbing. My eyes felt heavy. I was aware of being shaken. Sandra was handing me another large mug of black coffee.

"Can't drink any more of that shit! Wanna sleep."

Somewhere from the distant haze, I heard the doorbell ring. She ran off to answer it. I drifted off into my stupor again, but I was aware of voices near me. Rough hands picked me up like a rag doll and put me onto the sofa. Someone was talking to me. With difficulty, I managed to focus on the face before me. It was Hansen Mulhenny.

The rest of the night was hazy. After throwing up several times, I was bundled in a car and taken somewhere. I awoke with a blinding hangover in a small prison cell-like room with a formica table and a narrow put-me up bed. There was a lady in the room sitting on a wooden chair in the corner. Mid-fifty, grey hair, overweight. No vision of loveliness that was for sure.

"Where am I?" She did not reply but stood up and went to the door.

"I need the bathroom!" I was insistent, so she stopped in her tracks and spoke quietly into an intercom on the wall. Within seconds Hansen and Penny appeared with two guys.

"He has requested the bathroom," said my observer.

"Take him!" Hansen directed his subordinates. I felt like total shit. When I returned, I was told to sit down at the table. Penny and Hansen sat opposite. There was a plastic cup of water waiting for me.

"Drink it."

I knew I was in for a grilling, but I didn't have the clarity of thought to sidestep any of their questions, so I played dumb. Hansen was the first interrogator.

"You have been less than honest with us yet again, Robin?"

"Really! Why is that then?"

"You hid the goods where it was impossible to retrieve them. Isn't that what you said?" I said nothing. Just lowered my head.

"**Isn't that what you said?**" His voice boomed across the room.

"Yes, I did!" But you knew that was crap, so why go over it? I assume you've seen the email?" I was going to add, 'from that lying scheming bitch' but thought better of it. Instead, I protested my ignorance about the deception.

"I didn't know who or what she was! I swear it!" I took a sip of the water as he continued.

"She is an outstanding actress. You were taken in and so were we."

"We did have our suspicions," Penny added. Hansen nodded in agreement.

"We couldn't understand why she was with the old lady that day in Devon. The girl had never come up before as a member of any anarchist group and was definitely under the radar. She wasn't wanted in any country".

"That's why we wanted you two married," Penny commented. I glared at her.

"So, you could keep tabs on the both of us?"

"It was for your own safety as well as serving our interests." My head was hammering, but not from Hansen's cross-examination. He continued.

"Robin, we have known each other for several years, have we not? Don't think the worst of us. Our job is complex and often unpleasant. We have to lie and use people but believe me, we make a difference. We play an important role in the interests of national security. You must understand, my friend, that we are not the enemy." The interview or interrogation carried on in the same vein. I was taken back to the flat by an unmarked car. I had no secrets left to tell and for me, it was all over. I felt betrayed and empty.

Sandra greeted me, anxiously when I returned. I must have looked rough.

"Rob, I had to do it. I had to tell them!" Sandra seemed so worried about my reaction. At that point, I realised that she was my only true friend.

"It's OK, Sandra. I am glad you did." I felt incredibly weary.

"You have been detained for nearly forty-eight hours! Did they give you much of a grilling?"

"No, not really. It took me half a day to sober up."

"I told Hudsons you've been ill. They've phoned loads of times."

"What did you say was wrong? That I've just had my heart broken by a lying bitch? That I've been dumped and deceived? So fucking ironic!"

"Rob, please don't. I didn't say anything specific. I hate to ask at such a time as this, but what about the book? Should we still go ahead"?

"Why shouldn't we?"

"I thought it might be too painful, too soon. After what she's done to you?"

"Compared to losing Amy in the way I did. Ella was nothing. What hurt with that bitch was the lies, the deception." I felt tears welling up inside. Sandra put her arm around me.

"I believed everything she told me! How could I have been such a fool to be sucked in, deceived and lied to all this time? That's why I got pissed."

"Are we going to change the ending in the last chapter?"

"No. What's the point?"

"Well, it makes a good twist in the tail with Ella not being who she said she was."

"Don't we need a happy ending, though? Who wants to read about a guy who's had his guts ripped out and left looking a total betrayed idiot?"

"Because it's the truth. No more lies, Rob?" I thought about it a while and said I would speak to Charles. I went to bed for several hours, feeling sorry for myself and wanting to dull the ache in my heart.

Sandra let me sleep and then brought me a bacon sandwich in bed with a cup of tea. It was very welcome.

"You know Sandra," I said, tucking into my bacon bap,

"The more I go over things. There were signs, weren't they? I mean, how did she know the key to this flat was on that bunch of keys. She took it off and kept it separate. She's taken all the others."

"I guess she wanted all the jewels and diamonds then?"

"Yes. Things she did, things she said. I believed all of it. I'm so fucking stupid. I should have seen it coming! Jesus, I'm going mad!"

"Even when we went to Tenby, she said she had been wondering where I had hidden the stuff. Why would she do that?"

"Rob, stop torturing yourself. You couldn't have known. Did Penny say anything about the flat?"

"What?"

"Do we have to move out soon?"

"I never thought to ask. Didn't the email say that the flat would be sold? I wonder who it really belonged to?"

"Maybe it belongs to an illegal organisation? It's a shame because I like it here. It's rent-free and such a good address for me. What will you do, Rob?"

"I guess I will head down to Devon as soon as possible after the book business is out of the way. I'll check with Penny, but you stay here if you like until the sale."

"I don't want to be here on my own. What if members of the AF come calling?"

"I'll change the locks, tighten up security and get you a guard dog!" She laughed.

"If you want to come to Devon with me, I would love that! Sandra, I appreciate your friendship, you know that."

"I do, but please don't get slushy with me. Getting a dog, that's a good idea. I do so miss Scott." Sandra paused then added.

"Dogs never let you down, not like people," she remarked. "But I don't know how a dog would fit into my life at the moment. We've got a very punishing schedule over the next few months. Look at all these events that Hudson's emailed this morning." She showed me a long list of venues and places around the UK. She wasn't kidding.

The next few weeks were demanding and hectic. Handling the book launch, promotional interviews and book signings took my mind off Ella's betrayal. I was the centre of attention and everyone wanted to know about me and my background in the hotel industry. Strangely as it may seem, hotel staff are generally inconspicuous until there is a problem, so this was such a new role for me to play. One radio interviewer even introduced me as the man who met a French queen, which was an angle that generated even more interest. Getting around the absence of Ella was difficult, firstly with Charles and then everyone else. I made up some excuse about an illness then a family emergency. I knew these pretexts would only last so long, but I had to take things day by day.

I was also liaising with Top Notch about The Limes. I gave them full authority to make decisions on any interior design issues and they were only to bother me if there any major problems. After about eight weeks, Charles wanted a meeting to talk about initial book sales. The results were in. The reviews were generally good, not quite as spectacular as Hudson's had wished but steady. Sandra was keeping tabs on the business side of things and felt we would make some money. What she hoped for was being picked up by a TV company to do a dramatization.

I headed back to Devon, where my story began. I drove there in my newly purchased nine-year-old Toyota. I had managed after much searching, to find an identical car like the one stolen by Ella. Same make, model, and age. Even the colour was identical. After spending a vast sum of money on The Limes, I couldn't bring myself to spend excessively on a car, as Ella had wanted. The locals would think it extravagant and maybe not so good for business. It was then, with the sun sinking in the autumnal sky, I felt I was coming home. I passed all the landmarks so familiar to me. Haytor and then on the horizon, the sea. The peace in my heart was short-lived.

A text came through on my phone from an unknown number. It read,

'Got this all wrong. My fault. Have to see you. Ella'

My heart was racing at her words, yet I felt upset that she had made contact. I parked up on the seafront and was trying to think of a response when a second text came in.

"Hurt you so much. I know that, but I've something to say which has to be face to face. Don't deserve anything from you, but please give me five minutes before it is too late."

Anger was building up inside me. How could she come back into my life again after what had happened and just as I was starting a new life without her? I was about to dial Hansen's number then stopped as the tender memories of the night we spend in each other's arms came flooding back. How could anyone make love as she did without it meaning something? My head was all over the place and my hands were shaking. I needed to know. I needed to see her for one last time. It took me ages to get the words right in my head.

"I am in Devon for two nights. I'm staying at The Regent. I will give you ten minutes and then I'm calling the police!"

I felt I got the tone right and my text was not angry or abusive. Whatever bullshit she was going to come up with, I wanted to let her know it was over. I wasn't even sure if she would show up or not. I got a swift reply.

"*Watch the TV news tonight!*" Not the message that I had expected. Was she playing me? What the fuck was she up to?

I asked for Tom when I checked in and found that he had left. I couldn't get any explanation from the girl at reception, so I asked Harry, a middle-aged man at the bar. In my experience, bartenders are the best gossips. If anybody knew, Harry would. I ordered a pint of Badgers and engaged him in conversation.

"Looking for Tom! Any idea why he left?"

"Just announced one day he was leaving. Didn't see eye to eye with the management, if you get my meaning, sir."

"Any idea where he is?"

"Still in town, saw him about a week ago. Why do you ask?"

"Thought I might offer him a job!"

"Fair play, he is a good guy." Harry looked round to see if anyone were listening then whispered,

"Where is your establishment, Sir? Do you need a barman?" I smiled.

"Maybe! What's the matter with The Regent?" Been told it's the best hotel in town!"

"I don't think the place will be the same without Tom." He winked at me. "Do you know the town at all, sir? There is another hotel here called The Limes and it is having a big refurbishment. The word is that it will be the place for the best tips soon!" I smiled to myself, but I didn't let on who I was. It had crossed my mind about a manager and Tom would be an excellent choice. I took a sip of my drink. If Tom accepted, I would give Harry a job too, as he kept a good pint. I turned around on my stool to watch the large TV on the wall.

As the main story on the six o'clock news unfolded, I dropped my drink on the floor and the glass smashed.

'*Terrorists arrested in London!*'

I took no interest in the mess I had made and walked over to stare at the screen.

'*Several radical suspects from a terrorist gang have been arrested in London. This was a co-ordinated swoop with security forces working with the French. There have been simultaneous arrests in Paris, Geneva and Rome.*'

There was no mention of the Action Française, but I was drawn to the story. I knew it was to do with everything that had encompassed my life in the last few months. Then a minor piece from France to say that certain French state treasures had been uncovered in the form of documents and works of art. They had been anonymously donated to the Louvre museum. The camera went to a press conference inside the Louvre. I was utterly dumbfounded and couldn't believe what I was hearing.

'Certain treasures including the infamous 'French blue diamond' thought to be lost forever, have mysteriously shown up, delivered in several large trunks by DHL.'

I sat down to recover. My friendly barman came up to hand me another beer. I gave him a twenty- pound note.

"Keep the change! That's for your trouble."

"Are you OK, mate?" said Harry. "You look like you've had a shock! Would you prefer a brandy?"

"No, fine. It's Ok," was all I could say. My phone was beeping loudly, which brought me back to reality. It was Sandra in a state of excitement and agitation.

"Rob! Have you seen the news? Do you think Ella's been arrested too?" The thought hadn't occurred to me.

"I don't know. Sandra! Ella's messaged me. Says she's got something to tell me!"

"Oh, my God! Do you think she will now?"

"Christ knows. All the stuff has been donated to the Louvre. Is that Ella?"

"Gotta be! She's given back all the treasure! Apparently, there is going to be a statement by the Prime Minister tomorrow about the arrests and then…….." Sandra was still speaking, but I had stopped listening.

"Rob, are you still there? Rob!"

I couldn't move. I was struck dumb. My eyes were fixed on the girl walking towards me. It was Ella. Before I could say anything, she started talking.

"You said I had ten minutes, so here goes. I am pregnant. You are the father!" I think a bomb going off in the bar could not have had any more impact than that. Ella continued.

"I made a big mistake. I treated you like shit and I am so sorry. From the day I left the flat, I pined for the life we had together. But then, when I got control over the AF, I could see they were wrong. The cause was not a cause which people should die for. It was all a historical myth, that was all. You've seen from the news that I've donated the contents of the trunks, in particular the 'French blue diamond' to the Louvre. You said it should go to France and France is where it belongs. You were right. The modern AF is no more. I've disbanded it and given the names and identities of those who want to fight, to the authorities with evidence to convict them of the crimes. Have I had ten minutes yet?"

"You're pregnant? You're going to have a baby? Oh, Jesus, Ella!"

"Yes, Rob! In that order! It usually goes that way. That weekend, that beautiful weekend!

We could hear police sirens outside the hotel getting louder. People in the lounge were gathering together and muttering about why the police had arrived.

"I've already called them. I'm giving myself up. I want us to bring up our child together! Please say yes, Rob! I love you!"

At that moment, armed police rushed in, followed by Hansen, pointing a revolver at Ella. It was chaos. Uproar. Panic. Shouting. Masked figures in black uniforms, faceless. They surrounded her at gunpoint. People in the bar, screaming and running, tables overturned, glasses smashed. Ella motionless. She slowly put her hands above her head to show surrender. I could do nothing but stare at her. Our eyes were locked together. I watch her being handcuffed and led her away. I shouted after her, "Ella!"

All I could think of to say was, "Only if we call it sprout!"

THE END

THE REAL FACTS!

Firstly, The French royal family. Any history book or google search will tell you Louis Phillipe was the last king of France, (1830-1848) and while in exile, he worked in Switzerland as a teacher in a boarding school. He taught under an assumed name. He started dating Marianne Banzori, the cook and got her pregnant, around 1794, so she was sent to Milan where the child was born in secret and raised in an orphanage there. What if, he had secretly married Marianne? The line of succession might be different.

Secondly. There really was a political movement called *Action Française.* It was founded in 1899 and supported the restoration of the French Monarchy. By 1914, it had become the best structured and the most vital nationalist movement in France. Although *Action Française* is not a major force in the right as it used to be, its ideas have remained influential. What if this movement still existed today as an aggressive underground, secret fraternity?

Thirdly, The French Crown Jewels. Again, it is well documented that they were stolen in 1792, during the French revolution when the *Garde Meuble* (Royal Treasury) was stormed by rioters. Most, though not all, of the Crown Jewels were recovered eventually. Neither the Sancy Diamond nor the French Blue Diamond were found in the years after. The Royal French Blue is believed to have been recut, and it is now known as the Hope Diamond. What if the rest of the treasure were found, including the uncut and original French Blue diamond?

Printed in Poland
by Amazon Fulfillment
Poland Sp. z o.o., Wrocław

59030840R00254